Golf Balls Are Female

Golf Balls Are **Female**

Robert C. Knox

Writers Advantage
New York   Lincoln   Shanghai

Golf Balls Are Female

Writers Advantage
an imprint of iUniverse, Inc.

For information address:
iUniverse, Inc.
2021 Pine Lake Road, Suite 100
Lincoln, NE 68512
www.iuniverse.com

ISBN: 0-595-25596-5 (Pbk)
ISBN: 0-595-65200-X (Cloth)

Printed in the United States of America

To Dave, for encouraging me to remain young at heart;
To G, for insisting that I some day grow up;
To Monte, for allowing me to do both.

Let's see…one in the pond, two out, three in the trap, two to get out, and three putts…

"Damn, put me down for another bogey!"

Monte Grant

CONTENTS

CHAPTER 1

ON TO OKLAHOMA

I left Albuquerque, New Mexico, in August of 1973, and headed east to attend the University of Oklahoma. Like most 18-year olds, I had no idea what I wanted to do with my life. My highest priority at that point in time was finding someone to help me lose my virginity.

I didn't bother to look at a map before I jumped on the interstate. I figured that as soon as I got to Oklahoma there would be all kinds of signs about OU football to guide me to the campus. I was about half way through Oklahoma City when I saw a sign that said "I-35 South to Dallas". I decided that south was as good a direction as any, so I turned right and started looking for football stadiums.

Luckily, my decision to change course also caused me to glance down at my fuel gauge. Even though I had no idea how to get to where I was going, I concluded that I probably ought to get some gas for the journey. I got off the interstate and pulled into the first filling station I came to. When I stepped out of my Mustang, I was hit with the most stifling blast of heat this side of Hades. Having grown up in the desert, I was used to the heat, but unaccustomed to the humidity, so I began to perspire almost immediately.

I pumped five bucks worth of gas into my car and walked inside to pay. The place was empty except for a middle-aged man in a sweat-drenched tee shirt sitting in a rocking chair behind the counter watching television. A small oscillating fan was blowing hot air back and forth across his cozy little nook. I laid down a twenty-dollar bill and waited for him to arise from his seat. It was apparent from the pace of his trudge toward the cash register that he didn't appreciate having his afternoon program interrupted. Even though it was obvious that the station didn't place a premium on customer service, I decided to ask for directions.

"I'm trying to find the University of Oklahoma. Am I heading in the right direction?"

My question was sufficient provocation to cause the cashier to launch into a tirade about Oklahoma football.

"So, you goin' to OU, huh? Gonna watch the Sooners play football? You better get season tickets, cause they damn sure ain't gonna be on TV this year. All 'cause of one dumb nigger."

I quickly deduced that the Klansman behind the counter was referring to the fact that the Sooner football team had been put on probation for using an ineligible player during the previous season. The cashier continued with his racial tirade as he rang up my purchase.

"You know, that whole probation thing is a buncha bullshit. I got firsthand knowledge that Texas and Nebraska both got a buncha illegal niggers. They just ain't been caught yet."

Although outraged by the attendant's unabashed bigotry, I knew that I'd better keep my liberal opinions to myself or there could be trouble; however, I couldn't just let his racist ranting slither by unchallenged, so I decided to rattle his racial cage with my cynical stick.

"I don't know anything about OU football," I lied. "I just need to get to the university before 7:00 p.m. or they might give my dorm room away to one of those shiftless darkies."

The attendant glared suspiciously at me as he counted out my change. I could tell he was having trouble deciding whether I was serious or just mocking him. After a long uncomfortable pause, he finally handed me my money and reluctantly spouted out directions to OU.

"You just keep headin' souf and get off at Linzy Street. It's 'bout 10 miles."

I walked out of the station feeling angry and confused. I wondered how many people in Oklahoma were as bigoted as the Grand Wizard I had just met. I certainly wasn't going to stay in any place that condoned racism; however, I was too close to Norman to turn around and go back home. I decided to give the people of Oklahoma at least more chance, so I got back on the highway heading south.

Actually, I was probably looking for any excuse I could find to turn around and go back to Albuquerque. I had never really been set on the idea of going to college. Even though I had graduated near the top of my high school class, I certainly didn't consider myself smart enough for college. Going to college was forced on me in a way when my grandfather died and left me a modest trust fund he hoped I would use to further my education. My mother had made it very clear that the only reason she had been put on this planet was to enforce my grandfather's wishes. With no other career plans, I had decided to give college a try, at least until the money ran out.

A few miles down the interstate, I saw a sign that said "University of Oklahoma, Lindsey Street Exit", so I pulled off and proceeded cautiously down the "main drag" in Norman. After about a mile, the number of fast food joints along Lindsey Street increased dramatically. This was a clear indication to me that I was getting close to the campus, and I actually felt a sense of excitement.

Just past the last pair of McDonalds' golden arches, Lindsey Street dipped down into a wooded residential area. Tall elm trees provided ample shade for the frame houses lining both sides of the street. I noticed that several of the houses had front porches with swings. I couldn't imagine Oklahoma ever being cool enough to actually enjoy a front porch swing.

As I emerged from the residential area, my excitement quickly turned into fear, bordering on out-and-out panic. The tall buildings of the campus seemed to jump up in front of me. I started to wonder just exactly what I had gotten myself into.

I finally saw a sign posted next to a traffic light that indicated the large buildings to my right were student dormitories, so I turned off Lindsey Street. The university had built three, triple-wing, twelve-story, high-rise dormitory towers in anticipation of the flood of baby boomers. Unfortunately, the baby boomers arrived later than planned, so one of the towers had been leased to the U.S. Post Office. The two remaining facilities, Walker Tower and Adams Tower, were brand new and now very much in demand.

I reached into my glove compartment and pulled out the papers that the university had sent me. My housing assignment said "*Kelly House, Cross Center*". I drove around the new high-rise buildings several times, before finally concluding that I needed to look elsewhere for my dormitory.

As it turned out, Cross Center was a set of old dormitories on the far south side of campus that had been closed, but the belated arrival of the baby boomers had required that they be re-opened. I pulled into the gravel lot that encircled the dorms and stopped to stare at the buildings in front of me. To say that I was disappointed with Kelly House, Cross Center would be somewhat of an understatement. All I could think was that I was never going to lose my virginity living in this dump.

I finally reconciled myself to the fact that I would have to endure living in the dorms for at least a couple of weeks, which was as long as I thought I would last before heading home to Albuquerque. There were just a few cars and plenty of available parking spaces, so I was able to park remarkably close to the building. I got out of my car, grabbed my suitcase, and reluctantly marched up the sidewalk leading to Kelly House, Cross Center.

The resident advisor's room was located on the first floor, just inside the glass doors leading into the building. Off to one side of the entrance was a lounge area that had a few old couches along with a television, pool table, soft drink vending machine and a foosball table. A couple of guys were sitting on the ragged furniture watching the television that was chained to a podium in the middle of the lounge.

I walked up to the resident advisor's door and saw a handwritten note that said: 'RA is in the study lounge. Will return at 8:00 p.m.'

This was just great. I was supposed to check in before 7:00 and the RA was in the study lounge. I wondered out loud, "What kind of dickhead studies before classes have even started?"

Just then, the door swung open and a large man with a receding hairline stuck out his hand and said, "Hi. I'm Don the Dickhead."

I was mildly embarrassed, but relieved to see him.

"That note was from last night. I've been expecting you and a couple of others to come straggling in late. Come on in and have a seat."

I walked in and sat down on a metal folding chair just inside the door. I waited quietly as Don looked up my room assignment in the logbook on his desk. He walked over to a cabinet on the wall, pulled out a room key and handed it to me. Then, he opened a closet and gathered up some bed linens, which he proceeded to plop down in my lap.

Don walked back toward his desk and announced, "You've been assigned to room 204 on the second floor. Your roommate has already checked in."

I stood up to leave, but Don caught me just as I got out of my chair.

"Sit your butt back down," he snapped. "I'm not quite through."

He grabbed a piece of paper off of his desk and returned to where I was seated. He shoved the paper into my chest and started into his lecture.

"You need to know that I'm a fifth-year pre-med student, and I'm busting my ass so I can get into medical school. Because I will be working hard, I won't have time to put up with any crap from the scumbags living in my dorm. You just obey these rules and we will get along just fine."

Although not overly impressed by his false bravado, I recognized that Don the Dickhead was in a position of authority and that I had just been demoted to a scumbag virgin. I simply thanked him and headed out the door and up the stairs to find my room.

Once I found the right room I had to fiddle with the key in the lock for a few seconds, but finally opened the door. My new living quarters were everything I could have dreaded and less. There was a small bed and wooden desk anchored to the wall on each side of the room. Twin-size mattresses were laid on top of the wooden bed frames, which had built-in drawers for storage. Along the back wall was a steam radiator and windows that could be opened by a hand crank. The front part of the room consisted of two wooden closets, not much bigger than the average gym locker. There was a phone on the wall near the door. The place wasn't big enough for one person, much less two.

It was obvious that my roommate, whoever he was, had already settled in. He had taken the bed, desk, and closet on the side of the room away from the phone and the door. Given that I wasn't planning on staying too long, I didn't give a shit which side of the hellhole I occupied.

By the time I dumped my luggage my shirt was heavy from perspiration, so I walked over and cranked open one of the windows above the radiator in a vain attempt to get some air flowing through the room. As I unpacked my suitcase, there came the now familiar noise of someone trying to jam a key into the lock on the door. When the door finally swung open, I turned to see what my new roommate looked like. He was at least a half-foot shorter than me, with sandy brown hair and a bushy mustache. After he retrieved his key from the lock, he walked in to the room, stuck out his hand and, without even taking a breath, proceeded to introduce himself.

"Hi, I'm Jack Jefferson. I'm from Carnegie, Oklahoma. You ever been to Carnegie? It's out west, near Hollis. We still play eleven-man football in Carnegie even though a lot of the other towns have gone to eight-man football. I was a fullback and linebacker. I scored two touchdowns in one game during my junior year. See, I still got the newspaper article and you can see it says, "Jefferson slammed over from six yards out". I was gonna play for OU, but I tore up my knee during my senior year. That's why I'm pre-med; I want to be a knee surgeon. I dated the same girl for three years, but me and Melissa broke up before I came up here. Now she's dating a guy who plays football for Southwestern in Weatherford. I'm glad for her and we still stay in touch. The last time we talked I told her that I am gonna find someone new up here and that she should just get on with her life. Gee, isn't this room great? I been here a week already. I come up early to go through rush with all the fraternities. There's three or four that say they want me to pledge, but right now I'm leaning towards the Pikes, that's Pi Kappa Alpha. I wanna be "Another Pike Goin Places", like it says on their pledge shirts. They're havin' a get together at the BSU tonight, wanna go?"

I stuck my hand out and said, "Hi. I'm Bob. What the heck is "mule shoe"?"

"No. B-S-U," he giggled. "The Baptist Student Union. There's gonna be lots of girls there."

"I'm not Baptist," I replied.

"That's okay. The reception is open to anyone so long as they ain't Jewish. What religion are you?"

I decided to toy with Jack a little, so I said, "I am a dyslexic agnostic."

From the perplexed look on his face, I could tell that Jack had no idea what I was talking about.

"You see, spiritually I am not sure whether there really is a dog."

Jack just stared at me without saying a word. After a few seconds of silence, I said, "That's a joke."

His continued catatonic gaze told me that Jack hadn't understood a single word I had said. I decided it would be futile to try and explain my humor to him, so I just turned and hung my clothes in the closet. Actually, I would have been hard pressed to even offer up an explanation because Jack decided this was an opportune time for him to fill me in on the details of his failed relationship with Melissa. He plopped down on his bed and continued talking. I didn't say another word for the next hour.

...   ~   ...

In spite of some initial reservations, I agreed to go with Jack to "mule shoe." The BSU building was on the far north end of campus, about a 15-minute walk, which meant that I was, once again, totally soaked in sweat by the time we arrived. There was a large crowd of students milling around outside the building, eating watermelon, and talking. I spotted several good-looking girls in the crowd and decided that I just might enjoy the evening after all. Jack and I grabbed a couple of slices of watermelon and headed inside the air-conditioned building. The cool air felt good on my skin, but as the goose bumps crept up my arms, a familiar sense of uneasiness swept over me.

Just then, an older gentleman shouted at the crowd gathered inside. He informed us that he was the pastor at the local Baptist church and wanted to welcome all of us to Norman and the University of Oklahoma. Then he asked that we all join hands for a moment of prayer before we continued with our night of fellowship.

I now felt extremely out-of-place and uncomfortable. Although active in the Episcopal Church as a youth, I was never comfortable with outward expressions of faith, by me or anyone else. While everyone else bowed their heads and closed their eyes, I scoured the room to plot my escape route.

At the conclusion of the prayer, the Pastor shouted that we were going to sing a couple of hymns, ones he was sure we all knew. He instructed the piano player to strike up one of his favorites, titled something to the effect of *"My Faith In Jesus Lets Me Pass Judgment on Thee."* As the crowd sang, I looked over and saw that Jack was belting out the words he obviously knew by heart. I walked over and whispered in his ear that I was leaving and heading to the S-S-B. In anticipation of his next question, I semi-yelled, "Store that Sells Beer." Then I made my way to the door. For some unknown reason, Jack decided to follow me.

I started to sweat the instant I stepped outside. The nearest SSB was two blocks away. All the sweating had made me quite thirsty. My pace quickened in anticipation of the first sip of cold beer. As we walked along, Jack babbled to me about the evils of alcohol.

"I know some kids from Carnegie who started out drinking beer, and that led them to smokin' pot and now they're just total dopers. Matter of fact, that's one of the reasons me and Melissa broke up. I told her..."

Not wanting to endure the Melissa story again, I interrupted by saying, "Jack, I guarantee that after a few beers you will forget all about Melissa."

Amazingly, my claim seemed to both placate Jack and, more importantly, shut him up.

When we got to the store I went inside while Jack waited outside. I grabbed two six-packs of Coors and laid them on the counter. The clerk at the register asked to see my ID, which was in my car back at the dorms. I left the beer on the counter and walked back out of the store.

"Jack, have you got your ID?" I demanded.

"Y-y-y-yeah," he stammered back.

I grabbed his arm and stuffed a ten-dollar bill in his hand. In a stern voice I ordered, "You have to go inside and pay for the beer."

Jack hesitated for a moment, but he could tell from the look on my face and the tone of my voice that I was in no mood to discuss the matter. He turned and slowly walked into the store. When he got to the counter, he hesitated for a few seconds before he pulled out his wallet and showed his ID to the clerk. After a few tense moments during which his ID was scrutinized, Jack managed to carefully hand the money to the clerk. As soon as he had my change, he quickly grabbed the beer and sprinted out of the store.

Once outside, Jack exploded into a fit of laughter. He handed me the sack of beer and gasped to catch his breath.

"Whew, boy! That's the most excitin' thing I ever done!" he exclaimed.

I thought to myself that Carnegie, Oklahoma, must not be the Sodom and Gomorrah of the Midwest. I immediately pulled a can of beer from one of the six-packs and shoved it in front of Jack.

"Here, drink this. You are about to have the most fun of your entire life."

After Jack contemplated my order for a few seconds, he reached out and hesitantly grabbed the can. He slowly popped the top on the can, and then proceeded to inhale the entire beer in a matter of seconds. Other than myself, I had never seen a man take to beer like Jack did.

"Am I drunk yet?" he asked.

"Don't get too anxious. It's only 3.2 beer. There ain't a whole lot of alcohol in it."

Jack took a second can and made short work of it too. I gave him the rest of his six-pack and told him to pace himself.

We walked through the main campus on our way back to the dorm. Jack finished his six-pack about halfway back. As we neared the dorm, we could see a couple of guys throwing around a football. A few outside security lights and the glow from lights left on in the dorm rooms dimly lit their playing field. Just before we reached the steps leading up to the dormitory, the short guy imitating a quarterback yelled, "Hey, youse guys wanna play some footbah?"

I had been looking forward to relaxing with my six-pack of beer, but Jack immediately screamed out that we would love to play. He bolted for the door of Kelly House, Cross Center and yelled back, "Let me get my cleats and my knee-brace. I was a fullback and linebacker at Carnegie before I tore up my knee."

Not only was I thirsty, but I also didn't particularly relish the idea of playing football with guys from Oklahoma. Although I was good enough to play, I rode the bench for most of my senior year in high school. The coaching staff felt that my attitude was not worthy of a starting position. They had constantly pressured me to lift weights in the off-season rather than play baseball, but I had steadfastly refused. About midway through my senior year, I got into an altercation on the practice field with one of "their boys", so I was suddenly demoted to second string defensive end and didn't play much at all after that. I probably should have quit the team, but that would have given them the satisfaction of running me off.

In spite of any real or perceived prejudices I may have encountered in high school, the fact remained that I had been a mediocre player on a lousy high school team, and I wasn't anxious to get my ass handed to me by some Oklahoma studs. I was, however, intrigued by the short quarterback's accent. I decided he must be from some place north of Oklahoma because he sounded like a damn Yankee. Reluctantly, I put my beer down, pulled off my sandals and walked over to join the game. I offered my hand to the short imitation quarterback and said, "Hi, I'm Bob. I'm not too big, but I am slow. Are you sure you want me to play?"

"I'm Pat Barrett. Dat's my brother, Paul. Now shut up and hike me da bah."

I had to laugh. This little runt had never met me before but he barked out orders to me like the Godfather. He yelled to his brother to run a post pattern and to be ready 'cause he was going to hit him "on da numbuhs".

I concluded that Pat was probably being mouthy just to show off, but I decided to test him to be sure. The little bit of action that I had seen in high school included serving as the deep snapper for the punting team. I bent over the ball and waited for the first sound out of Pat's mouth, at which point I sent a tight spiral speeding right at his nose. He was barely able to get his hands up in time to deflect the ball, which ended up about thirty yards behind him. I walked over to the sidelines to take a swig of my beer while Pat casually jogged after the football.

"So dats da way we're gonna do it, huh? Okay, wise guy, let's see how you handle a little smoke," he yelled.

Pat picked up the football and fired it at me as hard as he could. The ball started to wobble the minute it left his hand and ended up fluttering to the ground like a wounded bird, landing well short of me and my sack of beer.

Paul Barrett laughed and called his brother a pussy. He walked over to where I was standing, looked in my sack and asked, "You got anudder one of dem in dare?"

I took that to mean he was asking for a beer, so I said sure. He reached into the sack and grabbed two beers. He hurled one at his brother and screamed, "Don't drop that one, you pussy."

Pat snagged the beer and yelled back, "Hey, I've got something for you to suck on, right here," as he grabbed his crotch.

Although I was disappointed to see my beer supply disappear so quickly, I was somewhat mesmerized by the bantering back and forth between the Barrett brothers. Pat opened his beer and took a long pull off the can. He walked over, picked up his football, and headed toward Paul and me.

"You livin' in Kelly House?" he asked as he approached.

It seemed that "show off" time was now over, so I responded with, "Yeah. I just moved in this evening. I'm sharing a room on the second floor with the former fullback and linebacker from Carnegie.

"Yeah, my roommate is real dick too," he replied. Of course, he was referring to his brother, which set the two of them off into another exchange of mock insults and idle threats in their garbled Chicago slang.

At first appearance, it was hard to believe these two guys were brothers. Pat had wavy, sandy-brown hair, blue eyes and wore a pencil-thin moustache. Although he was short, he had a stocky muscular build. Paul was also short, but skinny with dark brown hair that he kept disheveled. He had a greasy little moustache on his upper lip that seemed tilted. This gave him a Snidely Whiplash appearance, which, as it turned out, wasn't too far from accurately depicting his personality and moral character.

Just as we finished our beers, Jack came running out of the dorm wearing football pants, cleats, and his old high school jersey. There was a bandana tied around his head to keep his hair out of his eyes and, of course, there was the extremely visible knee brace on his left leg. He sprinted over to us and asked, "Okay, what's the teams?"

Somehow, the Barrett brothers contained their laughter and managed to refrain from any insults. We split up into two teams. Three guys joined

Pat and me to form one team; Jack, Paul and three guys from an adjoining dorm formed the other team.

I felt prior to the first snap that the game would probably get ugly. I knew for a fact that Jack was a frustrated high school athlete, and I would have bet money that all ten guys on the field had, at one time or another, dreamed of playing football for the Sooners. We were away from home for the first time in our lives, and now it was time to act macho.

The game started out as touch football, which was fine with me. I laughed a lot and had a good time just getting to know everyone. Because of my total lack of speed, ability, and desire, I was designated to hike the ball and not do much else. After a few plays, I could see that Pat took the game seriously. My roommate, on the other side of the line of scrimmage, had also put on his game face. It was inevitable that one of them would propose that we change to tackle football, which we did.

Once we switched to tackle football, I became an instant, if unwilling, asset to my team. In the huddle, Pat asked who wanted to run one up the middle. Nobody answered, so he volunteered me to do it. I was too stunned to protest; we broke the huddle, and I reluctantly lined up behind Pat and waited for the snap. After he caught the ball, Pat wheeled around and stared at me. A look of genuine fear shown in his eyes because he knew would-be tacklers were bearing down on him. Pat started toward me with the ball but tripped over his own feet. As he stumbled by me, he lunged out and stuffed the football into my throat, which caused me to drop it. I bent over and pawed at the ball like a bear cub trying to pick up a beehive.

After what seemed like an eternity, I finally managed to grab the football and tuck it under my arm. I started to plod forward, gaining momentum with each step. I couldn't tell if the guys on the other team were seriously trying to tackle me or not. They bounced off me like handballs against a brick wall; the brick wall also being an appropriate analogy for the speed at which I moved up the field. Even my football star roommate didn't have much of an impact when he came over and laid a lick on me.

Finally, three of the defenders climbed on my back and dragged me down about five yards shy of the make believe goal line.

By Pat's reaction, one would have thought I had scored the winning touchdown in the Super Bowl. He ran over, helped me to my feet, and yelled something about us "ramming da ball right down dare throats." As the guys from the other team slowly struggled to their feet, they lavished me with praise. Even Jack said that he had never seen anyone run that hard before.

Although certainly pleased with my performance and the accompanying flattery, I knew something was seriously wrong with this situation. I had never even carried the ball in high school, but had certainly been run over by several guys who did. I had dreams of athletic stardom like every young man, but I wasn't delusional. Why was I suddenly the big stud football player I had never been before?

As it turned out, except for the former "fullback and linebacker from Carnegie" and me, none of the guys in the game played football in high school. In addition, Carnegie along with many other small towns in Oklahoma was only able to field eleven-man football teams by suiting up kids from the ninth through twelfth grades. When Jack "slammed over from six yards out," he probably did it by running over twelve-year olds.

The game continued for about an hour, then the inevitable happened. Jack's country bumpkin redneck pride ran smack into Pat's wisecracking Yankee attitude, and they exchanged punches. I stepped in and separated them, but I could tell neither one wanted too much more of the fight. It was late, so we all decided to continue the game some other time.

After Jack settled down, I suggested that we head up to our room and get to bed. The next day would be our first day of college and we were probably going to be running around like crazy. When we got up to the room, Jack took off his football gear, went over to his desk, and turned on the reading lamp. I guess the beer, football game, and short-lived fight had stirred his emotions. He announced that he was going to write Melissa yet another good-bye letter before he went to sleep.

I collapsed face down on my bed without undressing. The warm breeze coming through the windows actually felt cool as it blew across my sweat-soaked skin. I closed my eyes and wondered what the next day would entail. I drifted off to sleep while Jack put the finishing touches on his latest Dear Melissa letter.

. . . ~ . . .

I awoke early the next morning and went down to the community bathroom to take a shower. While toweling off, I noticed that I couldn't stay dry; it was only 7:00 a.m. and I was already sweating. I returned to my room and got dressed. Before I left, I walked over and shook Jack to wake him up. He took one look at me, rolled over, and went back to sleep.

I walked over to Couch Cafeteria where my meal ticket was valid. I checked in at the front desk, then proceeded through the serving line to get a plate of runny eggs, a couple of strips of burnt bacon, a slice of soggy toast, two glasses of diluted orange juice, and a cup of weak coffee. When I emerged from the serving line, I saw the Barrett brothers sitting together at a table, so I went over to join them.

As I was getting settled, Pat asked, "So Bob, what's your major gonna be?"

"I'm not sure yet," I replied, "probably math."

The two of them started snickering before Paul piped up with, "Yer gonna starve. Day don't pay mat majors shit."

Not yet annoyed with their critique of my career plans, I asked, "What are you two planning on studying?"

Without batting an eye, Paul chirped, "Pre-med. Minor in chemistry. Boat of us."

His response was so quick and direct, it was almost as if he had rehearsed it.

"What the heck is with pre-med? The RA is pre-med. My roommate is pre-med. You two faggots are pre-med. How many pre-meds actually get into medical school?" I asked.

Paul fired back with, "Don't mattuh. Sonny knows guys on da Regents."

"Who the fuck is Sonny?" I inquired.

"Dats our dad. He knows dese guys on da Regents. Says we're a lock to get in if we just make decent grades."

I found it kind of odd they referred to their dad as "Sonny". It also disturbed me that they were counting more on political connections than hard work to get them into medical school. I asked why they chose Oklahoma when there were plenty of schools in Illinois, closer to home.

Paul just shrugged his shoulders and said, "Sonny always toll us we was goin' to Oklahoma, and you don't argue wit Sonny".

As they stood up to leave, Paul said, "Yer gonna end up in da poorhouse wit a mat degree."

Pat giggled then continued the barrage with, "You ain't gonna need no mat skills to count yer money."

Paul followed with, "Maybe you can be our accountant? Of course dat will depend on how gooda blow job you give."

Pat inquired, "So Bob, are you a spitter or a swallower?"

They both cackled as they walked out of the cafeteria.

Due to their short stature, constant chattering and stinging insults, the Barrett brothers reminded me of the cartoon characters Chip and Dale. It felt like two juvenile delinquent chipmunks had just ganged up on me. I would have really been pissed if I knew what they had been talking about. After all, I was still just a scumbag virgin majoring in math.

· · ·   ⌐   · · ·

I managed to concoct a fairly decent schedule considering that I had waited until the first day of classes to enroll. As a first year math student, I was supposed to take calculus, chemistry, physics, and an English class. I also enrolled in an advanced French class; I had taken French in high school and done well in it, so I thought I'd better take at least one class I knew I could pass.

It only took me a couple of weeks to get settled into my routine. Each morning I got up, showered, ate breakfast, and went to my morning classes. After lunch, I pursued one of three options: attended my after-noon classes, went to the library to study, or screwed off playing foosball in the lounge until dinner. I became quite an accomplished foosball player during my first few weeks at OU.

It also didn't take long for Jack to find the woman who was going to replace Melissa. He met her at a social function the Pikes had with her sorority. I walked into our dorm room one day early in the semester and found them sitting on his bed, holding hands. Jack gazed longingly into her eyes as he said, "I knew I loved you from the minute we laid eyes on one nuther."

The young lady was obviously uncomfortable with the situation, and it had absolutely nothing to do with the fact that I had just walked into the room. She pulled her hands out of his grasp, and replied, "Jack, we have only known each other for a couple of days."

I knew what was coming next; Jack responded with, "Doncha feel the same way too?"

I'd had enough of the sickening scene, so I interrupted and asked, "Jack, how'd you do on that algebra quiz today?"

He had come to me for help the night before, so I tutored him briefly. I didn't think I had much of an impact because he left after 30 minutes to go over to the Pike House and drink beer with some of the upperclassmen. He didn't return until well after midnight.

"Not very well considering I didn't go to class," he replied succinctly.

The new Melissa and I both raised our eyebrows in concern. I said "Jack, you need to buckle down in that class or you're not gonna pass."

He countered with, "I don't need algebra to make it through life as long as I have you," never once taking his eyes off his female companion.

"Okay," I barked as I turned to her and asked, "how did YOU do on Jack's algebra quiz?"

She giggled briefly and said, "Jack, you need to become more serious about studying. Speaking of which, I need to get to study hall at the sorority house."

The new Melissa stood up and gathered her books. As she and Jack walked out of the room, I couldn't help but feel that I would never see her again, and I didn't. The next day Jack told me they broke up because "she didn't wanna get serious."

Although Jack professed to be heartbroken, he healed rather quickly. He nonchalantly dismissed his emotions and moved on to his next conquest. Thanks to the Pike's annual "Partake, Piss, Puke, and Pass Out Prom" he was able to find another girlfriend replacement the very next weekend. I actually found myself somewhat envious of his shallowness.

. . .　　　　　　～　　　　　　. . .

The third week of the semester proved to be crucial to my entire college career. I was headed toward my room when the Barrett brothers convinced me to go outside and throw the football around for a while. Pretty soon, several other guys were involved. Before I knew it, we had another full-fledged football game going. Of course, the friendly game of touch football evolved into another ugly exhibition of how not to play tackle football.

As fate would have it, once again I was tabbed to play running back. On my first carry, I ran a sweep to the right side. I must have envisioned myself as a very slow, white version of Greg Pruitt, because as I turned up the field, I tried to put some fancy moves on my pursuers. They didn't bite at any of my fakes, and four tacklers immediately smothered me. On my way down, I heard and felt something pop in my right knee. This time I did not bounce right back up. In fact, a few of the guys had to help me off the field and over to the campus infirmary. The doctor who examined me said that I had torn the cartilage in my knee. The next day, an orthopedic surgeon confirmed the diagnosis, and I was scheduled for surgery two days later.

When I returned from the orthopedist's office, I tried to summon enough courage to call my mother and give her the "good" news. I delayed calling her until that evening, when I knew she would be at home. She was surprised to hear from me given that it was the middle of the week. After she brought me up to date with the latest family gossip, she asked why I had called. I paused for a second then matter-of-factly said, "Mom, I tore up my knee in a pickup game of football, and I am having surgery later this week."

All in all, I felt she took the news rather well. There was a long pause of silence before she matter-of-factly started screaming at me.

"Now dammit, Robert, I didn't send you out there to play football. I sent you out there to get an education. Didn't I pay for enough knee operations when you were in high school? What the hell are you doing playing football when you should be studying? I hope you aren't hanging out with a bunch of lowlifes like your friends from high school. Your grandfather left you that trust fund to attend college not to be buying beer or paying for knee operations. I can't believe…"

I let the receiver dangle from the phone on the wall and hobbled downstairs to the vending machine to get a soda. I stopped by the lounge and bummed a cigarette and a light from one of the guys watching TV, then limped back upstairs to the waiting phone. I grabbed the receiver and put it back up to my ear.

"You remind me of your father when you pull stunts like this. You are supposed to be studying and staying out of trouble. I'll bet you were drinking when this happened, weren't you? You know I don't like for you to drink because they say alcoholism is inherited. Why do you do things like this to me? I work too hard…"

Once again, I let go of the receiver and lay back on my bed. I stared at the ceiling tiles as I puffed on my cigarette. Periodically I sat up and said something like "Yes, Mom" or "No, Mom" into the mouthpiece.

She finally stopped her tirade and asked if I wanted her to come out to Oklahoma. I told her not to bother because I had already lined up some guys from the dorm to take me to the hospital. The surgery wasn't serious, but I would be on crutches for about two weeks and would have to wear a cast for another four weeks. I told her I was sorry and not to worry.

Needless to say, I was totally disheartened to learn that I would be spending the weekend in the hospital. That Saturday was the first home game of the season, and I was anxious to see OU play football, even if the team was on probation. OU had promoted a young assistant coach to replace the departed Chuck Fairbanks, a move that had a lot of people predicting turmoil for the team. However, few could have predicted that they would not see Barry Switzer's team lose a football game for the next two-and-a-half seasons.

Being on crutches and in a cast for six weeks didn't make me the most popular guy to go barhopping with, so I grew accustomed to studying almost every night, including weekends. I had never really needed to crack a book in high school, so I learned some sorely needed self-discipline. My bleak social calendar translated almost immediately into improved class-room performance. It may have been that knee surgery was the best thing to ever happen to me.

. . .   ~   . . .

At the end of the fall semester, Don the Dickhead announced that he had been accepted into medical school and would not be returning. His replacement that spring was a dork named Keith, who was heavily involved in student government. Keith barely struggled through college as a history major, but by golly he found a way to get elected to the Student Senate every semester. His political connections helped him get appointed as a resident advisor, which meant he received free room and board while he floundered through school.

Keith's approach to running the dorm was to post a sign every time someone did anything or whenever he wanted to get people involved in one of his dorky activities. He took an immediate dislike to the Barrett brothers and me. He figured out early in the spring semester that we were the ones responsible for doctoring most of his dorky signs.

As spring break drew near, I scanned the signup lists for someone to share a ride with me to New Mexico. I wanted to go skiing, but needed a passenger to split the cost of gas and help with the long drive. I finally found a card on the signup board in the dorm that indicated someone wanted to share a ride to Albuquerque; the guy's name was Jim Fiedler.

I knew Jim vaguely from some of our dorm meetings. He was a cross-country runner who generally kept to himself. Jim was tall and slender with blond hair, blue eyes, and strong Aryan features. I didn't hang out with him because I figured that during any social situation, his good looks decreased my chances of losing my virginity by at least 100 percent.

Jim roomed with another non-scholarship cross-country runner on the fourth floor. I took his signup card off the board and went upstairs to confirm travel plans for spring break. When Jim answered his door, I smiled as I said, "Good news, Jim. I'm going to Albuquerque over the break. You wanna hitch a ride with me?"

I sensed excitement in Jim's voice as he said, "Okay," and quickly shut the door in my face.

On the drive to Albuquerque I learned that Jim was from a suburb of Chicago. I presumed out loud that he was probably a pre-med major like the two Barrett faggots. Jim was quick to set me straight with his long-winded answer of, "Nope."

After a few seconds of strained silence, I said, "Okay. I give. What are you majoring in?"

"Accounting," Jim replied as he stared straight ahead.

"Oh, boy," I thought. "I'm going to be cooped up with Mr. Excitement from Accounts Receivable for the next six hundred miles."

Suddenly, Jim pointed to a nearby field and yelled, "Look! Those cows are screwing."

Being a scumbag virgin majoring in math, I needed all the pointers I could get so I turned to look. Sure enough, there was a bull mounted on top of a cow. Jim laughed as I slowed down in order to get a prolonged look at the mating bovines.

For some reason, our first-hand exposure to animal husbandry seemed to loosen Jim up. He even joined me in a few beers while we drove. After awhile, he got kind of giddy and ultimately decided that he needed to set me straight about his name. We were just past Amarillo when he abruptly announced, "I prefer to be called Da Fieds."

"Fine with me," I said. "I prefer to be called Lord and Master Knox."

Jim responded to my clever reply with a sidesplitting, hysterical laugh that was barely audible. He then returned to staring intently out the front window as we drove through the flat, ugly plains of the Texas panhandle.

. . .   ~   . . .

It was near the end of the spring semester when Keith posted another one of his stupid signs that asked, "Those individuals who plan on returning to Kelly House, Cross Center for the fall semester, please sign up." There were already three names on the list when I saw it: *Pat Barrett, Paul Barrett, and Phil Barrett*.

I couldn't believe there was another Barrett coming to Oklahoma! At breakfast that morning I lit into the Barrett brothers.

"I saw the signup list. One would think that your parents would have stopped trying after their first two disastrous attempts at procreating."

I didn't get a reaction from either one of them, so I continued my taunting.

"Did your parents have any children who had actually lived? You two are obviously dead from the neck up."

Finally, Pat giggled as he said, "Dares even anudder one after Phil."

Actually, the dorm signup sheet offered me an opportunity to harass Keith, which was too good to pass up. It also didn't bother me to take a parting shot at the Barrett boys. After breakfast, I purposely walked back to the dorm to pencil in a few additional names. Now scheduled to return were *Pat Barrett, Paul Barrett, Phil Barrett, Momma Barrett, Papa Barrett, Baby Barrett,* and *Smokey the Barrett.* Pleased with the additions I had made to Keith's list, I quietly snuck off to class.

When I returned that afternoon, I found that more names had been added to the list. The roster of returnees now included *Teddy Barrett, Grizzly Barrett, Polar Barrett, Koala Barrett, Yogi Barrett, Grin and Barrett,* and *I Cant Barrett.*

I laughed because I knew the extra names were going to infuriate Keith. I went upstairs, grabbed my books, and headed over to the study hall. I saw the Barrett brothers and asked them if they were responsible for making a mockery of Keith's signup list, but they vowed that they knew nothing about it.

After a couple of hours of cramming for finals, we decided to go eat dinner. We went by the dorm to drop off our books and let Pat and Paul see the signup sheet. The list of names had grown to include *Pat Maweeny, Ben Dover, Jack Meoff, Heywood Jablowme,* and *Phil McCrack.*

That night, when Keith saw our collective handiwork, he went ballistic. He tore down the signup sheet and put up a second sign that said ONLY those individuals interested in living in Kelly House should sign up on the list. He included some asinine statement about the list being university property and that anyone caught defacing the sign would be expelled.

This time, the Barretts didn't even bother to put their names on the list. I started the second go around by penciling in *George Washington Barrett.* Within a couple of hours, the signup sheet was again full of names of fictitious individuals. This time, Keith decided to cut his losses and simply tore the sheet off his door.

After finals, I headed back to Albuquerque to work on a construction crew for the summer. Overall, I was pleasantly surprised by my first year at OU. Although I had yet to find the true love of my life, I had made some new friends. The Barrett brothers were irritating, but entertaining. Although Da Fieds wasn't really a laugh-a-minute, I somehow enjoyed his calm demeanor.

I had no way of knowing it at the time, but the most important acquaintance I made that year was my roommate, the former fullback and linebacker from Carnegie. Jack's courting woes seemed to defy common sense. He had brought all of his sexual frustrations and heartbreak on himself, mostly because of romantic overkill. On top of all that, he chose to ignore every bit of good advice he had been given. Inadvertently, Jack provided me with invaluable training that I would need, and frequently use later in life, after I made the mistake of becoming best friends with the most love-starved creature that God has ever strung a gut through.

CHAPTER 2

THE LITTLE LEBANESE LUSH

I returned to Norman for my sophomore year full of anticipation. The Sooners were ranked high in the pre-season football polls and there was talk of winning a national championship. I was looking forward to partying with Da Fieds and exchanging verbal abuse with the Barretts. Although I didn't relish the idea of having to break in another roommate like Jack Jefferson, I was anxious to make some new friends. Most importantly, I felt confident that this was the year I would finally lose my virginity.

I waited until the day before classes started to drive back to OU. This time my room assignment was in Kitchens House, Cross Center. I went to the RA's office to get my room key, fully expecting a lecture about not being a scumbag. I knocked on the door and heard a squeaky voice say, "Doe is open. Cum own in."

I opened the door and walked in. Sitting at the desk was a slender black man. He had a cigarette dangling from his mouth as he stared up at me through the wire rim glasses barely propped on the end of his nose.

"Woz happenin' my man?" he inquired.

"Hi. Bob Knox. I'm your newest scumbag," I said, trying to be funny.

He stood up and shuffled over to the cabinet of room keys mounted on the wall.

"Name's Mike Pierce. You can call me by either one but not boaf. You must be dat fool dem Barrett boys toll me bout."

"Well, before you jump to any conclusions, consider your sources," I replied.

He snickered and said, "Ain't dat da damn troof. Dem two little weasels is some strange motherfuckers. And they little bro, Phil, he's weirdest of 'em all."

Oh good, I thought, another demented weasel from Chicago. I just hoped and prayed that my new roommate wasn't a former linebacker and fullback from some tiny Oklahoma town. "Has my roommate checked in yet?" I asked.

"Yeah. He's a tall, quiet, white boy. Runs track or some shit. His name is Fiddler."

I couldn't believe my good luck. Da Fieds and I were going to be roommates.

"Actually, Mike, it's pronounced "feedler", but he likes to be called Da Fieds," I said.

Mike turned and glared at me for a few seconds before responding with, "Yeah, whatever," as he tossed me my room key.

He picked up a set of linens and handed them to me. Mike was obligated to give me a lecture about the rules of the house. He made it short and sweet.

"Man, don't pull any crazy shit, and I won't have to tear yo ass up."

"Don't worry about me, but you better watch out for the Barretts. I think they are all queer," I replied.

Mike laughed again and told me, "Get the fuck outta here."

       . . .   ~   . . .

Over the summer, I decided to switch my major from math to engineering. I read a book that overplayed the environmental problems the planet faced in true extremist fashion. Although somewhat impressed by the book, I thought it would be a lot more gratifying to work on developing solutions, rather than just screaming about the problems. I also had come to the conclusion that "day don't pay mat majors shit."

Near the end of the first week of school, I was in line to get lunch when the Barretts traipsed into the cafeteria. As usual, they were babbling and cackling at the tops of their lungs. Trudging along behind them was a very large black man, who I had seen a couple of times in the study hall, but had never met. The chipmunk versions of Al Capone and Bugsy Segal appeared to be taunting him; even though it was obvious he could have crushed either one of them with just his eyelids. The three of them threw their backpacks on a table, and got in line behind me.

When I got to the serving line, I grabbed a handful of paper napkins and some silverware and threw them onto a serving tray. As I started my way down the line, the lady serving entrees on the other side of the glass partition dutifully asked me, "Kin I hep you sir?"

"Yes, go kill the cook," I snapped back.

Unfazed by my remark, she repeated her question, "Kin I hep you sir?"

"Yes, give me some money to go to McDonalds," I replied.

Now, more than a little bit annoyed, she raised her voice and said, "Kin I hep you?"

"Is the poodle fresh?" I inquired in an obnoxiously sincere tone.

Just on the verge of getting angry, the server once more asked, "Sir. Kin I HEP you?"

I finally relented and said, "Just give me a scoop of that green shit."

I finished my trek through the serving line, then went and plopped down at the same table that the Barretts and King Kong had staked out with their backpacks. A few minutes later, the huge black man and the two weasels from Chicago joined me. As they sat down, Paul introduced me to their new friend.

"Knox, dis is G. Jew notice dat his knuckles barely scrape da ground when he walks?"

Paul's insulting introduction was followed by the most infectious laugh I had ever heard. The big, black behemoth was, in fact, extremely laid back and easygoing. He stuck his hand out and said, "Hi. John Gregg, but you can call me G."

G was from the ghetto of Houston. He had been recruited by OU to play football for Barry Switzer. The football players had to report to campus earlier than other freshmen, so initially he focused solely on football and moved up the depth charts as a linebacker. When it came time to enroll for fall classes, the coaching staff told G that he would have to take a limited number of classes in order to make it to football practice. G would have none of that; he had come to OU to become a doctor and only played football as a sidelight. He quit the football team, but still had a full academic scholarship to pay for his education. G had been reassigned from the jock dorms to Cross Center. The curse of being a pre-med major doomed him to have to interact with the Barrett brothers.

Growing up in Albuquerque, I had been exposed to people of color all of my life. As an Anglo, I was actually a minority at my high school. The majority of the school population was Hispanic, but there were also some Navajo Indians from the reservations and a few black students. Since I had grown up with friends from several different races, it wasn't any big deal to me that G and I immediately became good friends.

In fact, I actually used our mixed race friendship to mock the racism and prejudice prevalent in Oklahoma. I made an analogy of our friendship to that of the "caped crusaders", Batman and Robin the Boy Wonder. To me, we were "Blackman and Robert the Boy Whiter". Whenever the opportunity presented itself, I would initiate our conversations with, "Holy watermelon, Blackman!" I guess G didn't see the need for me to make my social commentary, because he usually responded with, "Shut up, fool!"

Because G was determined to get into medical school, he studied relentlessly. I soon found myself hanging out in the study hall more than I cared to. It was early in the semester when I noticed that the short, sawed-off, middle-eastern-looking guy in my general chemistry class also frequented our study hall. Although I would have bet money on something like Faruk or Abdullah, it turned out that his name was Danny. We had a passing familiarity with one another from the dorms, but I was relieved that we had never spoken; however, after the first chemistry exam of the semester, Danny decided to break the silence. He came up to me in the study hall and inquired how I had done on the test.

"Hey, how do you think you did on that chemistry exam?" he asked.

"Okay," I said without making eye contact.

Due to the large size of the class, the chemistry exams used coded answer sheets that could be read through a scanner for grading. We were allowed to keep the question sheets in order to review for the final exam. Danny pulled out his copy of the test questions and held them in front of me. He puffed out his chest a little bit and proclaimed, "Man, I nailed that exam. I even worked that damned stoichiometry problem."

I glimpsed at his question sheet and the answers he had marked. I could see he had circled an incorrect answer for the stoichiometry problem.

"That one is wrong," I said.

"What do you mean, it's wrong?" he demanded.

"You probably didn't balance the half-reactions correctly, but it's obvious you've circled the wrong answer," I said, as I looked back down at my book, wishing that this strange little man would go away.

"Are you sure?" he asked indignantly.

I snatched the sheet out of Danny's hand and went through the entire list of 25 questions, marking the ones he had gotten wrong. I marked seven incorrect answers on his sheet and shoved it back in his chest.

"At best, you only thumb-tacked that exam," I noted.

Danny grabbed his sheet of test questions, muttered something in his unique nasal camel-speak, and stormed out of the study hall.

At breakfast the next morning, Danny told a group of guys from his floor about the "know-it-all engineering prick" he met in the study hall the night before. He then hurried off to check his grade on the chemistry exam. Sure enough, he had only gotten 18 out of the 25 questions correct.

It was at that precise moment that Danny and I became friends. Well, if nothing else, he would tolerate me long enough to help him get into medical school. Danny was from a local Lebanese-American family in which all of the males were expected to become either doctors or lawyers. When we met, Danny was actually majoring in "getting his shit together." After two disastrous semesters at Oklahoma City University, he had transferred to OU and was desperately trying to get his grades up so that he could apply to medical school. Although use of drugs and alcohol had already taken a toll on Danny's mental faculties, he was still smart enough to recognize that my math-oriented brain was an invaluable technical resource to help him to achieve his goal.

As the semester wore on, Danny and I became better acquainted. He finally figured out that it was probably better to ask me for help with his chemistry before he took the exams, so I began tutoring him on a regular basis. We even started going out to the bars to chase women together. Our budding friendship was nurtured by the fact that I was the only person in the dorms who could match Danny beer for beer.

It was early in March when Danny suggested that we get a bunch of guys together and head to South Padre Island, Texas for spring break. Time was running short, so we decided to divide up the necessary vacation planning tasks. I was put in charge of lodging, so I called around until I found a cheap fleabag hotel on the beach that would let us sleep six to a room.

Danny was in charge of recruiting, so he sat down and developed a set of very strict criteria for screening candidates to invite on our excursion. First of all, each traveler had to be able to pay his own way. Second, they had to be able to tolerate the two of us for a full week. Candidates with mild to moderate drinking problems were given bonus points.

Glen "The Geek" was the first reprobate to pass our rigorous scrutiny. Glen had been an outstanding basketball player in high school, but came to OU to study electrical engineering. He met up with Danny and me during one of our bull sessions in the study hall and found us to be entertaining. Glen earned his nickname, "The Geek", by always talking shop whenever we went out drinking. Because he was tall and handsome, Glen tended to attract females, but his scintillating discussions about electrical field theory had driven away good-looking women on several occasions.

Once allowed into the inner circle, Glen nominated the two guys living next door to him in the dorm to join our group. Jack and Scottie had gone to the same high school in Oklahoma City and decided to room together in college. Scottie was majoring in business administration and manufacturing hangovers. Jack must have been majoring in animal husbandry, because there seemed to be no end to the stream of ugly pigs he drug up to his room. Collectively, the two of them seemed to exhibit sufficiently repugnant behavior to fit in with our troupe, so we extended them an invitation, and they accepted.

The last person we invited was Matt, an overweight architecture student from "Bastin" with an extremely strong New England accent. Matt didn't drink all that much, but we all found the unbelievable tales he told to be hilarious.

After planning our vacation for almost a full week, departure day finally rolled around, so I started packing. I stuffed a toothbrush, swimsuit, and a couple of shirts into a pillowcase. I then went to the liquor store and bought four cases of beer and put them on ice. It was a 14-hour drive to South Padre Island, and I wanted to be sure we had enough beer to get us there. With six people traveling, we ended up taking two cars, so I put a couple of cases of beer in each vehicle. Danny and Glen started off the trip riding in my car with me. Matt and Jack jumped into Scottie's car with him.

We were less than 90 miles into the trip when we pulled our two-car caravan into one of the roadside rest stops to take a piss. The wind was whipping out of the north, and the temperature outside was barely above freezing. We were all wearing our beach clothes even though we were still in Oklahoma. Danny had on a pair of overalls with the legs cut off to make them into shorts. He piled out of my car holding a can of beer. After the first blast of cold wind blew up his overalls, he decided to run to the bathroom. It took only a few strides for him to stumble and fall onto the cold concrete sidewalk. He bounced right back up without ever spilling a drop of beer; however, when he came out of the bathroom I could see that his shoulder was bleeding. With the number of beers he had already consumed, I knew he probably hadn't felt a thing.

We continued on our way south, making piss stops along the way with increased frequency. By the time we hit San Antonio, we were out of beer, so we pulled off the interstate to restock our ice chests. It was two o'clock in the morning and very few places were open. We wandered aimlessly for about an hour before we found an all-night convenience store.

In our quest for beer, we had gotten relatively far off the beaten path, so I asked the store clerk how to get back to the interstate. In a combination of Spanish and broken English, he managed to totally confuse me, so I decided we would just wing it. We pooled our money and bought a couple of cases of beer, then piled back into our cars. Danny always enjoyed having a variety of people to bother, so he jumped in the car with Jack and Scottie. Glen and Matt climbed in with me. Before we pulled out of the parking lot, I told Scottie to just follow me and I would get us back to the interstate.

With the aid of a road map, Glen was able to figure out where we were and how we could get back to the main highway. Unfortunately, the route he chose had recently been narrowed to two lanes due to construction. I decided to just press on rather than weave back through town and potentially get lost again.

We hadn't gone more than a mile when all of a sudden Scottie whipped his car out from behind, passed me, then quickly pulled over to the side of the road. I immediately pulled over behind him. Scottie stepped out of the driver's side and tilted the seat forward to allow someone to climb out of the back seat. After a few seconds, Danny spilled out of the car and onto the ground. I thought to myself that he probably just needed to throw up.

Danny crawled on the ground for the first few feet before he managed to stand up and start stumbling toward my car, weaving back and forth with each step. I actually became worried that he might veer out into traffic and get hit by one of the cars rushing by. With the headlights of my car shining on him, I could see dried blood on Danny's shoulder from that afternoon's sidewalk wound; I could also see that he had wet his overalls.

As he approached my car, I rolled down the window to ask what he wanted. He put his left hand on the hood to steady himself for the last few feet. When he finally managed to stagger up to my window, he looked at me as seriously as he could through his bloodshot eyes and slurred out, "Lemme see da map."

I let out a loud scream as I shoved open my door. I jumped out of the car, grabbed Danny by the back of his overalls and drug him back to Scottie's car. I yanked open the passenger side door, threw Danny into the back seat, and proceeded to scream at Scottie.

"Are you out of your fucking mind? You pulled over to let the drunken camel jockey take a look at the map? Jesus Christ you guys, Danny can't read a map when he is sober. You do realize that he has wet his pants don't you? Do not pull over again unless it is to piss or puke!"

When I got back in my car, Glen and Matt were howling with laughter. I didn't find the incident all that amusing until a few days later. We were all lying by the pool drinking beer when I asked Scottie if he truly felt that drunken camel jockeys who wet their pants make the best navigators.

...   ~   ...

After seven days of nonstop drinking, our vacation came to an end and it was time to head home. On our way back to Oklahoma, Danny asked me to stop in Dallas so he could see his friend, Monte. I had only met Monte briefly during one of his trips to Norman, but I had been able to deduce that he was a little bit weird. Initially, I was inclined to just keep on driving, but Danny convinced me to pull off by assuring me that Monte would have plenty of drugs and alcohol.

Monte had actually started college at OU; or more correctly, he had enrolled at OU while he did drugs and drank heavily. One fateful Friday night, he managed to get his father's Lincoln Continental stolen from a bowling alley because he left the keys in it. The very next night, he was pulled over in his mother's car and arrested for driving under the influence of alcohol. Possession of marijuana charges were tacked on when the officers found a bag of pot, in one of the most obscure hiding places, sticking out from beneath the driver's side floor mat. Monte always maintained that he was drunk, but not stoned, when he was arrested. Actually, he was rather bothered by the fact that he hadn't even had a chance to sample his stash.

With his one phone call, Monte called Dick, his adoptive father. Dick carried his weight well for a man standing over 6-foot-4 and weighing in excess of 250 pounds. Dick knew Monte's mom, Diana, from high school. After serving in the Navy, he started playing drums for a western swing band that toured around southeastern Oklahoma. It was during one of Dick's weekend gigs that he and Diana became reacquainted. Diana had recently divorced, so she and Dick started dating. Soon after they were married, Dick adopted Monte and his brother, Bubba. He immediately fell in love with the two little boys and grew to love Diana.

Although he had always been a reasonable and understanding father, this time Dick knew that Monte needed outside help. He decided to let Monte spend the rest of the weekend in jail, to sober up and think about his screwups. After bailing him out, Dick offered Monte two alternatives; he could join the Navy, or he could join the Navy.

Less than a week after his arrest, Monte announced that he had decided to join the Navy. That weekend, Danny and several other high school buddies threw an impromptu going away party for him. It took two kegs of beer and almost an ounce of weed for everybody to say their goodbyes to Monte.

Two days after the going away party, Danny decided to blow off classes and go to one of the local beer joints to drink a couple of pitchers of beer, play a little foosball, and try to figure out what was causing his grades to suffer so badly. It was about three in the afternoon when he stumbled into the Jockey Strap Saloon. It took a couple of seconds, but when his eyes finally adjusted to the darkness he was surprised to see Monte sitting in the corner booth. He had a half-full pitcher of beer in front of him and was bouncing a golf ball on the table.

Somewhat in disbelief, Danny walked up and said, "Mont, I thought you went to join the Navy?"

Monte replied, "I did, but when I got there my blood alcohol level was too high. They wouldn't take me."

Danny thought for a moment before pointing out, "Well, Mont, you sure are doing all you can to get that blood alcohol level back down."

Three days later the US Navy relented and allowed Monte to enlist; a move that probably saved his life. The structure and discipline of military life was just what Monte needed to help him grow up. Bear in mind that everything in the Navy is kept "spic and span". In essence, Monte had been sentenced to four years in neat freak heaven.

After finishing boot camp in San Diego, Monte was stationed in Dallas. The fact that there was a Naval base in the middle of Texas struck me as a little bit strange; however, given that this was one of Danny's friends, it somehow seemed appropriate for him to be landlocked while in the Navy.

I pulled off the interstate just outside of Dallas. Scottie followed me into the parking lot of a convenience store. Danny hopped out of my car and went inside to call Monte for directions to his place. Glen decided he would rather squeeze into Scottie's car than accompany Danny and me on our quest for drugs.

"Knox, I'm not going with you two dumb shits. I need to get back to Norman and work on some electrical circuits homework," he reasoned.

"Fine with me. I'll get your luggage," I replied.

While Glen struggled to get out of my back seat, I went around to the rear of the car. I opened the trunk, grabbed his suitcase, and heaved it as far as I could across the parking lot. As Glen scurried over to retrieve his belongings, I walked up to Scottie's car to give the rest of the group a very special good-bye. I pulled down my Bermuda shorts and planted my bare butt against the driver's side window. I rotated my cheeks in a circular motion, which left an unmistakable smudge print on the window. When I turned around to admire my masterpiece, Scottie threw me a finger from inside the car, a gesture that I returned to him as they pulled out of the parking lot.

It took over two hours for Danny and me to find Monte's apartment. As it turned out, he actually lived closer to Ft. Worth than Dallas. When we finally arrived, Monte greeted us at the door holding a couple of beers and a water pipe.

"Here Danny. You guys take a hit and then I'll give you a tour of my apartment."

Although I was grateful for the bong hit and the brew, I wasn't exactly thrilled with the notion of touring the apartment. I thought about asking Monte why in the hell he thought anyone would want to tour a one-bedroom apartment that two sailors shared, but I decided to humor him in order to keep the beers coming.

Monte started off the tour by pointing out and naming each one of the two-dozen fish in his aquarium. I wondered why anybody would bother with an aquarium in such a small apartment. He proceeded to elaborate on the details of his stereo system, which filled up most of the living room. He was quick to point out that his albums were in alphabetical order, based on the artist. I couldn't understand why in the hell anybody would go to all the trouble of alphabetizing albums. Monte seemed to be especially proud of all of the crap he had piled on the shelves around his living room. It seemed strange to me that a man would go to the trouble of collecting a bunch of worthless trinkets.

Once we reached the kitchen, Monte gave us a twenty-minute briefing on all of his cooking utensils. I found it kind of weird for a man to be proud of his cookware, but I didn't mind the lecture all that much because I was able to grab two more beers from the fridge. He then led us down the hall to show off the new toilet seat cover and shower curtain he had gotten for his bathroom.

When we finally arrived at the bedroom, I could see there was just one queen-size bed. Somewhat curious, I decided to inquire as to the sleeping arrangements Monte had worked out with his roommate.

"Monte, where does your roommate sleep?" I asked.

"In here. We share that bed," he replied rather matter-of-factly.

The opportunity was too much for Danny to resist.

"Mont, have you sucked his dick yet?" he asked, which caused me to giggle.

"Not yet, Danny, but I have let him screw me in the ass a few times," Monte quipped back, which made Danny laugh out loud.

I wasn't totally comfortable with Monte's response, but since Danny laughed I decided it was probably all in jest.

We finally made our way back to the living room. Monte sat down and rolled us a couple of joints for the drive back to Norman. Danny and I had blown all of our money during drinking binges on the beach, so I offered to write Monte a check for the dope. He told me I could just pay him the next time he came up to Norman. Danny wasn't satisfied with the drugs on credit arrangement, so he decided to barter with Monte over our tab.

"Mont, I'll let you suck my dick, but it's gonna cost you two more joints and a six-pack of beer."

Monte declined by saying, "Sorry, Danny, but I only have three beers left."

Danny and I walked out the door with a fresh stash of drugs to continue our trip back to Norman. Thankfully, our low cash reserves prevented us from buying more beer to wash down the marijuana smoke.

Although Oklahoma is located just above Texas on the road map, by the time we hit the border Danny and I were high enough to be in Canada.

· · ·   ~   · · ·

Due to the influence of my newfound Lebanese friend, the rest of the semester became one long drunk; however, we somehow managed to squeeze in a little bit of study time in between happy hours. With a minimal amount of effort on his part, and a large dose of my tutoring, Danny's test scores started to rise. As word of his academic improvement spread, I got requests to tutor other members of his family. Soon I found myself getting paid to tutor Danny's sister, his younger brother, and two cousins. Near the end of the semester, I told Danny how thankful I was that his entire fucking family was stupid.

In addition to being a borderline alcoholic, Danny was every bit as filthy and lazy as me. Whenever we returned from an evening of imbibing, he would stumble toward his room, peeling off clothes as he went. When he got down to his pants, he would reach into his pockets and simply pull them inside out so the contents would fall to the floor. This system made it a lot easier to find his keys the next day.

It was thanks to Danny's slovenly behavior that I came to learn that Monte was a little bit peculiar when it came to cleaning. Whenever Monte came up from Dallas, I noticed he was almost too anxious to tidy up Danny's room. At first, I thought he did it just to get money. A month's worth of Danny's pocket discharges to the floor would be enough for a couple of pitchers of beer and several hours' worth of quarters for the foosball table. But Monte didn't have to clean to make money; he had other sources of revenue.

One evening just before finals week, Danny came into my room and informed me that we were going to have a very important meeting later that evening. He told me to gather up the usual group of reprobates, buy some beer, and meet in his room at 8:00 p.m. sharp. I went to the liquor store and bought a case beer, came back, and rounded up half-a-dozen of my fellow dorm denizens.

When I arrived at Danny's room, I almost didn't recognize the place. Monte had picked up everything off the floor, made the bed, vacuumed the rug, washed the windows, dusted the blinds, and even organized the books on Danny's desk. In addition, he had set up a small classroom, complete with chairs and a makeshift chalkboard.

As we filed in, Monte told us all to take a seat. Once we got settled, he took off the pillowcase that had been concealing what he had written on his chalkboard. He whipped out a yardstick from behind his back and tapped the chalkboard as he announced, "Tonight's lesson is about D-R-U-G-S, drugs."

Monte proceeded to give us a thirty-minute lecture on drugs. His talk wasn't about the evils of drugs; in reality it was a sales pitch for the drugs he was marketing. On the chalkboard he had listed his bargain basement prices. He gave us a detailed description of the hallucinogenic impact each drug would have on us if taken in combination with sufficient alcohol. It was readily apparent that Monte was speaking from years of experience.

CHAPTER 3

THE STRANGEST CREATURE

My third year at OU started off with a newfound sense of maturity and responsibility. Not for me, of course, but for G. He'd applied to become an RA the previous spring and had been selected. Through some political maneuvering, Danny and I were able to find out which dorm G had been assigned. We signed up for single rooms and paid our deposits in advance to ensure we would get the two rooms on the first floor. G had his office and bedroom just off the front entrance; Danny and I had single rooms across the hall from one another. Thankfully, the Barrett brothers had been banished to the third floor.

G was ideally suited for the job as RA. Because he was totally committed to getting into medical school, he set a good example academically. Although not terribly outgoing, he was quite personable with everyone he met. Most importantly, his physical size was a strong deterrent to any "scumbag" behavior on the part of the dorm dwellers.

Early in the semester, G scheduled the obligatory dorm orientation meeting for the residents. He put up signs inviting everyone to gather in the T.V. lounge at 7:00 p.m. That evening, G stood at the entrance to the lounge, shook hands and handed out printed materials to the attendees as they filed in. I noticed there were quite a few faces that I did not recognize. G started off the meeting by having everybody stand up and introduce themselves. Getting down to business, he went through the checklist that had been provided to him by University Housing. Just before the last item on the list, G made a point to stress that he was there to help if anyone had any problems.

The final topic on the checklist was "Dormitory Rules and Disciplinary Measures". G stared down at his list for a few seconds without saying a word. Then, he slowly stood up and methodically tore the sheet of paper into little pieces. When he finished shredding the document, he raised head, glared directly at me and announced, "I don't do no paperwork. You fuck up in my dorm and I kick yo motherfuckin' ass."

On his way out of the lounge, G walked straight over to me, grabbed my hand, stuffed the shreds of paper into my palm, and closed my fist around them. Every guy in the lounge stared at the two of us; most of them trembled in their seats. They had no way of knowing that we were the best of friends, so his little show was quite effective.

It didn't take long for me to fall into my semester routine, which consisted mostly of drinking and studying. In my spare time, I devoted all of my energy to harassing my two floor mates. In fact, I guess I have to shoulder some of the blame for making Danny such an ornery little runt.

Danny's father had yanked him back to Norman after he drank his way to a sparkling 1.8 grade point average over two semesters at Oklahoma City University. Hooking up with G and me was good for Danny in terms of improving his academic performance, but rooming across the hall from me halted any behavioral development his father may have hoped for.

I came home from class one day early in the semester and found G's door closed, which meant that he was either gone or asleep. There was absolutely nobody in the T.V. lounge for me to bother, so I headed back to my room to see if Danny was available for some pestering. As I opened the door to my room, I heard shower water running in the bathroom that we shared. After I dumped my books in my room, I quietly snuck into the bathroom and saw Danny's silhouette through the transparent shower curtain. I waited quietly for him to start shampooing his hair, which meant that he would have to close his eyes. When I saw Danny raise his arms to start scrubbing his scalp, I carefully reached into the shower and slowly snaked my hand along the wall until I felt the cold-water handle, which I proceeded to turn all the way off. I scurried back to my room, flipped open a book, and pretended to be studying.

A few seconds later I heard a blood-curdling scream followed by, "MOTHERFUCKER!"

Danny came running out of the bathroom, dripping wet, with suds in his hair and a big red welt on his back from the hot stream of water that had damn near scalded him.

When he saw me he yelled, "KNOX. That's not funny!"

"Oh yeah, then explain to me why I'm laughing so hard," I replied.

As Danny re-entered the bathroom, he made sure to lock the deadbolt on the door; however, I wasn't nearly through messing with him. I got up from my chair and walked across the hall to his room. I pulled my pants down around my ankles and sat down directly on his pillow. I picked up a newspaper off the floor and pretended to be reading while taking a dump at the head of Danny's bed.

When Danny came out of the bathroom the second time, he took one look at me and yelled, "Get the fuck off my pillow."

I responded with, "Be with you in a sec, Danny. Hey, where do you keep the toilet paper?"

He grabbed a shoe off the floor, flung it at my head and screamed, "Get the fuck out of my room!"

I pulled up my pants and pretended to storm off in a huff. I couldn't leave without a snotty parting remark. As I exited his room, I said, "Okay. I know when I'm not wanted. You don't have to hit Bob Knox with a shoe."

. . .   ~   . . .

Living across the hall from Danny also caused me to become better acquainted with Monte, his strange friend from Dallas. Together, the two of them formed a very odd pair. From just their physical appearance, one would never conclude that they had much in common. Monte was tall and slender, with blond hair and blues eyes; his Aryan features were quite a contrast to those of Danny, who was short and skinny, with thick, salt-and-pepper hair that probably started turning gray in elementary school. Monte was truly graceful, using his long legs to help him glide along almost effortlessly. Danny, on the other hand, was truly chaos in motion. He was a whirling dervish, whenever he found enough energy to get up and actually do something. Whenever they were together, Danny took on the appearance of a spinning moon on an out of control orbit around the planet Monte.

In spite of their contrasting appearances, Danny and Monte shared a set of common desires; they both had very strong cravings for drugs and alcohol. They also possessed similar moral values; there's not much they wouldn't do in the pursuit of pussy. Most importantly, they shared a deep-rooted core belief that the world revolved around OU football. In fact, Monte drove up from Dallas and roomed with Danny for every OU home football game that fall.

It didn't take long for me to conclude that Monte was more than just a little bit neurotic when it came to OU football. Early in October, he drove up from Dallas to pick up Danny and drive back down to Dallas to attend the OU-Texas game that is played in Dallas. After the game, Monte was going to bring Danny back to Norman from Dallas, then turn around and drive back down to Dallas. Given the two characters involved, it was almost logical for their plans to make absolutely no sense at all.

On the Friday before the game, G and I got up early to go eat breakfast. As we walked to the cafeteria we discussed the logic of Monte driving back and forth to Dallas numerous times just to be with Danny. All of the sudden, we heard the roar of a car engine and turned around in time to see Monte's Firebird accelerating as if it were going to run us down. We jumped up on the sidewalk as the Firebird screeched to a halt in front of us. When the driver's window rolled down, we saw Danny seated behind the wheel, with a beer can between his legs. Monte was bent over in the passenger's seat, fiddling with something below the dashboard.

"We're off to Dallas!" Danny slurred, as beer dribbled down his chin.

I was curious as to why on earth Monte would let Danny drive his car on the trip back down to Dallas, so I leaned my head inside the window and inquired about this incredible act of stupidity.

"Monte, have you lost your fucking mind? Why are you letting Danny drive?"

Monte sat up and proudly displayed a big fat joint as he announced, "So I can roll. Danny's joints fall apart too easily."

G wheeled around and hurried off to the cafeteria, not wanting to be part of any conversation dealing with drugs. I decided to issue a few last minute instructions to Danny and Monte before they left for Dallas.

"Danny, drive careful! We'll meet you guys at the Anatole Hotel around 7:00 p.m. tonight."

Danny started to rev the engine of the Firebird, so I screamed at Monte, "Keep him sober until I get to Dallas!"

Monte laughed out loud as Danny floored the accelerator and the two of them sped off.

G and I didn't leave Norman until late that afternoon. We both had exams that we couldn't afford to miss. It was obvious that not all faculty members had been enlightened to the fact that the OU-Texas weekend included a full day of drinking on the Friday before the game, and a full day of recovering on the Monday afterwards.

After our exams, G and I piled into my car and headed for Dallas. We had just crossed the Red River when we came upon the support trailer for the "Run to Dallas" charity event. Every year, sororities and fraternities from both OU and UT would organize groups to run from the two campuses all the way to the Cotton Bowl. The runners would carry footballs autographed by their respective teams. The groups from both schools would start out on Thursday, winding up at the Cotton Bowl around mid-night on Friday. The event was designed to raise money for needy Greek students who couldn't afford new BMW's, or some such worthy cause.

As we passed the OU caravan, G blurted out, "Ain't dat just like a bunch of dumb ass white boys. Running down da middle of da fuckin' interstate all da way to Dallas. Man you fuckers is crazy."

I turned and glared at him, then asked, "How crazy do you think it would be for a black man to get kicked out of a car on the interstate in Texas and have to hitch-hike his way to Dallas?"

He just laughed and told me, "I'd jus grab dat football from one of dem crazy white boys. Ain't nobody gonna hit a nigger runnin' wid a football in Texas."

Once we got to Dallas, I managed to find my way to the Anatole Hotel. The hotel lot was nearly full, so we ended up parking fairly far away from the actual building. As we walked into the lobby, I stopped to gawk at the expansive structure. I was not encouraged at our prospects of actually finding Danny and Monte inside a building bigger than most shopping malls.

Then it dawned on me. All we had to do was find the hotel bar and we would find Danny and Monte. So I walked over to the concierge and innocently asked, "Where is your bar?"

He just looked at me with a blank stare and replied, "Which one? We have six."

I thought for a moment before replying, "The one most likely to have girls and dancing."

The concierge directed me to *Crocodiles*, a disco bar at the far end of the lobby. As we made our way across the lobby, G and I stared in amazement at the size of the vast enclosed expanse. Halfway to our destination I stopped at one of the small island bars in the lobby. I wasn't sure how long our journey would last, so I decided to get a beer for the trip.

When we finally arrived at Crocodiles, G told me to go in and look for Danny and Monte while he checked out all the "good lookin' pussy" wandering through the lobby. I walked over to the entrance to the bar and reached out to grab the door handle. Suddenly, the door burst open and out sprinted Danny, followed in close pursuit by an obviously irate female. Danny immediately recognized G's unmistakable frame, so he ran over and crouched down behind him. The livid young lady chased after him, and they soon began circling G like Wylie coyote chasing the Roadrunner.

G finally grabbed Danny's pursuer by the arm and said, "Whoa! Slow down. Woz da matta?"

"I'm gonna scratch his fucking eyes out, that's what's the matter!" she screamed as she lunged at Danny, who was still cowering behind G.

Instinctively, G swooped the livid young lady up in his arms and carried her to the nearest sofa to sit her down. With the coast now clear, Danny sauntered over to me, grabbed the beer out of my hand, and took a swig. I, of course, was on the verge of a major aneurysm from my fit of laughter.

About this time, Monte ran out of Crocodiles, obviously in search of Danny and his female pursuer. When he spotted us, he veered over to where we were standing.

I confronted him with, " Monte, what the fuck was that all about?"

Barely able to speak between fits of laughter, Monte said, "Danny asked that girl to dance, but she turned him down. So he called her stuck up and walked away. When I tried to go over and apologize to her, Danny shouted, "Mont, don't apologize to that cunt." Bob, she flew out of her chair and chased Danny out of the bar. I had to pay the tab before I could leave."

"I told you to keep him sober until I got here," I whined at Monte.

Monte put a serious look on his face and said, "Bob, I was doing real good, but somehow Danny got ahold of some pot," trying to insinuate innocence on his part.

I growled at Monte, but resisted the urge to wrap my hands around his throat.

G finally managed to calm down the young lady enough to escort her out to her car. When he returned he said, "I don't wanna know. Les jus get outta dis place before he gets us arrested."

When we left, I took G to our downtown hotel to get checked in. His girlfriend had come up from Houston, so I knew he was through for the evening. It was getting late so I decided to just check into my room and rock a twelve-pack of beer to sleep. Danny and Monte had checked in earlier that afternoon, so they decided to go down and become part of the scene on Commerce Street. Before they left, I once again instructed Monte to keep an eye on Danny.

The scene on Commerce Street was truly unique. Every year, the city of Dallas would cordon off the downtown district and let the revelers from both schools walk up and down Commerce Street screaming at each other. Cars would inch along with people hanging out the windows, shouting all kinds of obscenities at fans wearing the wrong school colors. Mixing alcohol with the heated rivalry between the two schools always led to numerous altercations. There was an unofficial contest to see which school could post the higher number of students arrested on Commerce Street.

Danny and Monte left the hotel and walked with the crowd on Commerce Street. After one block, Danny abruptly turned around and started to walk the "wrong way" down the sidewalk. Three of Dallas' finest descended on him like kamikaze pilots. They wrestled him to the ground, slapped handcuffs on him, and whisked him off to the paddy wagon before Monte was even able to discern what was happening.

When Monte checked with the police, he was told they had taken Danny to jail for the night. Monte became frantic. He ran back to the hotel and came straight up to my room.

"BOB! Danny's been arrested. We gotta get him out," he screamed.

I choked on a sip of beer as I blurted out, "Good Job, Mont! That's the way to keep an eye on him. You know the rules. They will let him out about 4:00 in the morning, after he has had a chance to sober up. You might as well go to bed, which is precisely what I plan on doing."

Monte would never let Danny go through his prison ordeal alone. He marched out of the hotel and straight down to the police station where Danny was being held. He went inside and asked the desk sergeant when Danny would be released and was told exactly what I had said just minutes earlier.

Monte walked over to some wooden benches, but was too restless to sit down, so he lit a cigarette and started pacing back and forth, stopping periodically to empty the ashtray he held in his hand. After an hour of nervous pacing, he decided to tidy up the area around him. When Monte commented out loud as to how filthy the place was the desk sergeant told him that he could either shut up or leave, so he went outside and continued to pace back and forth while he waited for Danny to be released.

It was just before 5:00 a.m. when Danny stumbled out of the police station. Monte had spent nearly six hours waiting for him. Danny, on the other hand, had been asleep in his cell the whole time.

. . .   ~   . . .

It wasn't until after the OU-Texas game that Danny and I settled in for the semester and got serious about our studies. We strived to cut back our carousing to five nights per week by mid-October, at the very latest. It was during this late semester period of self-discipline that Danny somehow managed to start dating an extremely cute high school student. Charlotte was very petite, with dirty blond hair and beautiful blue eyes. She was a junior at a private high school run by the Baptist church. I'm not sure exactly how they met; it certainly wasn't because Danny was going to church.

Although Danny enjoyed being in the company of an attractive woman, he certainly didn't give a shit about having any kind of meaningful relationship. The only things in life that meant anything to him were having sex, getting drunk, or any combination of the two. He was about as subtle as a train wreck when it came to dragging Charlotte back to his room to have sex, so it wasn't long before every guy in the dorm knew what was going on.

Danny's supposed romance with Charlotte continued over the Christmas holidays and on into the spring semester. Unfortunately for Danny, the change of seasons forced him to alter his dormitory sex routine. Because the dorm rooms weren't air conditioned, he had to leave his windows open to get some air circulation. This meant that his room was highly susceptible to surreptitious eavesdropping, for anyone devious enough to do so.

I came back from class one afternoon and saw that Danny's door was shut, his windows were open, and the blinds were down; the telltale signs that he was not alone. I found the opportunity too good to resist. I went into the lounge and recruited some of the guys watching TV to accompany me on a clandestine eavesdropping mission. It only took a couple of minutes to convince several of the sexual deviates to come with me to listen in on Danny and Charlotte in the throes of passion.

I led my perverted troupe out of the lounge and around to the back of the dorm. I put a finger to my lips to quiet the others as we carefully crawled over to the sill beneath Danny's window. We slowly raised our heads up to get our ears close to the open window. At first, all we could hear were rustling noises inside the room. These were followed by some muffled moans of human origin, but there were certainly no screams of ecstasy. Silence fell over the room for a few seconds, only to be broken by the melodious tones of Charlotte's voice.

"Danny, is Mr. Worm through playing?" she asked sweetly.

I covered my mouth to keep from spitting up a lung as I wheeled around and sprinted back to the safety of the TV lounge. My fellow voyeurs followed close behind me, barely able to contain their laughter. Once inside the lounge, we all broke into hysterics. Needless to say, we taunted Danny with Mr. Worm catcalls the minute he emerged from his love nest.

Danny was totally oblivious to our teasing. He didn't give a damn about what we had heard. It was also obvious that he didn't care about Charlotte's reputation. He continued to use absolutely no discretion while parading her in and out of his dorm room for afternoon recess with Mr. Worm.

One night about midway through the spring semester, I convinced Danny and the Barrett brothers that we had studied enough for the week and that we needed to go to the local beer joint for some well-deserved relaxation. It was the middle of the week, so the place was almost deserted. The stage had musical instruments for the rock-and-roll group that played on weekends, but this night there was only a DJ playing records.

We had just sat down when the DJ put on "*Wont Get Fooled Again*". This was another opportunity too good to pass up. I looked over at the Barrett brothers and said, "Let's do it."

We all sprinted up onto the stage and went into our imitation of *The Who*. I played fake drums, Pat Barrett was on air bass guitar, Paul Barrett was on air guitar and mock vocals, and Danny was the mock lead vocalist.

At first, the DJ appeared annoyed, but he soon got tickled with our antics as we jumped around the stage just like the real band did during their concerts. After the first song, the DJ came over and asked us the name of our band. Without batting an eye, Pat told him that we called ourselves "Gary and the Firing Squad" in honor of a death row inmate who had chosen to be executed just a few days prior to our debut on stage.

The DJ laughed and asked if we would do another song, which we gladly agreed to. This time, however, he grabbed his microphone and announced the name of our band to the sparse crowd inside the bar. I have always felt that it's a good idea to let everyone in a public place know that I am demented and that I only hang around with other sick individuals. Surely, that has to improve my chances with the ladies. Strangely enough, it worked for Danny that night.

There were two girls sitting at one of the tables near the dance floor, talking and trying their best to ignore our antics up on the stage. After our second performance, we went back to our table to concentrate on draining our pitchers of beer. Danny immediately struck up a conversation with the two girls and soon they were sitting with us, laughing at Danny and, as I noticed, drinking more than their fair share of our beer.

The more attractive of the two ladies was named Teri. She was a senior at OU, majoring in nursing and would be graduating in a few months. Teri took an immediate shining to Danny. One thing led to another and Teri ended up going home with Danny that night, leaving her dog-faced roommate behind for the Barrett brothers and me to fight over. However, we weren't able to coax enough beer into the basset hound to get her to even consider going home with any of us.

After that night, Danny soon fell into a pattern of "afternoon delight" with Charlotte, followed by "night moves" with Teri. Because Charlotte was just a junior in high school, she had an early curfew. So Danny would bring her over to his room in the afternoon, let Mr. Worm out to play, and then rush her back to her high school. He would then come back to the dorm to eat dinner and study for a few minutes before he headed over to Teri's dorm room to spend the night with her.

Being the laziest creature on the planet, Danny soon tired of all the extra effort he was being forced to exert just to get laid. He didn't mind having sex with two different women, but actually having to get his carcass up and walk or drive was too much physical exertion for him. So he made the executive decision that all sex would occur in his dorm room. In order to simplify the logistics associated with his sexual rendezvous, he gave keys to his room to both Charlotte and Teri. The entire dormitory was totally flabbergasted over the incredible stupidity of his decision.

It was bound to happen. One evening, Danny had Teri in his room when he heard Charlotte put her key in the door. He sprang out of bed, pulled on his boxers, and bolted over to the door before Charlotte could get it open. He then ran out in the hall in his underwear and shut the door behind him.

"You can't go in there," he told Charlotte.

"Why?" she asked, showing her naiveté.

"Because you aren't allowed in my room. You aren't even supposed to have a key," he countered.

"But Danny, you gave me the key?" she countered back.

"Well, you better get out of here before someone finds out that I gave you a key. Then you would really be in big trouble."

Unbelievably, Charlotte bought Danny's line of bullshit and left without incident. However, it would only be a matter of time before Habib Heffner would again get busted in his dormitory bachelor pad.

...   ~   ...

While Danny was busy trying to share his affections with two different women, I had set my sights on a Costa Rican girl who lived in an adjacent women's dorm. Although physically attractive, the fact that Lydia set the curve in my engineering math class was what really turned me on. I had tried to approach her in the cafeteria on several occasions, but it seemed that every time I gathered enough nerve to strike up a conversation, there was the same dorky guy hanging around her table and commanding all of her attention. I needed to figure out a way to somehow get rid of dork boy if I was ever to get an opportunity to unleash my incredible charm on Lydia.

My big break came on the night of our spring dormitory party. Lydia showed up stylishly tardy and sure enough, the dorky guy immediately started hovering over her. He was wearing white pants and a white satin shirt, trying his best to look just like John Travolta in *Saturday Night Fever*. The dork kept asking Lydia to dance, never once letting her alone for more than a few seconds. I could tell she wasn't interested in him, but was too nice to tell him to buzz off.

Early in the evening, I lamented my romantic frustrations to Pat Barrett.

"Pat, I've got a problem. I'm never going to get to play hide the enchilada with that Costa Rican chick, because dork boy is always lurking around her."

Pat listened intently to my dilemma, then, in his deepest east side Chicago mobster accent, he said, "Bob. Not a problem."

Pat walked over to the horse trough situated in the corner of the room and scooped up a glass of recently mixed "jungle juice." Our drink for the evening was a combination of orange juice, apple juice, cranberry juice, grape juice, and every imaginable kind of liquor we could get our hands on. When mixed together, the fluids took on a dark purple color because of the grape juice.

I watched intently as Pat walked towards Lydia's table. About three feet from his target, Pat went into his best "Oops I Tripped Over A Crack In The Floor" routine, and threw his drink all over my nemesis. He jumped up and pretended to be embarrassed, while he smeared the jungle juice all over the guy's pants. Pat apologized profusely to the poor dork boy who now had to go home to change clothes.

This was the opening I had been waiting for. Before the commotion from the apparent accident had dissipated, I swooped down on my prey. While Pat escorted his victim to the nearest exit, I slid into the seat next to Lydia.

"I enjoy Lagrange polynomials much more than Fourier transforms, don't you?" I asked.

Lydia stared at me in disbelief for a few seconds before she asked, "Did jew estage that whole escene?"

"Nope. I don't know either one of those guys," I lied.

She started to grow suspicious as she pointed out, "But Pat, he leaves in jew dorm?"

"I thought he looked familiar," I replied.

I followed up my introductory lines with some equally entertaining snippets about differential calculus. After a few nervous moments, Lydia giggled and actually thanked me for rescuing her from the dork boy.

Eventually, I coaxed Lydia out onto the dance floor. It wasn't long before I suggested that we go out on a date some time, and she accepted my invitation. With my primary mission accomplished, I could now focus on getting drunk.

Danny had been conspicuously absent from the party for most of the evening. It wasn't like him to be late for any event that involved alcohol. He finally came strolling into the party around midnight with Teri on his arm. I knew that he had been with Charlotte earlier in the day because his blinds were drawn when I came back from class.

I walked over to the watering trough and scooped out three glasses of jungle juice. I then made my way over to where Danny and his date were standing. I kept one glass for myself and handed the other two glasses to the little Lebanese Don Juan and his female companion. Danny choked on his first sip, but managed to chug the remaining contents. In order to keep up with Danny I was forced to slam my drink in one gulp. We spent the rest of the evening competing to see who could consume the most alcohol.

When I woke up the next morning, I declared myself the unofficial winner of the previous night's drinking contest. I felt like I had been drug through the jungle by a pack of hyenas. Judging from the taste in my mouth, they must have drug me face down through a pile of their dung. I somehow managed to get out of bed and go to breakfast with G, who felt fine because he didn't drink at all. I was picking over my watery scrambled artificial eggs when G asked, "Knox, did you axe her?"

"No John. I did not take a hatchet to her," I snidely replied.

"Fuck you. You know wadda mean. Did you axe her out?" he inquired.

I mocked him by saying, "Yes, John. I axed her out," then returned to stirring my eggs.

Danny straggled in a little bit later than the rest of us because he had spent the night at Teri's dorm. After he made his way through the serving line, he came over and sat down at our table. As he shuttled the plates from his tray to the table, Danny puffed out his chest and announced, "Knox, I slept with two women on the SAME day."

Then, in a voice loud enough to carry through the entire cafeteria, he yelled, "Knox, have you slept with two women in your entire life?"

I didn't have the guts to admit that I hadn't, so I just sat there silent while everyone at the table laughed at me.

   ...   ~   ...

Danny really enjoyed his notoriety as "the guy in our dorm who was sleeping with two different women." He certainly wasn't shy about pointing it out to everyone. However, given the fact that he had yet to get his own little house in order, trying to juggle two women would soon prove to be a task way beyond his capabilities. In fact, his tenure of sleeping with two women was relatively short-lived.

On the Monday after our jungle juice party, Charlotte busted Danny in bed with Teri again. This time, however, she actually caught them in the act. Charlotte screamed at Danny that she never wanted to see him again and stormed off in tears. It seemed as though Mr. Worm was through playing with her forever.

Danny was now forced to focus his affections solely on Teri; however, he soon found out that Teri felt no such fidelity obligation towards him. On Wednesday, Danny noticed that he needed to scratch Mr. Worm more than usual. On Thursday, he discovered a strange rash around his pubic region, so he called and made an appointment with his uncle, who was a nephrologist. On Friday, a quick examination revealed that Danny had "the crabs". His uncle wrote him a prescription for some pills and medicated shampoo to get rid of his affliction.

As expected, I was totally sympathetic to Danny's plight. After learning second hand of his medical condition, I immediately went out and bought a bottle of Clorox. I thoroughly deloused our communal bathroom and then hung a reassuring note of support on Danny's door that read:

"DANNY, IF I GET THE CRABS FROM YOUR INFECTED CAMEL JOCKEY CARCASS, I WILL PERSONALLY CUT OFF YOUR DICK AND SHOVE IT UP YOUR ASSHOLE.

LOVE, BOB."

On the following Friday, we were watching TV in the lounge when Charlotte showed up unexpectedly. From her bloodshot eyes I could tell that she had been crying. She apprehensively made her way into the lounge and stood next to Danny for a few seconds. He refused to even acknowledge her presence.

"Can we talk in private?" she finally asked in a soft low whimper.

Danny stood up and walked out of the lounge without a saying word. Charlotte followed him as he made his way back to his room. Once they reached the privacy of Danny's room, Charlotte announced that she had missed her period.

News of Charlotte's condition spread like a wildfire. Needless to say, Danny's notoriety throughout the dorm community plummeted. His reputation immediately went from "stud pussy monger" to "disease-ridden moron." Although he professed to be unfazed, I could tell that Danny was truly stressed out by the difficult situation in which he had gotten himself.

As fate would have it, a third woman had to step in and save Danny's ass. One week after her surprise announcement, Charlotte called Danny and told him that she had been to see her doctor. It turned out that she was late for her period but not pregnant. Thanks to Lady Luck, Danny and Charlotte had been bailed out of their dilemma.

Although relieved to find out that the rabbit hadn't died, Charlotte was still heartbroken and angry. She decided that she needed to tell Danny off in person one last time. Monte had come up from Dallas for the weekend, so the three of us were sitting in Danny's room when Charlotte appeared in the doorway. I stood up and excused myself to leave, but Monte remained seated. After I left, Charlotte walked into Danny's room and started into her well-rehearsed speech.

"Well, it's over. Everything is okay. I'm not pregnant and you're off the hook. I know that all you cared about was getting yourself out of the mess you created. I hope you are real happy."

Charlotte's voice cracked so she paused for a few seconds, but was unable to regain her composure. She just broke down and sobbed. Danny was glib and acted totally uninterested in her plight. When he did finally speak, he simply told her to get the hell out of his room. Charlotte burst into tears and ran out of the dorm.

Monte came into my room and said, "Bob, Danny's being real mean to her."

This time I had to agree.

"Yeah, Mont, he hasn't handled this very well at all. I feel sorry for her."

I am quite certain that a whirlwind romance ended by infidelity and followed up by a pregnancy scare would be quite a traumatic series of events for any young girl. However, the trauma in Charlotte's life was not yet over. The very next day, Monte called her up and asked her out on a date.

Of course Charlotte was totally perplexed as to why one of Danny's friends was asking her out. She turned Monte down and immediately called Danny to find out what he was up to. Danny said he had no idea what she was talking about. When she told him what Monte had done, Danny became livid.

I was studying in my room when Monte came over that night. The minute he walked through the door, Danny tore into him.

"Monte, why in the fuck are you calling Charlotte? She called me this afternoon and started whining about my friend asking her out."

Monte, of course, tried to lie his way out of the situation.

"Danny, I just called to tell her I felt sorry for her."

"That's a bunch of bullshit," Danny screamed. "You just want to fuck her because I did. That little whore has already caused enough problems. She doesn't need any help from you. Just stay the hell away from Charlotte."

Danny grabbed a pile of books off his desk and marched out of his room. He left Monte standing in the hallway looking dazed and embarrassed. Even though I knew Monte probably deserved the ass-chewing he had just received, I couldn't help but feel a little bit sorry for him.

I got up from my desk and walked over to the doorway. I pulled two cigarettes out of the open pack in my shirt pocket. I put one between my lips and stuck the other one out as a gesture to Monte.

"Mont, I need a smoke break, and you look like you could use one too. Come on in and sit down."

Monte accepted my offer. He followed me back into my room and sat down on my bed. As I bent over to light his cigarette, I said, "Mont, after what Danny just said you better check to see if your ass is bleeding. I don't want blood all over my sheets."

Monte just shook his head back and forth. I could tell from the wobbly cigarette between his fingers that he was trembling.

"Man, what got into him?" he asked sincerely.

His question told me that he had yet to fully grasp the complexities of the issue at hand. I decided that I had better explain how inappropriate it was for him to go after Danny's ex-girlfriend, especially right after a nasty breakup.

I began with, "Mont, you don't plant in your neighbor's field right after he's had a bad harvest."

Monte gave me a perplexed gaze, which told me I wasn't getting through to him, so I decided to try an analogy that he could relate to more readily.

"Okay, Mont, how about this? You would never take your neighbor's used bag and put it on your vacuum cleaner, would you?"

Although Monte shook his head from side to side, from the blank stare on his face, I could tell I wasn't getting anywhere with him. He either still didn't understand me or was totally disregarding the point I was trying to make. I decided to cut my losses and get out of the impromptu counseling session that I had gotten myself into.

"Mont, just stay the hell away from Charlotte."

CHAPTER 4

BIG D

My last year in the dorms started out just like the previous one. G was the RA, with Danny and me living across the hall from each other on the first floor. Although nobody expected any maturing on my part over the summer, I still had to start off the semester by pulling the most embarrassing stunt of my entire life.

I came back from class one afternoon early in the semester. G was waiting in the lounge and immediately beckoned me to his office with, "Knox, lemme show you sumpin," which meant that he was struggling with an algebra problem and needed my help.

I followed him into his office and stood quietly as he sat down at his desk and opened up a notebook with some pencil scribbling on one of the sheets of paper. I pretended to listen intently as G described the intricate procedure he had gone through to solve a rather simple algebraic equation. He concluded his explanation with, "and dats how I come up wif 2 equals 0," then turned and gazed innocently at me, as if seeking my approval.

I waited for a few seconds before I responded sincerely with, "Well, G, you might be right," then paused briefly before I giggled out "but then all of the mathematicians since time began would have to be wrong."

"Oh, fuck you!" he screamed as he slammed his notebook shut. "Get out my office."

I was near hysterics as I walked back to my room, opened the door and flung my books in whatever direction they wanted to go. It was at that instant that I came up with my brilliant idea. I decided to go back into G's room, apologize for having laughed at him, and offer to help him with his algebra problem. However, for some reason I thought it would be funny to go in with my dick hanging out of my pants. So, I pulled down my zipper, unleashed Jasper, and headed back toward G's office.

When I reached his door, I grabbed the handle, turned it, and barged in as if I owned the place. I wasn't more than a couple of steps into my grand entrance before I realized that somehow, in the 45 seconds since I had left, G's new girlfriend, Gaylene, had managed to walk in and sit down in the chair facing the door. I stopped dead in my tracks. We both looked at each other with terror on our faces. I turned and sprinted out of the office and ran up four flights of stairs, all the while trying desperately to get my tool back into my pants.

After a few uncomfortable seconds, Gaylene started laughing hysterically, which caused G to bolt out of the room and chase after me to find out what had happened. He finally cornered me on the top floor of the dorm.

"What the fuck you did?" he demanded.

After a few seconds of pondering my options, I decided to just confess my sins and brace myself for the beating I knew I would receive.

"Well, John, I, uh, came back, uh, to help you, uh, with that algebra problem. Unfortunately, I, uh, came back, uh, well, uh," I stammered. I then took a deep breath and blurted out the remainder of my confession.

"I came back in with my dick hanging out of my pants!"

G stared at me for a few tense seconds then just shook his head from side to side. He mumbled something about "stupid-ass white boy what ain't got no good sense," as he turned around and traipsed back down the stairs to his office.

· · ·   ⌐   · · ·

As the semester wore on, football season eventually rolled around and soon it was time to head to Dallas for the annual drinking contest disguised as the OU-Texas game. Danny and a few other guys decided to drive down to Dallas early Friday morning, so he borrowed a car from his parents. I drove down late Friday with Fieds and his new girlfriend, Sandra. G decided to drive down by himself on Saturday morning so he wouldn't have to put up with any of our liquor-induced nonsense.

Friday night turned out to be relatively uneventful, so Danny and I were able to gather everyone up and head over to the fairgrounds early Saturday morning. We were anxious to stake out our usual spot next to the beer stand closest to the Cotton Bowl. G met up with us about an hour before kickoff, but rapidly became bored with our seemingly endless procession to and from the beer stand. He tapped me on the shoulder and said, "I'm goin' in to watch da pre-game."

Even though I didn't understand how anybody could become bored with beer drinking, I chugged the last of mine and followed G inside the stadium. We moved down to some seats one row up from the field to watch the Sooners and the Longhorns go through their pre-game warm-up routines. When the Texas first team offense lined up to run through a series of plays, G immediately announced, "Uh oh, we in trouble."

I looked out onto the field and saw exactly to what he was referring: the massive thighs attached to Earl Campbell. Earl was a senior tailback and the leading candidate for that year's Heisman trophy. During the week leading up to the game, the press had asked Barry Switzer how he was going to prepare OU's defense for tackling Earl Campbell. He replied, "That's easy. We just have Leroy Selmon line up at tailback for the scout team." Leroy Selmon was OU's All-American defensive tackle, and the leading candidate for the Outland Trophy.

G's premonition turned out to be right on target. Although OU's defense was able to keep Earl in check for the better part of the first three quarters, it was inevitable that he would wear them down. He ran wild in the fourth quarter and Texas eventually won the game.

G left right after the game, but the rest of our troupe re-congregated at the beer stand to consume our traditional two dozen post-game beers. When we ran out of coupons needed to buy beer, I suggested that we go back to the hotel and get cleaned up so we could go out drinking again that night. As we walked out of the fairgrounds, I noticed that Danny was starting to do his familiar drunken Lebanese stumble. When we got to our cars, I told him to follow me and not do anything stupid. Unfortunately, my instructions fell on drunken ears.

Traffic around the fairgrounds was still heavy, but I finally managed to weave my way out of the parking lot and turned onto a major thorough-fare headed in the general direction of downtown. Danny was busy drinking beer and bullshitting with his passengers, so he fell behind me almost immediately. In order to catch up he needed to pull some fancy maneuvers, so he blew through a stop sign and pulled out in front of a car full of Texas fans, which incited them to honk and swear and shoot him the finger. Of course, Danny was totally oblivious to their outrage.

After the first few stop lights, traffic started to move steadily at about 35 miles per hour. The two lanes headed in our direction were separated from traffic going the opposite direction by a concrete center island. Left-hand turn lanes were cut into the center island at every other crossing street.

As usual, Danny was paying absolutely no attention to his driving. At the first crossing street he whipped into the left hand turn lane, thinking he had just found a clear path past all of the traffic. Without even bothering to look where he was going, he tromped on the accelerator and sped past me. Having failed to make the intended left hand turn, Danny's car barreled straight for the next concrete island. Sparks flew out in all directions as the car slammed into the concrete curb and bounced up onto the center island without ever slowing down. Danny never once thought about hitting the brakes as he cruised down the center island. He just swerved periodically to avoid the streetlights mounted in the middle of the island.

I watched the whole scene with my mouth agape. I couldn't help but wonder what the people in Danny's car thought as they weaved back and forth across the traffic island. Da Fieds was laughing so hard he had to hold his stomach to keep from vomiting. From the back seat Sandra repeatedly asked, "Oh my! What is he doing?"

After about a quarter mile, Danny could see he was coming to another crossing street and would soon be exiting the center island, whether he wanted to or not. Without panicking, Danny deduced that, in Texas, it was probably illegal for him to exit a concrete center island without signaling first, so he calmly put on his blinker, yanked hard right on the steering wheel and bounced his car back into the designated traffic lane, accompanied once again by a shower of sparks from the collision between metal and concrete.

When we finally arrived back at our hotel, I went over and immediately confiscated Danny's car keys. I told him there would be no more demolition derby on the streets of Dallas; he was too drunk to argue. I hauled him up to our room and threw him in the shower. It took the better part of an hour to get him sober enough to go out drinking that night.

Because we had been late in making our hotel reservations, eight people ended up sharing two single rooms. Danny and I decided to let Fieds and Sandra have the bed in our room, and we would sleep on the floor. When we returned from drinking that evening, the four of us clamored into our room and prepared to pass out. Before we turned out the lights, I decided that we needed to reminisce about Danny's concrete island adventure earlier in the day.

"Danny, what on earth made think you needed to turn on your blinker before exiting that median? Hadn't you already drawn enough attention to yourself with that little slalom run between the light posts?" I asked.

Da Fieds again started to laugh uncontrollably. Danny was slouched down in a chair, drooling on himself and unable to speak, so I decided to drop my inquisition.

I stripped down to my underwear and piled my clothes in the corner of the room to form a makeshift bed. Fieds also stripped down to his underwear, but Sandra chose to sleep in the shorts and blouse she had worn to the game. I headed toward the bathroom to take a leak before I passed out. On the way back to my pile of clothes, I stopped by Danny's chair, stuck my butt in his face, and said, "Kiss me goodnight, Danny."

As I turned to walk away, I heard some Lebanese mumbling to the effect of "here's a kiss for you". Danny then stood up and kicked me right between the legs. The shot to my balls dropped me like an anchor. Danny fell back into his chair and drifted off to sleep.

For the next hour, I lay on the floor writhing in pain and moaning "Oh my balls". I managed to crawl on my stomach over to my pile of clothes, knowing full well I had probably gotten what I deserved. After what seemed like an eternity, I finally passed out.

Everybody who ever met us said that Danny and I were a good acid test for any relationship. If a woman even spoke to a guy after meeting the two of us, she must truly be in love. The next morning, Sandra came up and thanked us for letting her have the bed and for being so entertaining. She even said she was looking forward to coming to next year's game. I knew at that moment that Sandra was the right woman for Da Fieds.

   ...   ~   ...

After the OU-Texas game, I fell into a daily routine of studying followed by drinking, except for the nights that I had my Costa Rican girlfriend stay over. Lydia was an enthusiastic and boisterous sex partner. When we had intercourse, she would moan loudly, occasionally yelping in Spanish, and would always end by screaming, "Oh, Boob!"

My sexual gymnastics did not set well with either Danny or G. One morning after Lydia had left, G sauntered into my room while I was getting ready for class. With a look of pure disgust on his face he said, "Knox, watch you doin' dat gull dat she has to be moanin' and shit?"

Danny had followed G into my room and joined in with, "Don't bring that disgusting pig over here ever again."

It was obvious that I needed to address the concerns of my two floor mates. I finally managed to silence them by offering up a suggestion as to how they could minimize the impact of the noise coming from my room.

"It's real simple; the next time you guys hear me screwing Lydia, all you have to do is go screw yourselves."

Of course their complaints had no impact on me whatsoever. I continued to drag Lydia back to my room to play "bury the burrito" on an as needed basis.

It was late in the fall semester when I noticed that G was starting to act peculiar. It seemed as though he purposely avoided me in public situations; a practice which was long overdue to salvage his reputation. I finally stopped him one night in the study lounge and asked what was wrong. He was evasive, but did say, "I'll letcha know sumpin aftuh dis weekend."

It wasn't until Sunday morning at breakfast that I found out what G had been doing. He bounced into Couch Cafeteria that morning and was obviously way too glad to see the Barrett brothers, Danny, and me sitting at our usual table. When he finally sat down with his tray of food, I started the inquisition.

"Okay, G. We give up. Have you really joined the Klan?"

"No. I, uh, hell no. Fuck you anyways," he replied.

"Well, tell us before we all explode," I pleaded half-heartedly.

G pulled a large manila envelope out of his coat pocket. He opened the envelope and produced what was obviously some sort of certificate of merit. Beaming from ear to ear he announced, "Last night, I was named Outstanding Black Man on Campus!"

This was, in fact, quite an accomplishment. He had beaten out every other black person on campus, including Leroy Selmon, the Outland Trophy Winner; however, we were not about to give him any credit for having won the award.

Danny started the assault by offering up, "G, you know, Outstanding Black Man on Campus is really one of those nothing awards. That's like saying I got the highest F on an exam."

The two hyenas from Chicago smelled blood and immediately joined in the carnage. Paul quipped, "I was the last guy cut from my high school baseball team."

Pat followed up with, "WOW! Outstanding Black. What's next for our dorm, Most Honest Mexican?"

I could tell G was less than amused with our taunting. I ended the foray by shouting out, "HEY! Leave him alone. This man has shown me that two equals zero. None of you have re-invented mathematics, have you?"

The four of us laughed as G grabbed up his tray and moved to a different table. If the truth were to be known, we were totally in awe of G and extremely proud of what he had accomplished; however, because of the way our group had evolved, there was no way we could ever come right out and openly express our true admiration for him. Even the slightest hint of sincerity would have been an open invitation for the verbal abuse to be redirected. In essence, none of us could compare to the Outstanding Black Man on Campus.

．．．   ．．．

Although drinking and carousing were the mainstays of our friendship, two years of my tutoring had also started Danny's grades on the long climb back up to where they needed to be. If he was to have any hope of getting into medical school, he needed to make a shitload of A's. He had already gotten all the C's and D's he could afford during his two-semester drinking binge at Oklahoma City University. As Danny's academic performance continued to improve, my standing with his family began to rise. His dad eventually came to the conclusion that "the kid with the big nose isn't such a bad influence on Danny, after all."

Danny's dad, Larry, was the chief administrator for the state mental hospital and a highly respected psychiatrist in Norman. He also owned several pieces of rental property and would periodically barter with his tenants over their past-due rent. It just so happened that one of his tenants had recently fallen a couple of months behind on his rent payments. In order to avoid eviction, the deadbeat renter gave Larry a beat up old Chrysler in lieu of the back rent. Larry, relieved by Danny's apparent academic turnaround, decided to reward him with the veritable pile-of-junk-on-wheels that he had just acquired.

I think the car was silver; it was hard to tell because Danny never washed it. Because the muffler had holes throughout, it spewed smoke and was very loud. What was left of the back seat wreaked of urine, so Danny used it only for dumping his trash. The front seats were filthy, but had some flimsy seat covers to sit on for anyone brave enough to actually ride with Danny. He once left the car running for over an hour in a shopping mall parking lot, but no one considered it worth stealing.

Monte came up from Dallas late in the spring semester. Now that Danny had wheels, the two of them could go out carousing without having to borrow a car. One day, the two rambling playboys roared into the dormitory parking lot in Danny's rattletrap trashcan. Danny yanked hard on the steering wheel and locked the brakes, which caused the bald tires to squeal as the tugboat lurched to a halt. Danny and Monte hopped out of the car and pranced up to the dorm like they were a couple of stud puppies.

One of the popular television series at the time was "*Starsky and Hutch*", a show about two good-looking detectives who tooled around town in a hot car while fighting crime. Since Danny and Monte were constantly riding around in Danny's mobile urinal, I dubbed them "*Barfsky and Crotch*".

Near the end of the semester, my family and my best friend, Brad, came out from Albuquerque to attend graduation ceremonies. After high school, Brad had chosen not to pursue a college degree, opting instead to simply sell acid and pot to college students. Brad wasn't necessarily all that impressed by my academic accomplishments. He viewed my graduation as simply a potential business opportunity, so he came to Oklahoma well stocked with a full line of his merchandise.

On the night before graduation, I had to go to dinner with my mother, but I also wanted to spend one last night with Lydia. She was heading back to Costa Rica for the summer and was going to "reely meece Boob". I was going to "reely meece" the steady sex. I decided to get Barfsky and Crotch to entertain Brad while I went to dinner with my mother, then spent the evening with "Oh Boob!"

Brad and Monte hit it off immediately. They compared drug prices, talked about bad acid they had bought, and discussed proper bong techniques. Brad and Danny both found each other to be a little bit strange, but they decided that as long as there was enough liquor to go around, they could tolerate one another for one night. That evening, the three of them piled into Danny's junk-mobile to head out on the town in search of women. Of course, Brad first had to fling enough trash out of the back seat to clear a place to sit. As they drove off, I felt that the three reprobates were destined for an eventful evening.

My premonition turned out to be quite accurate. The next day, Brad could hardly wait to relate the events of his night out with Barfsky and Crotch to me.

Brad said that they had gone to three different bars and were headed to a fourth when a car turned in front of them at a busy intersection. Danny laid on the horn as he slammed on his brakes to avoid running broad side into the other car. The engine stalled as his filthy tugboat screeched to a halt, but the horn kept on blaring. Danny pounded on the steering wheel in an effort to release the horn, but to no avail. When the light turned from red to green, he started to panic and said, "Mont, do something!"

Monte hopped out and raced around to the front of the car and lifted up on the hood, but couldn't get it to open more than a few inches. Danny shoved open his door and ran to help Monte. They both pulled up on the hood as hard as they could without success. Brad laughed as he leaned out his window and suggested that they try the hood release lever.

Danny ran back to the driver's seat and asked, "Where the fuck is it?"

Brad, now laughing harder, pointed to the lever on the driver's side and told him to just pull on it. Danny reached down and yanked the release lever as hard as he could.

Unfortunately, Monte was still trying to pry the hood open through brute strength. The hood flew up and smacked him squarely on the chin and sent him reeling backwards across the intersection. Brad claimed to be drooling at this point and unable to breathe.

Danny ran over and gathered up Monte. They stumbled back to the car and looked under the hood to try and figure out what on earth they might do to stop the horn from honking.

Monte reacted first by saying, "I know what to do, Danny. We just need to disconnect these."

He reached down and grabbed a bundle of wires leading from the firewall. With one mighty heave, Monte was able to yank the wires loose from their housing and proudly held them above his head.

Brad told me the last things he remembered before passing out from hysterics were the headlights going dark, the horn still blaring, and Danny yelling, "Good job, Mont."

. . .   ~   . . .

The day after graduation, I packed up my car and headed back to Albuquerque for the summer. I had already decided to return for graduate school in the fall, but G had been accepted into medical school, which meant he would not be returning to OU. Saying goodbye to G was probably the hardest thing I had done up to that point in my life. Having Brad with me made it a little less painful. Brad didn't provide all that much emotional support, but the killer weed and gram of cocaine he brought along made the long drive home a lot more tolerable.

CHAPTER 5

LITTLE ORAL ANNIE

When I got back to Albuquerque, I started looking for a temporary job for the summer. I knew that I needed to maintain a strong work ethic in order to prepare myself for the rigors of graduate school. I felt that following a routine schedule would also help me develop the time management skills necessary for completing my Masters degree. So, I spent the next six weeks drinking beer and playing golf during the day, then drinking beer and playing slow pitch softball at night. In spite of all my diligence, I somehow managed to remain unemployed.

Although I didn't have much success finding a job, I wasn't about to let the lack of gainful employment prevent me from taking a summer vacation. Just before graduation, Pat Barrett had announced that he was getting married that summer and asked me to be one of his groomsmen. Danny had also gotten an invitation to participate in the wedding, so we decided to organize a road trip involving our reprobate dorm buddies. Glen proposed that we meet him in St. Louis for a few days of fun before the wedding. He somehow managed to convince us that his mom and dad would love to meet us and that their house could hold us all. I am sure the truth was that his parents had reluctantly agreed to tolerate us for a few days, as long as he guaranteed to keep us out of their sight.

In early August, I flew up to St. Louis for our pre-arranged stopover on the way to the wedding. Danny and Monte flew in from Oklahoma City a couple of hours after I landed. Monte had become such a regular fixture in the dorms that he was considered part of the gang. Pat had invited him to the wedding in order to provide us all with some comic relief.

Glen picked us at the airport and immediately started droning on about all the great bars he was going to take us to that night. But first, he had to take us down to the riverfront to do the tourist thing. We went up in the Gateway Arch and walked around downtown. Glen babbled almost non-stop through the entire tour. Thankfully, we were never within earshot of any good-looking women so we didn't have to endure any of Glen's discussions of Ohm's Law or potential theory.

When we finally arrived at Glen's house, his mother told us to go over to the park and swim in the public pool. Her reasoning was sound; she pointed out that we could use the community showers at the pool a lot faster than sharing one bathroom at her house. However, I could sense that her real motive was to keep our time in her presence to a minimum.

When we got to the park, we found two separate pools; one for swimming and one for diving. The diving pool had both low and high diving boards. I decided to try to convince Danny and Monte to go jump off the boards with me. However, my playmates had discovered two girls laying face down near the edge of the diving pool with the tops of their bikinis unhooked. Danny and Monte were already making their way toward a couple of vacant lounge chairs next to the two sunbathing beauties.

"Let's go jump off the boards, you pussies," I challenged.

Danny turned around and smugly replied, "Knox, unlike you, we don't enjoy looking like dorks in front of babes in bikinis."

I hollered back, "With your scrawny bodies, it's a little bit too late to be worrying about looking dorky."

Glen finally agreed to go with me, so we walked over to the diving pool, laughing at the two scrawny dorks we left behind. I arrived at the high dive first, so I scampered up the ladder, then yelled down to Glen at the tops of my lungs to watch my "atomic turtle" dive.

Having gathered the attention of my own private audience, I began my pre-dive routine, which consisted mostly of me posing as if I were truly serious about the ensuing dive. After a period of time sufficient to make the other divers grow impatient, I trotted slowly out toward the end of the board. Just before the end of the diving board, I jumped up as high as I could. When I landed, the board groaned as it flexed due to my weight. The recoil of the board was able to hoist me several inches into the air. What started out as a beautiful swan dive soon turned very ugly.

At the apex of my ascent, I pulled my arms in and grabbed my knees. As I descended toward the pool of water below, I tucked my head into my chest, much like a turtle recoiling into his shell. Just before I hit the water, I caused my body to tumble forward. Upon entry, the combination of my weight and the rolling motion of my turtle shell sent a wall of water out of the pool that totally engulfed Monte, Danny, and the two bikini-clad girls they had hoped to impress. This was followed by a loud thud as water rushed back in to occupy the void I had created. The resulting splash sent water at least twenty feet into the air.

As I surfaced I thrust my fist into the air in mock triumph. I saw Glen standing on top of the high dive, laughing at my antics. I then looked over and saw Danny and Monte trying to towel off while they shook their heads in disgust. The two sunbathing girls were busily gathering up their belongings, which were now soaking wet. It was obvious that they were not the least bit interested in two scrawny dorks, especially not two who chose to hang out with *Orca the Diving Whale.*

It was at the diving pool that Glen proved to me that basketball players have to be the most gifted and coordinated athletes in the world. As I climbed out of the pool, he started his dive. He walked smoothly out to the end of the board, leaped straight up and came back down on the board, which flexed and threw him at least ten feet straight into the air. As he came off the board, he twisted and turned in effortless motion. He continued to twirl and flip as he descended, then straightened out his body just before he tore into the water, barely causing a ripple.

I was totally amazed. The guy was over six-foot six and was as graceful as any four-foot tall gymnast. He was the same way on the basketball court. He seemed to glide through the air and was always in control of his body.

I would never even think of giving Glen a compliment. When he surfaced I called him a pussy and said I would only be impressed if he could properly execute the atomic turtle. After a few more of my ridiculous splash dives, Glen suggested that we go take our showers. We needed to get back to his house in time to mooch a quick meal before we headed out to the bars to continue our never-ending search for lonely women.

. . .   ~   . . .

We must have scoured through at least ten bars before we actually found some girls willing to talk to us. I spotted a rather well-developed brunette standing by the dance floor and looking bored, so I sidled up to her and asked, "Would you like to dance or are you watching your girlfriend's purse?" repeating the lame excuse I had heard several times earlier that night.

To my surprise, she accepted my invitation. After a couple of dances, I offered to buy her drink, and she again accepted my offer. We sat down at an empty table to get better acquainted.

In the meantime, Danny, Glen and Monte had also found a couple of desperate females willing to dance with them. It wasn't long before Danny stumbled over to my table with a half-nelson around the neck of a short stocky girl.

"Bob," he screamed, "they make 'em healthy up here, don't they? Look at the thighs on this ones," as he whirled his prized catch around in front of me.

Before I could get a word out, Danny started his drunken inquisition of the young lady with whom I was sitting.

"Wash yer name?" he asked.

Somewhat sheepishly, she replied, "My name is Renee."

Danny followed up with, "Well, Weenie, my name is Johnny London. I'm a medical student at the University of Hawaii. Didja know that Bob is the smartest linebacker on the OU football team?"

I couldn't believe Danny had put me on the spot like that. More importantly, I couldn't believe how lucky I was that Renee was naive enough to believe it all. I spent the rest of the night telling her how much I liked Coach Switzer. I informed her that, in my opinion, Billy Sims was a better running back than Joe Washington, but Joe was the better all around athlete. Of course, I had never even met any of them.

By the end of the evening, Renee seemed truly impressed by my OU football career. Since we were staying over for a couple of days, I asked Renee if she would like to go out to dinner the following night. She said yes and gave me her phone number.

The next day, Glen arranged for me to use his dad's car for my date. Somewhat jokingly he told me I had to have the car back by 6:30 a.m. because his dad had to go to work. I half-heartedly acknowledged Glen's concern, then grabbed the keys and took off.

I picked up Renee at her apartment, and we went to dinner, then back to the same bar we had met at the night before. We danced and drank until midnight then I proposed that we go back to her place. Renee was hesitant to go back to her apartment because her roommate was home. Conjuring up all the nerve I could muster, I managed to suggest that we get a hotel room. I nearly came in my pants when Renee agreed to my bold suggestion. We ended up checking into a room at the Holiday Inn for a total of four hours. I didn't mind the cost, because, for the first time in my life, I felt like I was a real stud.

When we entered the room, there were a few nervous moments as we both realized that we didn't know what we were doing. I tried to make small talk as I pretended to get nonchalantly undressed. When I turned around and saw Renee's totally nude body, instinct kicked into overdrive. I walked around the bed and grabbed her by the shoulders as I slid my tongue between her lips. After an extended kiss, during which I was sure I was going to explode, I swooped Renee up in my linebacker arms and carried her around the room, never once letting my tongue get away from her mouth. By the time I laid her on the mattress, we were both burning with desire. I may have come with my first thrust inside her, but it didn't matter. We made love at least a half-a-dozen times before collapsing in each other's arms in total exhaustion.

Just before I dozed off, I decided that I had better arrange for a wake-up call to make sure I got back to Glen's house on time. I called the front desk and asked for a 5:00 a.m. wake up call. The desk clerk told me that it was already 5:15 a.m., so I jumped out of bed and hopped in the shower.

When I came out of the bathroom, Renee was hurriedly trying to put her clothes on. I walked over and undid her bra that she had just finished attaching. I kissed her neck and massaged her breasts from behind. She whispered for me to stop, but moaned as I put my hand inside her panties. I gently slipped her panties down her legs and over her feet. As I carefully laid her back down on the bed, she undid my towel and grabbed my now fully erect penis. She put one hand on my buttocks and pulled me closer to her face. She caressed the head of my member lovingly before taking the whole length into her mouth. After a few exhilarating moments, I withdrew from her mouth and moved down to more familiar territory.

Having performed several times earlier, I was not about to come in just one stroke. I pounded away at Renee with a fury I had never known before. She squealed as she approached ecstasy, which only made me work harder and faster. I propped myself up on my arms and gazed down at my cock moving in and out of her at a furious pace. Renee grabbed her ankles and spread her legs wide open to receive me more fully. I thrust into her with a vengeance.

"I'm… coming," she whimpered in a voice that was barely audible, as she shook her head from side to side.

I asked her if she wanted to kiss me when I came.

"Yes!" she screamed. "I want you to come inside me."

With that, I exploded inside her and shoved my tongue deep down her throat. She contorted so violently that I thought I had hurt her. As I tried to back away, she pulled on my hips, which caused me to plunge inside her again. I finished with a few long slow thrusts. She moaned loudly then wrapped her legs around me and locked them together at the ankles.

"I want your cock inside me," she commanded. It was obvious I wasn't going anywhere, so I collapsed on top of her.

By the time we finished, the clock read 6:00 a.m. I told Renee about my 6:30 curfew, so we hurriedly dressed and I drove her home. I left Renee's apartment at 6:15 a.m. and sped toward Glen's house. I pulled into the driveway just as his dad came out of the house to go to work. I nonchalantly tossed him the keys as I walked up the driveway and told him to have a nice day.

Still on an emotional high from my night of passion, I snuck inside and worked my way to the back of the house. Everybody was still asleep, so I carefully toe-stepped toward the den to lie down on the couch for a few hours. As I passed by the last bedroom, I could see Danny asleep on the top bunk, with Glen snoring in the bed below. I paused for a few moments and smiled as I watched them slumber.

Suddenly, it occurred to me that I ought to share the details of my sensual experience with my good buddy Danny. So I quietly snuck over to the bunk beds and carefully slid my index finger under Danny's nose. I put my lips close to his ear.

"WANNA SMELL MY DATE?" I screamed as I planted my finger firmly on Danny's upper lip.

Dazed and startled, Danny flailed his arms in an effort to get away from me. He tried to sit up, but hit his head on the ceiling instead, which caused him to fall back onto the bed.

"Knox, get the fuck away from me," he yelled.

I laughed as I fell to the floor. The commotion I created woke up Glen in the bottom bunk. Monte heard all the noise and ran in from the other bedroom. All three of them begged me for details of my adventure, which I was only too glad to share. After I finished my story, we packed and headed for the airport.

. . .   ~   . . .

I was thoroughly exhausted by the time we reached the airport. I slept through the short flight from St. Louis to Chicago, but it seemed to be just enough to revive me. Da Fieds was waiting for us at O'Hare Airport. He drove us to the Barrett's farmhouse, which was north of Chicago, just a few miles from the Wisconsin border. Paul Barrett had warned us to be ready for one hellacious bachelor party. He hit it right on the nose, because it turned out to be the bachelor party from hell.

The accommodations provided by the Barretts were everything we had expected and much less. We were directed to throw our suitcases upstairs, which meant the loft above the barn that had been converted into makeshift living quarters. At the top of the stairs, there was a half-dozen cots with sleeping bags, which I assumed were for us. I wasn't able to stand erect without hitting my head on the ceiling, so I had to do my best Quasimoto routine in order to move around our spacious living quarters.

Not accustomed to living in the lap of Barrett style luxury, I was perplexed by the drawn shower curtain in the corner of the room. I hunchbacked my way over to the curtain and drew it back to reveal the most filthy toilet and sink I had ever seen. There was also a makeshift shower comprised of an old bathtub with a handheld nozzle attached to the end of a garden hose.

In addition to having never been cleaned, the bathroom fixtures had also been stained yellow by the "sulfur water" supplied to the barn from the well. Although it didn't impart a noticeable taste, the sulfur in the water did stink to high heaven. We also found out that the sulfur had a strong laxative effect a few hours after ingestion. This was truly unfortunate for the six of us who shared the same facilities. Luckily, the smell of the sulfur water engulfed the room to such a degree that it overpowered any noxious fumes that came from the toilet. The Barrett brothers had also replaced actual toilet paper with a pile of old MAD magazines stacked next to the toilet. It was a simple system: read a page, rip it out, and wipe.

It was obvious that Paul had put about as much effort and expense into his brother's bachelor party as he did for his yearly trip to the Laundromat to wash clothes. He had purchased one twelve-pack of beer and a handful of submarine sandwiches for a dozen guys. After I saw the gourmet food and beverage buffet Paul had provided, I told him that I was truly underwhelmed by his generosity.

I knew better than to ask Paul if he had gotten any stag films for us to watch, so I went to Pat and inquired where the nearest adult bookstore was. He said that we would have to go across the state line if we wanted to get any really good porno tapes. It just so happened that Paul and he frequented one such establishment. Pat whipped out his car keys and motioned for me to follow him. I jumped in the passenger's side and off we drove, in search of smut.

The Barrett's favorite adult book, film, and novelty store was located on the outskirts of a small town just across the Wisconsin border. I was sure that any place at which the two Barrett weasels hung out had to be cheap, filthy, and disgusting, and I wasn't disappointed. The place appeared to have been an automobile repair garage in its previous life. As we entered the store, Bucky, the clerk behind the counter, acknowledged Pat with a nod of his head. His protruding front teeth were the obvious source of Bucky's nickname; it was also obvious that he could have benefited from the use of some hot water and a bar of soap.

Pat walked over to the counter and asked Bucky if he still carried any 8-millimeter films; brother Paul had been too cheap to buy or borrow a

VCR, so we were stuck with using his parents' twenty-year old movie projector. Bucky directed Pat to an aisle near the back of the store.

Having only recently gotten my first blowjob, I certainly was a neophyte when it came to all of the accessories and sexual toys lining the shelves of Bucky's store. I gawked in disbelief at the dildos, handcuffs, whips, and various lubricants.

As I wandered down the aisle of edible panties and penis-shaped chocolate bars I accidentally bumped into one of the other patrons of the establishment. When I turned around to excuse myself, I saw that the other discerning shopper had a pair of large nose rings and a full head of purple hair. As I looked around the store, I noticed that each one of the half-dozen shoppers had some unique physical feature, such as pierced nipples, to accompany their multi-colored spiked hairdos. I felt uneasy, so I decided to find Pat, and get the hell out of there as quickly as we could.

I rushed over to the aisle where Pat was perusing through the limited selections of 8-millimeter films.

"Bob, which one would you prefer, 'Little Oral Annie' or 'Backdoor to the Orient'?" he inquired earnestly.

"I don't care. Get both of them. Let's just get out of this place. These guys give me the creeps."

"Relax; dare harmless. Besides we haven't even taken in any of da peep shows yet. Bucky told me day got some new releases."

"The what?" I replied quite befuddled.

"Come on, I'll show ya," Pat quipped as he grabbed the two films he had been scrutinizing.

We walked to the back of the store where there was a series of makeshift viewing booths. The front wall of each booth had a television and VCR behind a Plexiglas window. On the back wall was a small wooden bench, which could easily seat two people uncomfortably. On the arm of the bench was a coin slot for depositing quarters, which activated the VCR. Of course, privacy was essential for viewing these films, so each booth had an old blanket nailed to the top of the entrance.

"Come on, Bob. Let's try dis one," Pat said, as he walked into the first booth.

I was right on Pat's heels, not wanting to be left alone in the store for even a few seconds. We pulled back the blanket and sat down on the bench. Pat was obviously experienced in the procedure, because he had come prepared. He reached into his shirt pocket and pulled out a roll of quarters. He peeled away the paper wrapping to expose a couple of coins.

"Let's see what we got here," he said nonchalantly as he dropped two quarters in the slot.

After a few seconds, lights came on the VCR behind the Plexiglas window. A test pattern appeared on the television screen momentarily, then abruptly switched to action from the film. At first, all I could make out on the screen were two bodies contorting wildly. The audio portion of the film was of extremely poor quality, but the grunts and groans accompanying the thrashing action on the screen seemed to be coming from men. When the camera angle of the film changed, I could see one man sitting on another man's lap, and they were kissing. The two figures broke from their embrace and the man on top squealed, "Fuck me you faggot!"

Pat stood up and said, "Whoa! Wrong booth, Bob. Let's try da next one."

"Pat, let's get the hell out of here. My shoes are sticking to the floor!" I replied rather urgently.

Pat laughed as we made our way to the front of the store. At the checkout counter, Bucky asked if we had found everything all right. Pat told him that I had particularly enjoyed the peep shows. I handed Bucky a twenty-dollar bill and waited impatiently for him to ring up my purchase. I was uncomfortable with him touching my hand as he counted out my change. A couple of Bucky's regular customers were waiting to check out, so I started out of the store without my receipt.

Just as we cleared the doorway, Pat stopped abruptly. He turned and pointed back inside the store and asked, "Bob, didja see dat thing hanging from da ceiling over dare?"

"What thing?" I asked naively, as I walked back inside the doorway to take a look.

Pat stepped back out of the doorway to let me get a better view. He waited for me to get a couple of steps inside the store before he cupped his hands around his mouth and screamed, "PERVERTS!" He then turned around and sprinted towards his car.

Every person in the store immediately turned to see who was yelling and there I stood in the middle of the doorway.

"Oh, you little son-of-a-bitch!" I half-giggled as I turned and ran out of the store to catch Pat. We laughed uncontrollably as we jumped in his car and sped away.

Back at the farmhouse, we gathered in the upstairs hayloft/guest house to view the films. After three or four showings of each film, I decided to call it a day. My lack of sleep from the night before made my cot seem more comfortable than it looked.

After the fifth rerun of Little Oral Annie, everyone complimented Pat on his choice of films; everyone except Monte, who said he couldn't understand why a nice-looking girl like Annie wasn't married. I drifted off to sleep to the melodious sound of aluminum clanging on the floor as they all took turns heaving their empty beer cans at Monte.

CHAPTER 6

NERVOUS NELLIE

It only took a year for me to finish my Master's degree, so I decided to just stay in school for my Doctorate. I told everyone the rationale for continuing my education was that I needed much more in-depth training to solve the world's environmental problems. In reality, I was simply having too much fun in college to consider leaving and getting a real job.

Danny finished his undergraduate degree that same year. He had already applied to medical school twice, but had not been accepted. The two-semester massive alcohol consumption experiment early in his college career had kept his grade point average near the bare minimum for applying to medical school, much less actually getting in. His medical college admissions test (MCAT) scores weren't high enough to allow the review panel to overlook his borderline grade point average either. After his second rejection, I suggested that Danny get a Master's degree, while he studied to retake the MCAT. I told him that a Master's degree would look good when he re-applied for medical school. The truth of the matter was I just wanted him to stick around and keep me entertained.

In order to save money, Danny moved into one of his dad's rental properties near OU. I rented a duplex on the other side of campus, but our behavior wasn't all that much different than when we lived in the dorms as undergraduates. During the fall, we were drunk before noon for every home football game. Since money was tight, we sold parking spaces in Danny's front yard to pay for our pre-game libations.

That season came fresh on the heels of the Iranian hostage crisis, so I developed a brilliant marketing strategy. I stood out in the street with a hand-held sign that read:

"PARK HERE—
KICK A CAMEL JOCK"

Interested passers-by would slow down and gawk at my sign. I would then point in the direction of my drunken Lebanese parking lot attendant. Those who realized the sign was a spoof would laugh. Those who bought my racist hook would pull into Danny's front yard and spew angry rhetoric about "getting even with them god-damned rag heads". I decided to swallow my liberal pride and collect their money without saying anything to further incite them.

Our two-man circus eventually attracted several regular customers. They liked our location close to the stadium, the easy access in and out of Norman, and our prices, which were below those of our nearest competitors. The fact that we were overly generous with our liquor also appealed to several of our regular patrons.

Thanks to Danny, our part-time revenue generating business almost came to a screeching halt one Saturday. I had just flagged in one of our regular customers, a wealthy attorney from Dallas who drove a big silver Cadillac Seville and always asked to park close to the street in case he had to leave early. I gave him the usual "thumbs up" signal and motioned for him to back in to the spot where Danny was standing. It was Danny's job to help the guy maneuver into his accustomed space and collect our fee, so I headed back out to the street to drum up some more business.

As I was walked away, I heard Danny slur out parking instructions, " Moan back. Zairz plenny a room."

I turned to check on Danny. He was waiving his arm in a circular motion, slinging beer from the can in his hand in all different directions.

"Zats it. Jus a lil more," he slobbered.

The attorney tapped his accelerator to nudge back for what he presumed were the last few feet. Unfortunately, he was mere inches from the car behind him. His Cadillac slammed into the other car with sufficient force to shatter brake lights on both vehicles. My drunken traffic cop raised his hand up and said, "Dats far nuff."

...   ~   ...

The only thing different about home football game days that fall was the absence of Monte. Earlier in the summer he had gotten orders transferring him to the east coast for a year. Having spent three years in Dallas, Monte didn't want to go clear across the country and couldn't understand why he was being sent there. Danny pointed out that it might have something to do with the fact that he was in the Navy and that the east coast actually had an ocean. Monte wasn't the least bit swayed by Danny's reasoning.

Less than one month after he moved to Boston, Monte called Danny and triumphantly announced that he had met the perfect woman. Translation—he had stumbled across someone so desperate she would actually tolerate him. It only took another month for Monte to knock up Marilyn. Less than three months later they were married, for the first time.

Marilyn and Monte were still living on the east coast when she gave birth to Corey. After Monte was discharged from the Navy that summer, he gathered up his bride and their newborn son and moved them back to Oklahoma. He always wanted to return to Norman, and now was his chance. Monte was absolutely thrilled with the idea of settling down and becoming one big happy Oklahoma family.

There was just one problem with Monte's plan—Marilyn's mission in life was to make him as miserable as she possibly could. Norman was the perfect place for Marilyn to salve her conscience about her unrelenting domination of Monte. She portrayed him as an inconsiderate husband who only cared about hanging out with his boyhood friends and totally disregarded his wife and son. After two tempestuous months in Norman, including several pointed arguments staged for the benefit of all of Monte's friends and family, Marilyn moved out and went back home to Cape Girardeau, Missouri.

Monte called me about mid-afternoon with the bad news.

"Bob, you are not going to believe what happened," he announced.

"Marilyn left you," I snapped.

"That's right! How did you know?"

"Pure serendipity, Mont. Marilyn, the queen of the 90 mile-per-hour flying ash tray has left you? Boy, knock me over with a feather," I answered.

Monte ignored my sarcasm and asked if I would come over and help him move some of his stuff. I reluctantly agreed, but decided that Danny needed to be a party to the latest episode of the Monte and Marilyn soap opera, so I went by and picked him up on my way over to Monte's.

As we pulled into Monte's driveway, we saw a garden hose leading out the front door onto the lawn. We got out of my car and followed the hose in through the front door. The house reminded me of Whoville the day after the Grinch had paid his visit. The furniture was gone, along with all of Monte's precious knickknacks. Marilyn had taken all of the appliances that Monte had bought while in the Navy. Gone were all of the sheets, towels, rugs, shower curtains, drapes, and washcloths. She had bundled up Corey, along with every toy and article of clothing that Monte's family had ever bought for him. She had packed up all of her clothes; she had even packed up all of Monte's clothes. Marilyn had left him with nothing more than the clothes on his back, a garden hose, and a half-drained waterbed.

It took almost an hour for Danny and me to stop laughing. All the while we hurled insults at Monte about what a fine choice he had made in picking out a wife. Finally, I asked, "Mont, what do you need help moving? There's nothing left."

"I know. I really just need a ride over to my mom's house," he replied.

"Why? Are you moving back home?" I asked.

"Heck no. I'm a grown man and I can take care of myself. I'm not about to move back in with my mom. I just need to grab some food, borrow some money and get her car. Marilyn took mine back to Missouri."

Danny pointed out, "Yeah, Mont. You are your own man, all right. Have you checked to make sure Marilyn didn't take your penis and testicles with her?"

. . .   ~   . . .

After the dust from his breakup had settled, Monte moved in with Danny. As Danny soon found out, a small one bedroom duplex is not nearly big enough to get away from Monte and his non-stop neurotic behavior. Within two weeks, he'd had a snoot full of Monte and told him to go live elsewhere. As luck would have it, my roommate announced that he was moving out to get married, so I invited Monte to come live with me. Thus, began the most bizarre eighteen months of my life.

Monte was, without a doubt, the most neurotic, anal retentive, impatient, nervous neat freak I have ever had the displeasure of having to tolerate. He was always washing, sweeping, dusting, wiping, soaking, mopping, or scouring something. He did more laundry than a small hotel even though most of it was clean when he started. You could eat off any surface in the house. Although it was ludicrous to even suggest that any germs could survive Monte's disinfectant deluges, if there were any in our house, I guarantee they were sterile.

Chaos was also one of Monte's mortal enemies. When he wasn't busy cleaning, Monte would while away the hours by stacking, arranging, alphabetizing, or categorizing some collection that had already been stacked and re-stacked, rearranged, alphabetized, and categorized hundreds of times.

Monte's cleaning fetish certainly didn't come from his personal health or hygiene habits. He had been smoking cigarettes since high school, and God only knows what a job he was doing on his liver with all the alcohol he drank. His obsession with organization certainly didn't spill over to his personal records, because he was perennially in trouble with the IRS over his taxes. For some reason however, Monte was completely obsessed with keeping everything in his immediate surroundings clean and tidy.

At first, Monte was both a novelty and a convenience. I no longer had to waste half-a-dozen minutes cleaning my house every six months. Monte kept the place continuously spotless. However, I paid the price for having a clean house by enduring all of his peculiar traits and quirky habits. Initially, I tried to ignore Monte's strange cleaning rituals and go on with whatever I was doing. After awhile, his routines became so annoying that I was compelled to add some spice to them.

Monte came home from work one day and, as usual, he bee-lined straight to the closet, whipped out his trusty Hoover and started to vacuum up the imaginary debris field he envisioned on our immaculately clean dining room rug. I got up from the table where I was studying, walked over to the area where Monte had just vacuumed, flicked the ashes from my cigarette onto the carpet, turned around, walked back, and sat down; I never once took my eyes away from my textbook. Monte let out one of his patented groans of exasperation, then wheeled the Hoover around and sucked up my freshly deposited ashes. As soon as he was finished, I stood up, walked over and deposited a fresh load of ash. This cycle continued until I finished my cigarette. Monte never said a word to me, nor I to him. The way I looked at it, I was making him happy by giving him a reason to vacuum.

In addition to being a terrific housekeeper, Monte was a dynamite little cook. I told him that some day he was going to make someone a great little housewife. I never realized how close I came to describing Monte's ultimate dream.

Each night, after he was sure the house was spotlessly clean, Monte would fix dinner and bring my plate to me, usually as I was parked in front of the television in the living room. He would sit there impatiently, watching my every move to make sure I didn't spill anything, which would, of course, wreak total havoc on modern society. Before I could finish chewing my last mouthful, Monte would grab my plate and take it back to the kitchen. He was absolutely certain that somehow, in the twenty some odd feet between the living room and the kitchen, I would suffer some catastrophe which was sure to result in a mess of cataclysmic proportions.

Although I was oblivious to most of Monte's idiosyncrasies, it soon became apparent that he was more than a bit neurotic. He was not just a neat freak; he was totally incapable of relaxing. Monte couldn't even sit still long enough to watch a sit-com episode on TV. He enjoyed having people come over to our house, but only so he could remain busy by taking care of them. Thanks to Monte, I learned there is a fine line between "doting" and "pestering".

One weekend, we invited a group of friends over to watch an OU football game on TV. Just before kickoff, I parked myself in front of the set with a beer in one hand and a cigarette in the other. When I finished my beer, I crumpled up the can and tossed it into the middle of the living room floor. The clang of the empty can on the hard wood floor startled everyone in the room, so there were a few seconds of total silence. Although mortified by my slovenly act, Monte tried to pretend that the can sitting in the middle of the room didn't bother him. With me, it was no act. I never once took my eyes off of the television.

After a few tense moments, Monte stood up and slowly walked over to where my beer can had come to rest. As he bent over to pick up the can, he glared at me like I was a misbehaving child. He picked up the can and headed toward his sacred trashcan in the kitchen. I waited until I heard the sound of the lid closing before I bellowed out, "Mont, while you're up, could you bring me another beer?"

Monte grabbed a beer and returned to the living room at an annoyed gallop. He sternly, but not forcefully, set the beer down in front of me. He would never take a chance with something that might foam over onto his freshly polished coffee table.

"Bob, I am NOT picking up any more beer cans," he scolded. "You throw this one and you can pick it up yourself."

After the twenty or thirty seconds it took me to finish my new beer, I flung the empty can into the middle of the room, then leaned back and belched. All of our guests giggled as Monte let out another exasperated groan. We repeated the scene again and again, amid increasing laughter each time.

The *Felix and Oscar* relationship that developed between us was inevitable. With Monte there to provide around-the-clock chef and maid services, I was able to totally abandon all domicile responsibilities. I became a bigger slob than I had ever envisioned for myself. Although he loved to cook and clean, Monte also enjoyed portraying himself as the long-suffering soul of the household. His act served to heighten my image as a slob, but I really didn't need his help.

Although Monte and I were at opposite ends of the domestic spectrum, we did share a common hobby—we both loved to play golf. On Friday afternoons we would meet at the university golf course, rent a cart, take off our shirts, and head out for an afternoon of sunning, slicing, drinking, hooking, cheating, lying, drinking, laughing, and drinking. We easily averaged one beer per hole. A little advanced algebra will tell you that we were both throwing down close to a case of beer each time we played golf.

Monte was actually an incredibly gifted all around athlete with a long, sweeping, natural, inside-out golf swing that most pros dream of. However, for various reasons, he was not always able to make effective use of his natural abilities. At times, he could easily drive the ball 300 plus yards. He could also, just as easily, completely whiff at the ball, which invariably sent me into convulsions of laughter.

Although Monte was typically a hack, when it came down to crunch time, things were quite different. In a critical situation, with the tournament on the line, I can't think of any other golfer in the world, amateur or professional, that I would want keeping score, more than Monte. With the scorecard in Monte's hands, we would never be out of any match.

Monte introduced me to his Modified Grant Scoring System during our first round of Friday afternoon golf. The system was based on one simple guiding principle—don't get bogged down by complicated interpretations or enforcement of the rules of golf. For example, if his tee shot drew left and trickled into the water, he felt that shouldn't count, so he fished the ball out, got himself a really good lie in the fairway, and he was laying one. When he blew his next shot over the green into the bunker, he was laying two. When his first swing left the ball in the bunker, he took his mulligan. The next swing managed to get the ball out, so he was laying three. His first putt was two feet short, so he was now laying four. He nonchalantly tapped the next putt like he wasn't trying. If he made the putt, everything was fine. If he didn't make it, he just proclaimed, "that was in the rubber", so he either way he supposedly made a five on the hole.

Monte never apologized for his blatant cheating. In fact, he guaranteed me that if I would just switch to his scoring system I could shave ten strokes off my score.

In spite of all the fun we had, I eventually became frustrated with Monte's incessant, non-stop, nervous energy. I decided to turn to Danny for help. His father was a practicing psychiatrist and his brother was a psychoanalyst. Danny had been accepted to medical school on his third try and was planning on becoming a psychiatrist himself. I was convinced that someone in Danny's family had to be able to identify any and all of the neuroses that Monte was suffering from. We could then seek some professional help. In the back of my mind, I was hoping for a quick cure through some intense drug therapy, but I realized that it would most probably involve a strict counseling regimen.

When I approached Danny with my request for a professional psychiatric opinion about Monte's mental health, he pondered the situation for just a few seconds before returning his simple, yet elegant, diagnosis, "Bob, Monte is retarded."

Ironically, Danny's sarcastic assessment of Monte's mental health had a soothing effect on me. I was just glad to hear someone else confirm my opinion. I reconciled myself to the fact that my roommate was an incurable neurotic neat freak. I decided to do the humanitarian thing; rather than try and change Monte, I would just continue to exploit his strange personality for my own personal entertainment.

...   ~   ...

As fall rolled around, Monte and I made plans to attend the OU-Texas game in Dallas. The football game itself is only a small part of the OU-Texas weekend. It is preceded by a variety of hedonistic activities, most of which involve alcohol. The game is always scheduled for the first weekend of October, which just happened to coincide with Monte's birthday, as though we needed a reason to drink more.

Since Danny was now busy with medical school, he would not be participating in the festivities. In memory of all of the previous games that the three of us had attended, Monte and I decided to dedicate the weekend to Danny. We both committed to pickling our livers in Danny's honor.

Because we were poor college students, neither one of us had a car that could be trusted to make the three-hour drive to Dallas. Monte's mother, Diana, usually drove down to the game with his grandmother, Maggie, so we decided to ask if we could borrow Maggie's car for the weekend. Of course, Maggie said yes, but Diana outlined some very strict rules of behavior we had to follow with her mother's car. Most of her rules were directed toward my unusual behavior. She topped it off with, "Bob. No smoking or drinking in mother's car. Do you understand?"

I nodded my head in agreement as Monte grabbed the car keys. We left and headed straight for the liquor store. Not only were we ignoring Diana's most pointed edict, we were going to do it with six-point beer.

On the drive to Dallas the next day, Monte went into his *Nervous Nellie* role. He told me to put on my seatbelt, he wouldn't let me smoke, he turned the radio down, and he made me put all of my empty beer bottles in a trash sack rather than fling them into the back seat.

By the time we made Purcell, 24 miles south of Norman, I was already giddy and needed to piss.

"Mont, pull off and find me a tree to pee behind, " I ordered.

Monte pulled off the highway and found a grove of trees along a dirt road. After he parked the car, he started whining at me.

"Bob, you are drinking too much. Do you realize how long it is gonna take to get to Dallas if we have to stop every 24 miles?"

As I stepped out of the car I asked, "Mont, would you mind holding my wiener for me? I want to drink my beer while I piss."

Monte started to fume and shot me the first pouty face of the weekend.

When we got back on the highway, Monte launched into his silent treatment in an attempt to get me to straighten up. With nobody to talk to, I decided to investigate Maggie's glove compartment. My perusing made Monte ill at ease, so he broke his self-imposed vow of silence.

"Bob, get out of there. We are supposed to take good care of grand-mother's car and not get it dirty," he lectured.

I ignored him and continued pawing through the contents of the glove box, spilling most of them onto the floor mat at my feet. Finally, I found something I could use, a tube of bright red lipstick. I pulled down the passenger side visor so that I could see myself in the mirror.

Monte, now very nervous, inquired, "Bob, what are you doing? Put that away. That's grandmother's favorite lipstick."

"It's my favorite too," I replied as I smeared on a thick coat of lipstick. I mashed my lips together as I had seen my mother do before. I turned to Monte and asked, "How do I look Mont?"

Monte took one look at me and screamed, "BOB! Take that off."

"Give me a kiss and I will," I replied.

I puckered my lips and moved ever closer to Monte. Before he could push me away, I planted a big wet kiss on the side of his face, which left an unmistakable imprint from the lipstick. My kiss sent Monte into Nervous Nellie ballistic overdrive.

"BOB!" he screamed, "I am going to wreck grandmother's car. Stop kissing me. That's it. No more beer for you."

I laughed as I opened another bottle of beer and flipped the cap into the back seat. Not yet through tormenting my chauffeur, I grabbed a cigarette from my pack, fired it up, and blew smoke rings at Monte through my ruby red lips. He knew there was no reasoning with me, so he focused on driving without saying another word.

. . .   ~   . . .

As we approached the outer limits of the Dallas metroplex, I asked Monte where he wanted to go that night. He said he was going to take me to Arlington to hit some of the bars he used to frequent when he was in the Navy. He guaranteed me that we would be able to hit on loads of women.

When we walked into the first bar that night, I could tell Monte was right at home. He had also been right on the mark with his guarantee; there were plenty of women in the place and every single one of them was a load. I felt a little out of my element. Not only were all the women in the place bigger than me, most of their male companions appeared to be bikers.

We sat down at a table that probably hadn't been cleaned since the last time Monte had been in the place. There was a band up on the stage at the front of the bar, but they were just tuning their instruments. There appeared to be some sort of screen in front of the stage, but Monte informed me that it wasn't a screen; it was chicken wire to protect the musicians from beer bottles and other things thrown at them. Just then, one of the bikers sitting at the table next to us stood up and hurled a bottle toward the stage and politely requested that the "lazy motherfuckers fire it up".

"Mont, the natives appear to be getting just a wee bit restless. Since we stand out like a couple of cue balls here, why don't we go some place else?" I reasoned out loud.

Monte turned around and said, "Bob, don't worry. Bikers and sailors get along great."

I started to point out that we were members of neither one of those blue-blooded families, but the lazy motherfuckers suddenly decided to fire it up. The music blaring from the speakers was so loud I couldn't even hear myself think, so I just sat back and tried to ignore the sound waves as they passed through my body.

After about ten songs and at least thirty broken beer bottles, the band decided to take a break. Monte had been pounding rum-and-cokes throughout the whole first set and was now feeling no pain. I suggested that he give me the car keys so that I could drive us home, but he slurred out something about obeying Diana's rules.

We went to a couple more of Monte's previous hangouts, but none of them even approached the sophisticated ambience of the first bar. I had gotten so paranoid about our environs that I switched from drinking beer to sipping water. My designated driver, on the other hand, had switched from guzzling rum-and-coke to throwing down shots of tequila. Around midnight, I finally managed to convince Monte that we should leave because we had a thirty-minute drive back to our hotel.

Against my better judgment, I let Monte get behind the wheel. I helped him navigate Maggie's car back onto the highway that led to Dallas and figured he would be all right as long as I kept him awake. It was about 1:00 a.m. when we finally arrived back at our hotel. The parking garage was packed, so we ended up driving to the uppermost level before we found a place to park. Monte carefully maneuvered Maggie's car in between the lines of the empty stall, then he stepped on the accelerator to pull forward.

We couldn't have been going much over 25 miles per hour when we jumped the concrete bumper and slammed into the wall of the parking garage. Monte hurriedly threw the car in reverse and backed up over the bumper. He put the car in park and shut off the motor.

I jumped out of the car to go survey what was left of the front grill. Monte stumbled out of the driver's side and slurred out, "Bob, do you sink granmudder will notice?"

I thought for a minute before replying, "I'm afraid so Mont. Your grandmother is definitely going to know we smoked cigarettes in her car."

...   ~   ...

The next morning Monte and I both awoke with raging hangovers. Mine was attributable to the case of beer I drank on the drive down. Monte was suffering from the effects of mixing rum and tequila the night before. There was only one way to cure our afflictions; we needed to get to the Cotton Bowl and start drinking.

By the time we reached the fairgrounds it was already 90 degrees outside. I was drenched with sweat and very much looking forward to my first cold beer. Just as we cleared the turnstiles, Monte turned to me and excitedly announced, "Bob, I can't wait to play all the neat games on the midway."

I glared at him before offering up my reply.

"We are NOT going to waste valuable beer-drinking time trying to win worthless shit on the midway."

Monte broke into his patented pouty face and continued to whine at me.

"Bob, I always win a lot of stuff on the midway. I have great hand-to-eye coordination."

I countered with, "Mont, why don't you try some hand-to-gland coordination between my legs," as I grabbed my crotch. "We only have three hours before kickoff and I am getting thirsty. We ain't going to no fucking midway."

My argument had no impact on Monte whatsoever. He just turned around and picked up his pace. From the direction he took, I could tell that my first beer was going to have to wait awhile.

Once we approached the midway, Monte bee-lined for the first game he could find. He laid down a dollar and proceeded to throw three bamboo rings around a milk bottle. For his performance, he won a Texas State Fair glass ashtray. At the next booth, Monte shot a large basketball through a small hoop hung much higher than a regulation goal. In fact, he swished all three attempts. For this feat, he won a six-foot long snakelike stuffed animal. The next booth involved flipping dimes onto glass plates and Monte won a half-dozen filthy, chipped dishes. After that he threw darts at balloons, shot a water gun into a clown's mouth, and catapulted rubber frogs onto floating lily pads. He excelled at every mindless game on the midway, and at every booth he won some cheap trinket.

By the time we left the midway, both of us had our arms full of Monte's worthless winnings. As we walked toward the beer stand outside the Cotton Bowl, I decided to inquire as to how Monte was going to store all of his treasures.

"Mont, what in the fuck are you going to do with all of this crap during the game?" I asked.

"Bob, I'm not taking this stuff into the game. We're going to take it out to the car before the game starts," he replied.

I let everything in my arms drop straight to the ground and kept on walking as I shouted back at Monte.

"WE aren't taking a fucking thing to the car. You want it? YOU can take it. I'll be at the beer stand."

Monte pondered the situation. It was a long way out to the car, he really had won absolutely nothing of any value, and it was almost noon and he hadn't had a single beer yet. He decided it would be best to just get rid of all of his worthless crap, so he started handing trinkets to little kids walking by. He had so much junk that he actually attracted a small crowd.

After Monte finished doling out his treasures, he sprinted to the beer stand in order to get there before I did. He bought a couple of beers, snuck over to one of the picnic tables, sat down and fired up a cigarette.

All the walking we had done had built up my thirst. When I got to the beer stand, I ordered four beers and started looking for a spot to park my butt. I spotted Monte sitting at his table, sipping a beer, and smoking his cigarette. I didn't really care how he had gotten there; I just wanted to relax and enjoy my beers. I walked over and sat down across the table from Monte. Just as I took my first sip of beer, Monte said, "Bob, that stuff was just a bunch of worthless junk so I gave it all away."

Acting out of instinct, I immediately threw my beer at Monte and screamed, "Mont, I told you that two hours ago."

Monte was able to dodge my beer and started laughing. He was more pleased with the fact that he had managed to irritate me than he was with all the crap he had won on the midway.

As game time drew near, Monte and I devised our plan to sneak beer into the Cotton Bowl. I went inside the stadium while he ordered six beers. Once inside, I walked over to the iron grate fence that surrounded the stadium and nonchalantly fired up a cigarette. Monte snuck up to where I was standing and passed the beers to me through the fence. I then placed them under a large red Oklahoma cowboy hat that I had set on the ground.

When Monte came into the stadium, he went straight to the concession stand and ordered two large Cokes. He dumped the coke out of the cups and walked over to where I was standing guard over our beers. We took turns watching for security guards while we poured the beers into the empty coke cups. Once we were armed with our illegal refreshments, we headed into the stadium to find our seats.

The Cotton Bowl has individual folding chairs rather than bleachers. Although this prevents extra people from crowding into a section, it also hampers crowd mobility. When the seats are folded down, each row becomes essentially impassable. In order for someone to get to or from their seat, everyone on the row has to stand and collapse their seats in order to let people by.

Our seats were near the playing field, but in the corner of the south end zone. By the time we arrived, our row was nearly full, but I could see two empty seats about halfway down the aisle. We were just about to start side-stepping to our seats when the Pride of Oklahoma marching band struck up "Boomer Sooner". Everyone on the south side of the stadium stood up and roared. It was obvious that we weren't going anywhere until the fight song was over.

Monte decided to take his chances by walking on the folded down seats rather than waiting to scoot by everyone in the aisle. He stepped up on the first seat, then turned to me and yelled, "Follow me, Bob."

Although his first two steps were a little shaky, Monte pressed on. On his third stride, he stepped too far back on the seat, which caused it to fold up abruptly. His left foot went down to the concrete floor and the seat collapsed on his leg. Momentum was now carrying him forward, so he attempted to step on the next seat with his right foot, but his left leg was caught in the collapsed chair. The abrupt arrest of his forward motion caused him to spill his beer all over the couple standing in front of the next two seats.

The man wheeled around to see what in the world was going on. He shouted at Monte and drew back his arm as if he was about to throw a punch. His wife grabbed his arm and pleaded, "George, don't. He is obviously retarded."

After the band finished the OU fight song, I somehow managed to stop laughing long enough to excuse myself down the aisle to my seat. As I passed by the still irate George, I hollered out, "Excuse me. Has anybody seen a balding retarded man come by here with my beer?"

Several people around us laughed; George did not.

When I got to my seat, I found Monte bent over and wiping blood from the wound he had just inflicted on his ankle.

"How you enjoying the game so far, Mont?" I asked.

He looked up and shot me his second pouty face of the day as he said, "Bob, the worst part is that I spilled my beer."

I then suggested, "Mont, why don't you ask George to go out and get you another beer? He's closer to the exit ramp."

Monte shot me yet another pouty face.

I reached down and grabbed Monte's empty cup and poured half of my beer into it. As I handed him the cup I said, "Mont, this time try and throw your beer on a girl so we at least have a chance of winning the fight."

He shot me one last pouty face then chugged down his beer.

Late in the third quarter, I started to get a little bit anxious. Texas had been favored to beat OU, but the Sooners were still in the game. OU had moved the ball fairly well against the Longhorn defense, but we had trouble getting into the end zone. Our much heralded freshman running back, Marcus Dupree, had only played sparingly, but had been impressive when he was in the game.

Just before the end of the quarter, Texas punted and pinned OU deep in their territory. During the brief intermission between quarters, Monte told me he felt like we were going to break a long one on the next series. I totally ignored him because he tended to say that every time OU got the ball.

On the first play of the fourth quarter, Dupree took a handoff and broke through the Texas defensive line. He cut to the outside and sprinted toward the goal line in a footrace with the safety. Monte threw his hands around my throat and started to shake me, which dislodged my sunglasses. When it became obvious that Dupree's world class speed would carry him past the last Texas defender, Monte jumped up and down, which caused me to spill beer on myself. When Dupree finally crossed the goal line to put OU ahead, Monte wheeled around, grabbed my head with both hands, and gave me that kiss on the lips I had begged of him the day before.

While everyone in the OU section cheered wildly, I collected my belongings and wiped beer off my shirt. I excused myself down the aisle and went outside to the beer stand. I wasn't sure if they had enough beer to get the taste of Monte off my lips, but I was sure going to find out.

•••   ~   •••

For the most part, Monte and I truly enjoyed being roommates. Alas, like all good things, our time together was coming to an end. We were soon to be torn apart by the one force that neither one of us was strong enough to withstand—that irresistible male urge to make a complete ass of himself over a woman.

CHAPTER 7

DARRYL, IS THAT YOU?

The perception of being gay was something Monte started battling early in his adult life. A good deal of that false impression can be attributed to his quirky behavior: the cooking, the cleaning, the use of cosmetics, his love of shopping, and the unbelievable degree of ass-kissing he would do for any woman who paid the least little bit of attention to him. Monte also had some effeminate gestures; there were times I felt he swished a little too much when he walked. However, Monte never had any sexual desires for men; I think.

In fact, Monte was one of the horniest heterosexuals I have ever met. Like most men, he did a majority of his thinking with his dick. His every waking moment was driven by the desire for sex. I often told him him that "the squirt" was the only thing in life that really mattered to him, and he never denied it.

As much as Monte craved physical gratification, it paled in comparison to his overwhelming desire to be loved. However, he was so incredibly insecure that whenever he did meet a girl who showed any interest in him, he absolutely smothered her with attention. As I can attest, a little bit of Monte was enough to drive most people crazy, but non-stop, incessant, constant, omnipresent Monte had to be a veritable nightmare.

When I first met Monte, he had already been engaged once; to a girl he met while stationed in Dallas. As a caring mother, Diana, had paid for the engagement rings for both the bride and groom. She truly wanted to believe in the dreamboat relationship that Monte had painted for her. However, this was just the first of many times that Diana shelled out money for her son's impending nuptials only to watch as her investment in the dreamboat slammed onto the jagged rocks of lunacy surrounding *Monte Land.*

After he rushed into the engagement and hurriedly planned the wedding, Monte had gotten unceremoniously dumped before he could make it to the altar. He told me that his fiancée just woke up one day and said, "Monte, I don't love you."

I corrected him by saying, "You mean she just *sobered* up one day and said Monte, I don't love you."

After the failure of his first engagement, Monte took company with numerous women of questionable morals, ethics, and personal hygiene standards. Being in the Navy, he also participated in several sexual hi-jinks traditionally associated with sailors. He once told me about going to a bar the night before one of the guys in his outfit was to be married, in essence, a two-man bachelor party. The groom-to-be managed to pick up the fattest, ugliest girl in the bar, and the three of them headed off to a nearby fleabag hotel.

Once in the room, Monte's buddy got physically rough with the woman. He slapped her, ripped her clothes off, and sodomized her. He then screamed at her, "Go sit on Monte's face, bitch!" Monte told me that he felt it would have been rude to decline such a generous offer.

It wasn't until Marilyn (engagements two and three) came along that Monte showed how incredibly desperate he was just to be loved. That might have been possible if it weren't for the fact that he equated sex with love and vice versa. Monte believed that if you loved him, you should have sex with him. Moreover, if you had sex with him, the two of you were in love. For most mature adults, some variation on these themes is true, but no one ever took it to the illogical extremes that Monte did.

Although desperate for true affection, Monte was not very picky when it came to picking up women. He believed in the old Mickey Gilley song, "The girls all get prettier at closing time." Unfortunately, he also believed that at closing time "Some girls appear hundreds of pounds lighter and not nearly as sleazy as when they first rode up on their motorcycles." Whenever Monte got horny, he headed out to the singles bars armed with a set of truck scales and some heavy-duty paper bags.

The one club where Monte and I saw numerous closing times was a place called Opie's, a cozy little honky-tonk with a DJ and a small dance floor. The first night I ever went into Opie's, I met the owner and quickly figured out how he got his nickname. His red hair and freckles gave him a strong resemblance to Opie Taylor from the Andy Griffith show. Opie and I rapidly became good friends because I was the ideal patron; I drank a lot of beer, I never caused any trouble, but most important of all, I always paid my tab.

Opie had returned to Norman after a voluntary four-year stint with the Marines in Viet Nam. To me, the notion of anybody volunteering to go to Viet Nam was incredibly stupid, so I asked him about it. It turned out that Opie had worked part-time while he was in high school and saved his money to buy a car. One night during his senior year, he went out and got drunk, then came home and passed out in the front yard. As punishment, his parents took away the car that he had bought with his own money. Opie thought that was incredibly unfair, so to teach his parents a lesson, he went down and enlisted in the Marines. He also managed to talk four of his friends into enlisting. All five of them went to Viet Nam and returned without a scratch, although I'm sure each of them suffered some psychological wounds from the atrocities of that war.

After Opie related the story to me, I asked him if his parents had learned their lesson. I told him I wasn't sure what he could possibly do to get back at them if they ever acted up again.

Opie originally made his mark by bringing nudity to Norman. After he returned from Southeast Asia, he opened a strip joint called *Walter Mitty's*. He ran it for a number of years before he decided to switch to a less stressful occupation. It seems that watching beautiful women take their clothes off night after night can really take a toll on one's liver. Actually, Opie decided to take advantage of the cowboy dance craze that erupted as a result of the movie *Urban Cowboy*. Ultimately, it was a good business decision because country & western music remained popular, especially in Oklahoma.

A couple of years after he opened the honky-tonk, Opie started sleeping with one of the waitresses he had hired, named Missy. Although he had been to bed with many of the strippers from Walter Mitty's, Opie had never gotten serious with any of them. Things were different with Missy. Opie would actually acknowledge her in the presence of others.

After about six months of sleeping together, Opie announced that he and Missy were getting married. He told me they were just going to a judge's chambers for the actual wedding ceremony, but I was invited to the private reception in the afternoon. Although I couldn't afford it, I decided to get the happy couple a wedding present. Opie hadn't bothered to register at any department stores, so I was on my own in trying to find a gift. After seven or eight excruciating minutes of shopping, I bought a set of steak knives with deer antler handles. The cost of the knives all but wiped out my checking account for the month, so I was glad that booze at the reception was free.

To the surprise of almost no one, Opie's marriage to Missy didn't last very long. He moved out and begged his way back in at least a dozen times over nine months before they finally decided to split up for good. After his divorce, I decided that Opie needed a little fatherly lecture. I told him that I did not appreciate spending all of my hard earned money on fancy steak knives just to have Missy and him throw them at each other. I also rode him about the fact that Missy took the knives as part of the divorce settlement.

For some strange reason, Opie's favorite holiday was Halloween. He made a big production about Halloween parties at the club the very first year he opened it. Never one to pass up the opportunity to make a complete ass of myself, I decided to dress up and try to win the costume contest. I put on a cowboy hat and a pair of long handle underwear. I filled a surgical glove full of water and hung it from my crotch to resemble a cow's udder. Opie soon adopted my depiction of "the real cowboy" for his club's logo.

Oddly enough, Opie did not appreciate my most creative work. The next year my costume was simply a man with his head cut off, but carrying the head in his hands. I worked for over a month to make a plaster-of-paris head that looked like Opie with his mouth wide open. I placed the head in the palms of two fake hands dangling from a shirt, with blood all around the collar. Opie didn't mind my costume so much as the sign I had printed on the back of my shirt, which read, "Opie Gives Good Head".

      ...   ~   ...

A couple of days after we returned from our OU-Texas weekend, Monte and I decided to go out to Opie's and have a few dozen quick beers, then call it an early night. We didn't believe in burning the candle too late on Tuesdays.

The place was all but empty when we arrived, so Monte and I sat down and reminisced about our weekend in Dallas. It was around midnight when a couple of trailer park pachyderms waddled into the bar. Monte bent over and whispered in my ear, "Pssst, Bob. There's that mother-daughter team I told you about."

He claimed to have had a threesome with the two women the week before the OU-Texas game.

I leaned over and whispered in Monte's ear, "Pssst, Mont. NO FUCK-ING WAY! They are NOT coming into my house!"

Monte glanced up at me with his famous pouty face. As he tried to put on his best act of feigned interest, he said, "Bob, I'm not gonna bring them home. That mother is crazy. She wants to take me shopping and buy me some cowboy boots."

As I stood up to go take a piss, I repeated my warning to Monte.

"Mont, you are NOT bringing home anything heavier than a Volkswagen. Understand?"

I was just wasting my breath. When I came back from the restroom, I found the younger pachyderm wallowing by herself at my table. I immediately scoured the bar, but there was no sign of Monte or the mother hippo.

As I approached the table, the daughter hippo wiggled her ears in excitement. She stuck out one of her front paws as she introduced herself. I shook her hoof then politely inquired as to Monte's whereabouts so that I could go choke the living shit out of him. She told me that Monte and her mother had stepped outside for some fresh air and that she was to keep me company until they returned. I thanked her for the offer, but noted that it was getting late. I damn sure didn't want to see what this woman might turn into at midnight, so I gathered up my belongings and headed for the door. I figured that Monte could fend for himself when it came time for a ride home.

When I stepped outside the bar, I was startled by some rustling noises in the hedges next to the entrance. I walked over to investigate the source of the commotion. When I peered into the bushes I saw Marlin Perkins and the mother hippo going at it, not more than ten feet from the front door.

I cleared my throat and loudly asked, "Excuse me, sir. What size cowboy boots do you wear?"

Monte never missed a beat. He simply finished his business, pulled up his pants and went back into the bar to continue drinking.

· · ·   ~   · · ·

Over the next few months, Monte must have brought home at least two-dozen different women, but he never was satisfied with one-night stands. More than anything else in life, Monte wanted to be married. Just when it seemed that Monte was destined to spend the rest of his life dragging home bar flies and bimbos, along came Tony.

Tony was a short, attractive dark-haired woman of Lebanese descent whom Monte had met at work. She had a somewhat sordid past. For a while, she dated a former OU football player who went on to play in the NFL. She then started dating Darryl Jones, a former OU basketball player who had been dismissed from the team after being charged with multiple counts of rape.

Tony's parents were less than pleased that she was dating a former athlete with serious legal troubles. I'm sure it didn't help matters that Darryl was of different skin color than Tony. They had been pressuring her to find a nice Anglo boy. She found the perfect sucker in Monte.

In order to take the pressure off, Tony started going to dinner with Monte and periodically parading him in front of her parents. Of course, she had absolutely no intention of ever getting serious with Monte and certainly didn't plan on sleeping with him. In spite of Tony's true ambivalence, Monte fell in love, or at least he convinced himself that they were meant to be in love.

After a couple of weeks of dating, Monte started to get frustrated because the relationship had not proceeded in the direction that he had envisioned, i.e., into the bedroom on the way to the altar. We were out at Opie's one night when I noticed that Monte was acting stranger than usual; he was unusually quiet and reserved. In the hour we had been there, he had barely been able to choke down five double rum-and-Cokes. Finally, I decided to ask Monte what was bugging him.

"What's the matter with you, Mont? Did your vacuum cleaner break down or something?"

He paused for a moment then blurted out, "Bob, don't girls get horny?"

"Well, Mont, I'm not a girl, but I'm pretty sure they do. Obviously they do or we wouldn't be here," I answered.

Monte paused for a few more seconds then said, "Well, what's the matter with Tony? On our dates we always end up making out, but that's as far as she lets me go."

"Mont, did you ever stop to think that she might be getting it elsewhere?" I asked.

"No, that can't be it," he immediately countered without even considering my suggestion.

After our brief counseling session, Monte started pounding the rum-and-Cokes. Finally, closing time rolled around and we left. On the drive home, Monte kept on whining about not getting past first base with Tony. I tried to take his mind off his sexual frustrations by saying, "Mont, you know she wants it. Maybe you aren't being aggressive enough."

As we drove on, Monte said something about going over to Tony's house and confronting her. I detected a potentially embarrassing scene in the works, so I tried to defuse the situation by saying, "Mont, what have you got to lose?"

When we pulled into our driveway, Monte announced that he was going over to Tony's to get what was rightfully his. I made one final desperate plea for calmer minds to prevail by saying, "Go for it, Mont!"

I gave my car keys to Monte, then went inside and passed out in my bed. About 20 minutes later I was awakened by the slam of the front door. I heard Monte stomp down the hallway and slam his bedroom door. I giggled as I deduced that he had probably been told to go home and now had to go to sleep with a raging hard on.

The next day, Monte told me the whole story, which was probably a bigger mistake than what he had done the night before. He said that he went over to Tony's house, snuck up to her porch, knocked on the door and stepped back into the shadows. Tony had the security latch on the door and couldn't see who was on the doorstep. She slowly cracked open the door and whispered, "Darryl, honey, is that you?"

Obviously, Tony had still been seeing Darryl and was just using Monte as a decoy for her parents.

This was the first of numerous times when Monte should have just kept his mouth shut. I was the last person in the world he should have confided in. This incident also earned him a new nickname. After that evening, every time I came home, I would swing the door open and scream, "Darryl, honey, I'm home!"

· · ·   ~   · · ·

In a strange bit of irony, it was on New Year's night at Opie's when Monte introduced me to Lisa, the first love of my life. Lisa and Jamie were twin sisters whom Monte had known since they lived next door to each other as kids. The twins were attractive and extremely vivacious. Both had recently divorced and each had a young child. I was immediately attracted to Lisa and started to pursue her with a vengeance. I also fell head-over-heels in love with her two-year old daughter, Jaclyn.

Anybody who has ever done it will tell you the same thing; you don't date one twin, you date both twins. Lisa and Jamie were inseparable, and I soon realized that I had to keep both of them happy if I wanted to keep either one of them happy. A couple of months after we started going out, Lisa conned me into coaching a girls softball team. To top it off, Jamie coaxed me into asking Opie to sponsor the team, which he gladly agreed to.

Actually, coaching a girls team can be a lot of fun, if one doesn't take the game too seriously. Because Lisa and Jamie recruited most of our players from Opie's bar, I knew we would be horrible. I figured that most of the other teams would be just as bad, so with a little bit of practice and some judicious player selection on my part (also known as bringing in ringers), we were able to win more games than we lost that summer.

Near the end of the season, I scheduled an early morning batting practice session in order to avoid the summer swelter. Even though we started early, the heat began to build, and I could see some of the girls were starting to wilt. I decided to call it a day and told everyone to go sit down under a nearby shade tree and cool off. The girls went over to the tree, plopped down, and immediately started gossiping about whoever wasn't there to defend themselves. I brought over a cooler of water and handed out paper cups.

After everyone grabbed a cup of water, I stood up and started to read out the schedule for the remainder of the season. When I looked up from my paper to see if any of girls were paying attention, I immediately noticed the muscular legs of our shortstop, who was lying back on the grass, propped up on her elbows. Kim was a short brunette who had played softball in high school. She had a habit of wearing short shorts to highlight her butt and tight tops to display her chest. Kim was married to a friend of mine, but everyone knew she screwed around on him a lot.

Instinctively, my gaze moved up her legs and when I got to her shorts, it was obvious that she did not have anything on underneath them. I looked up at Kim's face and she smiled and winked, which meant that she knew exactly what I was gawking at. She took the opportunity to shift positions so that she could give me a brief, but totally unobstructed, view of her wares that she had been marketing around town.

I felt myself starting to blush. I looked over at Lisa and was relieved to see her mouth going ninety miles an hour in an effort to get a word in edgewise with the other gossipers. By ignoring me, she hadn't seen Kim shoot me the beaver.

That night, Lisa and I went out to Opie's to have a few drinks. We sat at the counter near the entrance where Opie usually stood to greet customers as they came in. Opie asked me how the softball team was doing, and I said great. I then started to tell him about being flashed by one of the girls at practice. This time, Lisa was paying attention, and she was not at all amused by my story. When I told Opie the part about the unobstructed view of Kim's twat, Lisa let out a snort of disgust and turned her head away.

I decided I had better do some damage control, so I looked at Lisa and said, "Don't you worry, dear. Yours is a lot bigger."

Opie spit out the cigarette in his mouth and started to choke and laugh at the same time.

Lisa turned back toward me and calmly replied, "Well, it's too bad you won't get to see it ever again."

"What? Was it something I said?" I fake-pleaded with Lisa while giggling the whole time.

Lisa and I soon became regulars at Opie's. Since Jamie usually went with us, it was inevitable that people would get the two of them mixed up. One night, Opie asked me how in the world I was able to tell the difference between Jamie and Lisa.

I replied, "Opie, it is real easy. Lisa is the one that I'm dorking."

Before Opie could even start laughing, Lisa piped up with, "Not anymore, pencil dick," and walked off to find her sister.

From that day on, Opie referred to me as Dr. P.D. In fact, for my birthday later that year, Lisa and Jamie delighted in presenting me with a bouquet of pencils, in front a large crowd at Opie's. Most men would have been embarrassed or humiliated, but not me. I reveled in the attention because I was falling in love with Lisa.

...   ~   ...

Lisa and I continued dating on into the fall, which meant that I no longer devoted my football weekends to getting drunk with Monte. He soon became frustrated by the fact that I had found someone with whom I was very comfortable, and he didn't have anyone. To him, there was one obvious solution; he should be with Jamie.

In typical Monte fashion, he totally misconstrued the little bit of attention he received from Jamie and equated it with true love. The next thing Jamie knew, Monte was smothering her with flowers and cards at work and babysitting her son; he even left barbecued chicken on her front porch so she wouldn't have to cook when she got home from work. Jamie never really knew what was behind it all because she continued to treat Monte like she always had, as a friend.

When Jamie unknowingly rebuffed Monte, he became despondent and fell back into Marilyn's tentacles. It was just before Thanksgiving when Monte told me that he was going to Cape Girardeau, supposedly to see Corey. I knew right then that he was probably going to do something stupid. In spite of my concerns, I sat down and tried to reason with him.

"Monte, when you go up there, think with your head and not with your heart," I pleaded.

I didn't aim low enough. I forgot about the organ that does all of Monte's thinking.

Marilyn was very manipulative and a lot smarter than Monte. She knew that if she got Monte in bed, she could convince him to come back to her. This time, she'd get him back on her terms, in her hometown, and under the thumb of her family. During the course of his short visit, Marilyn gave Monte more sex than she had the entire time they had been married. Actually, it probably only took one blowjob to win him over, but Marilyn wasn't going to take any chances. On the last night of his visit, Marilyn let Monte screw her in the ass.

When he returned to Oklahoma, Monte announced that he and Marilyn had worked out all of their differences, that they were getting back together, and that he was moving to Cape Girardeau. As if I needed further convincing of his stupidity, Monte topped off his revelation by telling me all about his night of anal sex. I simply shook my head without saying a word.

As usual, Monte couldn't be patient about the whole affair. He had already decided to pack up and leave that very same day. He owed me money for back rent, repairs to his car for which I had paid, and some utility bills. When I reminded him of his debt, he nonchalantly dismissed my concerns. He said he would send me some money as soon as he found a job in Missouri.

I wasn't comfortable with Monte traipsing off to "Never, Never Rear Entry Land" when he still owed me a bunch of money. When he went over to break the good news to his mother, I packed up all of his clothes and locked them in the trunk of my car. When he returned and found his clothes missing, he angrily confronted me.

"Bob, where the hell are all my clothes?" he demanded.

"In the trunk of my car. When you send me my money, I'll send you your clothes."

Monte clenched his fist and charged toward me. He stopped just short of getting in my face, but I could tell he was furious.

"Give me my clothes motherfucker!" he yelled. His face was beet red with anger.

I paused for a few seconds before I responded.

"Monte, I'm just sending you back to Marilyn the same way she delivered you to me—with nothing more than your waterbed and the clothes on your back."

Monte stormed out of the house and hopped in his car that Marilyn had given back to him. He put the key in the ignition, started the car, buckled his seatbelt, adjusted the rearview mirror, carefully backed out of the driveway, and slowly accelerated down the street. It simply was not Monte's nature to leave in a cloud of dust.

. . .   ~   . . .

Immediately after Monte made the ill-fated decision to return to Marilyn, his father, Dick, moved in with me. Dick and Diana had been having a difficult time with their marriage and finally decided a divorce was the solution. Because Dick had been so good to me over the years, I was eager to have him move in with me. Even though there was twenty years difference in our ages, we became quite good friends. As I was nearing completion of my Doctorate, Dick taught me about dressing professionally; what suits to buy, how to combine slacks and jackets, and how to color coordinate ties and shirts. I, in turn, kept him in stitches with stories about Monte, Danny, and me.

Dick also enlightened me about Monte's relationship with his deceased brother, Bubba. We were driving to play golf one day when I finally got up the nerve to ask about Bubba. At first, Dick smiled and recounted all of the wonderful things he remembered about Bubba. His face turned empty as he recited the details of how Bubba had died.

It was one night during their junior year in high school, when Danny and Bubba headed out looking for girls. While cruising the usual spots along the main drag, they met up with one of their buddies and a girl they all knew from school, who happened to have some marijuana. They decided to head out of town to get high and fired up a joint as they drove along one of the deserted country roads east of Norman.

The details of what happened are kind of sketchy; we don't know if the girl's bra was already off or just in the process of coming off, when Danny swerved on to the shoulder of the road. For some unknown reason, Bubba reached over and grabbed the wheel, which caused the car to go off the shoulder and into the drainage ditch. Danny tried to steer the car back onto the road, but the wheels were caught in the ditch and wouldn't turn. Danny hit the brakes just before the car slammed into the only tree along the entire stretch of road. Ironically, no one in the car had more than a scratch on them except for Bubba; he had been thrown out of the car and his skull was crushed. Danny administered mouth-to-mouth while the others went to call for help, but it was already too late.

Dick had been the one to go in and identify Bubba's body at the hospital. He had to physically restrain Diana from going into the room because of how badly Bubba had been mangled. I could see tears rolling down Dick's cheeks from underneath his sunglasses. His voice started to break up slightly as he said "I wouldn't wish that kind of thing on my worst enemy."

Dick confided to me that he thought Diana had stayed mad at him all those years for not letting her go into that room. I wondered if, under those circumstances, I would have had the courage to do the right thing, like he had.

Through all the years I had known them, Dick and Diana had always treated me like one of the family. I always thought that was kind of strange because I was just Danny's friend with the big nose. To them, however, any friend of Danny's was a friend of theirs. Although I knew it was a painful memory for Dick, I asked him how he and Diana could love Danny the way they obviously did after what had happened.

Dick responded to my question by saying, "Why should we ruin that kid's life? There was nothing we could do to bring Bubba back."

Dick perked up as he recounted how Diana had run over to Danny in the hospital and hugged him when she saw that he was distraught. She had held him in her arms and rocked him back and forth as he cried. She told him that it was not his fault and that everything would be all right. This time I found myself wondering if I would have had the courage to do the right thing, like she had.

CHAPTER 8

MONT, YOU'VE STILL GOT IT

After Monte went back to Marilyn, my life returned to normal, or as normal as possible in my case. I continued to share a rental house with Dick, but spent most of my time at Lisa's place, with her and Jaclyn. In the back of my mind there was the notion that Lisa and I would some day get married. The impending responsibilities of having to provide for an instant family convinced me to get serious about completing my dissertation. I even went so far as to buy a small house with the intention of staying in Norman after I graduated.

Ironically, finishing my Doctoral degree actually thrust me into an extremely difficult situation; for the first time in my life I needed to find a real job. Sending out unsolicited resumes to local consulting firms brought no immediate offers, so I started to look for an academic position. Given my late start, the only available opening I could find was at a small school in Louisiana. I interviewed for the job and the faculty voted unanimously to offer me the position, due in large part to the fact that I was the only applicant.

At first, I was somewhat apprehensive about moving to Louisiana. I wasn't sure whether or not I wanted to teach college for a living. I was also unsure whether or not to take Lisa and Jaclyn with me. Although Lisa was ready to make a commitment, I knew that moving away from her twin sister would not be easy for her. After weighing all of the factors, I finally decided to go to Louisiana by myself.

I sat down with Lisa and explained my decision. I told her that I didn't want any undue stress to affect our relationship. I indicated that I was more than a little bit worried that she would miss her sister and get home-sick for Oklahoma. I also pointed out that I needed to focus on my career for a few years in order to build a strong financial foundation for our future life together.

Thanks to one heck of an acting job, I managed to get Lisa to buy the whole pile of crap. The truth of the matter was that I wasn't ready to get married and I saw an opportunity to sow some wild oats without running the risk of losing my steady girlfriend. I put on an even better show when it came time for the tearful goodbye. In fact, my act was so good I almost convinced myself that I was sincere.

I quickly grew to love Louisiana and the Cajun way of life; they never let anything get in the way of having a good time. One of the celebrations I enjoyed most was called "Contraband Days", commemorating when the pirate Jean Lafitte sailed into town and raped and pillaged the locals. In a place where people were willing to throw a three-day drunken festival for absolutely no good reason, I was bound to fit in.

After he graduated from medical school in Tulsa, Danny had decided that Dallas was the best place to do his internship. Since Dallas was close, I was able to visit him fairly often while I lived in Louisiana. I was more than a little bit curious as to how Danny would handle his new responsibilities. Through the course of a handful of weekend visits, I found out that in order to start his career in medicine, it was important for Danny to do a lot of late night carousing, play golf at least three times a week, take frequent vacations, and get started on a life-long addiction to gambling. In all the times I visited, I never once saw Danny even walk into a hospital.

Having parted on bad terms, I didn't hear from Monte for over a year. He somehow managed to track me down while I was in Louisiana and apologized for the way he had left. His decision to marry Marilyn a second time had taken him to Missouri. Even though he steadfastly proclaimed that he and Marilyn were going to make it work the second time around, I wasn't convinced. The fact that he had gone to the trouble to look me up was a clear indication that their relationship had already started to deteriorate once again.

Louisiana was fun, but my stay turned out to be all too brief. After only two years I was offered a tenure track position back at the University of Oklahoma. I was going right back to where I had started. Getting the job at OU was a godsend, given that I had a house in Norman that I had been unable to sell when I left. Oh yeah, I was also going back to Lisa.

. . .   ~   . . .

My return to Oklahoma did not meet with nearly as much affection as I had anticipated. Although we had managed to see each other on a regular basis during the two years I had been gone, Lisa seemed distant. She was, at best, cordial to me for the first few weeks after I returned.

Things took a turn for the worse early in the fall when I announced that I had scheduled a weekend trip to Arizona with Danny and Monte. We were going to watch Monte's brother, Eddie, play football for Arizona State University. I felt certain that Lisa would be excited for me, especially after I pointed out that the Sun Devils were going to take on OU's arch nemesis—Nebraska. However, having been on a two-year sabbatical from our relationship, my decision to immediately take a trip with my buddies was not well received.

Lisa's first response was to tell me that I was the most inconsiderate, selfish, immature asshole on the planet. She then pointed out that I had all but abandoned her and Jaclyn for two years. She concluded her remarks by noting that all I cared about was drinking and carousing with my reprobate friends.

I got the distinct impression that Lisa was less than pleased with my travel plans. I decided that I had better make some drastic changes. Lisa sat beside me and fumed as I picked up the phone and called Danny.

"Listen Danny, Lisa says I'm not getting enough exercise. I think we ought to fly out a day early so we can play some golf."

Lisa jumped up and stormed off to her bedroom, then slammed and locked the door behind her.

When Friday rolled around, Lisa and I were barely speaking to one another, so I decided not to waste my breath by asking for a ride to the airport. I was feeling a little bit guilty when I boarded the plane. I didn't want to ruin the weekend for Danny and Monte by moping around just because I had a fight with my girlfriend; that would be selfish and immature. I decided it was time for me to take some responsibility for my actions and rid myself of any sense of guilt. After takeoff, I made a concerted effort to try to drink every last beer on the beverage cart. By the time the plane landed, I was guilt free and ready to help Danny and Monte enjoy their vacation.

Monte's dad had followed Eddie to Arizona about the same time I moved to Louisiana. Since Dick lived in Phoenix, he was able set up tee times for us at a fairly nice municipal course. After we checked into our hotel, we headed straight out to the golf course. Dick declined our invitation to hack around the course with the three of us, opting instead to play with a couple of ASU boosters. That turned out to be a very wise move on his part.

Danny and I decided to share one cart; we put Monte and two cases of ice-cold beer in a second cart. With the desert heat contributing to our thirst, we soon made a major dent in the beer supply. By the time we made the turn, I was feeling absolutely no pain. It was on the back nine that I pulled one of the most crude, disgusting, vulgar, immature stunts of my entire adult life; Danny loved it.

On the 15th hole, I was the first one to tee off. After I hit my tee shot, I nonchalantly walked back to the two golf carts. Monte was next on the tee, so he dutifully teed up his ball and got ready to swing. As he addressed his ball, Monte heard Danny start to snicker, so he backed off.

"What's so funny?" he asked, but Danny didn't say anything.

Monte returned to his pre-swing routine, but quickly came to the realization that I was not in his field of view, which meant I had to be up to absolutely no good. He immediately aborted his golf shot and wheeled around in search of my whereabouts. When Monte spotted me, I had my shorts down around my ankles and was basking my face in the warm Arizona sunshine as if I didn't have a care in the world. I was also pissing in Monte's golf cart.

"BOB!" he screamed, as he ran over to the cart, "You are peeing in my cart!"

I snapped to attention, regained my composure and innocently replied, "Oh, I'm sorry Mont. Is this YOUR cart?"

Monte flashed me his most profound pouty face, then broke into emergency cleaning procedures. He took the melted ice water from one of the coolers and used it to flush the floor of his cart several times. He pulled the cart up onto the tee box so he could keep his eye on it while he hit his tee shot. For the rest of the round, Monte never let me, or the cart, get out of his sight.

By the time we finished our round, all three of us had a pretty good buzz going, so we were content to just head for our hotel room and crash. After breakfast the next morning, I loaded Danny and Monte into our rental car and set out to buy some liquor to sneak into the stadium. Within a matter of just a few blocks, Danny spotted a liquor store; Danny had a good eye for spotting liquor stores. I pulled into the parking lot and told Monte to go in and buy a couple of pints, because they would be easier to sneak into the game. When he emerged from the store, Monte had a fifth of rum in his hand.

"Very good, dumbass. How in the hell are we gonna get that into the stadium?" I inquired.

"Bob, I'll just take my shirt off and wrap it around the bottle. Nobody wears a shirt in this stadium because it's too hot," he replied.

I had my doubts about Monte's plan, but it was getting late. I needed to get to the stadium to try and find a ticket. As a player, Eddie was only allowed four tickets and one sideline pass for each game. He gave Diana and her new husband the pair of tickets that were on the shade-protected west side of the stadium. Dick got the pass to prowl the sidelines. Eddie gave the two tickets in the student section to Monte and Danny. As the odd man out, I ended up having to purchase a ticket from a scalper outside the stadium.

Surprisingly, Monte's plan for sneaking in our bottle of booze worked like a charm. He marched right past the ticket-takers without so much as a glance from any of them. In fact, we probably could have taken a keg of beer in with us if we so desired. The ushers working the turnstiles didn't give a shit about what anybody was carrying, so long as they had a ticket. As it turned out, the police inside the stadium were not nearly so open-minded.

Once we were inside the stadium, we bought three cokes and headed down to the student section where we knew it would be safe to mix our drinks. After I was sure we were sufficiently surrounded, I poured half of each coke on the ground and filled the void in each cup with rum. I handed Danny and Monte their drinks without stirring them, then watched as both of them choked on their first sips. I gave the bottle of rum to Monte and told him to take care of it until I came back at half time.

I started to make my way out of the student section. Just as I got to the aisle of stairs, I heard the sound of glass break. I turned around and saw that Danny had already kicked over the bottle of rum and broken it. A cop at the other end of the row had heard the commotion and was now hurriedly making his way toward Monte and Danny. I decided I had better get my butt far away from the crime scene, so I sprinted up the stairs.

I paused at the main concourse and turned back to check on my two rum smuggling buddies. The cop was standing next to them holding the remnants of the bottle of rum as he made them pour their drinks out on the ground. I laughed when I saw Monte's famous pouty face expression. I held my drink up in a mock toast to Monte and Danny, took a long sip, and headed off to find my seat.

The game was a sellout so the ticket I bought was for a seat near the top of the upper deck on the sun-drenched east side of the stadium. I didn't really care where I sat; I was just thankful that I still had a refreshing beverage to enjoy during the game.

In an extremely exciting game, ASU lost in the final minutes to a powerful Cornhusker squad. It was this game that propelled the Sun Devils into national prominence. The next year, ASU would win the Pac 10 and go on to defeat Ohio State in the Rose Bowl.

After the game, the three of us decided to take Eddie out for a night on the town. Although he wasn't legally old enough to drink, his status as a football jock managed to get him into all of the bars. The evening was actually quite an ego trip for Danny, Monte, and I. At every bar we went into, people would whisper and point at Eddie, the stud football player. Monte was totally taken up by all the attention we were receiving.

"Bob, I wonder what position they think I play," he naively wondered out loud.

Before I could answer, Danny interjected with, "Mont, they probably think you spend a lot of time on your knees in the locker room."

At the last bar we visited, we were introduced to the "shot girl", an attractive young lady, semi-dressed as a cowgirl, with bottles of tequila in her gun holsters and shot glasses on her bullet belt. This was the first time Danny and I had ever seen such a wonderful person. I bought the first round of tequila shots. I raised my glass in the air and offered up my favorite toast, "Here's to Monte's upper lip."

Danny bought the second round and dedicated it to Monte's lower lip. I don't recall how many rounds of shots we had, but I know we toasted every orifice on Monte's body.

It was after midnight when we finally decided to head back to our hotel. On the drive home, Eddie announced that he was hungry so we pulled into a Whattaburger restaurant. Monte, of course, bolted out of the car and was the first one into the restaurant. He marched straight up to the counter and placed his order. The girl behind the counter dutifully repeated Monte's order into the microphone next to the cash register. She followed the exact same procedure for Eddie, Danny, and myself. Then, she made a crucial mistake; she turned her back on us to fill our drink orders.

Danny was first to seize the opportunity. He grabbed the microphone and announced to everyone in the restaurant that he had a "Whopper" in his pants that Monte could eat if he was really hungry. Never one to be outdone, I sprinted over to the other cash register, grabbed the microphone and started serenading Monte with a heartfelt rendition of "*We Take It Up The Ass In Cape Girardeau*" (sung to the tune of "*I Left My Heart In San Francisco*").

I was barely into my second verse when the manager stormed out from the back of the restaurant and informed us, in no uncertain terms, that the microphones were for use by employees only. He told us that we should take our food and hit the road before he called the police.

On our way out, Monte couldn't resist the urge to add a few last stinging comments. He looked the manager straight in the eye and told him that his tile floors were filthy, his tables needed to be bussed, and his napkin dispensers were all empty. We left before Monte's inflammatory remarks provoked the manager into taking off his apron and challenging Monte to broom duel.

Somehow, Jose Cuervo and I managed to guide the rental car back to our hotel without getting us pulled over. When we got up to our room, I fell face first onto my bed and passed out without eating a single bite of my food. Danny and Monte actually managed to ingest a couple of mouthfuls before they called it quits. Eddie ate everything he ordered then called one of his girlfriends to come pick him up so he could go get something else to eat.

The next thing I remember was being awakened by the sound of the TV. I had a throbbing headache and could only manage to pry open one eye. Through my one blurred portal, I saw Monte standing at the dresser taking his shirts out of the drawer, carefully unfolding them, then re-folding them and delicately placing them into his suitcase. Of course, you can't fold clothes without watching the television. At 5:30 in the morning, the only shows on are children's programs, so Monte was watching *"Mr. Rodgers Neighborhood"* while he folded shirts.

I actually had to reach up and pull my lips apart in order to overcome my severe case of cottonmouth. When I tried to speak, my voice cracked due to my dry throat. I finally managed to squeak out, "Monte, what in the hell are you doing?"

"I'm packing, Bob. We fly out today and I want to be prepared to unpack when I get home," he replied matter-of-factly.

I rubbed my one good eye in disbelief and responded, "Monte, your flight is not until three fucking o'clock this afternoon! Turn the damn TV off."

Monte was not swayed by my logic. He announced, "Fine. I'm almost through packing. I'm gonna go down to the lobby and get a newspaper."

He closed his suitcase and left, never once contemplating the fact that nothing would be open in the lobby at 5:30 in the morning.

Although near death, I felt an obligation to help Monte finish packing. It took all of the courage I had never before displayed in my life to pull back the covers on my bed. I rolled over and fell onto the floor. Gamely, I struggled to my feet and stumbled towards the dresser. Once there, I carefully removed half-a-dozen of the recently re-folded shirts from the suitcase. I then inched my way towards the garbage can using the edge of the dresser for support. As I bent over, I could feel myself starting to black out, but I summoned enough inner strength to prop myself up. I carefully reached into the trashcan and retrieved the sacks containing the uneaten food from our previous night's foray at Whattaburger. I shuffled backwards along the dresser until I reached Monte's suitcase. I stuffed the garbage sacks into his suitcase and carefully replaced his meticulously re-folded shirts. I shut the suitcase and collapsed back onto my bed.

That night, back in Oklahoma, I got a call from Monte in Missouri.

"Bob, why did you put that stuff in my suitcase?" he demanded. "It stunk up my car and ruined all of my clothes."

"Mont, I knew you were gonna have a long day ahead of you since you got up so fucking early. I just didn't want you go hungry on your drive home."

   ...   ~   ...

After the Arizona trip, I decided it was time for me to seriously consider my future with Lisa. I had purposely left her behind while I was in Louisiana because I truly felt that our time apart would allow us to reflect on what we meant to each other. I was extremely fond of her and totally head-over-heels in love with Jaclyn. After thinking about it for a couple of days, I finally asked Lisa if she wanted to get married.

I could have sworn that I asked, "Would you like to be my wife for evermore?" However, I must not have not pronounced my words clearly because it soon became obvious that Lisa had answered "yes" to the question, "Would you like to fight more than ever before?"

It turned out that our time apart had made me independent and Lisa bitter. She didn't understand the time demands of my career in academia. Moreover, she wasn't willing to play second fiddle to my job, my friends, or my hobbies, no matter what the circumstances. She felt that if I truly loved her and Jaclyn, I should devote all of my time and energies to just them. Whenever I deviated from her expectations, Lisa would make it very clear to me that she wasn't pleased. She would pay me back by refusing all of my advances. However, I wasn't willing to tolerate what I considered to be her emotional blackmail. After a few weeks of nonstop bickering, I finally broke up with Lisa.

Without a doubt, the hardest part of the breakup was not getting to see Jaclyn. She and I had become great pals, and we truly enjoyed our times together. Although I missed Jaclyn immensely, I knew it was best that I not have any contact with her for a while. I was tired of battling with her mother. I also knew if I called Lisa too soon, we would probably end up getting back together, which would ultimately just lead to more bickering.

Although Lisa was furious at me, she knew how much I loved her little girl; she also recognized that I was the only positive male influence in Jaclyn's life. After about a month, Lisa finally broke down and called me. She said that Jaclyn had been asking about me every day. She then asked if I wanted to see Jaclyn. To her credit, Lisa eventually allowed me to take Jaclyn every other weekend, even though I had no legal rights to see the little girl.

...   ⁓   ...

It was early in the fall when Monte once again surprised Danny and me by announcing that he wanted to go to the OU-Texas game. Since Marilyn loathed me, detested Danny, and hated football, I was able to deduce that she would not be accompanying Monte on the trip. I started to suspect that all was not right in Missouri.

Monte came down to Oklahoma on Thursday then he and I drove down to Dallas the next day. Since Danny's apartment was small, sparsely furnished, and filthy, I decided we would be much more comfortable if we spent the weekend in a hotel. We picked Danny up at his apartment and drove straight over to check into the Embassy Suites hotel. After we unpacked, the three of us headed out for one of our typical wild Friday nights in Dallas.

After we hit a few topless bars in Greenville, Monte convinced us to go check out a country and western bar. He had bought a new white cowboy hat and was sure it would attract females, even with me standing next to him. Once inside the bar, it wasn't long before a short, fat migrant farm worker came up and asked Monte if he would like to two-step. He jumped at the invitation and strutted off like a stud bull.

Danny had gone to the bathroom and when he came out he asked, "Bob, where is the gay caballero?"

"Some short Filipino woman whisked Señor Monte off to dance," I replied as I pointed in their direction.

Fred and *Ginger* were certainly easy to spot on the dance floor. Monte was at least three feet taller than his dance partner, so he had to bend over like a straw just to put his hands on her shoulders. Even though she was standing on the tips of her toes, her short stubby arms barely reached Monte's elbows. Danny turned around and rolled his eyes at me. As I glared at the freakish looking couple stumbling around the dance floor, I got the feeling that we might be in for an evening full of Monte's romance-inspired stupidity.

It only took one dance for Monte to become totally enamored with his newfound dance partner. Unfortunately, she had come to the bar with several pickup trucks worth of friends and relatives. In order for Monte to make his move, he needed to find some way to get her away from her entourage. Danny and I spent the next three hours ignoring Monte's pleas that we ask her friends to dance.

Monte eventually came to the realization that we were not going to help him out in his pursuit of romance. When I finally suggested it was getting late, Monte told us he just wanted one more dance before we left. We reluctantly agreed to his request, but I also gave him my sternest "NO FUCKING WAY" warning about dragging anything back to our hotel.

It was after midnight by the time we made it back to our hotel. The bedroom in our suite had two king size beds and the couch in the living room folded out into a third bed. Normally, I was relegated to the couch because of my snoring. However, when I opened the door to the suite, Monte walked over and immediately folded out the couch. He claimed that he wanted to stay up and watch some television. I knew he was probably lying, but I was too tired and drunk to argue with him. I went into the bedroom and passed out in one of the beds; Danny did the same in the other bed.

I should have known that, against my direct orders, Monte had told his dance partner exactly where we were staying. It was about 2:00 a.m. when Monte finally heard the knock that he had been so anxiously awaiting. However, when he opened the door he found his Filipino floozy standing in the hall holding up one of her girlfriends, who was "muy baracho".

After he invited both señoritas into our suite, Monte snuck into the bedroom and quietly woke up Danny. He whisper pleaded with Danny to come out and fool around with the very drunk friend. I, of course, snored through the whole scene. Reluctantly, Danny got out of bed, walked into the living room, quickly surveyed the situation, and turned on the old Lebanese charm.

"Get the fuck out!" he screamed at Monte's visitors, then turned and stumbled back into the bedroom.

Monte managed to convince his lady friend that Señor Danny was just joking, then offered her something to drink. By this time, the drunken friend was slumped over in a chair with her face smashed down on the small glass dinner table next to the kitchenette. Just as Monte started to make his way toward the fridge to get some beers, she puked on the table and all over herself.

Monte's dance partner quickly stood up and announced that she should probably take her friend home, but once again he insisted that they stay. He wrestled the upchuck queen out of the chair and dragged her over to the corner of the room. He laid her down on the floor, where she was free to throw up some more. He hurriedly cleaned up the vomit on the table, dragged his lovely señorita into bed with him and screwed her.

When I walked out of the bedroom the next morning, I found the remnants of Monte's romantic interlude scattered across the living room. I demanded an explanation and Monte was more than eager to tell us the whole story. When I finally stopped laughing, I started to lecture Monte about his stupid little stunt.

"Monte, I specifically told you not to bring Corizon Aquino back to our hotel. I can't believe you let her come in here when we were asleep. You don't know anything about her. That slut could have taken all of our money, or even worse, stolen our liquor."

Once again, I was just wasting my breath. Monte was proud of his conquest. As we were getting ready to leave for the game, he looked in the mirror, adjusted the few remaining wisps of hair on the top of his balding head, pointed his finger toward the mirror and proclaimed to himself, "Mont, you've still got it."

Danny was not amused as he pointed out, "Yeah, Mont, after last night you've got it all right. You just better hope that you don't give it to your wife."

                ...   ~   ...

After that weekend, I didn't see Monte again until he and Corey showed up in Norman unexpectedly for the Christmas holidays. When I inquired as to Marilyn's whereabouts, he made up some story about her needing to stay home because of a sick relative. I didn't give a damn why she wasn't with him, but it sure did seem suspicious that they would spend the holidays away from each other. I got the distinct impression that perhaps Monte's marriage wasn't doing too well again.

In the spring, I heard from Monte with increased frequency. Every time we talked, he would speak longingly of Oklahoma and of his desire to one day get back to Norman. He would always assure me that his career was going great and that it was only a matter of time before his company would transfer him to Oklahoma. He never spoke about Marilyn, nor did I ever ask.

At the start of the summer, I called Monte to organize a trip to Dallas. I wanted him to see firsthand just how little work Danny was doing during his internship. I told him that we would hit a few bars, play some golf, and even take in a Texas Rangers game. I sealed the deal by pointing out that it was getting close to harvest time and there would probably be thousands of short lettuce pickers in town for him to dance with.

Monte and I arrived in Dallas early on Friday, so we checked into our hotel and waited for Danny to show up. That night, Danny took us out to the *West End*, an older part of the city whose buildings had been renovated into upscale shops, exotic restaurants and, of course, a variety of fine drinking establishments. Our tenth bar of the evening was a loud, smoky discotheque. The place was packed, so we had to take a table in the rear of the bar. This was a good thing because Danny was feeling no pain; hence, he would have no inhibitions about yelling disgusting remarks to the women out on the dance floor.

Although he was short and skinny, Danny could consume alcohol like a top fuel dragster. The good news was that alcohol helped rid Danny of his inhibitions, which allowed him to show off the one physical feature he was most proud of; his prodigious tallywhacker. Whenever the need arose for a penis to appear in a public setting, Danny could whip out his manhood with lightning like speed. The bad news was that Danny's special attribute didn't mix well with alcohol. There had been several instances during which he had stumbled across the fine line separating drunken horniness from inebriation-induced impotence. This night, however, Danny would prove that he could always put his drunken pecker to good use.

When the waitress came to our table, I ordered a beer and Danny ordered scotch-and-water. As he stood up to go to the restroom, Monte ordered his favorite, rum-and-Coke. The waitress returned a few minutes later and placed our drinks on the table. Conveniently, Monte had stayed in the restroom long enough for me to get stuck with the tab for the first round. Upon his return, Monte sat down and grabbed his rum-and-Coke and took a sip. The drink was so strong that he choked and immediately spit it back in his glass, spilling some down the front of his shirt in the process.

"Man, that's strong. They need to stir their drinks better," he whined as he stood up to return to the bathroom to wipe off his shirt.

After I tipped the waitress, I turned to watch one of the young lovelies on the dance floor, knowing full well that I had absolutely no chance of ever meeting her, or any girl like her. After a few moments of gawking at the young vixen's tantalizing gyrations, I turned to ask Danny what he thought my chances would be of getting to dance with her. Although the bar was dark, the glow of lights from the dance floor provided sufficient illumination for me to see that Danny had his dick out of his pants and was getting ready to take Monte's drink off the table. Never startled by anything Danny did, I nonetheless had to inquire as to what he was up to.

"Danny, why do you have your dick out of your pants?" I calmly asked.

"Don't want Mont to choke anymore, so I'm gonna stir his drink for him," he answered.

Danny lowered the glass down between his legs with his right hand. Then, with his left hand he plunged his one-eyed swizzle stick into Monte's drink and swirled it around.

Realizing that this could turn into a potentially embarrassing situation, I said, "Keep stirring, Danny. I'm gonna get one of them flowery umbrellas to put in there when you're through."

When Monte returned to the table, his drink was sitting on a new napkin and had a pink umbrella sticking out of it. More than a little bit suspicious, Monte inquired, "Bob, why does my drink have an umbrella in it?"

"Mont, you should have been here. Danny was so outraged about you choking that he went up to the bar and demanded a fresh drink at no charge. He chewed them out about you ruining your shirt. He went to great lengths to make sure that your drink is properly stirred this time."

Satisfied by my bogus explanation, Monte turned and thanked Danny, then took a large gulp from his glass. I was thankful that we left after just one drink. There was no telling what Danny would have done had Monte ordered a second round.

. . .   ~   . . .

When I awoke the next morning, I felt like something had eaten me and shit me over a cliff. Monte and the impromptu bartender felt even worse. We were supposed to tee off at nine that morning, but I was quite sure that I would be pronounced dead well before we got to the first tee.

Somehow, the three of us managed to get up and drag our carcasses out to the golf course, which was a big mistake. In the summer, Dallas is hotter than two queers with lockjaw. We spent the next five hours hacking our way around the course, while sweating out everything we had drunken over the past few years. I was proud to be the only one to shoot below that day's high temperature of 105.

After surviving the hell of 18 holes of golf, we drug ourselves back to the hotel room to cool off and crash. I left a wake up call with the front desk so we wouldn't miss the Rangers' game that night. When the phone rang, we grudgingly crawled out of our beds, showered and headed out to watch some baseball.

Most major league players will tell you that the old ballpark in Arlington, Texas, was easily the hottest place on the planet, and this night was no exception. As we filed into the stadium, we learned that it was "bat night"; a promotional event at which all kids entering the stadium received a souvenir baseball bat. Ironically, I suddenly had a chilling premonition that 15,000 bats in the hands of children were not going to help my hangover.

Although our seats weren't the best for viewing the game, they were very easy to find; they were one row down from the blimp overhead. I thought the climb might do us some good, but Danny bitched every step of the way. Upon arriving at our seats we found ourselves fortunate enough to be seated right behind the Mongoloids, a real nice family from Grapevine, Texas. There was Billy-Ray Mongoloid, his extremely large wife, June-Anne Mongoloid, and the seven little Mongoloid vermin, each armed with a souvenir bat.

Our metal seats were attached to the metal bleachers that formed the metal upper deck. I guess that my six years of post-graduate education in engineering momentarily escaped me because I plopped down into my seat wearing shorts, but no shirt. The instant my bare skin made contact, I jumped up and started swearing. For a moment, I actually considered sitting back down and finishing the job, but I decided that searing my skin off would be a coward's way out of having to spend an evening with the Mongoloids from Grapevine, Texas. I spread my shirt out over the chair and slowly sat back down.

After I got situated, I looked over and saw Danny had his head between his legs and was gasping for air. Monte was staring blankly out at the ball field way off in the distance and several hundred feet below us. The beads of sweat on his forehead had coalesced to form a small stream that ran down the side of his face.

Deciding to make the best of a lousy situation, I turned my attention to the ball game. Although I could barely make them out, there did appear to be figures standing on first and second base; the home team was starting a rally. Just then, the geniuses in the press box decided they needed to stir up the crowd by playing a rally cry over the loudspeakers. So they cranked up the "We will, we will, ROCK YOU!" refrain from Queen.

Instead of clapping their hands or stomping their feet in time with the music, every one of the armed little masochists in the stadium started pounding the metal bleachers with their souvenir bats. The deafening noise and vibrations reverberating throughout the upper deck made me feel like I was inside a huge bass drum.

Monte looked over at me and yelled, "Bob, maybe we should get some beers? That might make us feel better."

I screamed back, "Mont, if we are gonna get anything then I suggest we GET THE HELL OUT OF HERE!"

I heard no argument from either one of them; thirty minutes later we were sitting in the air-conditioned lobby bar of our hotel. Danny ordered martinis for all of us. The place was deserted except for an attractive woman sitting on a couch near the piano. Since we didn't get to see much of the baseball game, I thought I might as well give her my best pitch.

"Are those Gucci flip-flops you have on?" I asked politely.

Having never heard anything so stupid in her life, she had to smile. I then invited her over to our table for a drink and she accepted.

Monte immediately launched into his usual "I'm nice and have a really clean house and these guys tease me too much, so can I get a pitty fuck?" routine. Whenever there were women around, Monte would play his "poor pitiful me" act to the hilt. Danny and I were only too glad to help Monte convince this woman that we did, in fact, tease him too much.

As the night wore on, it became obvious that the woman had absolutely no interest in Monte or me. However, she did appear to be more than a little bit enamored with Danny. Through the course of five rounds of martinis, we found out that she was a recent widow. Her late husband was a Lebanese doctor, just like the little drunken dromedary sitting across the table from her. When the lobby bar closed, she invited all three of us up to her room for a nightcap, which none of us needed.

When we got up to the widow's room, there was nothing to drink so she called the concierge to order a couple of bottles of liquor. Danny, being the suave little charmer that he was, decided to make his move. He walked over and started to grope our hostess while she was talking on the phone.

"DON'T!" she pretended to resist. "You are gonna rip my blouse."

I looked at Monte and said, "We are obviously interrupting Danny's courting ritual. Let's get out of here."

We got up to leave the room just as Danny tried delicately to undo the buttons on the woman's blouse by grabbing her collar and yanking the whole garment up over her head while she still had the phone up to her ear. The last thing we saw was Danny tugging on her brassier as she struggled to get untangled from the blouse and phone chord noose that he had managed to wrap around her head. Monte and I cried with laughter all the way back to our room.

The next morning, Danny woke up in a strange room, in bed with a strange woman whom he did not remember meeting. Startled and frightened, he jumped out of bed and started putting on his clothes. The lovely widow was not so lovely early in the morning when you have yet to have your first martini.

"Where are you going," she cooed.

"I'm getting the hell out of here," he replied.

Once he got his pants and shoes on, Danny threw his shirt over his shoulder and hurried over to the door. He grabbed the handle, yanked it open, sprinted into the closet, and smacked his head on the clothes rack.

Without panicking, Danny calmly backed out of the closet and politely asked, "Where the fuck is the door out of here?"

Alas, there were two more choices, but his lovely maiden from the night before was not going to give him any hints. Of course, his second choice led him straight into the bathroom. Danny whirled around and stomped out of the bathroom. He finally grabbed the correct door handle, opened it and ran out into the hallway.

About the time that Danny reached the elevators he realized that not only did he not know the woman in the room he had just fled, he didn't remember our room number either. So he went down to the lobby, picked up the house phone, and had the front desk call our room. When I answered the phone, Danny asked, "Knox, where in the hell am I?"

When I finally stopped laughing, I got up and went downstairs and led the little Lebanese Romeo back to civilization.

Thus ended the last of Danny's pre-marital flings. After three years of hedonism in Dallas, Danny was getting ready to move to Rochester, Minnesota, to begin a residency in psychiatry at the Mayo Clinic. It would be during his stay in Rochester that the avowed woman-hater would meet his future wife.

CHAPTER 9

THE WEDDING

It wasn't long after the Dallas trip when Monte called and told me that he and Marilyn had finally decided to call it quits, for the second time. Since he had established himself as a fairly successful insurance agent and, since Marilyn was willing to give him joint custody of Corey, Monte decided to stay in Cape Girardeau. Although he tried to paint a rosy picture of the arrangement, I could tell that Monte did not relish the idea of living in Marilyn's hometown for the rest of his life.

Less than a year after his re-divorce from Marilyn, Monte received his first big break when his company announced an opening at an agency in Ponca City, Oklahoma. It wasn't Norman, but as far as Monte was concerned, it was a step in the right direction. He immediately applied for the job and was absolutely thrilled when it was announced that he had been selected. I am quite sure that Monte is probably the only person on this planet who has ever coveted a job selling insurance in Ponca City, Oklahoma.

Once he received the good news, Monte eagerly announced his promotion to everyone in the Cape Girardeau office. His best friend decided to throw him an impromptu going-away party that same night. During the course of the celebration, Terry offered to help Monte move to Ponca City. He even agreed to drive the rental truck back to Missouri in order for

Monte to avoid the drop off charge. Monte gladly accepted his friend's generous offer. Early the next morning, the two of them loaded up the truck and headed south to Oklahoma.

Monte had leased a house in Ponca City, so he and Terry were able to complete the move in just one day. However, a couple of days after Terry left Ponca City, Monte got a call from the rental company wanting to know when he was going to return the truck. Acting out of instinct, Monte immediately conjured up a lie about an unexpected illness that had caused him to delay returning the truck. He assured the caller that the vehicle would be returned as soon as he felt better.

After Monte hung up, he immediately tried to call Terry, but the phone line had been disconnected. With nowhere else to turn, Monte decided to call his ex-wife and enlist her help in locating Terry and the missing truck. When Monte dialed Marilyn's number, Terry answered the phone.

It turned out that Terry had been sleeping with Monte's ex-wife for months. He'd taken the truck back to Cape Girardeau and used it to move all of his stuff over to Marilyn's house, but had not bothered to return it. Terry and Marilyn only had one vehicle between them, so they decided to use Monte's rental truck to run errands around town.

Monte was more shocked than angry. By this time, he didn't give a damn what Marilyn did or with whom, he just wanted to get the rental truck returned. After a few seconds to regain his composure, Monte asked Terry if he could speak with Marilyn. When she got on the phone, Monte calmly told her that he would not send any child support payments until the truck had been returned and the rental charges paid in full. He then slammed down the phone.

Marilyn was not at all impressed with Monte's newfound set of balls. She knew that Monte would never get to see his son if he was late on any of his child support payments. Marilyn and Terry continued to use the rental truck for another two weeks. Monte ended up paying the rental fees plus all of the late charges.

Terry and Marilyn married soon after he moved in and they immediately had a baby. A hasty marriage, followed quickly by an unplanned child, was a sure sign that theirs was not a match made in heaven. Coupling these events with the fact that he was a borderline alcoholic and she was too lazy to work, money soon became a problem. Rather than trying to embezzle more child support money out of Monte, Marilyn simply chose to give up custody of Corey.

Monte called me after Corey arrived in Ponca City. He was elated with his opportunity to play the role of the single parent. After Monte finished telling me of his great news, I called Danny to get his input. We concluded that it was a toss up as to which of his fucked-up parents should raise Corey.

Once Monte finally settled down in Ponca City, he was able to begin his search for the perfect woman. There seemed to be no shortage of tramps and whores from which to choose in Ponca City, and Monte made a concerted effort to drag every last one of them down to Norman so that I could have the displeasure of making their acquaintance. For some reason, he always expected me to elevate his female companions to sainthood status like he did. In *Monte Land* you can ignore all the sordid facts and obvious character flaws of a woman, just as long as you are getting laid. I referred to his psychotic form of hero worship as "re-virginating".

Monte also saw himself as the knight in shining armor for every woman he ever met. Invariably, he would convince himself that his latest low-life tramp could become the perfect woman, with just a little help from him. He would then try to sell me on his demented reasoning.

The story was the same each time. At first, Monte would assure me that he had found the perfect woman. Then, he would slowly but deliberately release little bits of information about the tragic life that his newest ideal companion had experienced prior to meeting him. He felt it was important to share her sad story with me because that would enable me to better understand why she had multiple children with different fathers, or some other endearing trait.

Monte discovered his first "damsel in distress" working as a manicurist in the Ponca City beauty salon where he went to get his haircut. Lee Ann was a divorcee with two children. Her ex-husband was well known around Ponca City for his alcoholic binges and wife beating episodes, and she had a reputation for sleeping her way around town. Lee Ann was good-looking and willing to go to bed with any man who would spend money on her. Monte was just the kind of lonely sucker she preyed on, so it was inevitable that they would get together.

True to form, Monte brought Lee Ann down to Norman for an OU football game so that his family and I could meet her. Although not the least bit surprised, I still had to cringe when Monte took me aside and told me that he was going to ask Lee Ann to marry him. He wanted all of us to put our stamp of approval on her so that he could get started on planning the rest of their lives together.

I knew from the minute I first laid eyes on her that Monte would never escort Lee Ann down the aisle. She had "home wrecker" written all over her. During her short weekend visit it became quite clear that she was more than willing to flirt with any man who paid her any notice. It was also obvious to everyone, except Monte, that Lee Ann was just using him.

My premonition came true one week later when Monte caught Lee Ann in bed with another man. Although he was willing to continue their relationship, Lee Ann mercifully broke it off before Monte could propose to her. It took almost a full week for Monte to get over his latest case of heartbreak.

. . .   ~   . . .

Unable to find a perfect woman in Ponca City, Monte soon received another career break that enabled him to cast his net a little wider. He found out that there was an opening for a new agent in his company's Norman office, so he immediately applied for the job. He came down to Norman the day before his interview, so we went out to dinner and then headed out to Opie's to have a few cocktails. I left early, but Monte was feeling so confident about his prospective job that he decided to stay a while and stake out his old stomping grounds.

It was almost midnight when a woman Monte knew from high school happened to wander in for a nightcap. He recognized Glenda the instant she walked through the door, so he went over and struck up a conversation with her. They continued to drink and get reacquainted up until closing time, at which point they decided to go back to her place, where eventual engagement number four was consummated.

There was never any question as to whether Monte would get the job in Norman. He was by far and away the brightest young agent in his entire firm. More importantly, his organization fetish made him perfectly suited for a job that didn't really require any brains, just good record-keeping. Monte called me a couple of days after his interview to share both bits of good news with me.

"Bob, I got the job!' he announced excitedly.

"That's great, Mont. I knew you'd get it. When it comes to sleazy insurance salesmen, you're at the top of my list."

"I have some more good news," he proclaimed.

"I'm on the edge of my seat, Mont," I answered glibly.

"Glenda and I are engaged!"

I didn't say a word. After a few moments of silence, Monte asked, "Well, what do you think, Bob?"

"Mont, I can't decide if you are emotionally resilient or just plain stupid. Less than a month ago, that whore in Ponca City dumped you. Don't you want to take some time off between heartbreaks?"

"Bob, love is a lot like riding a horse. Once you get thrown, you gotta get right back on or you'll never ride again," he reasoned.

"Mont, at the rate you're going, you're gonna wear out the stirrups on the saddle of love," I noted.

There was one small drawback to Monte's new career plans. He had to fulfill his commitment to the Ponca City office for six months before he could move to Norman. In order to avoid changing schools in the middle of the fall term, Monte decided to have Corey move in with Glenda and her daughter from a previous marriage.

Given that Corey was only seven years old, I wasn't very comfortable with the living arrangements Monte had conjured up. I had never met Glenda, so I really couldn't pass judgment on her, but I knew how quickly things were moving between her and Monte. I decided to call Monte and try to convince him that Corey would be better off living with me.

"Mont, why don't you let Corey stay with me until you get down here? He knows me and I'll take good care of him," I offered.

"That's not necessary, Bob. In addition to giving great blowjobs, Glenda is an excellent mother," he replied.

"Well, its good to know she has all the requisite maternal skills," I said, not totally comforted by Monte's answer.

In spite of all my pleadings, Monte carried out the hastily conceived plans for him and his son to cohabitate with Glenda and her daughter. During the week, Monte worked in Ponca City. On weekends, he would come to Norman to see Corey and help Glenda plan their upcoming wedding. Given the speed at which it was proceeding, I knew Monte's marriage train was heading for an early derailment.

October eventually rolled around, and it was time for us to make our annual trek to Dallas for the OU-Texas game. I made our usual hotel reservations; two rooms with a connecting door. Two days before Monte and I were scheduled to drive down to Dallas, he called me. I could sense panic in his voice.

"Bob, I can't go to Texas," he said.

"Why the fuck not, Mont? I've already made our reservations," I replied.

"Bob, you are not gonna believe this, but Glenda tried to commit suicide yesterday. She took a bunch of sleeping pills," he said in an overly dramatic tone.

"Mont, maybe she just got tired of being an excellent mother and needed a nap," I reasoned.

"BOB! I'm serious. Corey found her unconscious in her bed, so he called 911. The paramedics were able to revive her, then rushed her to the hospital," he responded.

"Mont, why on earth did she try to kill herself?"

"I don't have a clue. I'm supposed to meet with her doctor in the morning. I'll know more then."

I was barely able to hang up the phone before I burst out laughing. I knew exactly why Glenda had tried to kill herself. She woke up one day and finally figured out just exactly whom she was engaged to. I immediately called Danny and we proceeded to laugh ourselves sick over Monte's tragic news.

It turned out that Glenda had been through a series of personal tragedies and was extremely depressed. Her father had died of alcoholism, her mother had died of cancer, and her sister had been killed in a car wreck, all in a matter of months. She was drinking heavily and had also acquired an addiction to downers. To top it all off, in one of her drunken stupors, she had accepted an extremely premature marriage proposal from Felix Unger.

When Monte met with the doctor the next morning, he was given some disturbing news. The doctor told him that Glenda had been transferred to the mental hospital for observation. She was emotionally drained and mentally unstable. He didn't think she would try suicide again, but he wasn't positive. He said that Glenda needed to stay in the hospital for at least a couple of weeks and would need some long-term counseling.

Monte was outraged. He had rushed down from Ponca City to help Glenda hurry up and get through this difficult time so that they could hurry up and get married. It was clear to Monte that this doctor didn't know what he was talking about. All Glenda needed was to go home and let Monte screw her and everything would be just fine. So, against the advice of her doctor, Monte checked Glenda out of the mental hospital and took her home. While she was still semi-comatose from her suicide attempt and the medication they had given her in the hospital, Monte boinked her.

When Glenda finally emerged from her drug-induced fog, she told Monte the engagement was off and that she wanted him out of her house. When he didn't leave, she packed up her daughter and ran away. Engagement number four was over and Monte was, once again, temporarily devastated.

Corey ended up living with me until Monte finished his tour of duty in Ponca City. After Monte moved down to Norman, I sat down and talked with him about his failed engagement with Glenda.

"Mont, once again you jumped too far and too fast into a relationship. You don't have to propose to a woman the first time you have sex. You know, sometimes the best way to catch a woman is to play hard to get."

Monte thought for a moment then announced, "Don't worry, Bob. That's it. I've had it with women. No woman will ever make an ass of me again."

I was less than impressed with his proclamation.

. . .   ~   . . .

Contrary to Monte, who had spent most of his adult life desperately trying to find someone to marry, Danny and I had both avoided marriage like the plague. However, time had run out for Danny. He had met an attractive physical therapist while working at the Mayo Clinic and had become quite smitten by her, albeit grudgingly. After they had been together for a year, Martha told Danny that she wasn't interested in dating for the rest of her life. Danny managed to sober up long enough to realize what a prized catch he had, so he finally asked Martha to marry him, and she accepted. That was her first mistake.

Given our hedonistic past, I felt that a traditional bachelor party for Danny would just be boring. I decided that we needed to do something more creative, more entertaining, and more enjoyable. I called Danny to brainstorm as to what we should do for his pre-nuptial celebration.

"Danny, if we have a regular stag party you'll just end up getting shit-faced and wont be able to get it up. The last thing in the world I want to do is sit around and watch you hump and slobber on some fat, ugly stripper."

"Knox, it's too cold to fuck in Minnesota. I'm freezing my balls off up here. Let's go someplace warm," he replied.

"How about if the three of us go out to Arizona for a golf orgy instead?" I proposed.

Danny didn't have to think twice. A weekend of fun in the desert sun greatly appealed to him.

"Sounds great. You make the reservations. Be sure and get money from Monte up front so he can't back out on us at the last minute again."

"I've already talked to Monte. He is temporarily between marriage proposals, so he said a weekend of golf and liquor would be great. We'll see you in Arizona."

When I went by to pick up Monte for our weekend trip, I was surprised to find out that Mr. Organized didn't even have a flight bag for his golf clubs. I knew that the airlines would not accept his clubs unless they were covered, so we had to improvise. I told Monte to grab a plastic trash sack (I was sure he had plenty) and we could use duct tape to secure it over the clubs. Evidently my plan worked, because the Sky Cap let us check Monte's clubs through to Phoenix.

Monte was unusually nervous through the entire flight. He kept flipping through the same magazine without stopping on any page long enough to even glance at its contents. Finally, he turned to me and asked, "Bob, how long will Danny have to wait for us at the airport?"

"A couple of hours. Why?" I replied, without looking up from my newspaper.

"Do you think he will spend the entire time drinking in the bar?" he asked.

I could only speculate. After a fraction of a second of pondering the question, I responded with, "Of fucking course he will. Why?"

"Bob, its not a good idea to leave Danny unattended in an airport bar. You know how he gets," he said, as he turned to stare out the window of the plane.

"I wouldn't worry too much, Mont. Danny just likes to relax when he goes out of town," I falsely reassured him.

When we got off the plane in Phoenix, Monte uncharacteristically trailed behind me. Once inside the terminal, we found no Danny, so we headed off in search of the nearest bar. We were about ten yards away from the first cocktail lounge when I spotted our little Lebanese playing partner. As we approached his table, he stood up and let out his unmistakable camel jockey growl, "MONT!" which was followed by a beer can whizzing by us at about 90 miles an hour.

I turned to inform Monte of my findings.

"Mont, I do believe Danny HAS spent the entire time waiting for us in the bar."

We had a tee time early that afternoon so Danny didn't bother to order another beer. Instead, we headed out for the baggage carousel to claim our beloved golf clubs. I went to pick up the rental car while Danny and Monte retrieved our luggage. I had to circle the airport several times while I waited for them to come out of the terminal. When I finally spotted them, Monte was carrying all three sets of golf clubs plus two suitcases. Danny had his overnight bag slung over his shoulder and was talking on his cell phone while making marks on his tip sheet. I pulled up to the curb and popped the trunk lever. While Monte and I loaded the luggage into the trunk of the car, Danny hopped in the front seat and adjusted the air conditioning vents so that they were all blowing in his direction.

Once everything was secure, I jumped in the car and grabbed the road map that the rental company had supplied. I took Danny's ink pen and plotted a course to our destination—The Boulders in Carefree, Arizona. I gave the map to Monte and told him to help me navigate our way. I instructed Danny to be on the lookout for liquor stores. It was an hour's drive to Carefree and I wasn't going to attempt it without at least a six-pack of beer.

We arrived at the course just minutes before our scheduled tee time. We barely had enough time to pay our greens fees and load our carts with beer. As usual, we stepped up to the first tee not having hit any range balls or taking a single practice putt. It really didn't matter. No amount of stretching, warm up or practice swings would make any measurable improvements in our games. Besides, we were there simply to have fun. And there was nothing more fun than watching Danny help Monte with his golf game.

All golfers know that the mental part of the game is the hardest to conquer. Not only was Monte ill equipped to deal with this aspect of the game, but he also had to endure our constant mental tinkering. Danny had a special gift for saying just the right thing to throw Monte totally out of sync. Without a doubt, Danny's favorite modus operandi was to pump Monte up with a bunch of false bravado, then sit back and watch him fall flat on his face. Monte never flew higher or fell flatter than he did that day in the desert.

Monte played uncharacteristically consistent golf for the first seventeen holes and led both of us by at least half-a-dozen strokes when we came to the last hole. The 18th at The Boulders is a beautiful par 5; a large pond with decorative fountains runs along the right side of the fairway and in front of the green. On the 18th tee, Monte creamed his tee shot. At over 275 yards, Monte's drive put him within striking distance of the green in two; that is, if he had a short range mortar that he could put back spin on.

As we drove down the fairway, I heard Danny set Monte up to take the plunge.

"God, Mont. Look at your drive. You've got to go for it. We're talking eagle in Arizona!"

"I don't know Danny, maybe I...." Monte hesitated.

"MONT! You are only 230 yards out on a par 5. When are you going to get a better opportunity?" Danny reasoned.

"Yeah, but if I lay up, I…" Monte stammered.

"MONT! We did NOT come 500 miles to the desert so you could lay up, did we?" Danny demanded.

After a few nervous seconds Monte announced, "That's it. I'm going for it."

I somehow managed to contain my laughter.

After Danny and I each skulled our second shots, we drove down the fairway to reach Monte's mammoth drive. Monte hopped out of his cart and quickly grabbed his 'Pam Wood', a club he named after one of the many women who had made a fool out of him. All Monte had to do was think about how he had babysat for Pam while she went over and screwed that married guy, after she told Monte that she was going shopping at the mall for a new dress to wear on their dinner date that night, which she ended up canceling when she came back to pick up her son. With so much rage flowing through his body, Monte could really murder the ball, and this time was no exception.

We all watched as Monte's ball took off like a rocket, headed straight at the pin. The ball gained altitude as it roared out over the pond. After it reached its apex, it started a slow descent, seemingly right on top of the flag.

Monte yelled, "Go baby!"

Danny joined in, "That's right at it Mont!"

I was a little less excited.

"You're wet," I said smugly as I turned my back on the two of them and started walking toward my ball.

Monte's ball splashed down a full 20 yards short of the green and he was devastated.

"Why did you make me go for it?" he whined at Danny.

But Danny wasn't through tinkering with the expansive vacuum that Monte calls a brain.

"Mont, that's okay. Two in, three out. You get to drop up there. You pitch it up close, make the putt, and you've got par."

At the drop area, Monte contemplated his pitch shot. He still had a small arm of the pond to contend with in front of him and a bunker behind the green if he hit it too far. He wanted to simply chip it on to the fat part of the green, which took both the water and the bunker out of play, but almost certainly guaranteed him two putts or more.

Danny put an immediate halt to Monte's attempt at course management.

"MONT! What do you mean play it safe? You have got to throw it up there close if you want to have any chance for a par."

After a few nervous seconds, Monte decided to take Danny's advice, again. He hit his shot right at the flag, but it spun backwards off the green into the water: 4 in, 5 out. Danny then convinced Monte that he now had nothing to lose. In fact, he might even hole it out if he went at the flag. Same shot, same result: 6 in, 7 out. Monte swung so hard at the next ball that he skulled it straight right, into the pond: 8 in, 9 out. He finally did what he should have done the first time and chipped on to the fat part of the green in 10. He took three putts to get down for his 13, which was good enough to push him into last place.

I looked up after Monte's final chip and saw his pitching wedge go whirling overhead on its way toward the decorative fountain in the middle of the pond. I was near death due to lack of oxygen because of my hysterical laughing fit. Still, I managed to choke out a question to him.

"Mont, why did you do that?" I asked.

"Bob, sometimes you gotta teach your clubs a lesson. That one needs swimming lessons."

. . .   ~   . . .

After our weekend golf orgy, Danny had to return to Rochester to help Martha finalize plans for their wedding. Of course, he wanted to have

Monte and me somehow involved in the gala event. He reasoned with Martha that the responsibilities of the ushers were so simple that not even we could screw them up. Reluctantly, Martha finally agreed to allow us to be the ushers for the wedding. That was her second mistake.

It actually had been several months since Monte's last engagement, so it was about time for him to pull another screwup. Although he had professed to be through with women, I knew it was just a matter of time before he would find another loser to make a complete and utter fool out of him. Ironically, he found her at Danny's wedding.

Monte and I went up to Minnesota a week before the wedding to make sure that Danny stayed drunk for his last few days of bachelorhood. On the day of the wedding, we actually showed up sober and managed to seat most of the attendees without any major screwups. When the ceremony began, Monte and I dutifully took our places at the back of the church. I felt a sense of relief knowing that we had already fulfilled our most important usher responsibilities.

Because of his short stature and Lebanese bloodlines, I lovingly refer to Danny as the "sawed off, foul-breathed, alcoholic, camel jockey". That really is an unfair characterization; I seriously doubt that any of the lunatic fringe Middle Eastern countries would ever claim him. As I stared at the altar, I couldn't figure out how in the world the little runt had managed to pull this thing off. Martha was attractive, smart, even-tempered, sober and, most importantly, willing to put up with his shit for the next fifty years.

Although everyone knew that Danny was an unbelievably obnoxious little smartass, what perplexed me was the fact that he was also a sexist and an avowed woman-hater. This time I had to agree with Monte; life just wasn't fair. We were the nice guys and Danny was an asshole, but he's the one who gets the wonderful wife.

After the priest finished the last few sentences of the wedding ceremony, he told Danny that he could kiss his new bride. I cringed as old bactrian-breath bent over to kiss Martha, but I figured she had better get used to it. The priest turned to the congregation and announced, "Ladies and Gentlemen, I present to you, Dr. and Mrs. Daniel Farha."

Danny threw a quarter-nelson on Martha and started to drag her down the aisle at just under a full out sprint. That was our cue. Monte and I now had to complete our last job as ushers. I was supposed to get the limo and pull it up outside the front doors of the church. Monte would escort the happily married couple out of the church, open the doors of the limo and help Martha with her gown. We would then speed them away to the reception at the Rochester Country Club.

I turned around and started to repeat the instructions to Monte.

"Okay, Mont. I'll get the car."

But as I looked around, Monte was nowhere to be found. I whisper yelled, "Monte, where are you?" but got no response.

I decided it was time to improvise. I ran out of the church and over to the Cadillac limousine that Danny had rented for the week. I jumped in, fired it up, and sped toward the circle drive leading up to the church. Danny and Martha were already standing outside when I pulled up.

Looking somewhat bewildered, Danny asked, "Bob, where is Monte?"

I hopped out of the car and threw my arms up to indicate that I had no idea where my fellow usher was. I ran around the car, opened the door and helped Martha step into the limo without tripping over her gown. Then I grabbed Danny's arm and twisted it behind his back. I put my other hand on top of his head and shoved him into the squad car before he could make any more inquiries as to the whereabouts of my partner.

"I'll be right back," I said as I bolted back into the church to search for the elusive Monte.

When I opened the door to the church I saw the congregation starting to file out. This was not good. They would see the limo and crowd around it and we would be late getting to the country club. That was not how we had planned it. Danny and Martha were supposed to get to the country club first, so they could greet people as they came in the door. More importantly, it was almost three in the afternoon and I had yet to pop the top on a single beer. My hands started to tremble.

Just as I turned to go down one of the side hallways, I spotted Monte coming up the stairs from the basement. He was adjusting his cummerbund, obviously having just been to the restroom.

"Mont! Where have you been?" I whisper screamed.

"Bob, I've got diarrhea," he replied, not bothering to lower his voice.

"Let's go!" I scolded as we hurried out the doors.

By the time we piled into the limo, Danny had already fired up one of his El Putrid deluxe Cuban cigars. He was talking on his cellular phone to one of his bookies and checking off the games that had already been played. As usual, he was putting a lot of scribble marks in the loss column.

"Mont, where were you?" Danny asked as he hung up his phone.

"Danny, I've got diarrhea, bad," Monte answered.

Danny cackled out loud and inquired, "Mont, tell me about your diarrhea. What color was it?"

"It was all green and stringy," Monte replied earnestly.

Danny cackled even louder and asked, "Did it stink?"

"Danny, it was horrible! I know it didn't smell like that when I ate it."

Danny again laughed out loud. Monte then proceeded to give us a detailed accounting of his loose stool as I drove toward the country club. Danny periodically interjected some of his demeaning questions, such as, "Mont, have you ever smelled a woman's butthole after she's had diarrhea?" Martha remained even-keeled throughout the whole story. She hung on to Danny's arm and smiled; she even managed a polite giggle every now and then.

Here we were, on the biggest day of Danny's life, and these two were bantering back and forth about human excrement and laughing, just like they had done about thousands of idiotic topics since they were kids. These cerebral exchanges were truly unique to the two of them. Danny would usually come up with some disgusting hypothetical theme, almost always with sexual undertones, and start quizzing Monte about it. Monte would always light up whenever Danny showed any interest in him, no matter what the topic.

Monte finished detailing his most recent case of diarrhea just as we pulled up to the Rochester Country Club. He got out and opened the car door for the new bride and groom. After everybody piled out, I pulled the car around to the parking lot and then headed inside. I gave the car keys to Danny's dad who was going to return the car for us the next day. Danny and Martha had hired a large van to take people from the reception back to their hotels, in order to allow them to imbibe with no risk of trouble from driving while impaired. As fate would have it, I was destined to become one of the first passengers on the short bus.

The reception started with a formal, sit-down dinner. Unfortunately, the mental midget in charge of catering had decided to seat me at a table with absolutely nobody I knew. By the end of the meal, I had my elbows on the table and my head propped up in my hands while I listened to one of Martha's relatives explain why carrots are orange. Finally, I decided I could take no more; I needed a drink. I stood up and excused myself, then headed straight to the cocktail lounge.

Having escaped the titillating discussion about orange vegetables, I felt like I had been granted a reprieve. I wandered up to the bar, sat down and ordered a martini. Monte came in not long after me and ordered a rum-and-Coke. We were in the middle of exchanging stories about the exciting dinner conversations at our respective tables, when a couple of divorcées-to-be walked in and sidled up next to us at the bar. They were both nurses at the Mayo Clinic and were out to meet some of Danny's "doctor friends". The better-looking one of the two vipers sat next to me and started to make small talk.

"So what do you do?" she inquired, sounding very much like a tax accountant.

"You wouldn't believe me if I told you," I replied.

"Oh, just try me," she cooed.

"Well, I'm a professor of engineering at the University of Oklahoma. I educate tomorrow's leaders."

She giggled and replied, "Oh, Alicia said you were funny! Can I buy you another drink?"

I could almost feel her voice reaching for my checkbook. Although flattered and somewhat excited, I knew something was not right. I had spent a good deal of my adult life sitting in bars, but there had been very few occasions when a beautiful woman came up and asked to buy me a drink. I wondered if there was any way in the world I could screw this situation up. I should have known better; of course there was.

Alicia, the other home-wrecker, was a nurse who had worked with Danny for about two years. She had also dated Danny's friend, John, for the better part of those two years. In fact, when I first met her, she was John's fiancée. It was obvious that Alicia was no longer engaged and that she was intent on making John jealous. Alicia sidled up to Monte and asked, "So what's your name?"

At first, Monte was unable to utter a word; he simply drooled on himself. When he finally did answer Alicia, his reply sounded more like "Marry Me" than "Monte", so I knew the wheels of soon-to-be-doomed romance had already started turning.

Luckily, we were interrupted by the sound of music from the main ballroom before Monte could propose to Alicia. I knew that I didn't want to miss out on watching Danny try to dance, so I asked the gold digger hanging on my arm if she would like to go with me to the next room. She said she would love to and ordered both of us another drink. I pinched myself to make sure I wasn't dreaming.

As the night wore on, Danny started to get drunk. After about his fifteenth scotch-and-water, I managed to coax him into getting out on the dance floor. Danny's attempts at dancing always reminded me of an arcade game. He had absolutely no clue as to what he is supposed to do and totally lacked any sense of rhythm, so he spent most of his time bouncing off people like a pinball. When liquor was added to the mix, he became really unstable. It was while trying to regain his balance that Danny would manage to grope every woman he ran into. I loved to watch the women readjust their brassieres as they came off the dance floor.

It was during Danny's dance recital that I took the opportunity to introduce myself to the priest who had performed the wedding ceremony. I somehow felt obligated to inform him of Martha's terrible affliction. I walked up to the priest and introduced myself. As he shook my hand, I said, "Father, did you know that Martha has a drinking problem?"

A look of total bewilderment fell across his face. He had known Martha all of her life, having baptized her as a baby, confirmed her into the church as a young woman and, just two hours earlier, performed her wedding ceremony. Before he could utter a word of protest, I pointed to the dance floor and said, "It's true. She just married it."

When he turned to look at the dance floor, he saw Danny with Martha's wedding veil on his head, a cigar in his mouth, a drink in one hand, and some woman's breast in his other hand. The priest turned and looked at me, then shook his head as we both started laughing.

Since everything was going so smoothly, I should have known that I would not be spending the night with *Miss Overdrawn Checking Account*. After consuming at least a dozen martinis, I staggered out to the front lobby of the country club and collapsed in a lounge chair near the front door. It was around midnight when the driver of the courtesy van had to roust me out of a deep sleep and load me into the van. I fell asleep again during the 15-minute ride back to the hotel. I somehow managed to stumble off the bus and up to my room, then crawled into bed and passed out.

Monte never made it back to our room that night. He came straggling in early the next morning. He was carrying the better part of my tuxedo with him as he entered the room.

"Bob, what are all your clothes doing in the hall?" he asked.

"I was just a wee bit tipsy when I got back last night," I mumbled into my pillow. I sat up and asked, "Mont, where the hell have you been?"

Monte dove onto the other bed and pulled one of the pillows between his legs. He humped on the pillow as he said, "I went home with lovely Alicia and we had massive sex. She's coming down to Norman in two weeks for a football game. Bob, she is just the right kind of woman for me."

I just fell back on my pillow and groaned. I knew full well that Alicia was on her way to being re-virginated and elevated to sainthood in *Monte Land*.

Alicia did come down to Norman two weeks later. When I saw her after the football game, it was obvious that she had made the trip less than willingly. The next weekend, Monte drove all the way up to Minnesota to see Alicia, unannounced. Evidently, Alicia was not a very gracious hostess because Monte turned around and drove back to Oklahoma the very next day.

After I heard about Monte's futile roundtrip love excursion, I immediately called Danny. We laughed ourselves sick over Monte's stupidity, then Danny said he would try and get the real story from Alicia the next day at work. When he asked her what happened, she said very simply, "Danny, I just got so sick and tired of all those cards and flowers he kept sending!"

Reflecting back on it, Danny's wedding actually represented a microcosm of our lives. I drank the most and had more fun than anybody else, but ended up not getting a girl. Danny drank a lot, behaved the worst, but ended up with the best girl. Monte tried too hard, moved too fast and ended up getting dumped by a loser.

CHAPTER 10

DANNY TO THE RESCUE

Danny's marriage actually had a profound impact on me. Having watched my drunken dorm buddy take the first step toward exhibiting responsible behavior caused me to reevaluate my own priorities. I started to think that maybe it was time for me to grow up a little bit. I had advanced well in my professional career, but had yet to enter into a truly meaningful personal relationship. Ultimately, I concluded that the time was ripe for me to get serious about finding someone to ruin my life.

At first, I dated former students who had stayed around Norman. I soon came to realize that these women were probably exhibiting a mild form of hero worship. It was also obvious that all I wanted out of them was some relief from my severe case of horniness. Although I enjoyed their company, none of these brief relationships was what I would call emotionally fulfilling.

Undaunted by my failures with the student population, I decided to continue my search for a future mate by scouring the local bars. I went into Opie's one night to check out the scene and have a few dozen beers. As I sat down at the bar, I looked over at the waitress stand to check out the shapely behinds of the ladies serving cocktails. I immediately noticed a new set of buttocks protruding out from a pair of skintight jeans. When the owner of these magnificent globes finally turned around, I almost fell off of my barstool. She was absolutely drop-dead gorgeous.

The new waitress' name was Julie and she ended up waiting on me all night. Although overly friendly, I tried to dismiss the attention she afforded me as just doing her job. However, over the next few weeks, I frequented Opie's more than usual and always ended up talking with Julie. I finally managed to get up the courage to ask her to a pre-game party before the next OU home football game. When Julie accepted my invitation, the process of inflicting a total lobotomy on myself officially began.

Not only did Julie show up late to the pre-game party, but she also brought along a date. Having bragged to all my friends about the "babe" I was taking to the game, I now felt like a total idiot. I had an extra ticket to the game, which I hoped to have Julie use. Instead, I just gave her both tickets and told her to use them. Julie eagerly grabbed the tickets, then she and her escort left for the game.

When I realized that I had just pulled the biggest "Monte" of my life, I decided to get started on the next day's hangover. Hardly into my third beer, Julie suddenly walked back into the party, supposedly to use the bathroom. When she took me aside, I fully expected her to ask to borrow some money so she could buy her boyfriend a hot dog at the game. I was more than a little bit surprised when she told me she had tried to get rid of her date, but couldn't seem to shake loose of him. She had really wanted to go with me to the game, but he had asked her first.

I didn't bother to point out that the guy had asked her to the game but didn't even have tickets. Instead, I blurted out that I was going to the OU-Texas game in two weeks and, if she wanted to go, I would be glad to take her. She said it sounded like fun and laid a lip lock on me before she trotted out the door.

My uncontrolled hormones had just caused me to violate Danny's one cardinal rule: NEVER TAKE A WOMAN TO THE OU-TEXAS GAME! I thought about Danny's rule, and then I thought about Julie's buttocks in those skintight jeans. It was a no-brainer; I went for the but-tocks.

I had met some fun people in the OU alumni organization who had been begging me to go to the OU-Texas game with them. I called Tommy, who was president of the basketball booster club. I first asked if I could catch a ride to Dallas with him, then inquired if it would be all right if I brought along a date. As I expected, Tommy said the more the merrier. He told me that he would be by to pick us up at 11:30 on Friday morning.

I told Julie to meet me at my house around 11:00 a.m., giving her a 30-minute cushion, every bit of which she used. Tommy and his wife, Dawn, showed up right on time. Dawn glared suspiciously as I helped Julie into the backseat of the van. I could almost hear the hissing as Dawn curled her back and prepared to pounce.

"Glad you could make it," she said without the slightest movement in her lips that formed a genuinely fake smile, while she made an obvious gesture to check her wristwatch.

I quickly jumped in the back seat to intercede in the catfight before it started.

"Well, thanks, Dawn. I didn't know if I was going to be able to go until last night. You know Friday is my day to help the nuns at the orphanage."

Julie giggled as I continued to defuse Dawn's first cat bomb.

"The Mother Superior insisted that I go down to Dallas. She said I sac-rifice too much for them as it is. You know, Dawn, it's times like these that I thank God for me."

Dawn turned around to face forward as she muttered, "Yeah, Doctor Bob, you're a real prince."

I couldn't resist the temptation to taunt her just a little bit more.

"I'm glad you finally noticed, Dawn. You know, I could go on and on about myself. It is one of my favorite subjects."

Tommy interrupted me by shouting, "Oh no. I have to listen to that shit all the time out at Opie's."

As we pulled out of the driveway, Dawn began her interrogation of Tommy. Did he have the tickets? Was he sure he had made hotel reservations? Did he give them a credit card number to reserve the rooms since we were now behind schedule?

Tommy's answers were, "Yes. Yes. Shut up and drink a beer."

The remainder of the drive down to Dallas was relatively uneventful. Dawn dominated the conversation with her gossip and badmouthing of everyone involved with the booster club. I wondered what she told those people about me when I wasn't around, but I decided that if they weren't bright enough to consider the source, I probably didn't care too much what they thought about me anyway.

Tommy had made our reservations at the hotel in Dallas where most of the OU alumni club was staying. We checked in at the front desk and agreed to meet back in the lobby for drinks after we dumped the luggage in our rooms. On the way up to our room, I contemplated jumping Julie's bones, but I figured that would happen later. As it turned out, I would have been better served by making a move on Julie.

As Julie and I exited the elevator into the hotel lobby, I saw a crowd of about fifty people sitting in the lobby listening to the radio broadcast of a local sports commentator named Al Eschbach. I knew Al from my trips to Kansas City for the Big Eight basketball tournament; he was also a semi-regular at Opie's. Al was short and had an obnoxiously strong New York accent, but I found him to be entertaining, both on and off the radio.

When Al spotted me, he grabbed his microphone, stood up and announced, "Hey, dares Doctah Bawb. Come on ova heyah, Doctah Bawb."

I was a little bit apprehensive, but after some strong urging by Tommy, Dawn, and Julie, I walked over and sat down at the table with Al. There was a microphone in front of me, so I figured that Al was broadcasting his conversations with Sooner fans throughout the lobby of the hotel while music or commercials were playing on the radio. I figured very wrong.

"Dis is da famous Doctah Bawb."

"Al, I prefer *The Surprisingly Sober Doctor Bob,* just in case the president of the university is in the crowd," I replied.

He then asked, "So, Doctah Bawb, how long'd it take you to get heyah?"

"Well, Al, I can usually make it to Dallas in about three six-packs, but today it took us a little over one case of beer," I replied seriously.

Several in the crowd laughed.

"I see. Well, are ya goin' down on Commerce Street later?" he asked.

"No, Al, I had a bad experience on Commerce Street last year. I was arrested for urinating in public. They charged me with indecent exposure but had to drop the case for lack of evidence," I answered.

After that, Al quit talking and just let me shove both of my feet into my mouth. It turned out that Al's radio show was being broadcast over the entire Sooner Network. Literally, thousands of people were listening to me. The next day at the game, people I didn't even know came up and told me how funny I was on the radio.

In spite of my humiliating performance on the radio, Julie ended up having sex with me all weekend long, even after we got back to Norman. In essence, I had just made a deep incision in my scalp. A few weeks after the Dallas trip, I kidnapped Julie and took her to Las Vegas for her birthday. We had sex numerous times that weekend also. This was the emotional equivalent of sawing through my skull. Near the Christmas holidays, Julie announced that she was late for her period. She then started subtly pitting me against her ex-husband. I had several heated verbal exchanges with the dirt bag regarding his past due child support. Then, in a fit of macho showmanship, I proposed to Julie. I had now essentially pried open my skull and exposed my brain. I officially completed the medical miracle of a self-inflicted total lobotomy by plucking my brain out the following May, when Julie and I were married in Jamaica.

It turned out that Julie wasn't really late for her period after all. In fact, her periods came with increased frequency soon after we were married. The one thing that Julie truly was late for was her job, which ultimately caused her to be fired. She then announced that she wanted to finish college, but it seems that she was also always late for class, so her grades were horrible.

The one activity that Julie was never late for was shopping at the mall. She started buying all the things she and her two kids had never been able to afford before I came along. After I received the first wave of bills, I confiscated Julie's credit card, but she simply went in and took a book of checks without my knowledge and continued her shopping spree.

Julie's reckless spending soon exhausted my checking account and, for the first time in my life, I had a check bounce. Well, being totally honest, I had sixteen checks bounce. When I pointed out to Julie that writing hot checks was illegal, she became irrational. She noted that all of the checks she wrote had cleared the bank. In fact, I was the criminal because the checks that I had written to pay the mortgage and the utility bills were actually the ones that had bounced. She could see no fault on her part whatsoever.

I suddenly realized that I was now living with three children, one to whom I was married.

···   ~   ···

After he finished his residency at the Mayo Clinic, Danny decided to move back to Tulsa and quickly built a successful practice in child psychiatry. He was careful not to work too hard or too often in order to maintain a constant demand for his services. Danny wasn't worried about the competition taking a piece of his pie while he was busy relaxing. As he so delicately put it, "I just thank God there are a lot of fucked up children out there."

It was early in the spring when Danny called to tell me that he and Martha were taking a charter trip with several other couples down to the Princess Hotel in Acapulco. He used his irresistible Lebanese charm to try to convince me to go on the trip.

"Knox, most of these guys are real dicks and their wives are a bunch of dumb sluts. I can only tolerate Martha for short periods of time. I need you to come so I'll have a golf partner."

"Gee, Danny, you make it sound so enticing," I replied facetiously. "Do I have to bring my wife?"

"I don't know, Bob. If you take that whore to Mexico, are you sure you can get her back across the border?"

"The thought of deserting her in a foreign country is pretty tempting right about now. Let me talk to Julie and I'll call you back."

Of course, Julie jumped at the opportunity to spend more of my money. She was thrilled with the idea of taking an expensive vacation. In the back of my mind I hoped that maybe the trip would help rekindle the flames of passion between us, but I was skeptical. A lot of bad water had already passed under the bridge of our relationship. However, in spite of my overwhelming reservations, I reluctantly agreed to go.

It was supposed to be a romantic vacation, so the minute we arrived, Danny and I abandoned our wives in order to spend time with the things in life we truly loved—our golf clubs. Unfortunately, we were joined by one of Danny's friends from medical school and his extremely liberated wife. By the time we reached the first tee it was obvious to both Danny and I that this woman had never in her life been properly told to "shut the fuck up."

Since Danny was of the opinion that there was nothing wrong with a woman on the golf course, as long as she was driving the beverage cart, I got the feeling that we were not going to have a totally relaxing afternoon of golf. Danny soon proved me to be quite the clairvoyant.

The front nine was relatively uneventful until we came to a short par 3. Danny was not on his game that day as evidenced by his tee shot, which he sliced way right. After his ball bounced off the cart path leading up to the baños (bathrooms), he screamed, "God damn you little whore!"

His loud expletive scared off a group of Mexican peasants who had been waiting by the green to sell us some of their junk.

We eventually found Danny's ball in one of the urinals inside the baño marked Señores. Danny invoked the local "free drop from the urinal with no penalty" rule. He actually got up and down in six strokes to avoid the dreaded snowman.

On the very next hole, Danny began what appeared to be a remarkable turnaround in his game. He hit a monster drive, followed by a superb approach shot to the green. However, his sudden resurgence came to a screeching halt when he left his eighteen-inch birdie putt about three inches short of the hole.

Instinctively, I quipped, "Very good. Does your husband play golf?"

The militant wife in our foursome immediately jumped down my throat.

"Bob, that's a sexist remark. I'll beat your ass in golf any day you want."

I was already fed up with her incessant babbling, but decided to ignore her assault on my male ego. There was also more than just a little bit of doubt in the back of my mind as to whether I could meet her challenge. I just put the flagstick back in the hole and walked off the green.

As the irate feminist headed toward her cart, Danny sidled up next to her and asked, "Do you know why doctors spank newborn babies?"

She knew what an ornery little cuss Danny could be so she was a little bit leery. When she shook her head no, Danny responded with, "So they can knock the dicks off the stupid ones."

I buried my face in my golf towel and cried with laughter. When Danny hopped in the cart I thanked him for helping me defuse a potentially volatile situation. I told him that if that joke couldn't settle down an infuriated dyke, nothing could.

The trip to Acapulco did add some spark to my marriage, but not the kind I had hoped for. Julie used the occasion to sneak behind my back and buy worthless trinkets for every one of her low life relatives. When it came time to check out of the hotel, I was stunned when I found several hundred dollars worth of charges from the gift shop. When I tried to pay the bill, the cashier informed me that I had reached the limit on my credit card. I then had to endure the humiliation of borrowing money from Danny to pay my bill.

• • •   ~   • • •

When we returned to Oklahoma, I decided to make a concerted effort to turn my marriage around. I sat down with Julie and discussed our situation. I told her that I was committed to making the marriage work and that I wanted us to become one big happy family. I asked her what she felt we needed to do to improve our home life. Her answer was simple; everything would improve if I would just get her kids a dog. She pointed out that the responsibilities of caring for a pet would be good for the kids. She said that they needed something to focus their attention on other than her. She somehow managed to convince me that if her kids had a dog, she would be able to focus more affection on me.

I knew that Julie and her kids would probably lose interest in the dog once the cute puppy stage passed, so I decided to get the type of dog I wanted; a Siberian husky. I found a local breeder who had some newborn pups for sale, so I loaded up the family and went over to pick out our dog. I managed to convince Julie's kids that the lone male puppy was the cutest of the litter. I wrote a check to the breeder and we gathered up our puppy and left.

On the drive home, I suggested that we needed to come up with a name for our new dog. Julie's eight year-old daughter suggested "Bambi," but I immediately nixed it. There was no way I was going to name a Siberian husky after some stupid Disney cartoon deer. I proposed that we name the dog "Fellatio," which Julie quickly vetoed for obvious reasons. After several more mindless suggestions from Julie and her kids, I finally offered up a very simple, one syllable name—Hans.

Just as I predicted, Julie and her kids quickly grew bored with "Hans the Dog." The responsibility for filling his food and water bowls fell in my lap almost immediately. I knew that the dog needed to exercise, so I took him for a run every evening after work. I loved the exercise, plus it gave me a reason to get away from Julie and her two spoiled kids. It didn't take long for "Hans the Dog" to become totally attached to me, and me to him.

One night, after a particularly long jog with the dog, I returned to my house and found Julie sitting on the couch drinking a beer. Her kids were in bed, so the house was quiet. I could tell that she had already consumed a few beers and was now itching for a fight. I took the dog outside and filled his food bowl. When I came back into the house Julie confronted me by saying, "You love that dog more than you love me!"

I pondered her accusation for a few seconds before I replied, "So what's your point?"

Obviously, a family pet did not cure the problems between Julie and I. Our marriage continued to deteriorate and at the end of one year I was as miserable as I have ever been in my entire life. However, in one last attempt to give the appearance of a normal, happy relationship, I reluctantly agreed to let Julie throw a Fourth of July party and invite the horde of freeloaders she referred to as her family. I called Monte and begged him to come to the party so there would be at least one person there who I could actually tolerate. I made him promise, however, that he would not try to hit on any of the low-life sluts in Julie's family. Before he could even ask, I told him not to get his hopes up because every one of the females in Julie's family was a total loser.

Monte came over about mid-morning on the day of the party. He found me up on the roof of my house, already drunk. I was lighting firecrackers and throwing them at my wife's two kids, who thought it was the most fun they had ever had. Monte climbed up the ladder and on to the roof just before a police squad car pulled up. An officer got out of the car and threatened to arrest me if I threw one more firecracker. I managed to slur out something to the effect that the kids were actually throwing them at me. Thankfully, the officer left without pressing the issue. I sat down on the roof and started chugging a beer.

"Bob, how long are you going to stay up here on the roof?" Monte asked.

"I'm not coming down till all doze fugging freeloaders are gone, " I slobbered. "Matter fact, I sink I'll just take me a little nappy-poo while I'm waitin'."

I laid back on the baking hot shingles of the roof and fell asleep. After I passed out, Monte climbed down the ladder and went inside the house. Julie asked him as to my whereabouts and he told her I was up on the roof taking a nap. I woke up a couple of hours later, both hung over and sunburned. I didn't get much sympathy from my wife, but Monte found the whole episode terribly amusing.

For the next few months of my ill-fated marriage, I didn't see much of Monte, but he knew I was extremely unhappy. Not only was I miserable, but I also had to work overtime to pay off the tremendous credit card bills that Julie had run up. I had started doing private consulting as an expert witness in oilfield pollution cases. To me, spending countless hours freezing my balls off while taking water samples from contaminated farm ponds was far preferable to spending any time at home with Julie.

My marriage began its final out-of-control downward spiral about the same time that Monte started to hang out at the racetrack with some of his insurance buddies. I had a hard time understanding how insurance salesmen and claims adjusters could make a living when they took off work every day at noon to go to the track and bet on the ponies. When I finally talked to Monte about it, he told me that his companions were all so successful that they didn't really need to work.

"What about you, Mont? When are you going to retire independently wealthy?" I inquired.

"Sooner than you think, Bob. My business is going great! Plus, the guys at the track are teaching me how to handicap horses," he chirped.

"Monte, with your brain, you don't need another handicap," I replied, feeling a familiar sense of uneasiness about Monte's latest obsession.

It was at the track that Monte met Anna, soon to become his fifth fiancée. Anna lived in a trailer park in Oklahoma City, with a guy who beat her quite frequently. She desperately wanted out of her abusive relationship, but she didn't want to do anything irrational, such as getting a job. She had started hanging out at the racetrack in hopes of finding some lonely sucker who could support her. Monte fit her requirements to a tee.

Actually, Monte and Anna were truly destined to find one another. He was tall, good-looking, friendly, generous, and emotionally desperate. She was trashily attractive, conniving, and willing to sleep with anyone in order to avoid having to work. Less than two weeks after they met, Monte moved Anna from the trailer park where she lived with her abusive boyfriend, into his house with Corey and him. The situation had all the trappings of that classic *Monte Land* fairy tale: "*Low Life Loser Cons Prince Dumbass Into Unbelievably Humiliating Relationship*".

As coincidence would have it, the day after Anna moved in, I showed up on Monte's porch at four in the morning with my wife's two kids. Julie had stayed out all night carousing, then called me and said she was going to stay with a friend. I told her to go ahead and plan on staying wherever she was because she was no longer welcome in my house. I knew there would be a full-blown, knock down, drag out fight with Julie when she returned, so I decided to pack up her kids and take them somewhere away from the impending fracas. I turned to the only person I knew I could count on: Monte.

When he answered the door all I had to say was, "Mont, I need your help."

Monte never batted an eye. He took the kids in and fed and played with them while I took care of business. I went back to my house and waited for Julie to call or come home. When she finally called, I informed her that I was going to take some clothes and my dog and leave for one week, during which time she should pack her shit and get the hell out of my house.

Later that day, I returned to Monte's house with a suitcase and Hans the Dog. This time, all I said was, "Mont, I need a place to stay for a while."

Monte had already made me up my own little bedroom, very clean of course. He had set up a reading lamp, a TV, and a VCR; he had even made sure that I had my own Nintendo system. I was a little bit old for video games, but Monte had yet to outgrow them.

After I dumped my stuff, I gathered up Julie's kids and led them out to my truck. During the ride back to my house, they became confused and more than a little bit frightened, in spite of all my consoling. When I pulled into the driveway, I told them to go in and help their mother pack because they were going away. The little girl asked if I was going with them and I had to tell her no. She started crying uncontrollably as she jumped out of the car and ran to the house. I backed out of the driveway before my eyes welled up with tears. The kids had done nothing wrong and I felt bad for them. However, I was determined to put an end to the marriage disaster that I had brought on myself.

. . .   ~   . . .

I tried to establish a regular routine while I lived at Monte's house. Each morning, I would get up at 4:30, eat breakfast then go to the YMCA for an early morning titty-bounce class. At the office I poured myself into my work so that I wouldn't have to think about how miserable I was. Each evening after work, I would head for Monte's, stopping along the way to buy beer. When I got to his house, I would plop down in front of the television and proceed to drink an entire twelve-pack before I passed out. I would repeat the same sequence the next day.

When I came home from work the first evening, I found Anna alone in the kitchen preparing dinner. I asked where Monte was and she pleasantly replied that he had gone out to the garage. I grabbed two beers and stuck the rest of my twelve-pack in the refrigerator. I walked through the utility room and opened the door that led to the garage. I found Monte pacing around in a circle, smoking a cigarette and shivering.

"Mont, what are you doing out here? It's freezing," I inquired.

"Well, Anna doesn't like for me to smoke in the house," he replied.

Stunned by his answer, I had to think for just a moment before I pointed out, "Monte, it's your fucking house!"

Monte just stared blankly at me. I decided not to press the issue because I was sure that if worse came to worst, I would be the one Monte booted out. I turned and walked back into the house, leaving the spineless jellyfish alone to finish his frigid smoke.

Three days into my visit, Monte called and asked if I would mind watching Corey and one of his friends after school while he and Anna went shopping and I reluctantly agreed. I didn't really mind watching the kids, but I was suspicious of what Monte was up to. I had a feeling that he was going to the mall to do something stupid, like buy Anna some jewelry for her finger.

I left the office early that day so I could be at Monte's house when the two boys arrived home from school. After what seemed like an eternity of mindless Nintendo games, I proposed a new entertainment venue.

"Let's have some real fun. You guys go over to the mantel by the fireplace and pick out one of those knickknacks and crook it about 45 degrees. I don't care which one."

At first, the two little boys just stared at me. After a few minutes of forceful encouragement, they sheepishly strolled toward the fireplace. Corey was the one to actually reach up and carefully twist one of the small objects on the mantel. They both scurried back to where I was sitting, as if they were afraid of being caught.

Then I said, "Each of you give me a dollar. Whoever comes closest to predicting how long it takes Monte to notice that knickknack on the mantel what is crooked about 45 degrees wins the pot."

Corey's friend said something ridiculous like 30 minutes. Corey knew Monte a little better than that so he predicted 10 minutes.

"You're both crazy," I told them. "I'm getting divorced and need your money so I'm gonna say 2 minutes, but I know it won't take nearly that long."

That evening, when Monte got home, he grabbed a beer from the fridge and walked into the living room.

"Hi, Bob," was all he said as he walked past me.

"Hi, Corey, how was school?" he asked as he walked past his son without ever breaking stride. He proceeded straight over to the fireplace and straightened out the little knickknack on the mantel that had been crooked 45 degrees.

Needless to say, when I looked over at the two little boys, their jaws were slack, and their mouths were hanging wide open in amazement. Monte's behavior didn't faze me in the least. I just took my last swallow of beer, crumpled the can and threw it on the floor so Monte could pick it up on his way back to the kitchen. Then I pocketed the three dollars.

Of course, the next day Corey and his friend decided to crook everything in the house; Monte never again asked me to watch Corey.

On the last day of my stay at Monte's house, I got up to head off to my early morning exercise class. I felt the slightest tinge of a hangover as I fixed myself a bowl of cold cereal. Monte startled me when he walked into the kitchen in his bathrobe. He had obviously been up for a while.

"Bob, look what she did," he exclaimed as he pulled down his bathrobe and revealed a set of bleeding rake marks running down his back. Evidently, Anna had scratched him with her fingernails for some reason.

I pondered his wounds for a few seconds until I could finish my mouthful of cereal. I said, "Wow, Mont. Those look like they hurt," then turned my attention back to my bowl of cereal.

"Oh no, it felt great! She did it just as I came in her mouth!" he announced triumphantly.

Somehow I resisted the sudden urge to throw up. I looked at Monte and calmly asked, "Do you think she ever did that with any of her first six husbands?"

Yes, Anna had already been married six times. Of course, that didn't include the abusive boyfriend she was living with when Monte rescued her.

Monte glared at me in disbelief. He couldn't believe that I didn't recognize true love when I saw it. I just set my bowl in the sink and left without waiting for him to respond.

My time at Monte's gave me the opportunity to do a lot of soul searching. I was emotionally drained and on the edge of financial ruin. I couldn't believe how stupid I had been. What in the hell was I thinking when I got married? How did I let things get so out of control? I was ashamed of my marriage. I had always prided myself on my accomplishments and this was my crowning failure. I was truly embarrassed by the whole ordeal.

The situation at Monte's house also left me very confused. Having almost ruined my own life, I was in no position to pass judgment on anybody else's relationships. However, I was, once again, more than a little bit bothered by the pace at which Monte was pushing his relationship with a woman he knew so little about.

...   ~   ...

A couple of days after I moved back into my house, Monte's mother called and invited me to go to the race track with the entire family for her birthday. Although Diana's invitation was mostly out of pity for me, I knew she would probably buy my food and drinks, so I eagerly accepted her offer.

Diana is truly a remarkable woman. She married early after high school and had Monte, then Bubba. She'd gotten divorced soon after Bubba was born and married Dick, with whom she had Eddie. Although she worked part-time to help support the family, most of her jobs were simple secretarial assignments. When Eddie reached an age where he could take care of himself, Diana went back to school to get her college degree. After she finished her baccalaureate degree, she decided to become an attorney. It was while Diana was in law school that she and Dick started having marital problems, which ultimately ended in divorce. She met Gordon while serving as an intern for his law firm and they ended up getting married.

Diana had established her own successful law practice in Norman. She was one of the few hardworking, diligent, and totally honest attorneys I had ever met. I once told her that we were kindred spirits because we were both over-achievers. She cringed at the notion that she was like me in any way, which only made me respect her more.

It was obvious that Monte's good looks came from his mother. Diana was a fairly tall woman, with beautiful auburn-red hair. Unlike many redheads, she had a creamy white complexion, totally devoid of freckles. She had a melodic alto voice that instantly put people at ease when she spoke. Although I had never experienced it first hand, Monte, Dick, and Gordon had assured me that her voice could become not so melodic at times.

Gordon was a man of taste and didn't do anything half-assed. He was also head-over-heels, truly in love with Diana. He wanted this to be a special afternoon for her birthday, so he reserved two tables in one of the more exclusive clubs at Remington Park.

It was decided that we would all drive up to the racetrack together in one car. Gordon, Diana, and Maggie, were in the front seat. I rode in the back seat and watched Monte and Typhoid Mary play "kissy face" all the way to the track. Each time either one of them looked at me, I would reach for an imaginary barf bag and pretend to heave my guts up. Although Anna giggled at my antics, Monte knew I was making a theatrical statement regarding my opinion of their relationship.

When we finally arrived at the racetrack, Gordon pulled up to the valet parking lane next to the front door. Once we were inside, the concierge led us to our tables near the huge viewing window overlooking the home stretch of the track. After the waiter took our drink orders, I perused the racing form, trying to decide which horse to bet on for the first race. Out of the corner of my eye I noticed Anna repeatedly poking her finger in

Monte's ribcage. I decided that it was probably just another part of their kinky sexual relationship that I did not want to know about.

Suddenly, Monte stood up and started tapping his water glass with a spoon. After he had garnered our attention, Monte said that he wanted to take the occasion to announce that he and Anna were officially engaged. Anna thrust her left front hoof out toward the middle of the table to reveal the ring that Monte had indeed run out and bought for her on the day he asked me to watch Corey. Monte followed up his surprise announcement with a load of crap about how special the setting was because they had met at the very same racetrack just a few weeks earlier.

I could hardly believe what I had just heard. Monte had known Anna for less than a month, she had been living with him for two weeks, and all of the sudden he announces they were engaged. I couldn't decide whether to actually puke or simply reach over and choke the fuck out of Monte, so I just sat there silently.

I wasn't the only one in shock. I looked over at Diana after Monte finished his special announcement. Her head fell to one side, and she stared at him like a dog perplexed by a strange noise. By the look on her face, I could tell exactly what she was thinking, "Why is my son such an idiot?"

The rest of the afternoon was all but ruined by the nauseating display of public affection between a rather jubilant Anna and a somewhat hesitant Monte. I could tell he wasn't totally thrilled with the situation in which he had gotten himself. When I stood up to go to the betting window before the last race, Monte followed me. After I made my bet, I headed for the men's restroom with Monte not far behind. I situated myself at one of the urinals and Monte pulled into the stall next to me. I closed my eyes to relax and enjoy a nice leisurely piss.

Monte broke the bathroom silence by asking, "Bob, do you think maybe we're moving a little too fast?"

I pondered his question for a full millisecond before I responded.

"Mont, why in the hell should this relationship go any slower than all of the other disasters that you've jumped blindly into?"

Monte didn't reply.

When I finished pissing, I zipped up my pants and walked over to Monte's stall. I wiped my hands on his shirt, as if they were covered in urine. Normally, Monte would have squealed in disgust and shot me a pouty face. This time, however, he was too deep in thought to react.

. . .   ~   . . .

In the days that followed his racetrack announcement, I tried to talk some sense into Monte. We both knew that he had gotten in way over his head, far too fast. I pointed out that both he and Anna had lousy records when it came to long-term relationships. He grudgingly acknowledged that everything I said was true. I told him that he should, at the very least, postpone the wedding until he got to know Anna better. Initially, he agreed with me, but then he went home to Anna and she changed his mind with one of her fingernail-raking blowjobs.

Although totally against my nature, I knew this was one time when I needed to get directly involved in Monte's romantic life. Since he wouldn't listen to reason, I decided it was time for drastic measures. There was only one thing to do; I needed to get the little Lebanese lush involved, so I called Danny and invited him to come to Norman for a weekend of golf.

Danny drove down from Tulsa on Friday morning, and we played eighteen holes of golf that afternoon, during which time I briefed him on Monte's latest bit of love-struck lunacy. After golf, I took Danny straight out to Opie's, where we continued to discuss Monte's ordeal. For the next two hours, I made sure that Danny's glass of scotch-and-water was never less than half full.

After ten or twelve rounds of drinks, Danny started to get a little restless. It was still early, so I suggested that we shoot a game of pool. I shoved a couple of quarters in the slots and grabbed the rack from underneath the table. As I was racking the balls, a man and woman came over to our table and asked if we wanted to play a game of partners. I figured that a couple of games of pool would allow me time to pump some more liquor into Danny, so I accepted their challenge.

The man was a local attorney who I knew as a regular at Opie's, but I had never seen him with this particular woman before. For some reason, they both seemed a little ill at ease. I just attributed their nervousness to first date jitters, but Danny sensed that there was some emotionally sensitive issue between our two opponents, so he started to probe. During the course of one game of pool, he was able to ascertain that the woman was actually out on bail for killing her abusive husband. Her male companion was her attorney, with whom she was now sleeping.

Intrigued by the poor woman's plight, Danny politely inquired, "Just out of curiosity, how pissed off will you get if you lose this game of pool? Will you just break our arms or would you actually go get a weapon? "

The woman glared at Danny without saying a word.

Opie was standing near the front door, so Danny decided to ask him about house rules.

"Opie, if she loses this game, doesn't she have to put quarters on the table and wait until it is her turn before she kills us?" he screamed.

Opie ducked his head and hurriedly walked away from the scene without answering.

Finally, Danny turned to the husband killer and asked, "If you scratch on the 8-ball, will you get pissed off enough to kill yourself?"

"FUCK YOU!" the enraged woman finally screamed as she swung her pool cue at Danny, barely missing his head. Needless to say, she and her attorney/lover left without finishing our game of pool.

This was perfect. Danny was more obnoxious than usual. It was about eleven o'clock, so I said, "Danny, let's go over and see Mont."

When we arrived at Monte's house, we saw the lights on in the living room. We stumbled up the sidewalk and beat on the front door. Monte answered the door in his bathrobe and reluctantly invited us in. It was obvious that he had not yet been to bed. He confessed to us that he and

Anna had a fight and that he had been relegated to sleeping on the couch in the living room.

I, once again, had to point out, "Monte, this is YOUR fucking house!"

Danny, in his drunken state, told Monte all the things he needed to hear. Of course, he said everything at a decibel level high enough that Anna was also sure to hear. He topped off his lecture by saying, "Mont, don't marry the bitch."

My little plan worked like a charm. The very next day, Anna packed up and left; engagement number five was over.

A couple of weeks after our late night counseling session, Monte called me and admitted that he had screwed up. He thanked me for saving his life by bringing over the drunken little camel jockey to cuss him out and scream whore several times at the top of his lungs. I told Monte it was no big deal and reminded him that Danny behaved like that most of the time.

CHAPTER 11

SHE'S JUST LIKE MARTHA

After the Anna debacle, Monte decided that the racetrack was probably not the best place for him to search for the perfect woman. He needed a more reputable venue to look for a soon-to-be-bride and it didn't take long for him to find one, or so he thought. He was watching one of his porno-tapes when he received his latest romantic revelation. The preview advertisements for telephone sex services triggered the marital synapses in Monte's brain. Suddenly it dawned on him that that the perfect woman was just one phone call away—at the local dating service.

It turned out that there was a wide variety of lonely hearts organizations for Monte to choose from. They ranged from exclusive private clubs with extensive screening criteria to the classified ads published in the newspaper. Monte decided to try his luck with one of the telephone dating services he found printed on the rag sheet distributed free of charge at the local convenience store.

I was at Monte's house when he called to record his dating service ad.

"Hi, I'm Monte. I'm a single white male, 38, 6-foot-4, 180 pounds and very athletic. I'm a Christian, a non-smoker, and a non-drinker. My hobbies include golf, tennis, skiing, jogging, bicycling, bowling, and ballroom dancing. I enjoy long walks in the woods. I am looking for a soul mate. Call me if you are too."

I laughed as Monte read his contrived self-description into the phone, but he quickly shushed me. When he hung up the phone I asked what he was up to.

"Monte, what in the fuck are you doing?"

"I'm placing an ad in this telephone dating service," he replied.

"Who the fuck for? You're not six-four, you're six-two, max," I pointed out.

"Oh, I just fudged a little," he countered.

"Mont, you smoke AND drink," I noted.

"I won't when I go out on these dates," he explained.

"Monte, the only thing you are religious about is calling the escort service every Friday night. You've never been to church in your life," I proclaimed.

"I've been thinking about going to church for years," he tried to alibi.

"Mont, I've got news for you. A *ball*room is not a place where you go to screw. And what's this shit about long walks in the woods? The only walks you have ever taken in the woods were in search of a golf ball. You are never going to find somebody compatible if you lie to them about yourself."

"Bob, you've got to tell them what they want to hear," he justified back at me.

Monte's glib answers brought on an all-too-familiar sense of uneasiness. It was obvious that he was about to embark on yet another hopeless quest for emotional gratification. However, I had no way of knowing that his ensuing escapades with the dating services were going to provide me with so many laughs.

Monte arranged to meet his first service date at a local restaurant. In typical Nervous Nellie fashion, he arrived an hour early so he could sit and drink in anxious anticipation. He managed to drain half-a-dozen rum-and-Cokes while he waited for *Snow White* to waltz in and wake him from his slumber of sexual frustration. When his dream date finally arrived, Monte could hardly believe his eyes. Not only was she both taller and heavier than him, she wasn't nearly as pretty as he had hoped for or envisioned. In fact, she wasn't even a female; she turned out to be a man who'd had a sex change operation.

Early into the date, *IT*, as Monte later referred to the individual, reached across the table, grabbed Monte's hand and in a deep husky voice asked, "Monte, do you feel the chemistry between us?"

Unable to respond, Monte simply stood up and excused himself to go to the bathroom. He walked right through the kitchen, out the back door, jumped in his car, and sped off.

Once again, Monte should have just kept his mouth shut about what had transpired. Instead, he drove straight to Opie's, started pounding more rum-and-Cokes down, and told everyone in the bar about his experience. Benny, one of the regulars at Opie's, claimed that he actually pulled a stomach muscle from laughing at Monte's misfortune. Of course, the story got relayed to me, and I shared it with Danny. Over the course of the next few weeks, I recounted Monte's dating ordeal to at least several hundred people.

Undeterred by his first disastrous experience, Monte continued to pursue the dating service route to eternal bliss. A couple of weeks after he had left *IT* stranded at the restaurant, Monte called me and proclaimed, "Bob, I met the perfect woman through the dating service."

"You're lying," I told him, knowing full well that I was about to get a heaping helping of his romantic bullshit.

Monte immediately countered with, "No, I swear. She is five-foot six, 125 pounds, with blond hair and blue eyes. Never been married. Says she wants a relationship."

"Yeah, right, Mont. How many times have you been out with her?" I asked.

"Three," he answered.

"Have you slept with her?" I inquired.

"No. We both want to proceed with this relationship one step at a time," he replied.

"Horseshit!" I laughed. "You've never been that patient with a woman in your entire life."

Although Monte stuck to his story, I could tell he was trying to feed me a pile of crap. By the end of our conversation, I was able to deduce that he had yet to even meet the woman; they had only exchanged phone messages. As it turned out, they never even completed their first date.

After his transsexual experience at the restaurant, Monte was a little bit leery, so he arranged for his second dream date to meet him at his house and they would go out from there. He was peeking out his living room blinds when a beat up old Dodge came rambling down the street. The car was spewing smoke and rattling loudly due to the lack of a muffler. Monte breathed a sigh of relief when the car went right on past his house. However, he found his reprieve to be short lived when the car turned around and pulled into his driveway. Monte stared anxiously at the car as the driver's door opened. His anxiety was vindicated when out stepped a short, stubby, black female, weighing well in excess of 200 pounds, wearing tight orange stretch pants and a bright red wig.

As the perfect woman waddled up the sidewalk to the front porch, Monte began to panic. After she rang the doorbell, he started to pace back and forth trying desperately to think of excuses he could use, but none of them seemed good enough to get him out of this situation. The dream date on the front porch rang the doorbell a second time. Monte didn't know exactly what to do, but there was no way he was going to open the front door. After awhile, *Cinderella* on the doorstep grew impatient, so she beat on the door and screamed, "Open dis doe. I know you in dare."

Monte was now in full-fledged hysteria and had to think of something fast. He decided that the only thing a red-blooded American male could do was bolt out the back door, hop the fence and run down to the local convenience store, where he could call me to come pick him up.

Monte's urgent phone call interrupted me in the middle of my nightly twelve-pack, but I reluctantly agreed to go get him. When I pulled into the store's parking lot, I saw Monte peering anxiously around the side of the building. I drove up to the front of the store and motioned for him to get in. He looked both ways to make sure the coast was clear before he sprinted out from his hiding spot and jumped in my truck.

Before I pulled away, I demanded an immediate explanation. Monte was gasping for air even though he had only sprinted a few feet; his accelerated breathing rate was more from fear than physical exertion. Between gasps, Monte told me to drive him to Opie's and he would tell me what happened after he had a few drinks.

It was probably a good thing that Monte didn't recount his evening until we were inside the bar because I am sure I would have wrecked my truck. After I managed to control my laughter, I tried to reason with Monte to stop all his nonsense with the no-cost dating services.

"Mont, you are just damn lucky. That woman was probably going to hit you over the head, or worse, and take all your money. Quit calling this dating service. It's obviously some sort of prostitution ring."

From the blank stare on his face I could tell that my words went in one ear and right out the other.

. . .   ~   . . .

Monte had several more entertaining, but fruitless, dating service dates before he met Susan, a classical pianist and piano teacher. Susan was also a church-going woman, an active member of the local Methodist church. Evidently, the spirit of the Lord put Susan in the mood for kinky sex. Soon after they started dating, Monte called and told me about going to church with Susan, then returning to her place to have, as he put it, *massive sex*.

It would be hard to recount all of the stupid things that Monte did with Susan. However, the one incident that stood above all the rest involved the Super Bowl. Monte was, without a doubt, the world's most ardent Dallas Cowboys fan. He had grown up watching the Cowboys win under Tom Landry. When the team faltered in the late 1980's, Monte was devastated.

He would sulk for days after each loss. Finally, Jimmie Johnson was hired and started to turn the Cowboys around. In 1993, after a fourteen-year absence, the Dallas Cowboys were finally back in the Super Bowl and all was right in *Monte Land*, almost.

I called and invited Monte to go with me to watch the game at Opie's, but he declined, saying that he and Susan were going over to one of her friend's house for a watch party. From the tone of his voice, I could sense that he was less than thrilled with their plans, but was unwilling to challenge Susan's decision.

Although I was unable to coax Monte into joining me, I still went out to Opie's to watch the game. I drank beer and ate free hot dogs while I watched the Cowboys crush Buffalo. Being a Cowboys fan myself, I couldn't wait to revel in their victory. As soon as I got home, I called Monte to celebrate over the phone.

Monte sounded rather unexcited when he answered the phone. I asked him if he had enjoyed the game, but he didn't answer me, which was his tactic when he wanted to avoid a certain subject. His ploy didn't work with me; in fact, it only made me probe deeper.

"Well, Mont, what didn't you enjoy about the game? The Cowboys won!" I exclaimed.

After a few seconds of silence, Monte blurted out, "I didn't get to see the game!"

"Why not?" I demanded, somewhat in disbelief.

"Well, uh, we, uh, decided to do something else," he replied sheepishly.

"What in the fuck is there to do on Super Bowl Sunday other than watch your favorite fucking team in the whole wide world win the goddamn thing?" I demanded.

Reluctantly, Monte related the whole story to me. He said that when they arrived at the party, the game had just started. About midway through the first quarter, Susan stood up and abruptly turned the TV off. She announced that football was boring and suggested that they all play a game. For the next two hours, instead of watching his beloved Dallas Cowboys win the Super Bowl, Monte played Biblical charades.

Having known Monte for so long, I wasn't surprised that he had gotten himself into such an awkward relationship. However, even I was amazed by the fact that he didn't get up and leave to go watch the game somewhere else. On that very sad Super Bowl Sunday, Monte proved that there was absolutely no degree of ass kissing he wouldn't stoop to in his pursuit of pussy.

I ended our phone conversation by saying, "Monte, you make me ashamed to be a man."

Monte continued to date Susan in spite of the fact that they had absolutely nothing in common. He was certain that the psychotic, church-going, nymphomaniac pianist was the one woman who would finally impress Danny. Monte was forever striving to get approval from Danny for his female companions, but it never worked. Every one of the tramps or whores that Monte ever brought around did nothing to impress Danny; this was especially true of Susan.

Not long after the Super Bowl fiasco, Monte called Danny and announced that he was coming to Tulsa with his new girlfriend. He invited Danny and Martha to go to dinner, so they could meet Saint Susan. Just before he hung up, Monte said, "Danny, you'll like Susan. She's just like Martha."

I have to admit that, just like everyone else on this planet, I too was amazed at how Danny ever found anyone as nice as Martha. However, Monte always went to great lengths to extol the virtues of Martha. In fact, I once told Danny that when Martha finally did get her fill of his shit and decided to kill him, Monte would probably be the first one to call Martha and ask what she was doing after the funeral.

When Danny told me about Monte's comparison of Susan to Martha, I was compelled to ask, "Danny, when did your wife become a psychotic, hypocritical slut?"

Monte and Susan drove up to Tulsa on a Friday and checked into a motel. Danny and Martha joined up with the happy couple at the restaurant later that evening. After a relatively uneventful dinner, the four of them went to a piano bar to have a few drinks. Danny told me that the evening started to get uncomfortable when Susan decided to prove her artistic talent by arguing with the piano player about every song he played, then insisting that he let her play a song or two. He said that Susan wasn't nearly as good as the guy she had ousted. Danny also noted that Monte just smiled through the whole embarrassing ordeal.

Monte continued to date Susan on through the spring. He wouldn't let any of her psychotic behavior detract him from developing a totally demented perception of their idyllic relationship. In his mind they were the perfect couple.

Eventually, Susan started to pressure Monte about joining her church and he eagerly acquiesced. She decided that Easter Sunday, the holiest day of the year, would be the best date for Monte to join her church. He agreed and immediately set about making plans for the sacred event. Monte invited his whole family to attend the gala ceremony; he knew better than to tender an invitation to me.

Monte could never just join Susan's church; he needed to do it with a bunch of bogus hoopla and shallow fanfare in order to make sure the after-church massive sex kept coming. Not only did Monte agree to join Susan's church, he also pledged a tithe and signed up to teach Sunday school. Those Sunday school classes were going to be interesting given that Monte didn't even own, much less had never read, a Bible.

Once again, Monte's over-indulgent ass-kissing approach was more than even a totally twisted relationship could handle. The week after he joined the church, Susan abruptly dumped him to go back to her trumpet-playing ex-boyfriend. Of course, Monte reneged on his tithe pledge and never once taught Sunday school. In fact, he never again set foot in the church.

When he came over to my house to break the bad news to me about his split from Susan, I could barely contain my laughter. The opportunity to tear into Monte was almost more than I could resist. However, instead of taunting him, I simply asked, "Mont, who do you think will burn in hell first, you or me?"

Monte looked perplexed by my question, so I tried to explain it to him in terms he could understand.

"Mont, I'm an agnostic, which means I don't necessarily believe in a supreme being. If there is a god, I'm gonna be in a little bit of trouble when my time on earth is done."

Monte nodded his head in concurrence. I then asked, "However, how do you think He's gonna feel about you going to His church just to get pussy?"

Monte pondered my notion of eternal damnation for all of three seconds before he replied with, "I think I'll go home and call the escort service to help ease my broken heart."

. . .   ~   . . .

After the Susan disaster, Monte had a string of short-term relationships. With each new tramp, he would announce that she was "just like Martha". One day, Danny and I sat down and figured it all out. According to Monte's comparisons, not only was Martha a psychotic, hypocritical slut, but she had also now become a fat pig and an alcoholic loser.

Monte did date one woman who truly adored him for a short period of time, but he treated her horribly. There is probably something significant in that, but with Monte you throw all the traditional psychological theories right out the window. Joyce was a barfly who hung out at Opie's. She had slept with a number of my other friends, so it didn't shock me when Monte confessed that he had been "taking Joyce back to her trailer." He certainly didn't mind having readily available sex while he continued his search for the next Mrs. Grant.

I had always known that there was a kinky side to Monte, but I never realized how big a pervert he was until Joyce came along. I rollerbladed over to Monte's house one Sunday to watch some golf and mooch a couple of free beers. During the course of our conversation I decided to ask about the status of the video camera that he had borrowed from me, supposedly to record one of Susan's piano recitals. I didn't really give a damn about the camera, but given that they had been split for a couple months, I thought it was appropriate for me to inquire as to its whereabouts.

"Mont, have you recorded any good trumpet recitals with my video camera lately?" I tauntingly inquired.

My question caught Monte totally by surprise. His expression immediately turned stone cold serious. He paused for a moment then asked, "Bob, can you keep a secret?"

"Okay, what the fuck did you do with it?" I replied, fully expecting to hear an elaborate lie.

Monte looked around as if he was making sure nobody could hear our conversation. He then bent over and whispered in my face, "I used your camera to secretly film me and Joyce having a nooner."

I choked on the sip of beer in my mouth and laughed uncontrollably. After I regained my composure, I pointed out that what he had done was totally illegal. I told him that it would be a serious offense if the tape were ever to be made public. I then demanded that he destroy the tape, right after Danny and I had a chance to view it.

The three of us had already planned a golf outing for the next weekend. We were heading up to a resort in northeastern Oklahoma called Shangri-La. I told Monte that he had to bring the camera and the Joyce video and we would surprise Danny. He was only too eager to oblige.

On Friday after we played golf, Monte and I started into our little routine. We told Danny that we had some videotapes from our spring skiing trip to Santa Fe that we wanted to show him. Danny, of course, had no interest in watching a skiing video involving the two of us.

"Screw that. Let's go to the bar," Danny whined.

"Danny, you have got to see this one wipe out that Monte had. It was hilarious," I pleaded.

Danny finally agreed to stay and watch the video. I hooked up the VCR and plugged in the tape, which I had not yet seen either. From the view on the screen, it was obvious that Monte had hidden the camera in a closet and cracked open the door to give a clear view of his bed. The film began with a shot of Monte lounging on the bed in a bathrobe, flipping through the pictures of a Penthouse magazine while he waited for Joyce to arrive. As the film would later show, a man needs some strong incentives to get up for a nooner with Joyce.

Danny took one look at the TV screen, turned to the two of us with a scowl of pure disgust on his face and said, "What the fuck is this?"

The remainder of the video showed Monte attempting to have sex with Joyce. However, throughout most of the film, he was unable to maintain much of an erection. At one point, Joyce even rolled over and lit a cigarette and puffed on it while Monte furiously flailed away at his limp member in an effort to get it up.

The next day on the golf course, I burst out laughing every time I thought about the look on Danny's face. However, Monte was proud of his film production. He told us that he was thinking of sending it to one of the many porno distributors to which he subscribed. Monte felt sure they could market it nationwide, and he would become the next John Holmes and make a million dollars.

Danny started dictating the letter of rejection he was sure Monte would receive:

"Dear Mr. Grant:

We have no use for your film involving the terminally flaccid penis. In our movies, we like for the male to actually fuck the female."

. . .   . . .

It was obvious that Monte was not interested in a serious relationship with Joyce. Soon after he made the video, he quit calling her. He then returned to a more familiar pattern of dating tramps and whores, with periodic calls to the good old reliable escort service.

It was early in the fall when Monte decided to return to one of his more fertile female hunting grounds—the racetrack. It didn't take very long for the next perfect woman to come galloping into Monte's life. Tonya fit the familiar "trailer park trash" mold. She was a single mom with no job and was not interested in finding one. Most importantly, she lived in a mobile home with a guy who beat her.

Tonya and Monte had a couple racetrack dates and then got in bed, which of course meant that they were in love. He brought her down to Norman for a football game to parade her in front his family. She was immediately re-virginated, elevated to the status of sainthood, and promptly became engagement number six.

Monte's racetrack romance continued through the fall and on into December. A couple of weeks before Christmas, G invited all of us to a party. He had recently moved back to Oklahoma City and was anxious to show off his new house. Monte, on the other hand, was anxious to show off his latest fiancée. Since G was not aware of the circumstances under which the engagement had come about, Monte felt he still had a chance to garner G's approval. Monte hadn't dared to ask me for my opinion, because he knew I would have chewed him out for moving too fast.

About midway through the party, Monte made the ill-fated decision to sneak out to the back patio for a quick smoke at the same time Tonya decided to go freshen up her drink. On her way to the kitchen Tonya caught a glimpse through the sliding glass doors of someone smoking a cigarette. Upon closer examination, the glow of the red-hot ash revealed that the cigarette was moving to and from Monte's lips.

Tonya had lectured Monte numerous times about the evils of smoking and now she had caught him openly disobeying one of her commandments. Rather than simply confronting him, she decided to teach Monte a lesson by making him jealous. When Monte returned from his clandestine smoke break, he found Tonya on the dance floor, making sexually suggestive gyrations in the arms of another man.

Unfortunately, I was privy to the entire pathetic scene. Tonya humped her dance partner and periodically flashed wicked little smiles, all for Monte's benefit. He, on the other hand, stood in the corner of the room and pouted. I felt like I had been transported back to junior high school. I finally walked up to Monte and said, "Mont, tell her you want your letter jacket back and let's skateboard home."

Evidently, the ninth-grade soap opera continued during their drive home, because the perfect couple ended up splitting the blanket that night. Tonya at least had the decency to leave rather than relegating Monte to sleeping on his couch. She simply gathered up her belongings and threw them in the back of her pickup truck. Before she climbed into the cab, she screamed at Monte not to ever call her again. Then, Tonya and her engagement ring hopped in the truck and drove off in search of the first trailer park they could find.

Although I was relieved to hear of Tonya's departure, I never got a chance to chew Monte out about the whole ordeal. Less than a month after she left, Tonya called Monte and announced that she was pregnant. Monte couldn't have been happier with the news.

Without even considering whether the baby truly was his, Monte immediately set about building a nest for his new family. The first thing he did was trade in his Honda Civic for a Pontiac mini-van. When he showed up at my house with his new vehicle he tried to justify his purchase by saying, "Bob, I've always wanted a mini-van."

"Mont, guys dream about having a Corvette. No man has ever dreamed of owning a peter-puffer van!" I screamed.

The ensuing soap opera surrounding *The Virgin Tonya* was truly pathetic. Monte had an immaculately clean house and now that he had a puffer van, Tonya just had to marry him. However, after having stalled long enough to be past the time that an abortion could have been a safe and viable option, Tonya told Monte that she was going to have the baby, but she did not want to get married. My opinion was that if ever there was a situation that warranted a late term abortion, this was it.

. . .   ~   . . .

About a month before the baby was due, Danny and I convinced Monte to go back up to Shangri-La for one of our weekend golf outings. As Danny so delicately put it, we needed to celebrate the impending birth of Monte's bastard child.

The three of us drove up to Shangri-La on Friday morning. We checked in at the clubhouse, loaded our clubs onto our carts and sped off, only to find the first tee box packed. There were at least five groups waiting to tee off. By the time we teed off, there were probably seven groups stacked up behind us.

When our turn finally came, Danny was up first on the tee box. He hit his drive down the right hand side of the fairway, then stumbled over to his cart to take a pull off of his beer and fire up a cigar. I was up next. After I teed up my ball, I turned and asked the starter, "Is Mickey Mantle or any other celebrity out on the course?"

The previous year, we had been bumped from the course so Mickey Mantle and his entourage could play through. The starter told me that he hadn't seen anybody famous all morning.

After I hit my drive, I walked over and stood next to the starter while Monte made his way to the tee box. I cupped my hand over my mouth and loudly whispered, "This guy is a celebrity. Do you recognize him?"

The starter looked at Monte and obviously had no idea who he was or why he might be famous. In order to save the poor man from embarrassment, I quietly yelled into my hand, "Monte is President of the Oklahoma Gay Alliance."

About 40 complete strangers heard me and snickered. Monte turned bright red, and I could tell he was angry. While he was still fuming from my comment, Monte took a furious cut at his ball. His over swinging caused him to yank the ball hard left off the tee, narrowly missing the starter and myself. The ball hit a tree about fifty yards down the fairway, then rolled back to within a yard of where Monte stood on the tee box. Danny and I howled with laughter.

I yelled, "Hey, Mont. Step that puppy off. I'll help you count: One."

The crowd around the tee box giggled.

I then screamed, "Mont, the scorecard says this is a 420 yard par four. I've got you at about 419 for your second shot."

Several more in the crowd laughed openly.

Just then, Danny decided to rush to Monte's rescue. He shushed the crowd by yelling, "Hey, leave him alone. You try hitting a golf ball with blood and semen dripping out of your butthole."

Danny's little admonition did the trick. Monte had to hit his second shot in front of a crowd of strangers who now sat in stunned silence. Danny and I just drove off down the fairway, laughing as hard as we possibly could.

After golf, the three of us went in to get cleaned up and go to dinner. While Monte was in the shower, I decided to sneak out to the parking lot and decorate his new puffer van. The steeply sloped front windshield of the puffer van was designed to reduce wind friction, but interestingly enough, it also allowed easy access for a man with his shorts pulled down around his ankles. I planted my bare butt squarely on the driver's side and slid down the entire length of the windshield, leaving behind a definitive smear print. After I had finished my masterpiece, I pulled up my shorts and ran back to the room to get dressed.

As we walked out to the puffer van to go to dinner, Monte tossed me the keys and told me to drive because he planned on getting drunk. After everyone had piled in, I slowly backed the puffer van out of its stall and proceeded toward the exit. I slowed down as we pulled underneath one of the streetlights that illuminated the parking lot. From the reflection of the light it was obvious that there were two globes smeared down the wind-shield of Monte's puffer van.

"What in the world is that?" I asked innocently.

As he squinted to get a better look, Monte replied, "I don't know Bob."

I then stuttered to him, "Mont, it kind of…it kind of looks like…like you have two buttcheek imprints on your brand new windshield."

"BOB! You did that," Monte screamed as he hopped out and ran around the puffer van to clean the windshield with the sleeve of his shirt.

Danny immediately shut Monte's door and I pressed the automatic door lock. I drove slowly across the parking lot while Monte ran after the puffer van and screamed for me to stop. After a few hundred feet, he stopped chasing the van, opting instead to stand still and pout.

I drove in circles around Monte as he stood in the middle of the parking lot with his arms folded across his chest, trying his best to ignore us. I stopped the van about twenty yards away from him and pressed the button to open the automatic sliding door. As the door slid open, Monte made a mad dash for the van, but I stomped on the accelerator and pressed the button to close the automatic sliding door. We repeated the routine several more times, making a complete lap around the parking lot. I finally opened the door and slowed down enough that Monte was able to hop in while on the run. He was not at all amused by my antics.

At dinner that night, the subject of Tonya and the baby came up during our conversation. Since Monte had brought it up, I decided not to pull any punches with him.

"Monte, I am totally opposed to you and Tonya bringing a child into the world under any circumstances. First of all, you don't even know if the baby is yours. Even if it is your child, I think you will make a lousy father. You aren't doing a real good job with Corey as it is right now. More importantly, Tonya is a loser and she shouldn't be having kids just to satisfy her urge to be a mommy."

Monte became enraged. He jumped up and screamed at me, "Bob, you are no longer my friend."

I countered with, "Mont, I am your friend, and that is why I am telling you this. Bringing a child into the world is very serious shit. This is not *Monte Land*."

He then screamed, "You and Danny are always picking on me. Fuck both of you! You can just walk back to the hotel."

As Monte stormed out of the restaurant, Danny started to get up, but I stopped him.

"Danny, let him go. He won't get far. I've got the keys."

We purposely let Monte sit outside and sulk until we had finished our dinner.

   . . .   ~   . . .

I did not hear from Monte again until after Tonya had a baby girl. He finally called and told me that the DNA tests had confirmed that he was the father. Although I didn't relish the idea of further alienating Monte, I wasn't about to condone what he and Tonya had done.

"Monte, I wish I could find some reason to congratulate you, but I can't think of one. As I told you before, Tonya is a total loser, so I don't hold out much hope for your daughter."

Monte tried to protest, but I continued my barrage.

"Monte, there is absolutely no doubt in my mind that Tonya is going to screw you to the wall over child support."

Once again, Monte blew up at me, and deservedly so.

"Bob, I am gonna be a great daddy to that little girl. For your information, Tonya and I have already worked out an agreement about the child support. There is also a very good chance that we will someday get married. As a matter of fact, you're the loser!"

He then hung up on me.

After his telephone tirade, I didn't even try to contact Monte. I knew he was in for a rude awakening once Tonya's true colors came shining through. Thankfully, it didn't take long.

Less than a month after he hung up on me, Monte called and said he owed me an apology. It seemed that Tonya had filed a petition to have her child support increased even though Monte paid her more than the law required. She claimed that her rent and day care bills had increased. However, Monte's mother had hired a private detective who confirmed that Tonya was actually hanging out at the racetrack and living with some guy in yet another trailer park. On the few occasions that she did go to work, she would leave the baby with a neighbor. Monte concluded his apology by informing me that Tonya was a loser and that he was through with her. I just laughed as I hung up the phone.

I couldn't let Monte get away with his temper tantrums without some sort of payback. One Saturday morning in early April, I loaded my gardening tools into my truck and drove over to Monte's neighborhood. I parked up the block from his house and waited for him to leave.

Monte liked to get up early on Saturdays so he could get in line with the mall walkers before the mall opened. When the doors did open, everyone else would go inside and walk to get some exercise; Monte would go in and window shop, even though none of the stores were open.

The puffer van pulled out of Monte's garage at 8:45 a.m., right on schedule. When Monte was out of sight, I pulled my truck into his driveway. I unloaded my lawn spreader, filled it full of fertilizer, and pushed it into the back yard. I opened the valves on the lawn spreader all the way and traced out twelve-foot tall letters spelling T-O-N-Y-A. I then watered down the grass and left.

About a month later, Monte called me and announced, "Bob, me and Tonya are getting back together. I got a signal from God in my back yard."

"What on earth are you talking about, Mont?" I replied, as if totally ignorant about his lawn art.

"Bob, I think you know exactly what I am talking about. I've got twelve-foot tall letters spelling out Tonya in my backyard."

I couldn't hold out any longer and started to laugh and so did Monte. Unfortunately, it was one of the last times we were able to truly laugh about his bizarre love life.

CHAPTER 12

GETCHA ONE

After Tonya filed her bogus petition for more child support, I told Monte that he probably ought to throttle back on some of his sexual escapades. I pointed out that the judge in his case just might decide that the several hundred dollars he wasted each month on escort service girls should go to Tonya. Surprisingly, Monte was persuaded by my logic and decided to just work hard and keep his pecker clean until after his hearing. When I jokingly asked if he would mind cleaning my pecker, he replied, "Not until after the hearing, Bob."

On the day of the hearing, the private detective that Diana hired showed the judge pictures of Tonya going into the racetrack during the middle of the week, on six different occasions over a three-week period. The photographic evidence must have influenced the judge, because he concluded that not all of the money that Monte had been paying Tonya was being exhausted on rent and day care. In a rare example of judicial prudence regarding child support, Monte's monthly payment was actually reduced.

Although pleased by his victory in court, Monte was once again faced with the task of finding a suitable venue to continue his never-ending search for emotional gratification. He had already scoured the racetrack several times and perused through all of the local dating services; he had

even looked for the perfect woman in church. Never at a loss for strange
ideas when it came to matters of the heart, Monte somehow concluded
that the perfect woman had to be waiting for him at the local country
club. If nothing else, being a member of a country club was sure to
impress any new tramp or whore he might meet at the racetrack.

Monte called me one day and tried to explain his latest bit of twisted
logic.

"Bob, country clubs don't allow losers to join. More importantly, any
woman who can afford to join a country club must have money."

He was not amused when I pointed out, "Mont, that 'No Losers' policy
might derail your application."

I was floored when Monte called me a week later and proudly
announced that he had been accepted for membership at *The Happy Trails
Golf and Country Club*. Something must have gone wrong. The only
answer I could come up with was that the member selection committee
probably didn't bother to conduct serious background checks or mental
stability assessments on their applicants. To test my theory, I went down
and immediately filled out an application for membership. When I was
informed of my acceptance, I concluded that The Happy Trails Golf and
Country Club definitely needed to enforce their 'No Losers' policy a little
more rigorously.

For some reason, Monte's latest plan for attracting females suddenly
rekindled my interest in the opposite sex. It had been a couple of years
since my divorce, so I started to consider the notion of dating again.
However, unlike Monte's stupid country club idea, I decided to find
myself a nice woman through the more traditional route—by sifting
through the endless stream of bimbos that frequented Opie's.

One of the key tactics in my overall strategy to attract a female was to
show up hot, sweaty, and thirsty, so I started rollerblading out to the bar in
lieu of driving. Actually, there truly was a method to my madness. By skat-
ing to and from Opie's, I minimized the possibility of getting pulled over
and offered a free breathalyzer test by the local police. More importantly,

by not having a vehicle, I wouldn't be tempted to offer a ride home to any of the losers I might find attractive after ingesting one too many beers. I was determined not to make any of the same alcohol-induced hormonal mistakes that had led to my disastrous first marriage.

I skated out to Opie's one Friday night to have a few dozen beers and continue my search for a woman. Just as I stumbled into the bar, I heard a familiar shrill voice scream out, "Doctur Bob, what air those own yer fate?"

I looked over at the nearest booth and saw my good friend, Poison, sitting with one of her girlfriends. Poison was drop-dead gorgeous and as much fun as any guy I have ever known. Her long blonde hair, beautiful blue eyes, hourglass figure, and "drink till closing time" personality were a deadly combination. I dubbed her Poison the first night I ever laid eyes on her. I told her that I would just as soon drink poison than get involved with her only to have my heart ripped out. The nickname had stuck with her ever since.

When Poison came over to inspect the contraptions on my feet a little bit closer, she introduced me to her friend, Jackie. The waitress came by and I ordered myself a beer and told her to get each one of my lady friends a refill on their drinks.

It wasn't long before every guy in the bar had lined up to take turns drooling on themselves over Poison, so I spent most of the evening talking to Jackie. Through the course of our conversation I was able to find out that she had been married once and had a three-year old daughter. As the night wore on I noticed that Jackie was every bit as good looking as Poison, but not nearly as wild. She would probably have truckloads of guys coming on to her if she didn't hang around Poison. One thing led to another and I ended up asking her if she would like to go to the horse races that next Friday and she accepted.

For the next few days, I had trouble getting excited about my impending date. I was upset with myself for letting my common sense get run over by my hormones. The last thing I wanted was to get involved with another woman with a child and no career ambitions. I knew I wasn't interested in Jackie, but I had committed myself to spending an afternoon with her. By the time Friday rolled around, I was thoroughly complacent about my impending date.

Jackie met me at my house so we could drive up to the racetrack together. Once we arrived, I pulled up to the front entrance and had the valet attendants park my truck, because it was much more convenient than general parking located in the next county. I walked over to the ticket window and bought tickets for two reserved seats on the second level, which meant that we could enjoy the comforts of being inside while we watched the races through large glass windows.

Once we reached our seats and sat down, Jackie said, "Ya know, I never been on a date where they park the truck fur ya and the feller opens yer door fur ya."

Suddenly, I realized just what a country bumpkin I had on my hands. It was obvious that we had very little in common. However, I decided to just pretend like I was on a date with *Ellie Mae Clampett* and enjoy the afternoon.

After the races, we drove straight back to my house. I pulled into my driveway and invited Jackie in for a nightcap. We went inside and I grabbed a couple of beers from the fridge. I sat down in my recliner instead of the couch because I felt an impending romantic move by Jackie, a move that I was not interested in pursuing. We drank our beers and talked for a while, and then she announced that she had to leave.

As I walked Jackie out to her car, I could tell she was disappointed that we hadn't gone any further than just sipping beer. Feeling a little bit guilty, I said, "Well, maybe we can go have dinner some time."

"Ah'd luv to. What day we goin?" she semi-demanded.

I fumbled around and managed to schedule a second date for the following Friday. I felt a sense of relief when Jackie finally drove off. I went inside and lay down on my bed. I tried to think of excuses I could use to get out of my next date, but drifted off to sleep before I could conjure up anything even half-way believable.

When Friday rolled around, Jackie showed up at my house right on time. Through the course of dinner I was able to discern that Jackie had probably never been on a date "where the feller pulls yer chair out fur ya and pays fur dinner with a credit card." I could also tell by the look in Jackie's eyes that she wanted a romantic relationship. Although I enjoyed her company, I was not interested in getting involved with another single mom looking for a meal ticket.

After dinner, I took Jackie out to Opie's to drink a few beers and play a couple of games of pool. I purposely kept her at arms length in hopes of stemming any desires she might have for physical contact with me. After about an hour, I told Jackie that it was getting late and we should go because I had to get up early.

When we pulled into my driveway, I reluctantly asked if Jackie wanted to come in for a nightcap. She jumped out of the truck and bolted for the house before she even said yes. Once inside, she ran over and plopped down in my recliner, which forced me to sit on the couch. I had no sooner settled onto the couch, when Jackie sprang out of the recliner, jumped into my lap and laid a lip lock on me that I couldn't tear loose from, even if I had tried. Although I had convinced myself that I was not sexually interested in this woman, the big brain residing below my belt over-ruled the small one in my head.

After some heavy petting on the couch, we went back to my bedroom to resume our wrestling match. Near the end of round one, as I was about to climax, my little country bumpkin hollered out, "Getcha One, Dr. Bob!" Thankfully, the orgasm kept me from laughing.

It was after midnight when Jackie got dressed to leave. I escorted her out to her car and kissed her goodnight. This time, I controlled my emotions and didn't offer up the possibility of us getting together again anytime in the near future. In the back of my mind, I knew that I didn't want to go out with her again. I was also quite sure that she did not share the same feeling. I managed to finally convince her to leave by promising that I would call her some time.

I got up early the next day to play golf with Danny and Monte. Danny had convinced Martha that they needed to drive down from Tulsa so that the kids could see their grandparents. Evidently, letting the kids visit their grandparents didn't involve Danny, because he simply dumped everybody off on his parents' doorstep, then headed straight over to play 18 holes of golf with us.

When we came to the par 4 third hole I asked, "Can I just go up there and lay out in three or do I have to go through the routine of slicing the little cocksucker into that guy's backyard?"

Monte and Danny were not about to cheat themselves out of the joy of watching one of my power fades disappear over the brick wall surrounding the home on the right about 200 yards down the fairway. I didn't disappoint them. My ball cleared the wall and slammed onto the roof of the house, then slowly dribbled down the shingles before dropping into a flower garden next to the house.

Danny was up after me and he snap-hooked a worm-burner into the trees lining the left side of the fairway. When it was his turn, Monte hit a beautiful drive about 250 yards right down the middle of the fairway.

I drove my cart up to the approximate point where my tee shot had exited the golf course and dropped a new ball. I proceeded to skull a seven iron up close to the green. Danny took three or four hacks at his ball and was still in the trees. Monte hit his second shot too far and it rolled off the back of the green.

After we had all chipped on, I putted first. I lagged a chicken-shit effort up close enough to tap in for my six. I picked my ball out of the cup, grabbed the flag laying on the green, and backed away. I walked over to the backside of the green while Jack and Arnie lined up their putts. I reached down and picked up Monte's wedge, so he wouldn't forget it.

Danny ended up two-putting for his snowman. Monte was only about twelve feet away for his par. He stroked his first putt too firm, which caused it to ring around the rim of the cup and left him about 18 inches for a bogey. He walked up and nonchalantly stabbed at his ball, but it stopped just short of the hole. He finally tapped in for his six.

Before Danny and I could break into our customary barrage of insults, Monte took his putter and flung it underhanded as hard as he could toward his cart. However, he held on a little too long before he released the putter, which caused it to fly high up into one of the trees next to the green. It bounced off one limb, fell down to a second limb and stopped.

Danny managed to stop laughing long enough to quiz Monte.

"Very good, dumb ass. What are you gonna putt with for the next 15 holes?"

"I'll use my driver. I putt as good with it as anything else in my bag," Monte replied in a huff.

I decided to come to Monte's rescue and said, "Don't worry Mont, I'll get it down."

As I prepared to fling the wedge up toward the tree-locked putter, Monte yelled, "Don't bother, Bob. I was gonna get a new putter anyway."

My first throw didn't even come close. I went over and picked up the wedge and began the windup for my second pitch. Monte screamed at me once again, "Bob, don't bother. I hated that putter. It reminded me of Tonya."

My second throw was right on target. The wedge stuck up in the tree on the exact same branch as Monte's putter.

Danny laughed and called me a dumb shit. I giggled as I climbed in the cart and sped off to the next tee box.

As I was getting ready to tee off, Danny said, "I can't believe you two fucking morons both got clubs stuck in the same tree!"

Monte jumped in with, "Bob, I told you not to throw your club," never even considering the hypocrisy of his little lecture.

I stepped back from my ball and replied, "Mont, I have NEVER thrown any of my clubs."

Monte was stunned. A sick look swept across his face as he reluctantly inquired, "Well,…whose…. club…. was that?"

I started to address my ball once again before I replied, "Well, that was your pitching wedge."

Danny was taking a sip from his beer when I made my revelation. He started to laugh and choke simultaneously. Foam came out of his nose as he tried to spit out his mouthful of beer.

Monte gave me his patented, "BOB!" scream, followed by his famous pouty face.

I don't doubt that other members of the Happy Trails Golf and Country Club have lost a club or two after throwing them, but this had to be a course record. I checked with the pro in the clubhouse after our round. When he stopped laughing, he told me they didn't keep track of such statistics. He then asked Monte if he wanted the clubs retrieved. Monte replied that they were just fine right where they were.

All of the club throwing I had done on the course had made me thirsty, so I suggested that we head to the 19th hole for a few dozen beers. As with all men, the topic of sex eventually came up. Monte started off the discussion by asking about my date.

"Bob, did you have a good time last night?" which really meant that he wanted to know if I had gotten laid.

"Oh, we had a great time," I said with a giggle, which was a mistake because now both of them wanted details. I told them about ending up in the sack and how she had cried out for me to "Getcha One Dr. Bob!"

Danny snidely inquired, "Well, Bob. Did you get up and go get a beer?"

Monte, on the other hand, was totally intrigued by my sex story. I could always get his undivided attention by simply talking about women with whom I'd had sex. I had no way of knowing just how much my little story had piqued his curiosity, but I was soon to find out.

On Monday, I got a call at my office from Jackie. This concerned me because I had purposely not given her my work number in order to avoid the inevitable series of phone calls to talk about nothing. I dreaded the ensuing conversation because I just knew she was going to want to talk about "us" or "our future".

I was totally surprised when she started off with, "You sumbitch! If you dent wanna go out with me you shoulda just said so."

"Jackie, I have no idea what you are talking about," I lied.

"Oh yeah. Then why'd yer friend call me up sayin' that he heard we was broke up?" she demanded.

"We cannot be broken up because we were never really together. A couple of dates don't make a relationship," I countered." Who told you all of this anyway?"

"Yer friend Monte told me that when he called and asked me out. How'd he get my number anyways?" she demanded.

Since Jackie had brought up his name, I took a cue from Monte and lied through my teeth.

"I haven't told Monte anything about us because there is no us. Just remember that Monte is your insurance agent, which means he has ready access to your phone number, plus a whole lot more. I will talk to Monte, but I assure you, I had nothing to do with him calling you."

After my confrontation with Jackie finally ended, I picked the phone back up to call Monte and chew him out. However, I decided it would be more effective to confront him in person, so I hung up the phone before I finished dialing his number. Although Monte was undoubtedly the world's most accomplished liar over the phone, he was incapable of lying to me in person without giving it away.

After work, I drove straight over to Monte's house and confronted him with the charges, which he unequivocally denied, at first. He then slowly leaked out that, yes, he had called Jackie, but just to talk about her insurance. He admitted that he might have asked how we were doing. It may have even slipped out that Bob wasn't necessarily looking for a long-term relationship. However, he was fairly certain that he hadn't brought up the "Getcha One" incident.

I could tell by his stammering that Monte was lying. He had probably taken the opportunity to bad mouth me by letting Jackie know that I had told him and Danny about our sexual escapades. Although I didn't have any strong desires for Jackie, I was bothered by the fact that Monte was trying to vacuum the field I had just finished harvesting.

"Monte, remember our conversation after the Charlotte incident back in college?" I asked.

Monte tilted his head to one side, opened his eyes wide, and stared at me in total amazement, as if he had absolutely no idea what I was talking about. When I realized that nothing was registering with him, I simply said, "Mont, at least let me get my tractor out of the field before you come in with your vacuum cleaner."

...   ~   ...

I never called or heard from *Getcha One* after Monte asked her out. I decided it was probably for the best, because I wasn't interested in her and didn't want to hurt her any more than I already had, with Monte's help, of course.

One night after the dust of the Jackie incident had settled, I called Monte and invited him to go to Opie's with me.

"Mont, let's try something new. I'll go into the bar and start talking to the first good-looking woman I can find. If she starts laughing and acting like she might be interested in me, then you can come over and ask her for a date."

"Why would I do that, Bob?" he asked.

"Think about it, Mont. It would be a new record for you. You could shoot me out of the saddle before I even get my boots in the stirrups," I replied.

Monte didn't think my plan was very funny and declined my invitation. He claimed to be tired and wanted to get to bed early, which really meant he was going to call the escort service as soon as we hung up.

When I arrived at Opie's that night, there were no good-looking women to be found. In fact, the place was all but deserted, except for a couple of regulars. I saw the familiar face of my buddy, TJ, seated at the bar, so I went over, sat down next to him and ordered a beer.

TJ was a lot like Monte in that he always had woman problems. It seemed as though every time I ran into TJ, he was out on the prowl, even though he was involved in some relationship. He would always tell me that he was "gonna show that bitch" that he could find other women. Inevitably, he would end up going back to the same woman, time and time again. TJ was every bit as pathetic as Monte when it came to relationships, but at least he could talk a good game.

A couple of months earlier, TJ had found himself truly alone when his live-in girlfriend left town to take a job in Tennessee. Never one to be all by himself for too long, TJ immediately set out to find someone with whom he could start a new long-term relationship. He began his search back in his hometown of Woodward, Oklahoma.

In small town Oklahoma you never really graduate from high school, and the Thursday night football game is still the biggest social gathering in the community. TJ had gone to the Woodward High School football game in search of a new lover. As it turned out, so had an old girlfriend, named Noreen.

As happens all too often in rural Oklahoma towns, Noreen had gotten pregnant while still in high school. She married and had a son, but the marriage soon ended in divorce. She then slept her way around western Oklahoma while her parents raised her son. Eventually, she found another loser to take her to the altar. They had a daughter, but a second divorce followed soon thereafter.

When TJ and Noreen ran into each other at the football game, they immediately started reminiscing about "the good old days." After the game they went back to her trailer for a night of passion. One thing led to another and before TJ knew it, Noreen and her daughter, Courtney, had moved to Norman to live with him in a small rental house. Although TJ never really held a steady job, he expected Noreen to pull her fair share of the financial load. She had taken a job as a waitress at one of my favorite restaurants, "The Mont".

The fact that TJ was out at Opie's meant that all was not well between Noreen and him. Before I could finish my first beer, he slurred something to me about how he "didn't need to take her shit" and that he "could find new pussy any time he wanted". He offered to buy me a second beer, but I knew that meant I would have to listen to more of his trailer park soap opera, so I declined. As I was leaving, I told TJ that I would come by and see him the next time I was out rollerblading. He indicated that "the bitch will probably be gone" by that time, because he wasn't "takin' no more of her shit". I hurriedly made my way to the door and left.

As fate would have it, a few days later Monte called and asked me to go to lunch. Of course, he wanted to go to "The Mont". Monte always claimed that the restaurant was popular because it was named after him. I used to argue that if the restaurant was truly named after him they needed to change their sign to "The Anal Retentive."

Monte and I sat outside on the patio that afternoon. Sure enough, Noreen was our waitress. She knew me from the times I had dropped by TJ's house when I was out rollerblading. We exchanged pleasantries and I introduced her to Monte. After introductions, we gave her our lunch orders. Monte had his usual, the Mont Burger. I had my usual, two Bud Lights.

Noreen's face showed the toll from years of being rode hard and put up wet. However, even though she had thrown a couple of calves she still had a good figure with a shapely behind, which Monte noticed immediately. As Noreen walked away, I could see Monte's eyes locked onto her butt. I felt more than just a bit uncomfortable with the intensity of his stare.

As the weeks rolled by, I saw TJ out at Opie's with increasing frequency. That could only mean one thing; he and Noreen were still not getting along. Each time I saw him he would offer to buy me a beer just so he could start lamenting about his troubles with Noreen. He always seemed to be mad at her for spending too much money, even though he had refused to get a steady job himself. I had a little bit of trouble understanding his logic, but simply listened to his stories without ever making any comments.

TJ's incessant whining about his troubles at home convinced me to forego stopping by his house on my weekly rollerblading excursions, at least for a while. I decided that dealing with Monte's periodic lapses into lovesick lunacy was all the counseling I could manage.

One Sunday, I strapped on my skates and headed out for Monte's house. When I arrived, I rang the doorbell several times, then pushed the door open and barged in without waiting for Monte to come to the door. Once inside, I headed straight for the kitchen, opened the fridge and grabbed a beer. I scooped a handful of popcorn from the wicker basket on the counter and skated my way into the living room where Monte was watching a football game. I purposely left a trail of popcorn behind me so that I could find my way back to the beer supply.

Monte stood up and walked over to the closet to get his new power broom. As he vacuum-swept my popcorn mess, he told me about taking a client to lunch at *The Mont* and that Noreen had been his waitress again. His next statement made the hair on the back of my neck start to tingle.

"Bob, Noreen was flirting with me," he announced. "She's not happy living with TJ."

I felt that all too familiar knot of frustration begin to tighten in my stomach. In *Monte Land*, you can fabricate elaborate tales with absolutely no basis, but more importantly you can also choose to believe anything you want in spite of overwhelming evidence to the contrary. I could tell that Monte was trying to convince himself that Noreen was yet another damsel in distress who needed to be rescued by him.

Before Monte could say anything else, I cut him short with, "Mont, don't even think about it."

He shot me his famous pouty face before asking, "What do you mean?"

"You know exactly what I mean. Stay the hell away from Noreen. She is BAD news. Don't slap on your shining armor and mount your trustee steed to go in and try to rescue her."

Monte gave me a look of disgust and said, "Bob, I'm not gonna do anything," which was followed by a long pause of silence before he added, "but she is not happy."

I rolled my eyes in total exasperation, stood up and announced, "I gotta go." When I reached the front door, I turned and sternly repeated my warning, "Monte, stay the hell away from Noreen. She is BAD news."

He was too busy emptying popcorn from the dust bag on his power broom to pay any attention to me.

Even though Monte was a complete idiot when it came to affairs of the heart, his impromptu announcement about Noreen had convinced me that I should go by TJ's on my way home and check on him. As I skated up to his house, I could see TJ's truck, but Noreen's Volkswagen bug was gone. I made my way up to the porch and knocked on the front door. When TJ opened the door, he looked like he had been in a fight.

"What the hell happened to you? Where's Noreen?" I asked.

TJ motioned for me to come in. He walked over and sat down on the couch, lit a cigarette, and said, "I don't know where she is. The last time I saw her she was loading shit into her VW as I was being hauled away in handcuffs."

"Sounds like you two had a fun evening out," I said as I sat down to listen to the rest of his story.

TJ proceeded to tell me how they had gone out drinking and got into a heated argument. When they got home, Noreen started throwing things at him. TJ claimed to have done nothing to her, which I didn't believe. He said that Noreen had called 911 and pleaded for help. She claimed she was being physically abused.

Because TJ was drunk when the police showed up, the situation turned ugly. They could see that Noreen was upset, but the odd thing was that TJ was the one bleeding. I'm sure TJ opened his big mouth to the cops and they hauled him off. That's when Noreen grabbed her daughter, packed up their stuff, and left.

I decided to try to console TJ by saying, "Maybe you're better off without Noreen. You two did fight a lot."

Almost as if he had consulted with Monte before opening his mouth, TJ replied, "But Bob, I still love her."

Not wanting to hear TJ cry over Noreen's departure, I stood up to leave.

"I'll buy you a couple of beers next time I see you at Opie's," I said on my way out the door.

As I skated home, I seriously contemplated the notion of never going back into Opie's.

   ...   ~   ...

I didn't hear from Monte for a couple of days after I ordered him to steer clear of Noreen, so I decided to rollerblade over to his house and check on him. As I came around the corner of the cul-de-sac, I noticed a VW in Monte's driveway. The closer I got, the more familiar the VW looked, and the madder I became.

I skated up the sidewalk to the front porch. I beat on the door and rang the doorbell simultaneously. This time, I purposely waited for Monte to answer the door. I could immediately tell that he was not glad to see me. He turned and walked away without saying a word. I followed him into the living room.

"Who's VW is that, Mont?" I demanded, knowing full well to whom it belonged.

Monte was nervous and evasive. He said that the VW belonged to a friend. Just then, Monte's "friend" came walking out of one of the back bedrooms.

"Oh, hi Bob," Noreen said, trying to act as if there was nothing uncomfortable about the situation.

I glared at her without saying a word.

She turned to Monte and said, "Monte, me and Tommy are going to Oklahoma City and won't be back until late. Will you watch Courtney?"

"Yeah, no problem," he responded in a tone that told me he was less than thrilled with the assignment.

After Noreen left, I immediately jumped all over Monte.

"What in the hell is SHE doing here?" I yelled.

"Bob, I'm just trying to help a friend," he replied.

"That's a bunch of bullshit! Monte, I told you not to rescue her. She is just another Anna or Tonya or worse," I screamed.

Monte turned and walked into the kitchen, but I followed right behind him. He grabbed the feather duster from beneath the sink and headed back into the living room to dust all of the knickknacks on the fireplace mantel, even though there wasn't a speck of dust to be found on any of them. I was right on his heels every step of the way. Although Monte tried his best to ignore me, I continued my onslaught.

"Monte, you are putting me in a very difficult position. What the fuck am I supposed to tell TJ?"

Monte wheeled away from the mantel and pleaded, "Bob, you can't tell TJ anything. She's afraid of him. She doesn't want him to know where she is."

"Monte, this is NOT a good idea."

I could tell that I was getting nowhere with Monte so I decided to leave. I was so furious at him that I left without even saying goodbye. However, I made sure to give the front door a very poignant slam on my way out.

I was still steaming when I got home, so I called Danny and told him about the whole sordid situation. He couldn't believe that Monte had let a woman and her fourteen year-old daughter move in with him and his thirteen year-old son. Danny said he wasn't concerned so much that Noreen was TJ's ex-girlfriend, but rather that neither she or Monte had the emotional maturity to be raising one child, much less two.

It was obvious that Monte had let Noreen move in with him in hopes of becoming the next love interest in her life. However, after she left TJ, Noreen had immediately found a new loser to sleep with. The only interest she had in Monte was to use him for cheap room and board and free babysitting services.

Monte's roommate situation quickly evolved into a pattern of Noreen coming and going as she pleased, while totally neglecting her daughter. Monte, of course, stayed around the house to cook and clean and wash and pick up after Noreen. He soon became best friends with her fourteen year-old daughter, which was when I started to get real nervous.

The weekend after I discovered Monte "just trying to help a friend," Danny came down from Tulsa. We managed to coax Monte into a round of golf. This was one of the very few times in my life that I was totally serious with Monte. I started in on him on the first tee box and I didn't let up for the entire round. Not once did I try to be funny. I knew the situation had deteriorated to the point where Noreen was never home, did not pay her bills, and hardly ever interacted with her daughter. Every time Monte tried to justify what he had done, I would interrupt him with, "Monte, tell Noreen to get the hell out."

In the clubhouse after our round, Monte dropped another bomb shell on us when he let it slip out that the police had called him the day before because Courtney had been picked up for shoplifting. He tried to convince us that Courtney was basically a good kid, but that she was going through some changes and really needed her mother. He said he was going to tell Noreen that she needed to spend more time with her daughter.

Given that Monte was at least cognizant of the fact that Noreen was a lousy mother, I felt like we were finally making some progress with him. I ordered another round of drinks while Danny lit a cigar and checked the football scores flashing across the screen of the television above the bar.

My brief sense of encouragement was totally numbed a few seconds later when Monte said, "I'm also gonna tell Courtney she has to stop walking around the house in just her bra and panties."

The idea of Monte being home alone with a fourteen year-old girl parading around in her underwear was so disturbing that it deflected Danny's attention away from betting. For the first time since I had known them, Danny actually paid serious attention to something Monte said. He abruptly turned away from the television and glared right at Monte as he forcefully stated, "Monte, tell Noreen to get the hell out."

. . .   ~   . . .

I went by to check on Monte a few days after we had given him our clubhouse lectures. I walked into his house without knocking and headed straight to the kitchen. I grabbed myself a beer out of the fridge and went to the living room and sat down on the couch. Monte pretended to be deeply engrossed in the football game on TV. I reached over and grabbed the TV remote and pressed the mute button. I again started grilling Monte about when he was going to get rid of Noreen. Over the course of a six-pack of beer, I was able to discern that he had not yet even talked to her about moving out.

When Monte got up to fetch us a couple more beers, I decided that I needed to go make room for mine. On my way to the bathroom, I stopped to peek into Noreen's room. It was immediately obvious that she was a complete and utter slob; clothes were thrown everywhere, dirty dishes were scattered around the room, empty food wrappers were strewn across the floor, and crumbs from potato chips and assorted crackers were visible in her bed. Her room was filthy, even by my standards.

When I returned to the living room, I started in on Monte again.

"Mont, Noreen is a pig. She is just using you. You watch her kid and pay all the bills while she is out screwing Tommy. You need to get rid of her."

In an indignant tone, Monte replied, "Bob, you don't know that they are sleeping together."

By this stage in our friendship, I had learned how to deal with Monte when he said such outrageously stupid things. I simply closed my eyes and envisioned my hands around his throat, trying to choke the life out of him while I banged his head against a wall and screamed in his ear, "Monte! Wake up and smell the coffee!"

After a few seconds of my self-induced therapy, I took a deep breath and calmly repeated my mantra.

"Monte, tell Noreen to get the hell out."

I left without finishing my last beer.

That Sunday, Noreen came home from one of her long weekends of not sleeping with Tommy and complained to Monte that she wasn't feeling good. She went straight into her pigsty, shut the door and went to sleep. The next day, she woke up in serious pain, so she went to the emergency clinic. The examination revealed that she had Pelvic Inflammatory Disease or PID. She called Monte and asked if he would loan her the money to get a prescription filled. Of course, Monte picked up and paid for the prescription.

When I called Monte to administer my nightly ass-chewing, he let it slip out that Noreen was sick. He hoped that her plight would generate enough sympathy for me get off his back for a while. His plan backfired because I tore into him with renewed vigor. I ended our conversation with my usual command that he get rid of Noreen.

I immediately called Danny to find out what he knew about PID. He told me that having intercourse too frequently was the most common cause of PID. As soon as I hung up from talking to Danny, I re-dialed Monte's number.

"Mont, I just talked to Danny about Noreen's illness," I announced.

"Did he say what causes PID?" Monte inquired.

"Yes, he said there are two things that cause PID," I tauntingly replied.

"What are they?" he asked.

"The two things are TOO MUCH FUCKING!" I screamed. "No, Mont. She's not sleeping with Tommy, she's just fucking his brains out. She's a loser and she is making a complete fool out of you. Get rid of her!"

I guess I finally managed to get through to Monte, because the next day he decided that he'd had enough of Noreen. Although he didn't do what I had told him to, he did manage to get rid of her by announcing that he was "getting the hell out". Monte made up a lie about the IRS and taxes and how he had lost the lease purchase option on his house. I was glad to see him finally get rid of Noreen. However, I was not totally thrilled with his choice for relocating; he moved in two blocks away from me.

                ...   ~   ...

It was only about a month after he had moved into my neighborhood, when Monte called me and said, "Bob, I've got some really bad news. You need to come over to my house."

"Mont, what could be worse news than finding out that you are my neighbor?"

"No, Bob. I'm serious. We need to talk."

I laughed and told him that I would be right over. I gathered up Hans the Dog and headed over to Monte's house to receive my really bad news.

Although he was just renting, Monte's house was something to behold; it was an interior decorator's dream. For this house, he had decided on a southwestern motif. Just past the front door, was the living room that had two large-pillowed, sandstone-colored sofas, with Navajo throw rugs draped carefully across their backs. He had sand paintings on the walls and Indian pottery in every corner. The end tables were adorned with miniature saguaro cactus plants and desert-styled lamps. The big screen television cabinet had a bleached cow skull on top. In the corner was a kiva ladder with a red chile ristra hanging from one of the rungs. The place literally looked like a small pueblo.

There were two remote control units; one for the big screen television and one for the VCR. When not in use, these units were stored in an antique cigar box on the coffee table in front of the sofa. When in use, the two remote controls were placed parallel on the coffee table, six inches from the edge. The remotes were always pointed directly at the big screen television—not off at an angle, not turned around, and certainly never placed upside down.

The bookshelves on either side of the fireplace were devoted to Monte's entertainment library. One shelf contained several hundred compact discs; all categorized according to type of music (rock, country, classical) and alphabetized according to artist. The word "The" is not ignored when alphabetizing music discs. I found this out after I was unable to find any CD's by "The Beatles" with the other "B" artists.

The other bookshelf contained Monte's entire video library, except for his extensive collection of porno tapes that he kept hidden in his bedroom. I never understood why he bought videotapes, because, except for the porno tapes, he only watched them once. Regardless of the fact that he never watched them, they were all neatly arranged and alphabetized.

In the dining room there was an elegant glass dinner table adorned with decorative place mats, napkins and napkin rings. In the middle of the table, Monte kept a collage of decorative spices and candles.

I found out these items were for decoration only when I once tried to use one of the napkins to mop up some beer I spilled on the table. After nearly snapping my wrist in two while rescuing his decorative napkin, Monte proceeded to mop up the spilled beer with a towel, wipe down the table with a wash cloth, clean the table with window cleaner and paper towels, sponge-dry the front of my shirt, break out the emergency rug shampoo system (although no beer ever reached the carpet) and shampoo the entire dining room area, all before I could finish my second beer.

Monte's kitchen was always immaculate. Everything was stored in its proper place, including the southwestern style burner covers on the stove. The cupboards were organized according to their contents: foodstuffs and dishes above; utensils, pots, and pans below. The refrigerator was a model for anal retentives the world over. All of the spaces were occupied with exactly what they were designated for: vegetables were in the vegetable crisper; meat was in the meat compartment; milk, juices and sodas were aligned along the door, and the remaining space was efficiently packed with every size of tupperware dish one could imagine, all labeled as to their contents. On those rare occasions when I would visit Monte and bring my own beer, I would open the refrigerator door and cram my six-pack in until several tupperware containers fell out. I would then eat whatever was in the containers.

In Monte's bedroom was the infamous waterbed from his first marriage, neatly made with an Indian blanket and adorned with throw pillows. A circular glass nightstand housed pictures of Corey, Diana, and Maggie, his grandmother. In his walk-in closet there were a dozen pairs of shoes hanging on shoe racks, a half-dozen sport coats and suit coats, a tie rack with a couple dozen ties, each draped exactly like the others, and no more than three or four hundred shirts. Monte had shirts I am sure he had never worn, but they were all on hangers and categorized; short sleeves versus long sleeves, dress shirts versus casual shirts, golf shirts versus tennis shirts, etc.

Every single room in Monte's house was always immaculate; at least until I showed up. When I arrived at his house for our serious talk, I let Hans the Dog in through the front door, just exactly as Monte had asked me repeatedly not to do. Always excited about visiting Monte, Hans the Dog tore through the house looking for anything on which he could heist his leg. When Monte finally heard the commotion that my dog and I were causing, he came scurrying out from the bedroom and ran over to the sliding glass door to let Hans the Dog out into the back yard.

"Bob, I have told you a thousand times to come through the back door and leave Hans out in the yard," he whined.

"Sorry, Mont. I forgot," I lied as I headed toward the fridge. I grabbed a beer and a handful of popcorn and walked back to the living room. I made it to the couch with the beer and only half a handful of popcorn, having dribbled the rest on the floor along my way.

When Monte got up to go get his power broom and clean up my mess, I asked, "Okay, Mont. What's this really bad news you have for me?"

Monte stopped in mid-stride and slowly turned around. He came over and sat on the ottoman diagonally across the coffee table from me.

"Bob, I've got to tell you this. It's about TJ," he announced solemnly.

"What about TJ?" I asked.

"Well, the other night, I was at Opie's when Julie walked in."

It was kind of unusual for my ex-wife to hang out at the bar that I frequented, but since I wasn't there I didn't care.

Monte looked me right in the eye, as seriously as he possibly could and continued by saying, "Bob, you are not going to believe this, but Julie went home with TJ that night."

I just looked at him and said, "Good. They deserve each other." I took the final pull off my beer and went to get another one.

Monte was stunned. He couldn't believe that I wasn't just devastated by the fact that my friend, TJ, had taken my ex-wife home. Wasn't that the most unforgivable sin anyone could ever commit? Hadn't TJ harvested a vacuum from my field, or whatever it was I had said to Monte so many times before that he had always completely ignored?

I grabbed a beer and another three-quarters of a handful of popcorn. I walked into the living room and sat down on the couch. From the blank stare on his face, I could tell that I needed to explain my reaction to Monte.

"Mont, you need to understand something. When I told Julie to get the hell out, I didn't just mean get out of my house. I meant get out of my life. I gave her more than she ever deserved. When she proved to me that she wasn't worthy of my affections, I ended the relationship. It always bothered Julie that I didn't beg her to come back, but when you make those kinds of decisions, you have to be sure about them. I am ashamed of my marriage. I am ashamed of her. I wish I could erase the whole thing from my past, but I can't. However, I have absolutely no feelings for that woman. Whoever she sleeps with is none of my business, but more importantly, it is nothing I'm concerned about."

Monte's face showed the disappointment of a man who had just been told he had a terminal illness. He had been absolutely certain that his bad news would infuriate me, but it had done little to even phase me. He had hoped to either elevate his stature or bring my opinion of TJ down a couple notches in the aftermath of the Noreen debacle. However, Monte was most disappointed to find out that it was okay to sleep with my ex-wife. I know he would have done it had he been given the chance.

CHAPTER 13

THE GOLD DIGGER

In the wake of the Noreen disaster, Monte decided to confine his search for the perfect woman to the Happy Trails Golf and Country Club. That summer he spent every free moment playing golf or hanging out in the clubhouse bar. Through all the rounds of golf and the endless hours spent guzzling cocktails, Monte never met any single women. Early in the fall he began to question whether just being a member of a country club was enough ammunition to attract the perfect woman. After a thorough self-examination, Monte concluded that his marital dowry did not have sufficient material trappings. He needed something shallow and superficial to spice up his image, so he decided to get rid of the Puffer Van and buy a new car.

We were driving up to Tulsa when Monte suddenly announced, "Bob, I'm thinking about getting a new car."

"What? Give up the Puffer Van? You might need it if you knock up Tonya again," I replied facetiously.

"I'm serious, Bob. I'm thinking about buying a Mercedes. I'm single and I can afford it, so why shouldn't I get one?" he asked.

I couldn't argue with Monte. As far as I knew he did make good money, a heck of a lot more than I made. However, I felt there were a few other needs more deserving of his loot.

"You're right, Mont. You do make good money. I don't make your kind of money, but I can pay my own way. So let's not let Danny foot the bill for everything this weekend," I reasoned.

Monte agreed with me that we needed to pay our fair share of the tab. I took the notion to heart, but Monte forgot all about our conversation by the time we got to Tulsa.

When we arrived at his house, Danny had a surprise announcement. One of his doctor friends had managed to get us a tee time at Karsten Creek in Stillwater, Oklahoma. There was only one small problem; Stillwater was 70 miles from Tulsa and we had less than an hour to get there. We decided to take Danny's Mercedes and haul ass. As usual, I was picked to play chauffeur.

True to his impatient nature, Monte let the thought of buying a Mercedes become an immediate obsession. He bombarded Danny with mindless questions during our drive to Stillwater. Danny had bought a Mercedes because he wanted to get into Southern Hills, Tulsa's most exclusive country club. He needed to maintain a certain image if he wanted to be seriously considered for membership. Given that he had been blackballed for five straight years, it appeared that hanging around with Monte and me did more damage to Danny's reputation than any expensive car could ever repair.

I made the drive to Stillwater in just under 60 minutes. We met Danny's friend in the parking lot, then ran into the clubhouse and hurriedly paid our greens fees. We quickly threw our bags onto a couple of carts and headed out to take on Karsten Creek.

Karsten Creek is arguably the finest university golf course in the world; it is home to the Oklahoma State Cowboys, a perennial powerhouse in collegiate golf. It is everything one would imagine a course named after the founder of Ping golf clubs, who donated untold millions to help build it, would be.

We were playing one of the par 4's on the front nine when I had one of my proudest moments ever on a golf course. From an elevated tee box, I had to fly a creek that cut across the fairway and hit a narrow landing area lined with trees on both sides. I took out my three-wood and smacked one right down the middle. I was starting to think that I finally had this game figured out.

Danny proceeded to block his tee shot way right and walked off muttering something about not getting his hips through quick enough. Danny's friend snap-hooked his ball into the trees on the left and muttered something about getting his hips through too quick. Then, Monte skulled his ball into the creek down below the tee box, and stomped off muttering something about waxing his baseboards when he got home.

When I reached my ball in the fairway, it was only 80 yards from the green. My approach was slightly blocked by a tree on the left, but I could easily clear it with a wedge. I heard the group behind us gathering on the tee box we had just left, so I took a few practice swings with my wedge before I set up to make my shot. In my head, I went through my usual pre-shot routine: "Okay, drag it back low and slow, finish your backswing, keep your head behind the ball, DON'T SWING HARD, and follow through."

I did just fine for the first inch of my backswing, but then things started to fall apart. I dragged the club back neither low nor slow; I picked it up as fast as I possibly could. Not only did I not finish my backswing, I didn't even get the club halfway up before my brain sent down that all too familiar message: "Pull hard on that grip in your left hand. Right elbow, your not comfortable tucked in there. Swing that clubhead WAY outside the target line. Do it now!"

As if things weren't going bad enough, I began my downswing by "stepping in the bucket" with my left foot, much the same as when I batted in Little League baseball because I was afraid of being hit by the pitch. Every golfer knows not to take a step when they swing the club, but in this instance it was probably good because I had the clubhead coming so far outside-in that I would have severed some toes on my left foot had I not moved them.

The mid-swing adjustment I made to my stance caused me to clip the ball just a little bit thin, which is a nice way of saying "I skulled the motherfucker!" Because I didn't get the club under the ball, it took off low and headed straight for the tree that I was trying to go over.

My follow through consisted of getting the club only about belt-high before I looked up in hopes of watching the ball sail toward the green. What I saw instead was the little white son-of-a-bitch slam into the tree and then head right back at me.

Instinctively, I jumped up to let the ball go under me. Given my severe case of white man's disease, I was able to get every bit of three inches off the ground. The ball slammed into my right shinbone with such momentum that it knocked me off balance. I started to list forward on my way down, so I put my wedge out in front of me to regain my balance. However, the hosel got caught in the grass, which effectively planted the club directly beneath me.

Upon landing, I impaled myself on the grip end of the club, which knocked the wind out of me. As I stumbled forward, gasping for air, I tripped over the wedge and fell to the ground. I laid in the middle of the fairway for what seemed like an eternity until I finally caught my breath.

The worst part of my ordeal was that I still had to get up and go hit the little cocksucker again, this time about ten yards closer to my private gallery back on the tee box. As I was limping back down the fairway, Monte came climbing up out of the creek with his ball. He asked me what had happened. Instinctively, I lied to him that I had hit a beautiful shot, but it struck one of the branches on the tree. He told me that wasn't fair, they shouldn't even put trees on a golf course, and that I shouldn't count it. Actually, I was just grateful to still be alive.

. . .　　　　　　　　～　　　　　　　. . .

It was less than a week after our trip to Tulsa when Monte unexpectedly knocked on my door. It was quite unusual for him to ever come by my house given that there just might be some dust on an obscure knickknack in the far corner of the guest bedroom, or something even more disgusting. When I opened the door, I saw Monte standing on my porch. He was beaming proudly as he said, "Bob, come see my new car."

I walked outside and in my driveway I found a small, red Mercedes sedan, called a "Baby Benz". The car was more than just candy apple red; it was burlesque dancer, bleached blonde, I-slept-my-way-to-the-top, bright lipstick red.

"Mont, that's a chick car, " I spouted instinctively.

I couldn't help but laugh. Monte had gotten rid of the Puffer Van in order to get himself a stud monkey pussy wagon; instead, he wound up buying a "Puffer Benz".

I could tell that my statement stung Monte, so in an attempt to make amends, I pretended to gush over his new car. He urged me to take it on a test drive, so I hopped in the driver's seat and away we went. As we cruised around our neighborhood, I praised Monte for selecting such a well-built automobile. I commented on the incredible engineering that went into all Mercedes cars. I even lied about how much I liked the creamy white interior.

Near the end of our little excursion, we stopped at a red light. I bent over in my seat so that the people around us could not see anyone behind the wheel of the Puffer Benz.

"Bob, what are you looking for?" Monte asked.

"Nothing," I whispered loudly, "but if someone sees me in this car with you they will think I'm a queer!"

Monte let out one of his patented groans of exasperation.

When we pulled back into my driveway, I offered up a couple more insincere compliments about Monte's new car. I then suggested that we take the Puffer Benz down to Dallas for the OU-Texas game that next weekend. Initially, Monte perked up and told me what all I should bring for the trip. Suddenly, the look on his face turned very stern as he said, "Bob, no drinking, no smoking, and no lipstick in my new car."

Monte always seemed to save his most unusual behavior for our annual trek down to Dallas for the three-day drinking contest disguised as the OU-Texas football game. This year would be no different.

Monte showed up at my house with the Puffer Benz early Friday morning. We timed our arrival in Dallas to coincide with Danny's flight from Tulsa. When we got to Love Field, I was dispatched to go find Danny while Monte stood guard to make sure nobody tried to park too close to the Puffer Benz. I found Danny in the baggage claim area. He was standing beneath a "NO SMOKING" sign, puffing a cigar and talking on his cell phone to one of his bookies. His suitcase was the only item left on the luggage carousel, so I grabbed it and motioned for him to follow me.

When we arrived at the Puffer Benz, Danny threw his hands up in a mock attempt to shield his face from the glare and squinted his eyes.

"Mont, that's a chick car," he quipped instinctively.

In an instant, Monte went from beaming like a proud parent to pouting like a spoiled child. I laughed as I opened the trunk of the Puffer Benz and threw in Danny's bag. I purposely chose to sit in the back seat for the drive over to the hotel. I wanted to see just how nervous Monte would get from Danny mashing buttons and playing with accessories while not paying any attention to where his cigar ashes were falling. Danny certainly didn't disappoint me. By the time we pulled into the hotel parking lot, Monte was an absolute nervous wreck.

As usual, I had reserved two rooms with a connecting door. Monte chose to room with Danny, which meant I had a room to myself. Neither one of them liked to share a room with me, because when I snored it sounded something like a wart hog trying to snort Jell-O. Bunking alone was just fine with me, because I could keep my room as messy as I wanted.

Once we had checked in, Monte bee-lined straight up to his room. He couldn't relax until he had completed his unpacking ritual. First, he opened his suitcase and unfolded, then refolded his clothes, before he carefully placed them in one of the dresser drawers. Next, he had to iron

all of his shirts that he had picked up from the dry cleaner just before we
left Norman, and then hang them in the closet.

Of course, nobody was allowed to relax until Monte had unpacked and
painstakingly arranged his accouterments on the counter in the bathroom.
The outermost row contained his vials of pills; vitamins, aspirin, alka-
seltzer, ginseng tablets, and various other herbal health aids. The next row
was the cosmetic accessories; clay mask for his face, lemon juice to bleach
his beard, eye drops, ear drops, nose drops, hand lotion, face lotion, body
lotion, deodorant, antiperspirant, three types of cologne, shampoo, and
crème rinse. The very last row had the dental accessories; tooth brush,
tooth paste, tooth polish, tooth picks, dental floss, two different types of
mouthwash, and breath mints. Laid out to the side were the appliances: a
brush and comb for his hair, another comb for his beard, an electric beard
trimmer, and the blow dryer with three speeds and three heat settings.
Everything was arranged in nice, neat rows on one of the complimentary
towels provided by the hotel.

It didn't take nearly as long as for me to get settled in. I unpacked by
simply dropping my travel bag on the floor of the bathroom and throwing
my hang up clothes on one of the twin beds. I set the ice chest full of beer
on the nightstand between the beds. I then stripped down to my briefs
and let each piece of discarded clothing fall on the floor. I grabbed a beer
out of the ice chest, then walked over and beat on the door connecting our
rooms.

After Danny let me in, I walked straight over and grabbed the remote
control off the nightstand and turned on the TV. I plopped down on the
bed that Monte had declared to be his. I stuck my hand in my underwear to
get a good scratch, and took a long pull off of my beer. Danny sat down on
the other bed, lit up a cigar, pulled out his tip sheet and started to add up all
the money he had lost betting on minor league baseball games that day.

When Monte came out of the bathroom, he saw me lying on his bed
and shot me his familiar pouty face. I pried my dick out of my briefs and

waggled it back and forth. I patted the bed with my free hand, while I winked seductively and blew kisses at him.

"Mont, come over here and sit next to me," I cooed.

Monte rolled his eyes in exasperation, then went over and sat down in one of the chairs next to the window.

I put my dick back in my briefs and pretended to watch TV while I waited for Monte to drop his guard. When he finally got up to go investigate the devastation I had imparted on my room, I sprang out of the bed and snuck into his bathroom. I quietly shut and locked the door. With one fell swoop of my forearm, I instantly rearranged everything from on top of the counter to the floor.

When Monte returned from his inspection tour of my room, he quickly figured out that I was now in his bathroom. He ran over and stood impatiently outside the door, frantic over what I might be doing inside. He knocked on the door.

"Bob, what are you doing in there? Bob, come out of there," he demanded.

I really didn't have to say anything. I simply grabbed his beard trimmer and switched it on. The whir of the electric motor sent Monte into a nervous frenzy.

"Bob, what are you doing in there? Is that my beard trimmer I hear?" he asked.

Monte started to pace back and forth like an expectant father outside the maternity ward as he wondered what evil act I was performing with his beard trimmer. After a few nervous moments, he decided to try and flesh me out by loudly announcing that he was going over to investigate my bathroom. Of course, his feeble attempt at reverse psychology had absolutely no impact on me whatsoever.

I waited until Monte had taken several steps toward my room before I opened the bathroom door. I waved the beard trimmer in the air and yelled, "Danny, did you know you could trim the hair around your hemorrhoids with one of these?"

Monte turned and bolted for the bathroom door, but he didn't make it in time to catch me. I slammed the door and re-locked the deadbolt.

Next, I fired up the blow dryer. Monte burst into a similar pacing frenzy and questioned me through the door as to what I was doing with his blow dryer.

When he finally backed off, I opened the door and asked Danny if he was aware that you could "blow-dry your balls with one of these things." Monte made another valiant charge toward the bathroom, but I once again slammed the door just before he arrived.

After about a half-hour of torturing Monte without ever really doing anything, I decided to surrender the bathroom. When I opened the door and walked out, Monte flew out of his chair and rushed into the bathroom to assess the damage I had done. He immediately set about reorganizing all of his toiletries that I had scattered across the bathroom floor.

The next day at the Cotton Bowl, Texas clobbered OU so we were forced to drown our sorrows with a few dozen post-game beers. We were hot, drunk, and sweaty when we got back to our hotel, so we went straight up to our adjoining rooms to get cleaned up. I told Monte and Danny that we needed to hurry up and get back down to the lobby bar or we would run the risk of sobering up.

I walked into my room and immediately peeled off my sweat-soaked shirt and threw it on the floor. Then, I unbuttoned my shorts and let them fall to floor. I contemplated whether or not I actually needed to take a shower, but couldn't make up my mind so I decided to let Monte be the judge. I walked into the other room to ask him if he would smell my balls, but he had already occupied the bathroom to begin his primping ritual. I plopped down on Monte's bed and waited for him to come out so he could evaluate the stench of my scrotum.

Danny had stripped down to his boxer shorts. He was sitting at the coffee table, smoking a cigar, scratching himself, and trying to figure out which way to bet the over-under on the all important Northeastern Connecticut Tech versus Poughkeepsie State Teachers College night game.

He had to make up for tripling his wager on the Sooners just before kick-off earlier that afternoon.

It wasn't long before Monte came out of the bathroom wearing a pair of his magenta-colored, banana hammock underwear. He had dark brown clay mask smeared on his cheeks and a towel wrapped around his head. He was holding his electric beard trimmer. He switched it on, pointed it at me, and launched into his mock lecture.

"Bob, this is not for use on your hemorrhoids!"

I took one look at Danny and said, "You get the beard trimmer; I'll get the purple panties."

I bolted from the bed and caught Monte totally by surprise. I was able to tackle him before he could dash back into the bathroom. I grabbed his underwear and yanked them down his legs. In his struggles to keep his shorts, Monte inadvertently let go of the beard trimmer, which Danny picked up and threw in the toilet. After finally getting Monte's underwear off, I jumped to my feet and put his briefs on my head. I paraded triumphantly around the room with the trophy from our battle pulled down over my ears.

When Monte finally stopped laughing and caught his breath, he started to chase after me. Our little game of keep away was suddenly interrupted by a knock at the door. Without even contemplating the circumstances, Danny walked over and yanked open the door. In the doorway stood the female companion of one of our friends. We had told them to come by our room for a drink on their way down to the lobby.

I have often wondered what that poor woman must have thought. Danny had answered the door wearing only his boxer shorts. I was running around the room in my underwear, with Monte's purple panties on my head. Monte, totally naked except for the clay mask on his face, was chasing after me trying to get his underwear back.

By the look on her face, Danny could tell that our visitor was less than comfortable with the scene playing out before her. He needed to do something quick to make her feel more at ease, so he decided to invite her in for some refreshments.

"Oh hi. Come on in. Wanna beer?" he offered.

We never saw her again, literally. She ran down the hall and hopped on one of the elevators. Her boyfriend called about ten minutes later and said they were leaving to go back to Oklahoma that night. When he asked what happened to cause his girlfriend to act so irrationally, Danny told him that it was obvious that she just had too much to drink.

In spite of the good times that we always had, Monte could never truly relax when we went out of town. Inevitably, he would become obsessed with getting back home to his comfort zone. On Sunday, he got up early and began his packing ritual before Danny and I had even gotten out of bed. Due to Monte's rushing and hurrying, we ended up dropping Danny off at the airport three hours before his flight was scheduled to leave.

We had barely made the outskirts of Dallas when Monte launched into one of his typical nervous tirades. He started lamenting about all the things he had to clean or wash or cook when he got back to his immaculately clean house. I finally interrupted *Pooh Bear* and told him not to forget that he also had to "chase all the bees from the hive and count all the clouds in the sky."

...   ~   ...

It turned out that Monte didn't need the country club or the Puffer Benz to attract someone he could fall madly in love with. Late that fall, Diana invited him to an impromptu happy hour at her office so that he could meet Angela, one of her clients going through a divorce. Innocently enough, she thought Angela and Monte would be good for each other. Diana could have never imagined the emotional cocktail she had just mixed for her son.

Angela was tall and slender, with short dark hair. She was part Filipino so she had some sensual Asian features to her face. Her Caucasian traits included full, round hips and large breasts, which she wasn't ashamed to show off. Even though she'd had two children, she still had a shapely figure. The bottom line: she was very attractive.

It was near Christmas when Monte and Angela had their first official date. They started off the night at Monte's office party and then went to Opie's. This was one of the few times that I wasn't in the bar. Opie called me the next day and told me that Monte had come in with a woman who was a real knockout.

Opie's statement took me back. I had grown accustomed to hearing this kind of exaggerated line from Monte, but now I was getting it from an independent third party. In fact, Opie's comments had so piqued my interest that I decided to call Monte and quiz him about his dream date.

When Monte answered the phone, he immediately started lavishing praise on Angela, telling me how beautiful she was and what a fantastic body she had. He confirmed Opie's story about them coming in late to the bar. He said that every guy in the place had his eyes on Angela. Of course, he had to conjure up one of his usual bullshit fantasy statements.

"Bob, she came up and put her arm around me and laid a big kiss on me and said, Monte, I know all these guys have their eyes on me, but I just want to be with you."

I groaned and said, "No, Mont, that's what you wished she would have said."

As I hung up the phone, I was absolutely convinced that Monte was already suffering from romantic hallucinations and his delusional stupidity would soon be rearing its ugly head. I felt a familiar sense of frustration because I knew, from numerous past experiences, there was absolutely nothing I could do to halt the progression of Monte's lovesick lunacy.

Being so close to Christmas, Monte had the perfect opportunity to go out and make a complete ass of himself by buying expensive gifts for Angela. He went to the mall and bought her a jade ring, a jade necklace, and an expensive lace teddy, all of which he hoped to some day see her in, none of which he would.

The first indication that Angela was nothing but a gold-digger came when I went by to see Monte the day after Christmas.

"Mont, how'd Angela like all that crap you bought for her? Did you get laid?"

"Not yet, but I will," he replied confidently. "Angela said the stuff I picked out was nice, but she wants something different. So I gave her the receipts and she exchanged everything."

My immediate reaction was to laugh. Then I asked, "Mont, what did she get instead?"

He paused for a few seconds before saying, "Well, uh, nothing yet. She just exchanged them for cash. She wants to wait until she sees something really special. In fact, next month we are going to Dallas for a weekend of shopping."

I resisted the urge to tell Monte that Angela's stunt was the tackiest thing I had ever heard of. I knew he would never see it my way. I could tell he was already well into the process of re-virginating Angela and would very soon be elevating her to sainthood status. Little did I know that Angela would surpass this first despicable act on several more occasions.

After the New Year, Angela began training for a bodybuilding contest. She started working out regularly at a gym in Norman and began following a very strict diet. Her new regimen involved no alcohol and she would not go out at night. In spite of Angela's self-imposed Spartan lifestyle, Monte spent his every waking moment trying to convince her that they were in love. He decided that the best way to prove their love for each other was for him to put on a display of unrequited ass-kissing, the likes of which no man had ever done before.

Angela worked as a manicurist at a local hair salon and didn't have the resources to pay for a babysitter while she worked out, so Monte watched her two sons after work. Not only did he baby-sit for her, he paid her booth fee at the salon, and gave her some spending money each month.

Because Monte spent almost all of his free time kissing Angela's ass, I didn't hear from him much. On one of the rare occasions that we did talk, I inquired as to why Monte was always baby-sitting Angela's kids.

"Mont, why the hell do you have to watch her kids all the time? Why doesn't she just leave them at daycare?"

"Bob, this is just a temporary situation. Angela's ex-husband has stopped paying his child support. My mom is taking his ass back to court. The judge will force him to start paying."

As usual, Monte's story didn't quite add up. I knew that if the guy truly were a dead-beat dad, Diana would have had him arrested a long time ago. The truth of the matter was that Angela had lied during the hearing for her divorce. Afterwards, she had some feelings of remorse and called Diana to confess. Diana's ethical values being totally above reproach, forced her to call the judge and admit that her client had lied under oath. Because of all this, Angela had been awarded only minimal child support. Monte had made up the story about unpaid child support to somehow justify to himself why he was giving money to Angela.

It didn't take long for Angela to realize that she had a real sucker in Monte. As time went on, she milked more and more from him, but only because he kept offering it up. Angela eventually started whining about wanting a new car. She liked Monte's Puffer Benz, but he could not afford two brand new cars, so they decided to look in the paper for used Mercedes. When they found an ad for a used baby blue Mercedes sedan, they bought it. At first, Monte claimed he only co-signed on the loan, but that didn't make any sense. If Angela couldn't afford to pay for daycare, she damn sure couldn't afford a car payment. Monte was already paying all of her other expenses, so I figured he was probably footing the bill for the car too.

As his so-called relationship with Angela progressed, I noticed changes in Monte's behavior. Except for work and babysitting, he rarely ventured outside of his dark, but very clean, little dungeon. Although I didn't see him that much, the few times that I did go to visit Monte, he was impatient with me. If I didn't set my beer on a coaster, he would become visibly agitated, instead of just throwing his usual little hissy fit. If I spilled popcorn on the floor, he would sternly scold me, rather than just whining. Nothing was funny anymore. Monte was totally obsessed with maintaining order and control within his house. I had no way of knowing that he was under an ungodly amount of self-imposed stress due to what a complete and total fool he was letting Angela make of him. The grand master of clean was hiding a very dirty secret.

Late in February, Monte called G and asked to borrow some money. He made up some cockamamie story about how his paycheck had gotten screwed up. It seemed that the office that handles premiums had not sent him his royalty check and it would be a week before it arrived and he had to pay some bills so he needed to borrow $1500. At first, G bought the story hook, line and sinker. He agreed to loan Monte the money, but he only had $1000 on him.

When Monte arrived to pick up the money, he appeared anxious. He became upset when G told him that he only had $1000. G finally sensed something was wrong, so he pressed Monte for details. After he stalled for a few minutes, Monte finally came clean, or as clean as possible for him. He admitted to G that he was going to Dallas with Angela and that he didn't have any money because he wouldn't get paid for another week. He assured G that he would repay the loan as soon as he deposited his overdue paycheck.

G thought about giving Monte a lecture, but decided instead to just loan him the money. He felt certain that Monte would keep his word and pay him back in a timely manner. He couldn't have been more wrong.

What Monte didn't tell G was that he wanted the money so he could take Angela on a shopping spree. When they got to Dallas, the first thing Angela picked out was a very nice $500 jade ring. She had returned the one that Monte gave her at Christmas, because it wasn't big enough. Of course, she had long since spent all the money she collected by returning his Christmas gifts, so Monte paid for the ring.

Angela wasn't quite through spending all of the money Monte had borrowed. She decided to revamp her wardrobe to the tune of another $500. Monte went through every penny G loaned him and then some. He ended up putting the hotel bill, including numerous room service charges, on his company credit card.

After the shopping trip to Dallas, Angela immediately returned to her training regimen in preparation for the bodybuilding contest. Monte resumed his dual roles of babysitter and celibate sugar daddy. As the contest grew closer, I hardly interacted with Monte at all. Whenever I went over to his house, he was usually gone; if we talked on the phone, he was always in a hurry; he declined numerous invitations to play golf because he was busy doing something for Angela. It soon became all too apparent that Monte was, once again, suffering from lovesick lunacy, an illness for which the only cure is a cruel combination of humiliation and heartache.

Danny came down from Tulsa one weekend in early March and we finally managed to talk Monte into a round of golf at the Happy Trails Golf and Country Club. I immediately started grilling Monte about his relationship with Angela because I knew he was making a complete ass of himself. Although I hadn't seen much of him since she had come into the picture, in our limited conversations I had been able to deduce that Monte was "not getting any". We were on the tee box of the infamous third hole, when I decided to subtly bring up the subject of sex.

"So Mont, are you poking that gook yet?" I sensitively inquired.

"Bob, she is not a gook. She is half Filipino," he replied.

"Okay, are you boinking the half Filipino yet?" I shot back.

Monte walked off, trying to avoid the issue, but I had now gotten Danny's attention.

"Mont, I hear Filipinos are good tree climbers. Why don't you bring her out here and have her get your clubs down for you?" he asked.

Monte just ignored Danny's taunt, so I decided to ask him about their recent trip to Dallas.

"Mont, you mean you didn't even bang her when you went to Dallas? Let me guess, she's saving herself for marriage?"

Monte, obviously annoyed, turned and said, "Yes, we had sex in Dallas and it was great."

"You're lying," I countered.

"No, I swear. She has a shaved pussy too. I love shaved pussies," he said nervously.

Danny and I just laughed. Over the next couple of holes we coaxed Monte into elaborating on his mythical night of sex with Angela and her shaved pussy. The story became more improbable with each hole.

Now every male golfer in the world knows that the golf ball is a female. Anything that can bring you so much pleasure, then turn around and make you as miserable as humanly possible, has to be female. However, being males, we also refuse to accept the fact that it is our tools of pleasure that cause female golf balls to act so irrationally.

Every man who has ever played golf has also, at some point during a round, referred to his golf ball as "darlin", "baby", "honey", or some other moniker of endearment. These expressions are reserved for when the ball is headed in the intended direction. Terms such as "sorry slut", "filthy bitch" or "dirty lying little whore" are used to describe a ball that has sliced way right, failed to get out of a trap, or took the cellophane bridge across the cup on a short putt.

When we got to the green on the 18th hole, I had a fifteen-foot putt to save par. I stroked the ball firmly and it was tracking straight for the hole when it came up less than an inch short. I launched into an obviously well rehearsed outburst, supposedly directed at my golf ball.

"Why you no good, bald-pussied, tree-climbing, gold-digging, Monte-using Filipino slut!"

Danny had a good laugh over my contrived tirade, but Monte was not at all amused. He now realized that not only did we not believe his elaborate sex story, we were also suspicious of the entire fabricated, idyllic relationship. We had no way of knowing the incredible lengths to which

Monte had gone to try to get Angela to fall in love with him. Although our comments had been made in jest, they must have stung like daggers to Monte.

. . .   ~   . . .

As the date for the bodybuilding contest drew near, Monte started to get excited. He was sure that once Angela competed in the contest, she would have more free time and they could do things together, like pretending to have sex. When the night of the contest finally arrived, Angela told Monte to meet her at the auditorium. Unwittingly, Monte put on his best suit and tie and headed out to be publicly humiliated like never before.

The competition required that each contestant do a three-minute posing routine. Prior to their routine, they were given the microphone to say thank-you to whoever had helped them. When her turn came, Angela took the microphone and thanked Ray, who owned the gym where she worked out. She then said she was dedicating her routine to Ray's friend, an alcoholic who had died earlier that week when he choked on his own vomit in his sleep. Angela said absolutely nothing about Monte.

Even Monte can take only so much. He bolted out of the auditorium and went straight to Opie's and started throwing down rum-and-Cokes.

The next day, Monte came over and told me what had happened. He claimed to have called Angela and told her she was not classy at all; that she was just low-life trash. I felt a great big "I-told-you-so" well up inside me, but I didn't let it out. I could tell that Monte was truly hurt by what had transpired.

Because Angela had totally humiliated him with her cruel performance at the bodybuilding contest, Monte decided he wanted to get back some of the stuff he had bought for her. The only thing he could realistically go after was the Mercedes he had helped her purchase. He called one day to tell me of his plan to confiscate the car and sell it.

"Bob, I've decided to recoup some of my losses. I'm gonna get that Mercedes back from Angela and sell it."

"Monte, how in the hell are you going to get the car back? Angela's gotten accustomed to fucking you around. I don't think she is just going to toss you the keys. "

"Mom has already told her to return the car," he replied. Diana had some leverage because she was Angela's divorce attorney.

"Even if you get it back, how can you sell it without her consent?" I asked.

Monte was silent for a few seconds, so I knew something was up. Finally, he said, "Well, I made all the payments on it so I should be allowed to sell it."

Even though I knew this all along, I still had to act surprised.

"Monte, I can't believe you did that. I thought you just co-signed on the loan?" I moaned.

"Well, I did, but she couldn't afford the payments so I had to make them so the car wouldn't get repossessed," he reasoned.

"You shouldn't have bought the damn thing in the first place!" I screamed, not about to let Monte somehow justify to himself what he had done.

It took three months for Monte to get the car back. All the while, he continued to make the payments. When Angela finally did decide to return the car, she simply abandoned it in a vacant lot, then called Monte and told him where to pick it up. When he arrived at the lot he discovered that Angela had decided to pit out the car. Although there was no physical damage, the car was full of trash, empty cans, and uneaten food. The car was also filthy on the outside. Monte went straight to a car wash to clean, vacuum and wash the car. The next day he put an ad in the newspaper to sell it.

That night, I went over to see how sales were going at Monte's used car lot. I walked into the house without knocking and found Monte sitting on the sofa, watching television. I grabbed a beer from the fridge and sat down next to him.

"Mont, how much you asking for the Benz?" I asked.

Without making eye contact, he replied, "I won't take less than $13,000."

"Wow. That's pretty steep. How much equity you got in it?" I inquired.

"Not much. The payments were only $150 per month," he replied while staring blankly at the television as he switched channels.

None of this made any sense, so I continued to probe.

"How did you get such a low payment on a $13,000 loan?"

Monte was silent for a long period, before he finally blurted out, "Bob, I cashed in my IRA to buy that car for Angela. I only had to finance $3000."

I have to admit that even I was surprised by what Monte had done. I was, once again, disgusted by his emotional stupidity, but I knew now was not the time to lecture him. I waited for a few seconds before I said, "Mont, that was not very smart."

"I know," he replied quietly.

CHAPTER 14

CYBERSEX WITH DRAGON LADY

Soon after Angela disappeared from Monte's life the escort service girls started to reappear at his house. In spite of these brief flashes of his normal deviate-like behavior, I could tell this just wasn't the same old Mont. The humiliation Angela inflicted on him had taken a good bit of wind out of his sails. I needed to find something to get him back on track; blowjobs from call girls just weren't doing the trick. I didn't realize it at the time, but the answer to Monte's emotional doldrums was waiting out in cyberspace.

I had pestered Danny for a couple of months about buying a computer for his daughter. I tried to convey to him how important it was for kids to learn to use computers because they were rapidly becoming an important tool at all levels of education. Danny was totally uninterested in everything I had to say up until I mentioned that he could check his stock prices online. I was able to finally sell him on the idea of purchasing a computer when I pointed out that offshore betting services had proliferated on the World Wide Web. The thought of an electronic bookie appealed to Danny, so he invited Monte and me to come up to Tulsa for a weekend of golf and computer shopping.

It took all of thirty minutes away from golf and beer for Danny to grow impatient, so he ended up buying the first computer system he saw. When we got back to Danny's house, I immediately went about setting up the computer. I installed some software packages and hooked him up to his on-line service. I surfed the Web for a few moments in order to show Danny how easy it was to find information on almost any topic with just a few mouse clicks. He quickly grew bored, so I decided to spice up my demonstration by pulling up some pornography sites. The pictures of naked girls on the screen only momentarily amused Danny. Monte, on the other hand, was totally mesmerized by my electronic peep show.

On the drive back from Tulsa, Monte asked me all kinds of questions about computers. I told him what little I knew, and then suggested that he needed to get a computer for himself. That turned out to be both one of the best things, and one of the worst things, I could have ever said to Monte.

Inside of a week, Monte called and announced that he had bought himself an elaborate array of computing equipment. I went over to his house to help him set up his system. He had opted for a large monitor, but just a small dot matrix printer. He had a sound card installed on the computer and bought speakers to attach to it, purportedly so he could listen to CD's while he worked, but he eventually used it for downloading much more disgusting cyber sounds.

I truly felt that the computer would be good for Monte, because it would give him something to do other than clean and re-clean his immaculately clean house. I hoped that he might find enjoyment in using some machine other than his vacuum cleaner. However, I totally underestimated the influence that the computer would have on Monte's lifestyle.

He immediately started to spend almost every waking hour at his keyboard. He became obsessed with the ability of his computer to bring all of the information on the World Wide Web to his fingertips. Within a matter of weeks Monte surpassed me in terms of computer skills. He soon started downloading shareware files and surveying on-line discussion groups. He even participated in a couple of on-line chat rooms.

Unfortunately, Monte's newfound obsession with information technology could not have come at a more inopportune time for me. The president of OU had come under political pressure from right-wing conservatives to do something about pornography on campus. The religious zealots that pervade Oklahoma were concerned about the proliferation of child pornography on the Web, and they didn't want university computers contributing to the problem. They publicly demanded that the president ban all discussion groups and chat rooms that dealt with child pornography. The president folded like a house of cards and gave into their unenforceable demands. He issued a meaningless directive that university computers were not to be used for non-academic purposes and declared that all child pornography Web sites had been officially blocked from the OU campus.

One of my faculty colleagues made a big splash in the media by immediately suing the president and the Board of Regents for violating his right to free speech. Although sympathetic to his cause, I was bothered by the dishonesty of the whole fiasco. Nobody on either side of the issue ever admitted that it was technically impossible to ban any discussion group on the Web for any length of time. With a simple change of address, the same group of degenerates could exchange their twisted views again within a matter of days.

To make matters even more ludicrous, two days after his announcement the president fired a staff employee for using a university computer to distribute an off-color joke sent to him by a friend. I didn't feel a whole lot of sympathy for the moron, because he accidentally forwarded the joke to his supervisor, who was aligned with the right-wing religious vigilantes who had just gotten pornography supposedly banned from the university.

Just as the pornographic McCarthyism reached its fervent apex on campus, Monte figured out how to send messages with files attached. The week after the official ban of pornography from the university's computers, I received an e-mail message from Monte that read: 'Bob, look what I found.'

Attached to the message was an image file that I clicked on. What pulled up on my screen was the cover page from a hermaphrodite Web site. There was a frontal view of a nude female, which showed that she did indeed possess both sets of genitalia. I immediately closed the file and deleted the entire message.

I sent an e-mail response to Monte that read: 'Mont, please refrain from sending me anymore cyber-smut files. The picture of the naked girl with a tallywhacker bigger than yours could have gotten me fired. I do have two questions for you. First, how did you find the hermaphrodite home page? Second, why on earth were you looking for it?'

Monte never responded to my questions; he probably reveled in the fact that he had managed to cause me a little bit of cyber anxiety.

... ~ ...

Monte soon branched out in some of his on-line discussion groups. He was thoroughly intrigued by interactive communication with total strangers. It didn't take long for him to find a chat room in which the members discussed sex. He began chatting regularly with one lonely female whose alias was "Dragon Lady" and they were soon communicating via a private chat room. As usual, Monte used his tried-and-true lines about how clean and nice and wonderful he was and, because of bad luck, he had never found the perfect woman. Dragon Lady's sympathetic responses were right on target. She said just the right things to tingle Monte's cyber-erotic nerve.

Early in the fall, I went over to Monte's house to watch a Monday night football game. When I walked in, he was, as usual, on the computer with Dragon Lady in a private chat room. He paid absolutely no attention to me as I made myself at home and turned on the TV.

When Monte got up to go to the bathroom, I walked over to his computer and read the sickening drivel left on the screen. Rather than puking all over the monitor, I decided to type in a few messages to Dragon Lady. Initially, she didn't realize that I was now responding as 'Montbenz'.

DRAGON LADY: I wish I could come see more of you.
MONTBENZ: Parlez vous a hubba hubba?

DRAGON LADY:????????

MONTBENZ: Vous ne sentez pas bien.

DRAGON LADY: Monty, is that you?

MONTBENZ: C'est moi, Robert. Le grand Robert. Je suis bien sur que vous etes tres enchante de faire ma connaisance. Oui?

DRAGON LADY: Is this Dr. Bob? Please put Monty back on.

MONTBENZ: Voulez vous couchez avec le stud monkey ce soir?

DRAGON LADY: MONTY, PLEASE!

MONTBENZ: No can do, mademoiselle. Monsieur Monty is taking le dump.

DRAGON LADY: YOU ARE SICK! I WANT MONTY, NOW!

MONTBENZ: I hear ze toilette. Monsieur Monty must be finis avec pinching ze loaf. Au revoir.

After I typed in my parting sentence, I went back to the couch and pretended to watch the football game. When Monte returned to his seat he saw my last few lines of communication that were still on the screen.

"BOB!" he screamed, "what did you do?"

"Nothing, Mont. I just spoke some French to her. You told me she liked French, remember?"

"Bob, 'pinching ze loaf' is not French," he yelled, trying to contain his laughter. "Boy, I gotta do some damage control. She doesn't even know I go to the bathroom."

He then started typing at a furious pace.

Although pleased with my little bit of cyber-sabotage, I was bothered by the fact that Monte's chat room acquaintance knew my name. After Monte finished apologizing to Dragon Lady for my behavior, he logged off and came into the living room. I immediately confronted him.

"Mont, what are you doing with that woman?" I asked.

"Nothing Bob. We are just in the same chat room," he replied.

I knew there was more to the story, so I continued to pry.

"Monte, are you having cybersex with that woman?" I inquired.

He tried to ignore me, but I kept pressing.

"Monte, are you having sex with the Dragon Lady over the Internet?" I demanded.

Finally, Monte turned toward me with a big smile on his face and said, "Yeah, Bob, and it's great! The only problem is I can't type very fast with just my left hand."

I rolled my eyes and laughed. However, I was still bothered by Dragon Lady's familiarity with me. I decided I had better find out a little bit more about Monte's cyber love interest.

"Where does Dragon Lady live?" I asked.

"North Carolina," he replied, followed by, "She's married, but not happy."

His statement sent a familiar chill up my spine. I felt the onset of the same sick feeling I got every time Monte did something incredibly stupid with a woman.

"Mont, you are having cybersex with a married woman, and you have told her everything about yourself, haven't you?" I accused.

"No, Bob. I haven't told her anything," he lied.

"How did she know I go by Dr. Bob?" I demanded.

He then started into his routine of sequential confessions. Maybe my nickname had snuck out, but what could it possibly hurt if Dragon Lady knew that he was a very successful insurance agent for Farm Bureau named Monte Grant who lived in Norman, Oklahoma along with his teenage son, Corey, just around the block from Dr. Bob, who was a professor at the University of Oklahoma?

Now, I was more than just a little bit totally freaked out.

"Monte!" I screamed, "She is a married woman! What if her husband is the jealous kind? He could find out all about you and come out here without you even knowing it. You shouldn't be telling complete strangers everything about yourself. This is NOT *Monte Land*. You could get both you and her in a lot of trouble. AND DON'T USE MY NAME WITH ANY OF YOUR CYBER SLUTS EVER AGAIN!"

Monte dismissed my comments as just a bunch of pish-posh. However, my concerns soon turned out to be well founded. A few days after I screamed at Monte, one of Dragon Lady's friends was beat up by her husband after he found out she was having cybersex on the computer. The woman had forgot to log out and turn off the computer and her husband found the remnants of one of her cybersex escapades. In a jealous rage, he destroyed the computer and beat the hell out of her. Dragon Lady had related the entire story to Monte.

When Monte told me what had happened, I gave him my very best "I Told You So" lecture, but it had absolutely no impact on his behavior. He and Dragon Lady continued to have online masturbation sessions. They even started calling each other and exchanged photographs of one another. Unfortunately, Monte felt the need to share all of the details of his twisted cyber-relationship with me.

To the surprise of absolutely no one, Dragon Lady turned out to be a cyber-loser. She was an unhappily married mother of two, who fulfilled her sexual fantasies through cybersex on the Internet. The Polaroid snapshot she sent Monte showed her dancing nude on a coffee table. In addition to being totally devoid of any class, she was fat and ugly. None of this mattered to Monte; he was already blinded by cyber-love.

Dragon Lady quickly figured out that she had complete control of Monte in their cyber-relationship. She sent him some software to install on his computer that would allow her to page him electronically. Once installed, she could send an electronic signal to Monte's computer and the software would activate his voice card, which would chirp out "Uh-Oh". That sound was the signal for Monte to get his butt over to the keyboard and start typing.

I quickly grew to hate Dragon Lady's "call button" software. I went over to Monte's one Saturday to watch OU lose a football game on TV. Just after I sat down, the computer chirped out the first "Uh-Oh".

"Mont, you're being paged," I said.

"I am NOT going over there. I am mad at her," he quipped.

"Uh-Oh, Uh-Oh, Uh-Oh," the computer chirped.

"Mont, sounds like she needs you."

"I am not going over there. She can't just dictate to me like she does. I am not going to run over there each time she beckons me," he proclaimed.

"Uh-Oh, Uh-Oh, Uh-Oh," the computer kept squawking.

"Mont, this is great. You have all the disadvantages of being married with none of the advantages. She's able to nag you from North Carolina, but you don't even get to screw her."

"Uh-Oh, Uh-Oh, Uh-Oh."

"This is the last time I'll ever do this," he said as he stood up and headed toward the computer. He sat down at the keyboard and I didn't see him for the rest of the game.

Monte became so enthralled with computer technology that he started talking about getting a laptop computer. After a couple of weeks of pondering the idea, he called me and announced that he had procured a brand new laptop computer. Of course, he had to give me some crazy concocted story surrounding his new computer.

"Bob, guess what?" he asked.

"Dragon Lady is pregnant and says you're the cyber dad?" I replied.

"No, I just won regional salesperson of the year."

"Congratulations, Mont. What did you get for winning?"

"Well, in addition to a trophy, I got $500 cash and a brand new laptop! Now, I can take my computer with me wherever I go," he gleefully announced.

"That's great, Mont. Now Dragon Lady can nag you around the clock," I noted.

Monte didn't acknowledge my snide remark, so I decided to press him a little harder.

"Mont, let me have the laptop?" I fake pleaded.

"Bob, why should I do that?"

"Well, you already have a computer at home, but I don't. I'll hook up the laptop at my house and get on-line with you and Dragon Lady. We can have an Internet manage-a-trois. That's French for gangbang. What do you say?" I reasoned.

"Bob, she won't even talk to you. She is still mad at you for telling her I was taking 'le dump'. Besides, I'm gonna use the laptop for my business."

I didn't really want Monte's computer. I just wanted to ruffle his feathers about it. However, I was kind of suspicious of the coincidental nature of his story. He had wanted a laptop computer and all of a sudden he wins one at work. The whole thing seemed just a bit too convenient. Of course, by this time in our lives I was suspicious of almost everything Monte told me.

Monte continued his cyber-affair with Dragon Lady on through the holidays. After the New Year, he told me of his plan to bring her out to Oklahoma for a visit. I immediately warned him against doing anything that unbelievably stupid.

"Mont, bringing Dragon Lady out here would be a huge mistake," I warned.

"Bob, we won't get caught. She's gonna tell her husband that she's going to see her mother," he tried to reason to me.

I said, "Mont, I'm not worried about you two getting caught. I'm just concerned about structural damage."

"What are you talking about?" he asked.

I looked Monte in the eye and with a straight face I said, "Monte, as a licensed professional engineer, it is my obligation to inform you that your coffee table will not be able to support Dragon Lady's fat ass. If she attempts any of those nude table dances, the force of the collapse could crack your foundation."

Monte countered my sarcasm by musing out loud, "I sure do hope she has a shaved pussy."

I shook my head and we both laughed.

Luckily, Monte had a cyber-spat with Dragon Lady before he could get her to come to Oklahoma. She had invited a third person to join them in one of their late night cybersex chat sessions. Monte was under the impression that he was having a cyber-threesome with two females, judging from the lewd things that the other cyber-pervert wanted to do to his cock. However, just as Monte was about to blow a load all over his computer screen, the third party typed in a sentence describing how he would love to "ram his swollen rod up Montbenz's butthole." Monte immediately logged off and never again communicated with Dragon Lady.

···   ~   ···

It was early in the spring when Danny decided that we needed to take a golf trip to San Antonio. Although Martha wasn't thrilled with the notion of having to play single parent for yet another long weekend, Danny certainly heard no objections from Monte or me. We needed a fourth for our group, so I invited my old college roommate, Jim, to make it a foursome.

We kidnapped Jim for his birthday the previous year and took him on a surprise golf outing and he had a blast. At that time, Jim was in training for a marathon, which meant that he certainly wasn't in our kind of drinking shape. We convinced him to try a couple of birthday martinis on Friday night and he spent the rest of the weekend throwing them back up. He swore he would never drink again. Actually, Jim's wife was enthusiastic about him going with us to San Antonio. She hoped that we would expose him to some other bad habit that he would swear off for life.

Monte's cyber-sexual setback with Dragon Lady didn't deter him from pursuing his newfound hobby of playing on the computer. Early in the planning stages for our vacation, Monte announced that he would handle all of the arrangements over the Web using his computer. I was too busy at work to be of much help; Jim didn't know enough about golf to feel comfortable making any plans, and Danny was too lazy to even pick up a telephone, so we agreed to let Monte secure our plans over the Internet. The logistics of our ensuing vacation were a cyber nightmare.

Our afternoon flight from Oklahoma City involved layovers in Dallas, El Paso and Houston before arriving in San Antonio around midnight. At the airport in San Antonio, we were directed to a shuttle bus for a 30-minute ride to an off-airport rental agency. In order to get a car, we had to sign the most expensive rental agreement in the history of the industry. We hopped in the car and drove for over an hour before we located our fleabag hotel, which was 30 miles away from the golf course at which we supposedly had a 6:30 a.m. tee time. We got up at 5:00 a.m. the next morning and drove like hell to get to the course on time, only to find out that they had no record of our reservations. Because San Antonio was experiencing record rainfall at the time, the course wasn't very crowded, so we were able to tee off six hours later than we had planned.

In spite of all of Monte's computer glitches, we still had our usual great time. However, I did notice something different about Monte. The heat seemed to bother him more than the rest of us, so he wore a baseball cap. This was kind of unusual for guy who would go to the tanning salon in order to keep a beet-red look year round. He also complained about his butt muscle that he had injured while rollerblading. In fact, on Saturday, Monte played just 18 holes of golf, then went up to the room and took a nap while the rest of us played another 18 holes. At dinner that night, Monte was barely able to choke down a couple of glasses of wine before announcing that he was too tired to go out and chase women. When we got back to the hotel, Monte went straight up to his room without even bothering to ask the concierge if there were any good escort services he could call.

This was not the same old Mont.

CHAPTER 15

GOOD BYE, MONT

I didn't see much of Monte through the remainder of the spring and on into the summer. Whenever I called and asked if he wanted to go rollerblading, he would claim that his butt muscle was still bothering him. I invited him to play golf on several occasions, but he declined each time by making up some lame excuse. I attributed his lack of physical activity to the return of Dragon Lady or some other cyber-slut he might have met on the World Wide Whorehouse. Still, he just didn't seem like the same old Mont.

The Fourth of July finally rolled around, so I started making plans to celebrate the holiday. Danny was coming down to Norman to visit his parents, so we arranged a weekend golf marathon. I made tee times at the university's golf course for the entire three-day weekend. When I called to tell Monte about our special event, he declined to participate. He claimed that he was going to Tulsa to attend an outdoor barbecue with a woman he had met through one of his online chat rooms. I was tired of battling with Monte over his demented love life, so I didn't even bother to argue with him.

Monte headed up to Tulsa a couple of days before the supposed social event. He and Danny went out to play golf on Thursday. After they finished their round of golf, Monte told Danny that he just wanted to go home and relax. He said he wasn't hungry and didn't feel like drinking. In fact, when they got back to Danny's house, Monte went straight to bed without so much as a nightcap. This definitely was not the same old Mont.

The next day, Danny managed to convince Monte to blow off the alleged barbecue party and come back to Norman to play golf with us instead. Danny and I both had our doubts as to the validity of Monte's claims of an impending romantic interlude. His quick decision to forgo the party only served to confirm our suspicions.

On Saturday, the three of us teed off at about nine o'clock in the morning. It was an unusually cool day. In fact, it was so cold that Danny opted to wear long pants and a sweater. Monte had on shorts and a long sleeve shirt, but changed to long pants after nine holes. Even I noticed a distinct chill as we drove down the fairways. This was not typical Oklahoma weather for early July.

There wasn't anything spectacular about our round of golf; I was playing fairly well, Monte was playing fairly well, and Danny was making a lot of bets on baseball games using his cellular phone. When we got to the thirteenth hole, we all hit decent tee shots, which in itself was rather unique. Rarely did our collective golf carts leave a tee box and all head straight down the fairway.

All of our golf balls were fairly close to each other in the fairway. I waited until Monte had hit his approach shot before I addressed my ball. All I had was a short pitch shot to the green, so I was pretty sure I would find some way to mess it up. I stood over my ball for a few seconds before I attempted my shot. At the top of my back swing, somebody yelled, "Don't screw it up Knox!" which, of course, caused me to screw it up. I sculled the ball and sent it zipping across the green, ending up about twenty yards too long.

After I finished cussing at my ball, I looked around to find the moron who had screamed at me. The voice sounded familiar, but I knew it wasn't Danny or Monte. Over on the elevated tee of number seventeen, I could see two very large but familiar looking silhouettes. When one of the figures started to laugh, I knew immediately it was Dick, Monte's father. The other behemoth-like figure was Monte's brother, Eddie.

Dick had moved to Phoenix when Eddie went there to play college football then decided to stay in Arizona. He was in town for the holidays and had called Eddie to play some golf. There had been some sort of falling out between Monte and Dick, because they hadn't seen each other for over eight years.

After I recognized my hecklers, I immediately shot them the finger. We hopped in our carts and drove over to the tee box where Eddie and Dick were getting ready to tee off. I hadn't seen Dick in a number of years either, so I jumped out of my cart and ran over to shake his hand. A handshake was never good enough for Dick, so he gave me his characteristic bear hug until I screamed "uncle". Danny and I hadn't seen Eddie for a while either, so we exchanged a few quick insults with him. We all agreed that Dick and Eddie would wait for us in the clubhouse after they finished their round.

When Danny, Monte and I finished our round, we went to the clubhouse and found Eddie and Dick sitting at a table, playing cards. Eddie was munching on the second of three hot dogs and had three beers in front of him. Dick was sipping on a beer, in between dealing hands of gin rummy. We sat down and ordered some beer. By the time the waitress returned with our beers, Eddie had finished his hot dogs and announced, "Let's go get something to eat. I'm starving."

It was a foregone conclusion that we would go to "The Mont." The food was good and the liquor was cheap. However, the real attraction of "The Mont" was all the young college talent in shorts and halter-tops. With the unseasonably cool weather, we were guaranteed to see plenty of nipples that evening.

Danny decided to ride with me to the restaurant. Monte was in his bright red Puffer Benz, but he took off without even asking if Dick and Eddie wanted a ride, so they followed me. Once at the restaurant, we seated ourselves at a table near one of the outdoor mist makers in hopes that the moisture in the air would provide a "wet tee-shirt" effect on the young ladies sitting nearby.

All of us had our fill of beer on the golf course. Now, it was time to do some serious drinking. I ordered my usual screwdriver; Danny and Monte both ordered the house specialty, the swirl- a purple and white frozen concoction involving several kinds of liquor. Dick stuck with beer, but Eddie also decided to try one of the swirls.

I sat next to Dick, my former roommate, so that we could get reacquainted. Monte sat on the other side of Dick and started off the conversation with, "Gosh, Dad, I haven't seen you in a long time."

Dick responded with, "Yes, too long."

On the other side of the table Danny and Eddie were babbling to each other and laughing. Monte soon joined in their conversation, leaving Dick and me alone to discuss old times. The conversation between Eddie, Danny, and Monte soon lost its initial light-hearted tone. For some reason, the three of them started talking about Bubba, the brother who had been killed in a car wreck 24 years earlier. Monte had never bonded with Eddie like he had with Bubba, probably due to their age difference; Monte was ten years older than Eddie. The conversation soon turned serious as they discussed brotherhood, friendship, and the roles that they had played in each other's life.

Dick turned to me and asked, "Partner, would you like to go have a real drink?"

"You bet. This is getting way too heavy for me."

Dick and I stood up and went inside the restaurant and bellied up to the bar. We talked about all that had happened in the years since we had seen each other. Periodically, one of the three stooges we had left outside would come in and interrupt us. As the evening wore on, I noticed that Danny was getting drunk. Whenever he came inside, he would throw his arms around Dick and slur something about Dick being the greatest guy on earth, and how Dick and Diana had always been good to him.

After a couple of hours, Dick and I looked at our watches and decided it was time to head on home. When we got back out to the patio, we found out that Larry, Curly, and Moe had already made other plans.

Eddie stood up and announced, "We're all going to Sugars to watch women dance naked."

Monte jumped on the bandwagon and said, "Yeah, let's go to Sugars."

Danny also gave the idea his ringing endorsement as he slobbered out, "Lessy gobey soogars."

Dick and I were less than thrilled with the idea of going to the local strip bar. We were tired and had already had plenty to drink. I whispered to Dick that I was going to take Danny home. He nodded in agreement. I initiated my plan of deception by saying, "Come on, Danny. Let's go to Sugars."

I walked to my truck with Danny stumbling along behind me. He was swerving from side to side, drooling on himself and mumbling something about titties. Once we were inside the truck, I pressed the automatic door lock, then turned to Danny and said, "There ain't no fucking way we are going to Sugars. We are going home."

Danny was too drunk and too tired to protest. I drove over to his parents' house, opened the passenger side door on my truck, and poured him on to their front lawn. I waited long enough to watch him stumble up to the porch and eventually make his way through the front door. I then drove home and went straight to bed.

      ...   ~   ...

The following day, Danny and I were scheduled to play golf again, this time with Danny's brother, Greg, and a friend of his from high school whom I knew from working at the university. Monte had declined our invitation to make it a five-some. He wanted to spend the day cleaning in preparation for our outdoor cookout that evening.

The day was again unseasonably cool. I played fairly well, considering I was still tired and a little bit hung over from the previous night's excursion to "The Mont". Danny was still "swirling" from the night before, so his golf game suffered.

Out on the course, I talked to Danny about what had gone on the night before.

"Why were you guys so serious last night?"

"For some reason we started talking about Bubba. You know, what a great guy he was and how much we all three missed him. That kind of shit," Danny replied, as he stared off in the distance.

"Dick said it was a long overdue cathartic session for the three of you," I noted.

Danny didn't reply.

I then said, "Well, you guys sure were obnoxious. You kept coming inside and slobbering on us and telling Dick what a great guy he was. If he is so great, why did you slobber on him?"

Danny was unusually reticent about the topic, so I dropped it.

When we finished the round of golf, Danny and I beat a quick path out to my truck. We were both ready for a nap. When I dropped him off at his parents' house I told him that I would give Monte a call and get the low-down about our proposed cookout. This time, Danny was able to walk in somewhat of a straight line to the front door.

On the way back to my house, I stopped at a convenience store to get a twelve-pack of beer and some chips. I was looking forward to curling up on the couch with a beer and the TV remote control. When I walked into my house, I saw the message light blinking on my answering machine. I put the beer in the fridge, then went over and pressed the button to play back my messages. Little did I know that my life was about to be forever changed.

The voice on the machine was Eddie. He said, "Knox. We are at the hospital emergency room. Monte has had a stroke."

I couldn't believe what I had heard, so I replayed the message twice. This just didn't make sense. Monte was too young to have a stroke, not to mention the fact that he was in perfect health. I wondered if it was a practical joke, but quickly dismissed that notion. Monte and Eddie weren't smart enough to come up with something like this. I decided I had better talk to Danny, so I dialed his parents' number. When Greg answered, I told him to get Danny.

"Danny, have you gotten a message from Eddie?" I asked.

"No, why?" he replied.

"Well, I just got a message from him saying that Monte's had a stroke."

Danny didn't say a thing. I finally broke the silence by saying, "Danny, those two aren't smart enough to come up with this as a joke."

Danny was either skeptical of the message or in complete denial.

"Let's just wait and see what happens. They must be up to something."

"Okay. I'll go over to Mont's house and see if I can find out what they are up to," I said.

I had barely hung up the phone when it rang. It was Eddie calling from the hospital again. Monte had indeed had a stroke. Eddie's words to me were, "Bob, it's not good."

I called Danny back and told him what had happened. I said I would be right over to get him.

When we walked into the emergency room, we found Monte's entire family. Diana was sitting in a chair; her eyes were red from crying. When she saw us, she stood up and came over to hug both of us. After embracing her for a few moments, I asked her what had happened.

Diana said that when Monte woke up early that morning he was unable to talk. The left side of his face was paralyzed. He had called Diana, but she couldn't understand what he was saying. She rushed over to his house and found him lying on the couch. He was able to walk out to the car, so she took him to the hospital. In one of the all-time big medical blunders, the doctor in charge dismissed Monte's symptoms as being the result of heat and too much alcohol on the golf course the day before. He gave him a prescription for painkillers and sent him home, without even so much as taking his blood pressure.

When they left the hospital, Monte claimed he felt a little bit better. They went to the drugstore and filled his prescription. Diana then took him home and said she would look in on him later.

After dropping Monte off, Diana went home to get cleaned up. However, she just didn't feel right about the whole situation, having seen her son lose all muscle control in his face that morning, so she sent Gordon back to check on him. Gordon found Monte unconscious on the couch, so he called 911 and the paramedics transported Monte back to the hospital emergency room. The CAT scan later revealed that Monte had suffered a severe stroke with damage to 60% of the right side of his brain.

Danny and I stood for a few seconds in stunned silence. I asked if I could go see Monte. Diana said, "Yes. Dick is back there with him. You can only go in one at a time."

I walked over to where she had indicated and pulled back the curtain. I saw Dick in his cowboy hat, standing over Monte, who was obviously asleep.

"Hello pard," he said in a low tone.

"Hi Dick. How's he doing?" I asked.

Dick just shook his head, indicating that things were not good. I walked around to the other side of the bed to get closer to Monte. I reached down and grabbed his hand. There was some crust on the side of his face, so I wiped it off. When Monte felt me touch his face, he opened his eyes.

"Mont, you got something on your face, " I stammered.

With all the tubes running out of him it was hard for Monte to speak. He managed to mumble out that he had thrown up earlier.

I could feel my voice starting to break as I told him, "Mont, you just had to ruin our golf game, didn't you?"

His eyes slowly closed and he fell back asleep.

About that time, Eddie walked in with Danny. A nurse followed after them and said, "I'm sorry, but he's only supposed to have family in here."

Dick immediately responded, "Well, I'm his father and this is his brother," as he put his hand on Eddie's shoulder. The nurse turned toward me, but before she could say anything Dick jumped in with, "that's his other brother." She looked at Danny, but Dick never even gave her a chance, "and that's his other brother."

The nurse just smiled and said, "My, you have a large family," as she walked out of the room.

Danny reached down and grabbed Monte's other hand, which again caused him to wake up. They looked at each other for a moment, then Monte fell back to sleep.

A few minutes later, the nurse came back in and said that they were taking Monte upstairs to the intensive care unit. I knew we had to leave, so I bent over close to Monte's ear and told him that I had to leave, but would come see him the next day. He opened his eyes once again. He struggled to get his right arm up to his mouth and took off his oxygen mask. The last thing Monte ever said to us was, "Hey guys. I won't be playing golf tomorrow."

After they wheeled Monte away, we returned to the waiting room to hear what the neurosurgeon had to say. He confirmed that Monte had suffered a major stroke, which had caused severe damage to the right side of his brain, the side that controls his motor skills. Although Monte didn't know it, he was completely paralyzed on the left side of his body. The neurosurgeon was very concerned about controlling the swelling in Monte's brain, which was why they were moving him up to intensive care.

It took a few minutes for the news to really sink in. After contemplating the seriousness of what had happened, I decided to talk to the only person in the world I could trust to tell me the truth. I went over to the pay phone and called G. I told him everything that I had been told and finished by saying, "G, I don't know how serious it is, but they seem to think he will be okay."

G knew better. His years of experience in pediatric intensive care told him that the situation was not good. He immediately got in his car and drove to Norman. He knew Monte's family would need some help in understanding some of the complex medical issues they were about to encounter.

As I drove Danny back to his parents' house, we tried to be upbeat in our conversation. I noted that at least Monte still had his mental faculties, as limited as they were to begin with. Danny told me that some people recover a lot of their muscle control after a stroke. I laughed when he pointed out that Monte could still call the escort service, but he just might have to do it from a wheelchair.

After I dropped off Danny, I took the long route back to my house. I drove slowly. Although I had lived by myself for over a decade, suddenly I didn't relish the idea of being alone in my house.

I couldn't help but wonder how Monte would react to being paralyzed. I wasn't sure he would adapt to it very well. He had always been very active and athletic. For the first time since I played back the phone message that afternoon, I actually thought to myself that Monte might be better off dead. A sense of panic quickly swept over me. If Monte were to die, I truly would be left alone. Suddenly, I found myself needing the comfort of familiar surroundings. I stomped on the accelerator and sped the last few blocks to my house.

Although I felt somewhat relieved to be home, I couldn't get the thought out of my mind that Monte could possibly die. As I continued to ponder the horrible notion of Monte no longer being part of my life, I suddenly realized that I needed to call Jamie and Lisa, the twin sisters who had grown up with Monte. I called Lisa first, but she wasn't home so I dialed Jamie's number. I tried to tell her the bad news without breaking up. As my voice started to crack, I asked if there was some way to get in touch with Lisa. She said she would call her mobile phone and have her call me.

A few minutes later the phone rang. When I answered, Lisa asked, "Bob, what's wrong?"

I started to squeak as I said, "Uh, Monte has had a stroke and is in intensive care."

"Oh my God, Bob. What happened?" she asked.

"It seems that he had a minor stroke this morning, but they misdiagnosed it and sent him home, then he had a major one," I replied.

"Well, how is he doing?" she asked.

"Not good," was all I could manage to say before I began to cry.

. . .   ~   . . .

Monte never did show any signs of recovering. Two days after his stroke, I was scheduled to give a deposition, which took all day. When I returned to Norman that evening, I cleaned up and headed straight for the hospital.

As I walked up to the main entrance, I saw Lisa and Jamie standing outside, so I called out to get their attention. When they turned to look at me, I could tell that they both had been crying.

Lisa said, "You haven't heard, have you?"

"Heard what?" I asked.

"They are going to turn off the machines. Monte is not going to live."

Instinctively, I grabbed Lisa and hugged her as I wept. Although it had been many years since I had held her in my arms, this was the most sincere hug we ever shared.

After I regained my composure, I headed up to the ICU ward on the third floor. I saw Gordon sitting in the waiting room. He could barely look at me, so he just stared at the ground.

"Gordon, is there anybody in there with him?" I asked.

"Yes. G and the neurologist are in there discussing what to do. We want to donate Monte's organs."

I replied softly, "That's a great idea. Monte would have wanted that."

I then took the longest walk of my life, from the waiting room, down a long hallway, past two swinging doors, through the first door on the left into Monte's room. I didn't know what I was going to see and was as scared as I had ever been in my life. As I turned into the room, I saw G talking to the neurologist.

When I turned to look at Monte, I could see the shunt they had put in the top of his head to relieve the pressure in his brain. Small pulses of fluid were making their way through the clear plastic tube leading from his head. There was also a steady stream of fluid running through the tubes leading to his arm. Although they were pumping saline solution into him, I could see blood in the stream leaving his body.

I walked over to the side of the bed and grabbed Monte's hand, finally showing the courage I never thought I had inside me. I looked at Monte while tears welled up in my eyes as I said, "Mont, how could you do this? We were such a unique trio."

G grabbed the neurologist and said, "Let's leave them alone," and they left.

I spent the next few minutes patting Monte's hand. I told him how much I loved him and would miss him. Before leaving, I bent over and gently kissed him on the forehead.

. . .   ~   . . .

The next couple of days were the worst ones of my entire life. By cruel coincidence, my mom was driving out from New Mexico, and I couldn't get in touch with her. When she arrived in Norman, she called me, and the first thing I had to tell her was that Monte had died.

I took on the responsibility of planning Monte's funeral. And, oh, what a funeral it was! Because of his long-term association with Norman, the popularity of his mother and stepfather, and, undoubtedly, his longtime friendship with Danny and me, there were literally hundreds of people in attendance at the funeral. The church was not nearly big enough to seat all of the people. Monte had drawn a standing-room-only crowd.

Because he was a veteran, Monte's casket was draped with an American flag. The Veteran's Administration also provided a technician to videotape the ceremony at the church.

After the priest had done the obligatory introductory prayers, he turned the service over to G, Danny, and me for the eulogies. I went first, even though that was not the order we had agreed upon. Danny followed me and G was third.

For Diana's sake, we tried to do everything for Monte just as they had done for his brother years before. We closed the ceremony with one of Eddie's friends singing the same song they had sung at Bubba's funeral 24 years earlier; Ray Stevens' *"Everything is Beautiful"*. We then piled into the hearse and drove to the cemetery.

Monte was to be buried right next to Bubba. During the graveside ceremony, I chose to stand back, away from the family. Danny saw me and came over to where I was standing. He walked up and loudly whispered, "Knox, they fucked up his organs."

Just like everything else they had attempted, the hospital had screwed up Monte's organs, and they were not suitable for donation.

Somewhat outraged by the news, I asked, "Danny, how in the hell could they screw that up? Monte was a healthy young male. He was the perfect organ donor."

Danny thought for a moment then replied, "Bob, I'm not sure I would have given top dollar for that liver."

I turned and walked away as I covered my mouth so no one heard me giggle. In death, just as in life, Monte continued to provide us with laughs.

G saw Danny and me walk away from the crowd, so he came over to where we were standing. I was still snickering when he whispered to us, "I tell you one thing; Monte woulda sure been proud of all da pussy at dat funeral."

He was absolutely correct. Monte had finally managed to attract more women than he could handle. Once again, the opportunity was too good for Danny and me to ignore.

Danny got us started by saying, "When that priest began to talk about the women in Monte's life, half of the congregation hid their faces in shame. Thank God he only mentioned his mom and grandma."

I giggled as I asked, "Danny, how many engagement rings at that funeral did Monte buy?"

Danny shot back with, "How many cars in the parking lot do you think he paid for?"

We were now laughing loud enough for the family to hear us. G grabbed both of us by the arm and drug us away as he said, "Man, you two are horribo. Days a funeral goin' on here."

The truth of the matter was that none of Monte's six fiancées had shown up at the funeral, except for his ex-wife. Joyce, the star of the nooner video, had come and cried her eyes out. Susan, the church going nymphomaniac, had asked to play the organ for all of the hymns, and Diana had agreed. Angela, the Filipino gold digger, had the good sense not to show up at the funeral. Although Monte's family would never have said anything to her, I'm not sure I would have been able to control my tongue.

At the conclusion of the graveside ceremony, Corey asked that they open the casket because he wanted to put something inside. Some of the curious peeked inside; I refused to. I never saw Monte again after the night I held him in the ICU at the hospital.

After Corey and his friends left, and most of the crowd had filed away, I went over and sat down in one of the metal chairs near the gravesite. I had been too busy all week to reflect on what had happened. I put my face in my hands and rubbed my eyes. I just could not believe Monte was gone.

Diana came over, put her arm around me, and asked, "Bob, what are we gonna do without Monte?"

Without looking at her, I answered, "I don't know."

I stood up and walked over to the casket. I put my right hand on top of it, patted it a couple of times, and quietly whispered, "Bye, Mont."

. . .   ~   . . .

After the funeral, I took a couple of days off to be with friends who had come to bid farewell to Monte. I waited until they had all left Norman before I went back to work. Having volunteered to help take care of the business of burying Monte, I really hadn't had the chance to grieve. As I drove home that evening, I thought about the great times Monte, Danny, and I had shared. It was then that it hit me; there would be no more times like those, and I started to cry. At first I just felt tears welling up in my eyes, but soon they were rolling down my face, and I could hear myself wailing. I drove around Norman for about an hour just to let all my emotions out. I now realize how important it was that I allowed myself to finally grieve over the loss of my friend.

The next day, I went by Diana and Gordon's house to see if they needed help moving Monte's belongings out of his rental house. After I made my offer, Diana took me aside and whispered, "Bob, if there is anything of Monte's that you want you can go on over and get it. Eddie is taking the stereo and some of the furniture, but you are welcome to anything else."

I looked at her and stated quite plainly, "Diana, I want the feather duster."

I was referring to Monte's most treasured household cleaning appliance. The feather duster had interrupted my enjoyment of numerous television programs when we were roommates. It had also served as Monte's emotional security blanket during the many times I had yelled at him for doing something stupid in his pursuit of the perfect woman. Rather than listen to me, he had always grabbed his feather duster and retreated into his protective tidy mode. I needed to put that feather duster out of commission.

Diana said, "You can have all of Monte's clothes and knick-knacks. Why don't you take his rollerblades? Heaven knows I'll never use them."

I stared straight-faced at her and repeated, "Diana, I want the feather duster."

She started to suggest some other belongings I might take, but I interrupted her and sternly said, "Diana, I want the feather duster. I am going to put that son-of-a-bitch under lock and key, so it can never bother anyone ever again."

She started to laugh and cry at the same time, then threw her arms around my neck and hugged me.

Diana talked to Monte's landlord and negotiated an extra week to vacate the house. She waited until the weekend to begin the unenviable task of gathering up Monte's life and stuffing it into a bunch of cardboard boxes. When I arrived at the house, the first thing I did was ask Diana if she had found the feather duster. She said that she had looked everywhere but had been unable to locate it. I quickly went in the house and conducted my own search, but couldn't find it either. I decided not to make a big issue about it. After we had moved all of Monte's stuff from the house into the moving van, I said goodbye to Diana and told her I would come by to see her after things had settled down. I decided that she needed time alone, as we all did.

                    • • •   ~   • • •

I waited about a month before I finally drove over to see Diana and Gordon. When I turned onto their street, I saw several cars parked in front of their condo. I walked up to the door, but hesitated for a few seconds before I rang the bell. I didn't want to interrupt them if they had company, and I wasn't sure if I had given them enough time to grieve. My concerns were completely dismissed after they opened the door. As always, I was welcomed like one of the family.

Monte's ex-wife brought Corey down from Missouri, so they were having a small family gathering. After I exchanged greetings with everyone, Diana said, "Bob, I've got something for you."

"What is it? Does it involve liquor or deviate sexual behavior?" I inquired.

"Go see for yourself. It's out on the back porch."

I made my way through the condo with most of the family right behind me. When I reached the sliding glass door that led out to the back porch, I could see the circular glass nightstand in which Monte had kept pictures of his family. I couldn't quite make out what was inside the glass case, so I opened the door and stepped out onto the porch. After a few steps, I was able to determine that the object inside the case was Monte's feather duster. Diana had found it in Monte's house and had purposely hidden it from me.

"This is the greatest gift I've ever gotten!" I announced, then turned around, grabbed Diana, and hugged her.

I proclaimed to everyone in attendance, "I swear that this feather duster will never bother anyone ever again!"

They all laughed and then helped me carry my treasures out to my truck. I stood the nightstand up in the back seat of my truck for the short drive back to my house. I bid everyone farewell and headed for home.

I drove carefully on the way back to my house. I thought everything would be just fine if I just took it nice and slow. However, as I made the turn from the main street onto my block, the glass case tipped over. I quickly pulled over to survey the damage. Fear ran through my body as I hopped out of my truck. I just knew I had broken it. When I opened the back door of my truck I could see that the case had tipped over, but did not break. The little glass door had swung open and the feather duster had tumbled out, but everything else was still intact.

I stared at the mess for a few seconds before I grabbed the feather duster and ran out into the street. I looked up and shook the feather duster at the sky as I laughed and shouted, "No, damn you, Monte. This is mine now. It will never bother anyone ever again!"

                    ...   ~   ...

As ironic as it may sound, Monte's passing actually taught me a few things about life. The first thing I learned is that the finality of death ruins a lot of good times. Danny and I figured that if had he lived, Monte still had three or four more broken engagements with which he could have entertained us. Of course, Monte and I would have continued to have hysterics over the antics of Danny, the reluctant family man. There would have been endless hours of laughter for the three of us, the majority of which would have been spent on a golf course. Death ruined all of that for us.

Through his death, I also learned just how little I knew about Monte. Because I had taken on the responsibility to help coordinate Monte's funeral, I had to put together his obituary. G had warned me not to go looking for information because I might not like what I found. I somehow sensed he was right, but I felt an obligation to Diana and the family.

Much of the information I gathered about Monte was not particularly flattering. Although he sold insurance for a living, he did not have health or life insurance on himself. The laptop computer he supposedly had won was, in fact, being paid for by an automatic withdrawal from his paycheck and needed to be returned. At the time of his death, Monte was making a good living, but spent every penny each month. The only way he had been able to afford the puffer Benz was by having Gordon co-sign the loan. In addition, his account at the Happy Trails Golf and Country Club was several months in arrears. I wasn't as surprised by these revelations as I was saddened by the thought of the tremendous pressure Monte had put on himself in trying to impress everyone, including me.

I called G one night to talk to him about all the events that had transpired leading to Monte's death. I was still spooked by the tremendously coincidental nature of it all. We had run into Monte's dad, whom he hadn't seen in eight years, on the golf course. Monte, Danny, and Eddie got an opportunity to express their feelings with one another regarding Bubba. Monte had even spent two hours in the emergency room talking with Diana about future plans for his daughter with Tonya.

G thought for a moment then said, "Knox, I really believe Monte was saying good-bye."

His statement hit home with me. I thought about it all night long. I finally concluded that G was right; Monte had endured a lifetime of humiliation in his pursuit of women. In the process, he had painted himself into an inescapable corner of debt through his lies and deceit. Perhaps, he knew there was only one way out without having to face the shame that the truth would ultimately reveal. It made sense to me; Monte had always taken the easy way out. This time, he wanted to say goodbye before he left.

The most important thing I learned from Monte's death was how much I truly loved the man. Although he was a pathological liar throughout his life, I had always been able to trust Monte when I truly needed him. In spite of his neatness fetish and emotional desperation, I had always enjoyed his company. In fact, his personality quirks were what made him so entertaining. And, as I told the congregation at his funeral, nobody has ever had as much fun as Mont, Danny and Bob.

...   ~   ...

As a devout agnostic, I'm not totally certain where Monte is right now. However, I am willing to at least consider the notion that he has gone on to a better place and that place is called *Monte Land*. I know exactly what *Monte Land* is like. For the past twenty years I have been witness to a virtual travelogue for this very strange oasis.

The sun shines year round in *Monte Land*, just right for working on your tan and barbecuing chicken on the grill. Because the weather is perfect, each day you can tee it up for a round of pasture pool at *Monte Land*

Augusta, a golf and country club that does not allow shirts to be worn. The course has no out of bounds markers, each golf cart is equipped with a cooler stocked full of ice-cold beer, and the scorecard pencils have erasers.

After a round of golf, you can head over to Upper Opie's, the local tavern that serves free rum-and-Cokes. There are plenty of fat women with whom to two-step and a large screen TV to watch football. In *Monte Land,* Oklahoma always beats Texas, and the Dallas Cowboys win the Super Bowl every year.

Monte has probably found a house to rent in *Monte Land* and has filled it to the rafters with his crap, all of which is neatly stacked and arranged according to some totally indecipherable system. His stereo is connected to dozens of speakers, all of which reach to the ceiling. He needs all the volume he can get in order to hear the music over the roar of his riding vacuum cleaner. He has an industrial strength power-broom for the smaller jobs; I am sure there is not a spec of dust anywhere to be found. I doubt that there are any porno tapes in *Monte Land.* Monte probably doesn't have any interest in porno anymore, because he now has a whole slew of perfect women from which to choose.

I have to admit that I must be searching for some kind of spiritual fulfillment, because I am both amused and comforted by the thought of Monte pacing back and forth, without his trusty feather duster, while he waits on Danny and Bob to get to *Monte Land.*

0-595-25596-5